HIGH KI...

"Dead! Kenneth!" Cormac mac Farquhar stared at the older man. "The Ard Righ dead? The High King of Scots!"

"Dead, yes – slain. And, God help us, by my daughter!" Connacher, Mormaor of Angus tugged at his greying beard. "He deserved to die. He slew my grandson. And now Fenella has slain him. She was ever strong of will. She has avenged her son. But – what now? I fear, I fear . . ."

Cormac wagged his head. "Slain! And by a *woman*! This, this is truth, my lord Mormaor? Not some fable?"

The young man drew a long breath. Desperate! The murder of King Kenneth, his monarch and liege-lord. And he, it seemed, to side with the murderer, the woman, his own mormaor's daughter. To be faced with this, and so soon after he had become the new Thane of Glamis!

Also by Nigel Tranter
(in chronological order)

Columba
Druid Sacrifice
Kenneth
MacBeth the King
Margaret the Queen
David the Prince
Lord of the Isles
Tapestry of the Boar
Crusader
The Bruce Trilogy (in one volume)
The Wallace
True Thomas
Flowers of Chivalry
The Stewart Trilogy (in one volume)
Lion Let Loose
Black Douglas
The Lion's Whelp
Lord in Waiting
Price of a Princess
Chain of Destiny
The Master of Gray Trilogy (in one volume)
A Stake in the Kingdom
The James V Trilogy (in one volume)
Warden of the Queen's March
The Marchman
A Rage of Regents
Poetic Justice
Children of the Mist
The Wisest Fool
Mail Royal
Unicorn Rampant
The Young Montrose
Montrose: The Captain General
Honours Even
The Patriot
The MacGregor Trilogy (in one volume)
Highness in Hiding
The Flockmasters

High Kings and Vikings

Nigel Tranter

CORONET BOOKS
Hodder and Stoughton

First published in Great Britain in 1998 by Hodder and Stoughton
A division of Hodder Headline PLC
First published in paperback in 1998 by Hodder and Stoughton
A Coronet Paperback

10 9 8 7 6 5 4 3 2 1

ISBN 0 340 69669 9

Printed and bound in Great Britain by
Mackays of Chatham plc, Chatham, Kent

Hodder and Stoughton
A division of Hodder Headline PLC
338 Euston Road
London NW1 3BH

Principal Characters in order of appearance

Cormac mac Farquhar: Thane of Glamis.
Connacher: Mormaor of Angus.
Lady Ada of Glamis: Mother of Cormac.
Bridget nic Farquhar: Sister of Cormac.
Pate the Mill: Local stalwart.
Duncan the Tranter: Personal attendant of Cormac.
Constantine mac Cuilean: High King of Scots.
Fenella nic Aidan: Niece of Mormaor Connacher.
Lady Alena: Mother of Fenella.
Aidan mac Nechtan: Father of Fenella.
Donald of Arbuthnott: Thane of the Mearns.
Donnie the Crab: Ethiehaven fisherman.
Father Ferchar: Priest of Usan.
Ian the Wright: Boat-builder of Usan.
MacBeth mac Finlay: Son of Mormaor Finlay of Moray and Ross.
Malcolm mac Kenneth: Son of the High King Kenneth.
Kenneth, Mormaor of Atholl: The new High King, Kenneth the Third.
Finlay, Mormaor of Moray:
Neil Nathrach: Illegitimate half-brother of MacBeth.
Gillacomgain of Conon: Cousin of MacBeth.
Thorfinn Raven-Feeder: Son of the Earl of Orkney.
Nechtan mac Cormac: Son of Cormac and Fenella.
Uhtred: Anglian Earl of Northumbria.
Sigurd Hlodvison: Earl of Orkney.
Lady Donada: Wife of Sigurd, mother of MacBeth and Thorfinn.
Princess Gruoch: Widow of Gillacomgain.
Lulach: Son of Gruoch and Gillacomgain.

PREFACE

The following story is considerably more imaginative than most of my historical novels, if reasonably informedly so, this because of the sheer lack of reliable detail and information available for this period, of the first millennium, the so-called Dark Ages in Scotland's story.

When Edward of England, the Hammer of the Scots, came north in force in 1296, he deliberately set out to destroy all symbols of Scottish sovereignty, not only seeking to take away the Stone of Destiny and the Black Rood, piece of Christ's true cross, but burning all the national records. So for the centuries before that historians have had to rely largely on sources outside Scotland, such as the Norse and Icelandic sagas, the Irish monastic annals, the Anglo-Saxon Chronicles, and so on, together with much later accounts, traditions and folklore, often very doubtful as to fact, written to favour causes and especial interests, often mythical and frequently contradictory. So historians themselves have had to pick and choose what to believe, with consequent controversy and dispute. I fear that I have had to do likewise, selecting what seems a fairly likely sequence, and filling in with my own storyteller's linkage.

This novel starts in the year 995, one of the darkest periods, and a deal of improvisation, not to say invention has been required of me; but it is a period I did not want to miss out, for it was a sufficiently dramatic one most evidently. If some of this story contradicts not only various historians but even some of my own previous writings, kind reader bear with me. One glance at any academic history-book touching on the era will show you why.

Nigel Tranter

PART ONE

1

"Dead! Kenneth!" Cormac mac Farquhar stared at the older man. "The Ard Righ dead? The High King of Scots!"

"Dead, yes – slain. And, God help us, by my daughter!" Connacher, Mormaor of Angus tugged at his greying beard. "He deserved to die. He slew my grandson. And now Fenella has slain him. She was ever strong of will. She has avenged her son. But – what now? I fear, I fear . . ."

Cormac wagged his head. "Slain! And by a *woman*! This, this is truth, my lord Mormaor? Not some fable?"

"Think you that I would be here at Glamis, man, if I deemed it so? The word brought to me was sure – by Ewan, keeper of Kincardine Castle. It was at Fettercairn, in the Mearns. By some device, he said. I know that she hated Kenneth – as well she might. But not this! There will be great trouble, war it could be. I must go to her. And in strength. She is my daughter. You, Cormac, gather a company of your men. Bring them to me at Forfar. In two days, no more. I will raise others. Waste no time."

The young man drew a long breath. Here was a dire demand – and in a dire cause. Desperate! The murder of King Kenneth, his monarch and liege-lord. And he, it seemed, to side with the murderer, the woman, his own mormaor's daughter. To be faced with this, and so soon after he had become the new Thane of Glamis!

Cormac mac Farquhar was aged twenty-three years, fair-headed, open-featured, lightly built but broad of shoulder. His father, the Thane of Glamis, in Strathmore, had died suddenly only three weeks before, leaving him, the only son, as thane in his place. And now this, he who had never had occasion to lead armed men. And in such a cause! But he could not refuse his own mormaor.

"How many men, my lord?" he wondered, doubtfully.

"One hundred. At least. I will have the men of Dunnichen and Lethem, of Rescobie and Guthrie, of Brechin and Menmuir. Aye, and from the glens of Prosen and Clova and Isla and the Esks. Two days, and we ride north. See you to it. Your father would have raised your folk in a morning!"

Cormac schooled his features, open as they were. "Who will be High King now?" he asked.

"That is for us mormaors to decide. We must meet. I would think Constantine, Cuilean's son. Kenneth's son, Malcolm, is too young . . ." Mormaor Connacher was already heading for the door.

Cormac accompanied his lord out of Glamis Castle, on its mound, and down to his horses, where a dozen men waited.

"Forfar, then – in two days," he was told briefly, as the older man mounted, a little stiffly, and the party rode off.

Head in something of a whirl, Cormac climbed back up the steep, stepped slope to the high timber palisade which surrounded the castle, passed through the gatehouse and crossed the yard to the tall hallhouse, again timber-built but covered in hardened clay as defence against fire-arrows, whitewashed and painted with elaborate Celtic designs, the thanedom's banner flapping above it.

He ran upstairs from the main hall, where he had talked with the mormaor, to the withdrawing-room where his mother and sister sat at their needlework.

"What was Connacher of Angus wanting with you?" the Lady Ada enquired. "He looked grim, so I kept my distance. He does not often darken our door!"

"He had reason to look so!" her son declared in a rush. "He brought word that his daughter, widow of the Thane of the Mearns, has killed the High King Kenneth."

"Killed! A woman! *Killed*, you say? Fenella of the Mearns."

"So he has been told by the keeper of the royal castle of Kincardine at Fettercairn. It is scarcely to be believed. But he deems it the truth. And he is for the north, to go to her. Would have me accompany him. With one hundred men."

"But this is unthinkable! Fenella nic Connacher! I have known her always. She was ever proud, that one. Headstrong. But to kill! And the Ard Righ!"

"How did she do it?" That was his sixteen-year-old sister Bridget, interested rather than shocked.

"I do not know. Some device, he said. But what will happen now?"

"To slay the High King! Will she be hanged? Or burned at the stake?"

"Tut, girl!" Their mother warned her to be quiet. "Why does the mormaor want you and the men, Cormac?" she asked. "What does he intend?"

"I know not. He fears great trouble. There is bound to be. So he rides north with a large company. There will have to be a meeting of the mormaors to elect a new High King."

"He will seek to aid his daughter, no doubt. And as thane here, I can see that he may desire your presence. What, ah what, would your father have said to this!"

Her son and daughter were in no position to answer that.

"I have to raise the men," Cormac said. "I have never done the like."

"Go you and see Pate the Mill, down at the castleton. He will aid you to gather them. And Duncan the Tranter. They are able men. And you will require horses for them all. Some may not have suitable beasts. Pate will know who to send round for that. Probably Calum the Smith. Let us hope that you do not have to lead them into fight, Cormac. You who have done nothing of that! In the old days it would have been different . . ."

Her son was quite surprised at the Lady Ada's grasp on such matters. Of course, when she and her late husband had been younger, they had been much concerned with warfare against the ever-invading Danes, now the land was mercifully spared much of that, the Vikings turning their savage attentions to Ireland and the Isles.

Cormac went down to the castleton, which in fact was more than that, a quite sizeable village on the Glamis Burn, a tributary of the Dean Water. And at the burnside, a little way north of the village, was one of the two mills serving the area; here he found the miller, Pate, a massive man of middle years, with something of a reputation as a fighter in his younger days, against the Danes. To him, amongst his heaps of grain and chaff, the young thane explained the situation and his requirements.

"Hech, but this is a sore matter, lord," the other said, shaking his head. "Heads will fall over it, I'm thinking. We will have to be seeing that few of ours do!"

"Yes. It is bad that it should be our own mormaor's daughter who is the cause of it. He is bound to take her side, seek to aid her. Which could have us set against most of the rest of the realm; the other mormaors, and whoever is to be the new High King. That could be an ill matter for Angus, and therefore for Glamis."

"Och, Connacher is no fool, lord. He will not cut his own throat! Nor ours. This of a great company to go north with him will be to give him time, belike. Time to get his daughter away."

"I hope so. I have no wish to take up arms in aid of a murderess! But we will have to answer his call. Provide him with our Glamis men. He said one hundred."

"I will find them for you, lord. More if need be. You will want them horsed, I take it?"

"Yes. Can we raise sufficient good beasts?"

"Garrons, aye. It may take time . . ."

"He wants us at Forfar in two days. Calum, the Smith, will know best about the horses, since he has to shoe them."

"Aye, I will go see Calum. And the smiths at Inverarity and Eassie will help. These hill farms will have the more garrons."

Cormac went to see Duncan the Tranter, so called because he had started his occupation as such, the man who retrieved the game and the falcons after kills in the sport of falconry, but had later advanced to fly the hawks in the hunt, and even to breed them. Hawking was Cormac's favoured sport, and these two were close, as between lord and servitor. A man in his thirties, and said to be the illegitimate son of an abbot, tall and dark and wry of humour, Duncan agreed to go and raise the men of the Arnifoul and Kincaldrum areas amongst the Sidlaw Hills to the south.

Cormac returned to the castle. This was his first major act as Thane of Glamis, his first assembling of his people – and he still tended to think of them as his father's people. Would they all sufficiently respond and heed him, obey and serve him as they had done his sire? Farquhar mac Drostan had been a masterful man, and *he* did not think of himself as anything of that sort. A curse on Fenella of the Mearns!

Actually it was one hundred and thirty-two mounted men who left Glamis at first light two days later to ride the six miles eastwards to Forfar, the capital of the mormaordom of Angus, this more than anticipated, and all seemingly eager for this venture. It was early September, to be sure, and the harvest was safely in, the cattle not yet brought down from the summer's high pastures in the hills, and the ploughing not started. So men were not exactly idle but free, in the main, from demanding duties and toil, and cheerful about a break of this sort, however grievous the need for it. To be off a-horse amongst their fellows and friends and neighbours was a welcome change, apparently. None gave the impression of doubting their young lord's ability to lead them. Cormac's mother had given him much good advice before he left, and his ever-lively sister had said that she wished that she had been born a man, and could have gone with him.

So at the head of quite an impressive array he rode up the Dean Water, by the Haughs of Cossens and Drumgley, to Forfar Loch, and round it northabouts to the town. At the head of the mile-long loch, on the levels of the commonland, they came to a large encampment of men and horses, the mormaor's assembly point. Cormac left his people here to go on to the castle on the higher ground north-east of the town to report to Connacher.

He found the mormaor with his chieftains and vassals, all of whom Cormac had seen only three weeks before at the funeral of his father. Glamis was the only thanedom in Angus, so in fact he was next in rank to the mormaor himself, and was greeted with a mixture of respect for his status and scarcely hidden questions as to his fitness to succeed Thane Farquhar who, to be sure, had been a notable warrior; this partly responsible for his only son's self-doubts. He at least was able to announce the largest contribution to the muster, apart from the mormaor's own contingent, this making something of an impact.

They would ride at noon, Connacher said. He reckoned that they would amount to over eight hundred, and seemed satisfied with this, at least as to numbers, however unhappy he and the others were over the reasons for this mission.

After some suitable provision for the inner man, the great company, it was all but a host indeed, set off northwards, going by Montreathmont Muir and Aldie and the South Esk to Brechin, there to pick up more men, and on still northwards for Stracathro to the North Esk, and into the Howe of the Mearns. Fettercairn, their destination, lay amongst the northern slopes of the Howe, on the edge of the Highland mountains, some forty miles away. Even with so large a company they ought to get halfway there by evening, Stracathro perhaps.

Cormac chose to ride with his own people, flanked by some of his landholders and notables, but with Duncan, Pate the Mill and Calum the Smith nearby. Perhaps

Connacher would disapprove of this, thinking that he ought to be up at *his* side; but the Lady Ada had warned her son not to let the mormaor dominate him, as he possibly would seek to do. She did not greatly like their sub-king, and in the present grim situation too close an association with him could be to Cormac's disadvantage; admittedly he owed the mormaor allegiance, but he was Thane of Glamis, and held his rank and position directly of the Ard Righ, the High King of Scots, never forget that.

At Brechin, in the late afternoon, they collected another two hundred men, amidst some delay, so it was in the evening's dusk that they reached Stracathro and the River North Esk. This was the border between Angus proper and its subsidiary province of the Mearns, part of the mormaordom but a section of it another thanedom held direct of the High King, like Glamis, a situation which Connacher deplored and why he had had his daughter Fenella marry the late thane thereof. The Scoto-Pictish system of government had its peculiarities and inconsistencies.

They spent the night in what had been a Roman marching-camp on the right bank of the West Water just short of its confluence with the North Esk, the green embankments and ditches enclosing a notably wide area, possibly five or six acres – this almost as far north as those invaders had got in their unsuccessful attempts to conquer Caledonia.

Five miles more, in the morning, up the North Esk, past Edzell to Gannochy, and they would strike off eastwards another five, for Fettercairn. What would they find there? all wondered. Connacher, never a talkative man, had grown very silent. The situation ahead of them was utterly unpredictable. With over one thousand men, they ought to be reasonably secure from attack. But Finlay mac Ruaraidh, Mormaor of Moray, the nearest sub-king to the north, was a noted fighter, and by this time might have arrived on the scene of the Ard Righ's murder, and be for taking harsh action.

Connacher sent scouting parties ahead as they entered the Fettercairn district next day. It was a large area comprising most of the thanedom of the Mearns, fully a dozen miles by seven, including the hillfoots of Fasque, Glensough and Drumtochty on the north, and Thornton, Garvoch and Fordoun on the south, the Bervie Water making the eastern boundary and this Esk on the west, the Dowrie, Black Burn, Luther and Ducat Waters dividing it, these all draining the fertile centre of the Howe. The community of Fettercairn itself lay right in the middle, on another water, the Cauldcoats, with its three mills, its fairground, its clay pottery and ironstone smithies, which, with a monastery and a church made quite an important place. The scouts reporting no unusual activity thereabouts, to this township the mormaor led the way.

They approached the Lady Fenella's house cautiously, with groups out to north and south in case of opposition or any possible flight therefrom. Cormac had been here as a boy with his father, but did not remember much about it. The castle stood, typically, on a mound in the midst of a wide morass, not so large as Glamis but strongly sited, with only a single causeway through the mire to give access, this twisting and zigzagging for security. No signs of alarm or opposition greeted the company's arrival at the marsh edge. The mormaor's banner, of course, flew prominently above the leading group, and would be recognised.

Leaving almost all his people on the firm ground, Connacher rode out with a small group along the partly mud-covered stone causeway, Cormac included. Within hailing distance of the palisade a horn blew and a shout reached them.

"Is that the Lord Connacher who comes?" they heard. "Do you seek the Lady Fenella?"

"I do," the mormaor called back. "I am her father."

"Yes, Lord Mormaor. But she is gone. She went to the Green Castle these three days past. Men came from Kincardine, so she went. You will know the Green Castle? It is I, Fergus, keeper here, who speak."

"I know it, yes, man. I will go there now. But I may be back, Fergus."

They reined round carefully on that narrow and deliberately difficult firm pathway to return to their waiting men.

Connacher did not seem surprised by this of his daughter's move to Green Castle, some four miles away to the north-east amongst the hills, a small and remote hold at the mouth of Glen Sough in the Drumtochty Hills, so named from the site of an ancient Pictish fort on which it was built. It would be a useful refuge in her present circumstances, little known and difficult of access for any large numbers. Cormac had never been there although he had heard of it. For good reason, then, the mormaor decided not to take his force there, leaving all but about a dozen at Fettercairn village itself, there to intercept any possible move from Kincardine Castle. Cormac went with him.

This of Kincardine was something of a problem and complication, not only for the Mearns thanes but for Angus altogether. For it was a hunting-seat of the High Kings, set there in the midst of the Howe only three miles from Fettercairn, and moreover with its own deer-driving area up on the mountain skirts to the north, this with an elaborate system of deer dykes and gaps therein where the herds could be rounded up and driven through, for ease of crossbow killing on a large scale. It might well have been on such a sporting occasion that Fenella had lured her victim to his death, whatever was the device. Ewan mac Dairmid, the keeper of Kincardine, he who had brought the word of the High King's slaying, was friendly with the mormaor; but the fear was that the king's murder could have brought some enquiring and punitive host down upon the area, especially that of the somewhat dreaded Mormaor Finlay of Moray and Ross. Connacher desired no sort of clash with any such at this stage.

The small group, then, proceeded up into the steep hillsides, amongst corries, ravines and waterfalls, by Fasque and Craigmoston and the Hunter's Hill, to the higher Drumtochty range, where, within the mouth of Glen Sough soared the crag on which perched the Green Castle, a mere single tower rising amidst the grass-grown ramparts of the old Pictish fort. This, eyed warily by most there, who had never seen it before, demanded a very different approach from the Fettercairn one, a steep and difficult track winding its way upwards between the rocks and bluffs. Up this Connacher led his little party.

This time they were not hailed by any watchful guard, no doubt such being scarcely necessary. They reached the heavily barred door of the tower without interruption, and had to hammer thereon with sword hilts to gain any attention.

It was an elderly man who eventually peered down on them from an upper window, and no doubt recognising that banner, waved and indicated that he would admit them. The group dismounted, room to leave their horses limited.

The old man, one Donald mac Brude, and allegedly a Dane-fighter once, opened up and led the newcomers within. But at once he announced that he and his wife were alone in the tower, that the Lady Fenella was gone, where he did not know, this to the mormaor's exasperation.

But this veteran could inform them of other than his mistress's present whereabouts, and extraordinary information it proved to be, all but unbelievable indeed. It seemed that the Lady Fenella had been planning her revenge for the death of her son for some considerable time, sufficiently long to be able to achieve it in unique and bizarre fashion. She had had a lifesize figure of a young man designed and forged by one of the Fettercairn blacksmiths in iron and bronze, this with an arm outstretched holding a golden apple set with gems, to be a gift for the High King. This figure was set between two tall wooden coffers, painted with flowers and images, the whole a decorative and artistic creation. But when that apple was touched, hidden springs in the coffers opened the doors, and within were fixed crossbows, four of them, arrows fitted and strings taut, and these would immediately discharge their bolts into anyone standing before them, from each side.

Scarcely able to comprehend all this, Connacher demanded explanation, elucidation; also how his daughter could possibly have thought of and produced anything such?

Donald mac Brude said that she had devised it in conjunction with the smith Congal, in Fettercairn, which man had promptly disappeared when the deed was done, no doubt all arranged beforehand. He was evidently a scoundrel of wicked ingenuity. They had erected the contrivance in a handsome room of this castle, and when King Kenneth returned from hunting up at his deer dykes one day, pausing for refreshment at Fettercairn on the way back to Kincardine, the Lady Fenella had gone to him and told him that she had a gift for him, to prove her loyalty now that she no longer blamed him for the death of her wicked son, whom she now realised had been justly executed. She persuaded the monarch to go with her, alone, to her castle for the expected present, leaving his companions with the horses. There Kenneth had admired the statue and artwork, congratulating her upon it, and duly reached out for the golden apple. The coffer doors had swung open and the four crossbows, strings twanging, had discharged their arrows directly into the monarch, who had fallen, fatally pierced by the sharp and poisoned bolts. His slayer had left him lying there, and slipped out of the castle by a rear door and away. So had ended the twenty-four-year reign of Kenneth the Second, High King of Scots.

The elderly man's hearers could only stare at each other in astonishment, all but incredulity. Could all this be possible? Yet the High King was dead and Fenella had bolted. Donald assured them that his mistress had told him these details herself, and proudly. She had given him no hint as to where she had gone now.

The mormaor, needless to say, was in a quandary as to what course to take. His daughter could be anywhere, even fled into the Highlands. Did he wish to find her? Would it not be wise to distance himself from her, in more than mere miles? As one of the sub-kings, he wanted no seeming links with the murder of the Ard Righ. He could not deny being father of the murderess, but his condemnation of the deed should be made apparent to all. Connacher was not a man apt to heed and consult with others, but in this remarkable situation he did express his doubts and queries as to action now with his senior companions – not that they could be of any great help to him.

None certainly advised that he should go seeking Fenella. Some suggested that he would be wise to disband this host meantime and return to Forfar, lest he seemed to be in armed revolt in support of his daughter. Others thought that a visit to Kincardine Castle was called for. The king's body presumably would have been taken there, and it might be suitable to pay respects and discover what was likely to be the immediate outcome. After all, Ewan the keeper there had come to inform him of the slaying, so the mormaor's visit might well be expected. Cormac agreed with this as a first step. But – to take his host of men, or not? Connacher decided against this. Best not to appear in any way warlike. Probably he should not have assembled his strength at all. He had thought that he might have to protect his errant daughter, but this was clearly not now to be considered. Better to send the men back to Forfar, and go on with his present little party to Kincardine. Tell his people, however, to be ready to muster again quickly if dire trouble did erupt for them all.

So, the Green Castle being only a couple of miles north of Kincardine, although hidden behind hills, the mormaor sent two of his group back to Fettercairn to order his host to return whence they had come, and with the remainder rode off southwards over the high ground for the royal hunting-seat.

They found Ewan mac Dairmid was gone, his wife saying that, after he had returned from informing the Mormaor of Angus of the tragedy, a worried man, he had decided that he must likewise report the situation to the next nearest mormaor, that of Atholl; or not quite the nearest, but the Mormaor of Mar was a child. The High King's main seat and palace was at Forteviot, in Fortrenn, none so far south of Atholl lands, so he could discover what was necessary to be done there. It would be long riding through the mountains westwards to Blair-in-Atholl, but her husband had felt that he had to go.

They were taken to see the corpse of the slain monarch, being kept meantime in the castle's ice-house outside, used for the preservation of game and fish, however unsuitable a resting-place this might seem to be. In due course, no doubt, the body would be encased in a lead coffin and conveyed to the Isle of Iona in the Hebrides, where the Kings of Scots were always buried.

Kenneth, a man in his fifties, made a grim sight, for although his body was now wrapped in plaiding, one of the arrows had pierced his eye, and so directly into the brain, part of the short shaft still protruding, and dry caked blood and mucus covering the face. They did not linger long in that ice-house on account of more than the cold.

What now, then? Connacher decided that there was nothing for it but to return to Forfar to await decisions and events. He feared, admittedly, that his daughter might have thought to flee to him there for protection, and if so, what he would do he did not divulge. But there would almost certainly be a call for him to go to Iona for the funeral; always the mormaors attended the obsequies and thereafter met to elect the new Ard Righ. Even the father of the murderess would be expected to attend, and, needless to say, he would be concerned to use the occasion to assure all thereat of his innocence and complete ignorance and condemnation of Fenella's terrible deed.

They did not delay at Kincardine, therefore. Connacher did not get on well with Finlay, Mormaor of Moray and Ross, an ancient grudge, and although the latter's capital was at Inverness, far to the north, he was quite often in the upland hunting areas of lower Speyside and the Forest of Avon, none so distant. So he might have got word of the deed, and could come to Kincardine to investigate.

It was back home for them all meantime, the future uncertain to a degree. Cormac's first action as Thane of Glamis had been unprecedented and harrowing, but it had made no great demands on his qualities of leadership at least.

2

It was not long before the next summons arrived at Glamis, this for attendance at Iona for King Kenneth's funeral. His mother had warned Cormac that thanedoms, being held directly of the crown, were expected to be represented. Kenneth having reigned for twenty-four years, there had been no royal interment during Cormac's lifetime, so he had not heard his father talk of such. At least this ought not to represent any major test of his leadership, and in fact might well be an interesting and memorable experience, so long as there were no difficult repercussions because of his links with the Mormaor Connacher and his daughter's responsibility for this assembly in the Inner Hebrides. There was still no news of that wicked woman.

So, only five days after the return to Forfar, Cormac was picked up by Connacher's party at Glamis, on its way westwards. This time there was no call to take any "tail" of followers, although the mormaor did ride with an escort of some fifty, as apparently was suitable for his status as one of the seven sub-kings. Cormac took only his hawking friend Duncan the Tranter, with no ambition to create an impression.

And very much westwards they had to go, a lengthy, cross-country journey, and most of the way through the mountains. It was as well that the murder had not taken place in mid-winter, when their route would have been all but impassable. They rode out of Strathmore by Blairgowrie and the passes between the lochs of Rae, Drumellie and Clunie, to Dunkeld, that abbey town founded by King Kenneth mac Alpin, the first monarch of both Picts and Scots, where he had established a monastic settlement of the Keledei, the Friends of God, an especial grouping of the Celtic Church monks, which had given the place its name of dun-keledie. Here they spent the first night, and learned from the abbot that the night before he had had to act host to the Thane of Fife, MacDuff, and his party, on the same journey.

Next day it was on down Strath Braan to Amulree, and then north through Glen Quaich and its peaks to Kenmore at the foot of Loch Tay in Breadalbane, the dividing ridge or watershed of Alba, and along that lengthy loch to Killin for the night, a fifty-mile progress through very rough country, these Highland miles very much slower and more demanding riding than even the uplands of their own Strathmore.

From Killin they threaded long Glen Dochart to Crianlarich, under the twin peaks of Ben More and Stobinian, then up Strathfillan to Tyndrum, to their highest pass of all, then downhill all the way to the foot of Loch Awe by Glen Orchy. They were in Ergadia, or Argyll now; and winning through the savage defile of the Pass of Brander, scene of many an ambush in clan warfare, they came to salt water at last, the sea loch of Etive, at the mouth of which was Dunstaffnage.

Kenneth mac Alpin had brought the coronation Stone of Destiny here from their destination, Iona, when it was being ravaged by the Danes, this before it was finally taken to Scone. At Dunstaffnage they had to leave their horses, amongst hundreds of others, for here they must transfer themselves to boats, galleys and birlinns, even captured Norse longships, for the final leg of their lengthy journey to the Inner Hebrides. The fact that Scotland's High Kings were always buried on the hallowed isle of St Columba did involve a great deal of difficult travel for its magnates, especially as it had to be done all too often, for few of the monarchs achieved such lengthy reigns as had Kenneth the Second.

Fortunately it was a pleasant autumn and the seas were not rough. Cormac and Duncan found themselves embarked in a small, twelve-oared, single-masted birlinn with a group of Athollmen, parties all having to split up in these circumstances. There was much talk about the slaying of the High King, much of it erroneous, but Cormac kept his mouth shut, advisedly.

Their sail down the Firth of Lorne, past the isles of Kerrera and Seil, was scenic indeed, with azure and cerulean green waters, dazzling white cockleshell sand, skerries and reefs innumerable with their colourful seaweeds so different from the eastern Norse Sea sort, all backed by endless mountains on mainland and islands. At the firth mouth they swung westwards to round the lengthy Ross peninsula of the great Isle of Mull, past its dramatic headland of Erraid, and there, one mile ahead of them, was their destination, the sacred Isle of Iona, where Columba had brought Christianity to this land nearly five hundred years before, and set up his first mission-station and monastery. Small but hilly, it was Scotland's most holy place, often as it had been ransacked and savaged by the heathen Danes. It was but three and a half miles long by half that in width, rugged with colourful rocks, including much pale green marble, with little bays and cliffs, gleaming white sands, hilly to the north with its culminating peak of Dun I, the entire coastline dotted with islets and skerries.

Cormac had heard much of Iona of course, but mainly of its history and hallowed traditions, and he had never thought of it as quite so small as this, however beautiful.

Halfway up the mile-wide sound between it and Mull, their birlinn put in to a haven in St Ronan's Bay, so far as they could see the only harbour on the island. It was now packed with craft for this special occasion, however few would be there normally; indeed Cormac and his companions had to clamber over other moored boats to reach dry land.

At least there was no problem as to where to go, the abbey, monastic buildings and community all being near the haven. Crowds flocked about, and tented encampments were being erected. What the folk of Iona thought of this invasion was a matter for conjecture.

Cormac and Duncan found their mormaor's company eventually, although Connacher was not with them, no doubt closeted with his fellow great ones in the abbot's house. They learned that the burial ceremony was to take place on the morrow, so, glad to stretch their legs after all the riding and sailing, they set off to explore the island. Others were doing the like, but mainly up this eastern side; so they headed westwards, across rough but not hilly ground, to the other shore, this highly scenic, with little cliffs, bays and inlets, these floored with that pure white sand which, with the many-hued seaweeds, turned water and all into a lightsome wonder of translucent colours. The pair had already picked up little pieces of green marble as mementoes.

At a lonely cottage, a goatherd told them that one of the nearby bays, Port a Churaich, the bay of the currach he named it, was where St Columba had landed, back in 563, from Ireland; and climbing the hummock behind, had ascertained that he could not see his native land to the west, and decided that here, amidst all God's beauty, he would settle. Apparently he had taken a vow that he would not reside in any spot of what was to be his mission-field where he could still see Ireland, lest he be tempted to give up his efforts and return home – a touching indication of the saint's human strengths and weaknesses. He and his companions had landed at a few other places on this western seaboard, but always, across the Irish Sea, their land had still been visible. Here, not so.

From Port a Churaich the pair picked their way up that fascinating coast, a quite strenuous progress, with much clambering and circling and back-tracking. They saw a ship-barrow which the goatherd had told them of, with two standing stones marking it, allegedly to bury the boat which the missionaries had used to sail from Ireland; also a hillock named Sithean Mor, the Fairy Mound, with its stone circle of the ancient druidical sun-worshipping days, which Columba had not cast down, declaring that it was a place of worship, however mistaken the deity, and should remain so, setting up a cross there and blessing it in Christ's name.

At the very northern tip of the island they looked across to the further Hebridean vistas, magnificent as they were far-flung, and they decided to climb Dun I, no very major ascent but quite spectacular in its shape and isolation. The views therefrom were even more stupendous, in every direction; small wonder that the missionary-saint had come up here often to commune with the Maker of it all, dwelling on God's attributes of love, order, beauty and truth.

Returning down the east coast to the abbey area and encampment, hungry, they were made only too well aware that food for this multitude on a small island was a problem indeed. Supplies of beef and fish and meal had been sent for from the larger Mull, and this had not yet arrived; when it did, rations would be apt to be small. It occurred to Cormac to walk back again to the goatherd's cothouse, where they managed to purchase oatcakes, honey and cheese made from the goats' milk, and also spent some time pleasantly with the herd, his wife and daughters. Indeed, instead of making their way back to the abbey and its crowded encampment, they passed a quite comfortable night in the hay of the cotter's barn.

Next noonday, the service of burial of the murdered Kenneth the Second was, in fact, quite simple and brief, however significant, conducted by the abbot, with much blowing of horns, declaring of ancestry, chanting of victories won and famous deeds, to the tapping of drums. The Reelig Oran, where it took place, was not a large building, so that only the mormaors and members of the royal houses, with the abbot and monks, could get inside; so even thanes and chieftains had to stand around, with the horn-blowers, drum-beaters and chanters. At least there were no horses nor hounds to bury, this time, in the nearby ground, for there was a tradition enshrining such peculiar custom in that Columba had held that since love was of God, and eternal, animals which men loved would go on to the afterlife with them, and so should have a form of Christian burial; it was said that his own old horse, which carried his portable altar, had been heedfully interred.

The ceremony over, the mormaors returned to the abbey for the vital decision on who was to be the next High King. This Scots usage was unique amongst monarchies in being elective rather than purely hereditary or won by force of arms. The ancient Pictish royal succession had been matrilineal, that is passing through the female line, not the male. This had in time become fused with the Dalriadic Scots succession into two alternate royal lines, from which the mormaors chose the most able and suitable candidate. These mormaors were themselves kingly, sub-monarchs, seven of them, allied to the main royal lines in blood, however far back, and were territorial in designation and authority: Angus, Atholl, Moray with Ross, Mar, Strathearn with Menteith, Caithness with Sutherland, and Lennox. The present Mormaor of Mar was a mere boy, but he was there to give his vote. And the aged Mormaor of Strathearn had been brought all the way in a litter.

Cormac wondered how Connacher was faring with his fellows in this situation, especially with his enemy Finlay of Moray. Neither of the two royal families themselves, as such, was partaking in this age-old choosing, although some of the sub-kings were closely related. The general opinion was that Constantine, son of the former King Cuilean, whom the slain Kenneth had succeeded, would be chosen, a mature, sound man, whereas Malcolm mac Kenneth was only seventeen years old. Another Kenneth there, a younger son of the King Cuilean's father, Dubh or Duff, was Mormaor of Atholl, and was the uncle of Prince Malcolm on the female side, would probably be pushing his claim. And he had powerful support, if it came to trouble, for *his* younger son was Dungal MacDuff, Thane of Fife, this a great and rich appanage of the crown.

It took a long time for the electors to reach a decision, so clearly Constantine's nomination was not going to be unanimous. The rest of the assembled company waited anxiously, for the result could be important for them all in more ways than one.

When at length the mormaors emerged from the abbey, their faces were scanned keenly. Kenneth mac Duff of Atholl was scowling, and Finlay of Moray looking very doubtful, the others' expressions varying. That probably meant that Constantine had been appointed, but not without discord. Cormac had no particular preference, but assumed that the older and experienced man would probably make the more competent monarch.

At least Connacher did not look particularly upset, fairly grim as was his usual expression. Did that mean that he had been able to avoid any major blame and condemnation for his daughter's deed? He was not the sort of man who committed himself to confidence, nor indeed anything much in the way of converse with others, so his people were left to draw their own conclusions.

The Angus contingent was not long in taking its departure from Iona for the long journey home. But heading back for Dunstaffnage in Argyll, Lennox territory, Cormac did learn from others in his boat that the mormaors had condemned Fenella of the Mearns to death, this sentence to be enacted at the earliest; and Connacher, as her mormaor as well as her father, had been ordered to bring it about. How he felt about that was anybody's guess; but none was going to question him on the matter, particularly not the new Thane of Glamis.

3

Whatever Connacher's part in the matter of Fenella, and whatever orders he gave, he and his nobles, including Cormac mac Farquhar, were within the month on their way westwards again, not so far this time, for Scone on the Tay, near St John's Town of Perth, this for the coronation of Constantine mac Cuilean as the third King of Scots of that name. Fenella, wherever she was, had not yet been apprehended.

From Forfar to Perth was only some forty miles through fairly level country, so easily covered in a day. They found a great gathering assembling there, far more than at the Iona funeral. There was the significant absence of the Mormaor of Atholl, although the more notable in that his younger son MacDuff of Fife had an important part to play therein, the Thanes of Fife having the hereditary privilege of placing the crown on the High King's head.

The ceremony was in two parts, as the Iona one had been, the actual coronation taking place in Scone Abbey, on the east bank of Tay three miles north of Perth, and the fealty-taking outside at a mound called the Moot Hill, this last accounting for the large numbers attending, for only a small proportion of these present could gain entry to the limited space of the abbey-church. Fealty was required from all land-holders.

Thanes were amongst those entering the church, and Cormac duly took his place in the third row of benches, in the nave, the front row reserved for members of the royal families, the second for those of the mormaors. Behind were the chieftains, nobles and senior land-holders, such as could squeeze in.

The chancel was empty, save for the Stone of Destiny before the high altar.

When all was ready, to much blowing of bulls' horns, the Abbot of Scone and other senior clerics filed into the chancel and took up their places. Then the High Sennachie led in the mormaors, six of them, including the boy Mar and the frail Strathearn, he walking with a stick. Behind came MacDuff, Thane of Fife, carrying the crown on a cushion, to go round and stand behind the stone, the mormaors ranged at either side.

The drums started to beat in their regular rhythm, and Constantine mac Cuilean strode in alone. He was a grave-looking man in his late forties, bearing himself well, not exactly handsome but with striking features. All stood at his entry. He was growing bald, it was noted.

Cormac stood between the Thanes of Cromarty and Gowrie. Others with them were Muthill, Kintore, Cromdale and Breadalbane. There was presently no Thane of the Mearns, that thanedom having been forfeited to the crown over Fenella's treason.

Constantine went to stand in front of the Stone, not to sit yet, while the abbot commenced the service with prayer. Choristers up in the gallery then chanted a hymn of praise. This was followed by a long roll of drumming, and the High Sennachie, in his handsome robes, stepped forward to announce that here before them all was the High King of Scots, twelfth since Kenneth mac Alpin, and the thirty-sixth Ard Righ of Alba, Constantine mac Cuilean, mac Indulf, mac Constantine, mac Aedh, mac Constantine, mac Kenneth, he chosen by the mormaors to occupy the ancient throne. He then read out the names of the alternate line of High Kings, starting with the late Kenneth the Second, mac Dubh, mac Malcolm mac Donald; and thereafter catalogued the entire list of Pictish Ard Righ back into the mists of antiquity.

This lengthy peroration over, he went, bowing, to take the arm of Constantine and lower him on to the coronation stone.

"Whosoever sits on this stone shall rule this realm, and only he!" he declared resoundingly.

The abbot brought a cloak of purple and gold to drape over the new monarch's shoulders as he sat.

The Sennachie pointed imperiously to the Thane of Fife, who came forward with the cushion and crown. Handing the former to the Sennachie, he went to stand before Constantine, bowing, and held the crown high.

The drums beat, the horns blew, the choristers chanted, and throughout the church all cheered and went on cheering.

MacDuff lowered the golden circlet on to the new monarch's head. Many there no doubt considered the fact, as did Cormac, that the only mormaor who had absented himself was MacDuff's father, Kenneth of Atholl, a most notable circumstance. What did this imply? Were father and son at variance? Or was it that the younger man was concerned that none other should crown the King of Scots?

When the noise died away, the abbot took over. He blessed the Ard Righ, in the name of the Father, the Son and the Holy Spirit, then gestured to the waiting mormaors. There was no order of precedence amongst them save that of length of tenure. So old Strathearn came first. Even with his stick he had great difficulty in bending the one knee, as required. As well that he did not have to take the royal hand between his own two, in the fealty gesture, or that stick would have presented a problem; the *righ*, being sub-kings, did not have to offer fealty. He kissed Constantine's upraised hand, and bowed away.

Then came Lennox and Angus, then Moray and Caithness, and lastly the young Mar, all kissing the hand.

This done, the High Sennachie thumped his staff of office three times on the marble floor to indicate the end of the ceremonial. The abbot pronounced a general benediction on all. Constantine rose from the Stone and led his mormaors out of the chancel, to the cheers of the congregation.

Scotland had a High King again.

All left the church for the second part of the proceedings, Cormac feeling in the pocket of the jerkin beneath his thane's tabard to ensure that he still had the handful of Glamis earth that he had brought.

Joining the crowd outside, all flocked the short distance to the Moot Hill, a low mound amongst trees, irregular as to shape and with a flattish top. Around this the great company gathered, with some confusion, even argument as to precedences. There was much talk and discussion.

Presently, to more drum-beating, six men emerged from the church, bearing between them on a sort of hurdle their heavy and precious burden, the Stone of Destiny, to bring and place it on top of the mound. It was a massive oblong block of dark, almost black stone, polished and decorated with Celtic carving, of seat height with a shallow hollow on top, and curious rounded volutes, or handles, at each end for lifting it. There were various stories as to this object's origin. The Stone was probably a large meteorite, by the colour, for such were considered to be holy, having come down from heaven. Some said that it was Jacob's Pillow, of Old Testament fame, brought from Egypt by the Princess Scota, who gave Scots their name. Some that it had come from the Hill of Tara, whereon the Irish High Kings were crowned. Or again that it had been the seat of justice brought from Spain by Gaythelos. Even that it might have been a Roman altar. That it had indeed been an altar, probably, was now the generally accepted belief; Columba's own portable shrine, the hollow on its top scooped out for containing water for baptisms; it was known that the saint took such with him on his missionary travels. If in fact this heavy weight had been carried by the old horse buried at Iona, then the animal certainly deserved the honour.

Left up on the Moot Hill, it awaited events.

In due course Constantine and his train came in procession from the abbey, he and his mormaors to climb the mound. Then to the continued beat of drums, the fealty-swearing began, commencing with the thanes, the land-holders of Scotland mounting the hillock, there bowing, to empty their handfuls of soil from their land before the High King for him to place his foot thereon. Then to kneel before him, these on both knees, take his hand between both of their own, and vow allegiance. That earth was the symbol that in theory all the realm's land was the king's, and that he stood on it to receive the fealty of those whom he allowed to use it, this to save the monarch having to travel to every corner of the country for the submission.

MacDuff was the first thane to kneel, with Cormac the third. Perhaps he should not have done so, but the latter wondered how genuine was the former's vow of allegiance.

It took a long time for all that host of land-holders to make their obeisances, and all the while the heap of soil grew, and had to be pushed aside from the feet of the Ard Righ. This was how the knoll had been formed. And through it all the drumming continued without pause, a strange accompaniment.

When at last it was finished, the abbot and his monks brought out a feast of sorts to the assembly there around the Moot Hill, a major provision which they had not had to offer for long, thanks to King Kenneth's long reign. Always there was speculation as to how soon or distant would be the next occasion.

Thereafter most of the company found its way to Perth for overnight accommodation, only the very lofty ones being able to be housed in the monastic premises. The inns, taverns and hospices of St John's Town had a busy night of it, not all the citizens the better therefor.

In the morning it was back to Strathmore for the Mormaor Connacher's party, Cormac being dropped off at Glamis.

It was three days later that he learned the news. Fenella of the Mearns was dead. Apparently Connacher had left

Ewan, keeper of Kincardine's royal castle, to bring her to justice if he could. That man had heard that she was hiding in a herd's cottage in the low Hills of Garvock area some ten miles east of Fettercairn, and he had sought her there. Warned, apparently, she had fled still further eastwards towards the coast to escape her pursuers, and possibly to find a fishing-boat in the Gourdon Bay havens. But she had not got that far before her hunters caught up with her, this at the edge of a steep ravine where the Burn of Mathers plunged down towards the shore. And there, on the lip of the abyss, where a waterfall hurtled down amidst spray, seeing that there was now no escape for her, she had shaken her fist back at them and then thrown herself over to her death on the rocks far below, a woman distraught.

So had ended an episode unique in even Scotland's turbulent and bloody history – and possibly the best outcome in the circumstances. Possibly, also, her father heaved a sigh of relief.

4

The new reign of Constantine the Bald was not long in being plunged into trouble. The Danes, those bloodthirsty heathen marauders, who for so long had been the terror of almost all northern Christendom, had these last years left Scotland more or less in peace, raiding occasionally along the northern coasts from their bases in Orkney and Shetland, but making no serious invasions, changing their targets to northern Ireland, although southern England, and even Wales, were also suffering their attentions. But, a mere five weeks after his enthronement, the new Ard Righ was faced with a challenge indeed, a quite major Danish assault on Lothian. And at this time of the year, almost November, it could be no mere hosting, as the term went, a sort of summertime activity, all but holiday, which these sea-rovers indulged in gleefully after the long, land-based winter and spring humdrum affairs of family and food production. So it probably meant that this was invasion with a view to settling, at least for some period, as they had been doing in Ireland, and so would have to be dealt with, and in vehement fashion. From all accounts they had landed in large numbers along the south shores of the Scotwater, or Firth of Forth – and whatever else they were, they were doughty fighters. So it was a call to arms.

Lothian was a difficult and problem-forming part of the realm, and always had been. Indeed some in the north might claim that it was not really part of Scotland at all. It had formed the small kingdom of a Pictish tribe which the Romans had called the Votadini, and its king in the sixth century, called Loth, gave it its present name. But it had been so often invaded and occupied by the Angles of neighbouring Northumberland and Bernicia that it had all but lost its Pictish character, however often the Scots from Fife and further north sought to recover it, for it was a notably fertile land, with the two great vales of Tyne and Peffer between its Lammermuir Hills and the sea. Oddly enough, Lothian was an ominous name for Constantine, for a score or so of years before, his sister had been abducted by an Anglian princeling from there; and when their father, King Cuilean, had gone to rescue her, he had been slain there, and the daughter also.

Now it was the Danes, not the Angles, who were seeking to take it over, it seemed.

The High King had no army of his own for such campaigns, dependent on the forces of his mormaors, not all of whom would be eager to take any major part in battling for Lothian, that faraway appendage, especially those of the northerly areas like Moray, Ross and Caithness. But Connacher of Angus was anxious to prove himself helpfully loyal after the murder of the late monarch, and sought to muster his fullest strength. And this not only demanded a good Glamis contingent but involved Cormac in a rather odd task.

Connacher had had only the one child, Fenella, and his heir was his younger brother. This Aidan was a peculiar character for a mormaor's brother and son, a retiring, studious man, learned and inactive save for his mind, more suited for the Church than for the duties of rule and governance. He lived well apart from his brother, down on the coast at the Red Castle of Lunan, a good score of miles to the east. He was not good at raising his people, farmers, herds and fishermen, for military duties, nor interested; and Connacher, reckoning that any ordinary messenger would probably be ignored, asked Cormac to act the courier and to urge a good turnout of men for the mormaordom's muster, a thane's voice probably the more effective.

So, with Duncan as company, he rode for Lunan Bay,

leaving Pate the Mill and Calum the Smith to assemble his own manpower and the necessary horses. They went by Forfar itself, and Guthrie and Braikie, across the Muir of Rossie to the Lunan Water, and down that quite major river to salt water at its mouth in the great bay. And just where the river coiled in tight loops as it entered the sea, on a tall rocky knowe within one of the loops, soared the square keep and outer walls of Red Castle; and red it was indeed for, unlike most strongholds of those years, it was built of stone instead of timber clay-covered, the local scarlet stone much more readily available hereabouts than was suitable wood. A notable and challenging fortalice it made, wind-blown, sometimes no doubt spray-showered, like a great red fist shaken in the face of the turbulent Norse Sea, a strange retreat for the scholarly Lord Aidan, his hermitage as it were.

Cormac had never actually visited here before, although he had seen Red Castle from the higher ground of Lunan Bay's cliffs. This was a large bay, the largest on all the Angus and Mearns coast, fully five miles between Red Head and Boddin Point, fine sands in the centre, and with its own central harbour of Ethiehaven some two miles south of this castle.

It was not a hold to take horses up to, over steep and craggy rock, so the pair left their mounts at a couple of fishermen's cottages at the foot, to climb its zigzag track up. At the rock-top, irregularly shaped as it was, and of broken levels, the outer walls of the small courtyard were of odd elevations and angles, inevitably, and there was no gatehouse. The gates stood open, looking as though they were seldom shut. Into the rock-floored little yard the visitors passed, to go and hammer on the keep door. They got the impression that callers here would be few.

They had to wait some time for any response to their knocking; in fact they thumped a second time. But the answer, when it came, was worth the waiting, for it was a young woman who eventually opened to them, and an eye-catching one at that, red-haired as befitted her domicile, great-eyed and as lovely as she was well-built. She considered them with something like surprise but nowise unwelcomingly. She was dressed simply but in a fashion that did no injustice to her figure.

"I am Cormac of Glamis," she was told. "Come from the Mormaor Connacher to see the Lord Aidan. A good-day to you, lady."

"Ah, I have heard of the new Thane of Glamis," she said. "Greetings, my lord. I am Fenella."

Cormac blinked and swallowed, abruptly at a loss for words. He had never heard Aidan's daughter's name. Another Fenella!

"Come, you,"they were invited. "I will take you to my father. Here is a pleasant occasion, surely. And your . . . friend?"

"He is my tranter, Duncan by name." They followed her inside. Fenella must be a family name – so they were cousins. But, in these circumstances, what a name for this one to be saddled with!

"You have ridden today from Glamis?" they were asked, as she led them up the winding turnpike stair. "Then you will be ready for a meal, I think? And one is all but ready. Humble as it may be, for the Thane of Glamis!" That was not exactly mocking, but held a note of challenge almost. Had he looked too much askance at the announcement of her name? This one, Cormac assessed, might well be a lass of spirit.

Upstairs, through a hall more comfortably furnished and decorated than the grim exterior might have indicated, the walls, although of stone, were whitewashed and painted in bright colours with strange animals, designs and Celtic symbols, deer- and sheepskin rugs on the stone floor.

They passed into a withdrawing-room where a fire burned brightly and a middle-aged woman of strong and rather gaunt features and slender build was setting places at a table. She looked up surprised at the arrival of visitors, eyeing the girl enquiringly; clearly this was where Fenella got her red hair, her mother indubitably.

The Thane of Glamis was introduced, and his companion indicated, and the lady came across to greet them, more guardedly than had her daughter, sizing up the newcomers.

"I knew the Thane Farquhar – but long ago," she told Cormac. "Before I was wed. I heard of his death with due sorrow. I remember him as handsome."

"The thane comes from my Uncle Connacher, to see my father," the younger woman said. "I will go to fetch him." She glanced back. "These will be hungry, Mother – they have ridden from Glamis."

"Yes. Then they will eat with us. I shall go down to see to it."

The visitors were left alone, meantime.

Duncan looked uncomfortable. "Lord Cormac, I should not be here," he declared. "Not in such company. I am but a servitor. Shall I go down? There will be a kitchen. A cook, or other, no doubt . . ."

"If these ladies so wish, they will say so, I think," he was told. "If not, bide you with me. If we can ride and hawk together, and go to war, we can eat together! This is a strange family, to be sure. Who the lady was before she married, when she knew my father, I do not know. But I—"

He was interrupted by the arrival of this young Fenella with her father. Aidan mac Nechtan was a better-looking man than was his brother, but more slightly made, stooping, seeming older, and peering short-sightedly. Uncertainly, he extended an ink-stained and rather shaking hand when his daughter introduced Cormac.

"You are Thane Farquhar's son?" he asked. "And come from my brother. He, he does not often look my way!"

Cormac glanced at the girl, almost for guidance. "As to that, my lord, I do not know. But this is a time of troubles. Much trouble. The Danes have invaded Lothian in large force. No mere raiding. So the new High King, Constantine, must go there with an army, ä large army. And the Mormaor Connacher assembles his men, his fullest force. So he seeks your Lunan people, and sends me to inform you. And, and possibly to aid you in gathering them. My own folk are being mustered at Glamis."

The other wagged his greying head. "I do not greatly concern myself with such matters, my friend," he said.

His wife and daughter exchanged glances. "If the safety of the realm is at stake?" the former put in.

"My brother will attend to that well enough."

"But we have men here, many men. They are *his* men, also."

"I will help gather some," Fenella said.

Her father shrugged. "As you will. But blood shed in such affrays is blood wasted, a source of sorrow and against God's will."

"You would have us all slain by the Danes, Aidan?"

He did not answer.

His daughter added, "It is my uncle's command. The men are his rather than ours . . ." She paused as two women came into the room with trays of food and drink.

Embarrassed somewhat over this family dispute, Cormac was glad of the diversion. Glad also of the provision, for he was hungry. A move was made to the table.

The Lady Alena steered the converse away from controversy over the meal. It seemed that she was a daughter of the former Cellach, Mormaor of Moray, which made her distant kin to Finlay, Connacher's foe – possibly part of the reason behind the enmity. She spoke of Cormac's father, and asked after his mother whom she had never met.

Duncan the Tranter remained silent.

It was only early afternoon, so Fenella said that she would change into riding clothes and take the visitors to some of the communities around Lunan Bay where men could be reached and readied, mainly fishing villages but with inland farmeries also; Ethiehaven, Boddin and Usan in particular, but also the houses of Dunninald and Courthill and Inverkeilor. Grateful for this offer, and for the attractive company involved, Cormac expressed his appreciation.

There proved to be a stable-block and two more cottages hidden down in a further hollow of the river's coiling, where Fenella, clad now in a cloak and riding-boots, saddled her horse, with suitable assistance, and led them off northwards to the hamlet of Boddin, just beyond the thrusting point of that name which was really the northern horn of Lunan Bay. Here she informed some elderly men who were mending nets at the pier of what was required by their mormaor and this Thane of Glamis. These, who clearly knew the young woman well, were respectfully friendly towards her. They agreed that two of their number should go inland to tell the farmers and herds nearby of what was ordered, Boddin's younger men being presently out in their boats fishing. These would be told on their return.

As the trio rode on, still northwards, for the next hamlet, called apparently Ulysses-haven – why Fenella had never learned despite her father's erudition – but pronounced Usan locally, she declared that horses would be the problem for these people, fisherfolk not apt to own or need such. The farmers would have beasts, but insufficient to supply the others. Cormac recognised the difficulty and said that the mormaor would send garrons down for them no doubt, if he was told how many would be required; he himself could supply some. Connacher was giving four days for the muster, so three days hence mounts should be arriving.

It was the same situation at Usan, and again Fenella did the ordering, but in kindly fashion, her instructions well received considering what an upset this summons would be to the fishing community's families, the women as well as these older men greeting the girl amiably. Obviously she was popular with her father's people.

Inland, for Dunninald then, the hallhouse of a *duin'uasal* or tenant-in-chief, holding land directly of his mormaor, this a youngish man named Drostan, who declared himself prepared to rally and indeed lead his sub-tenants and cowherds, and could even provide half a dozen extra garrons. His mother would have provided refreshment for their visitors, but Fenella was concerned about the time and the onfall of darkness, for she wanted to reach Ethiehaven, four miles southwards, before that. It was the largest village of the Lunan Bay area, and many fishing-boats should be returning to harbour before nightfall.

Cormac was grateful for all this help. He and Duncan could not have achieved it on their own thus effectively and in this time.

Calling at Courthill, inland now on their way south, this older *duin'uasal* agreed to raise his people, but made no offer to lead them thereafter.

Just over another mile and they were at Ethiehaven, a long village of a single street tucked into the narrow strip of foreshore below high steep cliffs, with an equally lengthy boat-strand, on which fishermen were drawing up and emptying their craft as the mounted group arrived. Fenella went straight down to them, dismounting, and greeting them all easily, asking after their catches before announcing the mormaor's summons to arms. She was heard with varying reactions but no sort of resentment, some of the younger men actually sounding as though they could quite enjoy this departure from routine. Cormac and Duncan were eyed speculatively.

Fenella explained about the horse provision, and this led to some doubtful glances. But doubting about horsemanship did not prevent the young woman and her companions being presented with net hampers of fish, haddocks, flounders and rock-cod, to take back.

Obviously the visitors were expected to stay the night at Red Castle, and were nowise loth in present company.

Riding back along those splendid sands, where the lofty cliffs abruptly gave way to marram-grassy dune country, Fenella told them that the shallows here were excellent for the sport of flounder-spearing, something which Cormac had never even heard of, and was told that if he cared to come back in more summery weather she would instruct him in the art. She also mentioned that it was a splendid beach for bathing and swimming from, something which rather stirred his masculine imagination, although she went into no details.

Below the castle, Duncan was found overnight accommodation in one of the cottages beside the stabling; and Cormac thereafter was led upstairs in the castle by Lady Alena and shown into a bedchamber near the tower-top, with warm water for him to wash in.

The evening meal passed without controversy, Aidan proving that he could be a good enough host when awkward subjects were avoided. Afterwards, round the fire, with its cosy ingleneuks at either side, Cormac sat beside Fenella. Almost inevitably the subject of the other Fenella came up. Aidan said that even as a child she had been wilful and difficult, although beautiful, her mother despairing of her. What sort of a wife she had made for Malcolm, Thane of the Mearns, they did not know, for they had no contacts with her; but her son had grown up as hot-headed and awkward as was his mother and, his father dying fairly young, had led his thanedom in revolt against King Kenneth sufficiently seriously to deserve his execution by that monarch – all a sorry story indeed.

The two women thereafter struck a more cheerful note, or notes, with a clarsach and a lute, both mother and daughter proving to be possessed of fine singing voices to complement the instrumental music. So the evening ended pleasantly, and bed-going was not too long delayed.

Fenella it was who escorted the guest up to his chamber, to ensure that all was arranged for his comfort, the bed warmed, the fire blazing brightly and more hot water steaming thereby. Satisfied that all was as it should be, when he expressed his gratitude for all, and for the day's help, she declared that it was not often that they had a thane visiting them, and added, with a little laugh, one not too proud to travel with only a tranter. Were they particular friends?

"Friends, yes," she was told. "Duncan has taught me much, all my days. More than just the hawking. He is a dozen years older than am I, and a good and able man. The bastard of an abbot."

"I see. I wondered . . ." She turned for the door. "Sleep you well, then, Cormac the Thane. With kindly dreams."

"I might even dream of you!" he declared boldly.

She raised one eyebrow at him.

In the morning the three of them rode again, this time south-westwards, inland, following the Lunan Water's erratic course, issuing the same message as before. This was very different country, the river winding its way through low hills dotted with scrub birch and hawthorn, its banks reed-grown, cattle country. Their first calls were at the small hill farms of Ardbikie and Gighty on the northern slopes, then on to Inverkeilor on the south bank, fording the water, this another *duin'-uasal*'s establishment, where they gained promise of a score of men and, almost more important, extra garrons. This was because, it seemed, of the mills on the river further up, where more men were employed and horses required for the transport of the grain. The Lunan was renowned for its mills for the next few miles: Balmullie, Waulkmill, Boysack, Hutton and Kinnell. Just why so many mills had been established along this stretch was unclear, but it did cope with the grain of a large area round about, and made elderly Inverkeilor a wealthy man, they were told.

This was as far as the Red Castle influence went, and Fenella said that she would return from here by the farmeries of Inchock. She could deal with these herself, for here they were well on their way home for her two companions. But Cormac would not hear of her returning on her own, unescorted, after all her help and good company, she asking if they thought that she was unsafe in her own father's bailiwick? But she did not reject their accompaniment.

So it was back through cattle country, with herders to

be informed, to the great bay again, near Ethiehaven, Red Castle towering tall on its hillock ahead of them.

Nothing would do but that the visitors must have another meal before they started on their twenty-mile ride back to Forfar and Glamis. Parting, Cormac could not adequately express his appreciation of all the kindness and co-operation received; and was told that he could rely on Drostan of Dunninald to lead a sizeable contingent of Lunan men to Forfar the following day. Even the Lord Aidan gave them a friendly farewell, however little he might approve of their mission.

Fenella saw them off down at the horses; and when Cormac declared that he would be back one of these days she said that she hoped so – but that would depend, would it not, on him taking good care of himself on the forthcoming campaign against those fierce and bloodthirsty Danes, who were well known to be savage and dangerous fighters. She went so far as to ask whether Duncan would be going to war with his master; and when that man assured that he would, commanded him to look well after the thane and see that he did not seek to play the hero and valiant leader lest no return to Red Castle resulted.

This sent Cormac off far from outraged, and waving back until the river bends hid her.

5

Connacher's assembly at Forfar was such as to have even that undemonstrative individual expressing satisfaction, the Lunan party considerably better than he had anticipated. Drostan of Dunninald had brought over one hundred men. He attached himself to Cormac's Glamis contingent of almost two hundred. Altogether the mormaor's force reached some fifteen hundred, and all horsed.

There was little delay, and the companies, from all over Angus and the Mearns, moved west by south for Perth, to cross Tay and then south through Strathearn for Forteviot, the capital of Fortrenn, the royal seat. Here, where the Water of May joined the Earn, in the fertile strath, they came to the palace of the High Kings where, on the riverside meadows, a great host was already encamped.

At the rambling palace, no fort nor castle this, Constantine greeted the Angus mormaor and leadership, including Cormac, well pleased with their contribution to his army, the more so in that it seemed that the two mormaordoms of Atholl and Moray were not sending forces. This situation was ever the weakness of Scotland's elective monarchy, the mormaors being sufficiently independent and powerful as to withhold their services on occasion if so they desired. These two had been against Constantine's appointment, and now were demonstrating their disapproval.

However, the other five mormaordoms had rallied to the royal standard, the black boar on silver, and with Angus's augmentation the assembled army amounted to almost ten thousand men. The Caithness addition was still to arrive from their far northern fastnesses, but was known to be on its way.

Constantine decided not to wait for this, for the word was that Lothian was suffering direly from the invaders, and more of them kept arriving, this most evidently no mere raiding incursion but a planned takeover of the land. It was suspected that the dreaded King Olaf of Norway was behind it. So the sooner the aggressors could be assailed and driven out the better. This large force would be necessary, for it appeared that the Danish hordes had landed at many points along the south shores of the Scotwater, from North Berwick and Dirlington at the mouth of the firth right up to Dunedin, and beyond to the mouth of the Almond River, a thirty-mile stretch of the coast. Dealing with all this would demand much planning, diversion of effort, and many men.

They moved off then, due southwards now, in companies, great companies of up to five hundred, these inevitably stretching for well over a mile, for the roadways and tracks, and more particularly the fords over the many rivers and undrained marshlands, meant that not many horses could trot abreast. Cormac and his people found themselves towards the rear of the lengthy column with the Thane of Buchan and his men.

They rode by Dunning, an ancient abbacy, and on down the Allan Water valley, by Auchterarder and Ogilvie and Kinbuck to Dunblane, another abbacy, over twenty miles. All this was far further west than they would have wished to go to reach Lothian; but the Forth estuary of the Scotwater formed an impassable barrier, save by boat, and ten thousand men could not so embark without vast fleets of longships, such as the Danes themselves possessed; and the first crossing of Forth, for any horsed army, was at Stirling, this thirty-five miles west of Dunedin.

So large an army could not cover nearly so great a distance in a day as could individual riders; but they did manage to reach the head of the mile-long causeway across the soft marshland of the Forth River at Stirling by the evening, and camped on the firm ground below the mighty rock, topped by its former Pictish fort, the Snawdoun. There was quite a township here, at this very strategic point, and the leaders of the force at least were able to house themselves in fair comfort overnight, while their troops sought such provision as was to be had locally, mainly slaughtered cattle. Armies were seldom popular with the inhabitants of the areas they traversed, however much they might be necessary against invasion.

In the morning they all headed down Forth to where it widened into the estuary of the Scotwater at Airth. From here onwards scouting parties were sent ahead, for they were nearing the western bounds of Lothian, and it was not known how far the invaders had penetrated. Thus far, the local folk had no word of them. These Norsemen, sea raiders always, never liked to go far from their longships and the open waters, so the probability was that they might tend not to settle much further west than Dunedin.

They rode all day to within sight of the mighty isolated hill of Arthur's Seat, called after the famous sixth-century High King of the Britons, who had used Dunedin much from his capital at Carlisle, indeed whose daughter had been King Loth's first wife and grandmother of St Mungo; and there, at the crossing of the Almond, where that river entered salt water, they obtained their first word of the enemy. Apparently there was quite a large number of Danes at Leith, the haven for Dunedin, their longships moored there, Leith only some six miles ahead.

Constantine and his mormaors decided to wait there at Craigalmond, pronounced Cramond locally, until other, more inland, scouting parties brought further information as to the main concentrations of the Vikings, as they called themselves, the impression being that this Leith grouping was merely their westernmost outpost. Until they knew where the greatest numbers of the enemy were based, it would be unwise to move further. And they were always hoping that the Caithness contingent would catch up with them.

By noon next day their scouts were reporting back from quite far into the eastern parts of Lothian, as far as the Tyne and Peffer vales. It seemed that the invaders were taking over all the area east of Inveresk, at that river's mouth, but so far had based themselves, typically, near the sea and their vessels. So they were scattered in groups, some quite large, all along that coast, a score of miles of it perhaps, raiding and prospecting inland during the day and returning to their bases at night. Constantine and some seasoned warriors in his army knew that this was the enemy's weakness. By nature and habit they were pillagers and plunderers, not united campaigners, seldom coalescing in actual armies, save for sea battles in fleets. So the strategy would be to keep the groups of them apart, assail them in separate engagements, seeking to prevent them from linking up into any major host.

Therefore the Scots army should itself be divided up into perhaps half a dozen forces, these to ride eastwards through the hills which the Danes would have no urge to penetrate, and to descend each upon a given base area. With their numbers, each between fifteen hundred and two thousand, and horsed, they ought to be able to overcome the invaders piecemeal, and drive them back to their longships and away.

Constantine proved to be an effective general, and appeared to know this Lothian area better than most did. He assessed the most likely area for any major concentration of their foes would be at Gosford Bay, halfway between North Berwick and Inveresk, this with easy access inland for unhorsed seamen to the fertile Tyne and Peffer vales, and the main communities of Heyden's-town and Travernent. Aberlady Bay, just to the east, was larger and more sheltered; but it dried out at low tide, and these seafarers would not wish their vessels to be grounded and immobilised for half the time. So the High King would lead his greatest division against that area.

Connacher and his force were allotted the districts further east towards the firth mouth, their approach thereto being well inland through the skirts of the Lammermuir Hills so that the Danes would gain no warning of their danger.

With furthest to go, Connacher led his people southwards before the others, heading up Almond and then over towards the parallel Water of Leith to get behind Dunedin and its Arthur's Seat and rock-top fort, making for the next river, the Esk. There were many rivers of that name in Scotland, the word merely a corruption of the Gaelic *uisge*, meaning water, from which their drink, whisky, was also derived. This one would bring them to the higher ground between the Pentland and Lammermuir Hills, and so to the headwaters of two more of this land of rivers, the Tyne and Peffer, whereat they would be safely into the foothill country they sought, twenty-five miles, Constantine reckoned. After that, it was up to Connacher.

They rode off through Lothian, all totally new country to Cormac, as to almost all. It was quite populous, mainly upland but the hills never very high compared with those to the north. The folk here were descendants of the Southern Picts, of which Loth had been king, the blood diluted over the years by centuries of British and Anglian invasions, as the lands to the north had never been. Whether these folk were living in dread of the present Danish aggression further east the horsed host did not trouble to enquire.

They had no difficulty in reaching the Lammermuir foothills by darkening, in the Hunmanbie area, well south of Heyden's-town, where they camped, finding plenty of sheep to provide them with meat, this appearing to be notable sheep country.

At a conference with his leaders, the mormaor sought to plan his further moves, difficult as this was when none of them really knew the ground. Constantine had given him a very rough sketch, on a scrap of parchment, of the coastline and river courses; and from this they had to develop their strategy. Cormac found himself allotted a fairly far east assignment, to descend on the area of Dirlington, lying between Golyn and North Berwick, where, it was said, there was no actual haven but sheltered beaches, behind islets called Fidra and Eyebroughty, which the Vikings might well be using. He was given Dunninald's party and a group of Mearnsmen from Arbuthnott, but what he did with them seemed to be left to himself. As a totally inexperienced campaigner, he was less than confident as to his leadership. He would consult Duncan and Pate the Mill, nowise suffering from pride or self-esteem.

Early in the morning, with his four hundred now, he set off eastwards, up and down, up and down, around the many hillfoot hollows and ravines and slopes, some of these very steep for their horses. He had been told to make for the area directly north of the obviously highest of the Lammermuir summits, called Lammerlaw apparently, and then to turn directly towards the coast, which they would be able to see from this higher ground. They would discern the great V of Aberlady Bay, with the hill of Golyn just east of it; and if they kept well to the right of this they should reach salt water near Dirlington. Which, of course, was all very well – but what about the enemy? These would not be likely to be sitting beside their longships, waiting to be attacked. It was all very vague, from the point of view of tactics. Would they be able to link up with others of Connacher's companies, right and left?

Cormac mac Farquhar, at least, in very doubtful frame of mind, headed his people down towards the coast. They could indeed see Aberlady Bay, unmistakeable, Golyn Hill, the islets in the sea, and, away to the right, two upstanding heights, one on land the other in the firth mouth, North Berwick Law and the Craig of Bass, these all having heard of at least, dramatic features of the landscape. Nearer at hand was another isolated leviathan-like hill rising out of the Vale of Tyne, which Duncan said that he thought must be Traprain Law, law being the name for hills in these parts, where King Loth had had his capital.

They saw something else also: smokes, these arising into

the forenoon air ahead, three of them, black and ominous. Cormac did not have to be advised that these were almost certainly farmeries or hamlets being burned by the Danes. At least this would give them a recognisable objective. The nearest was not much more than a mile away probably. Drawing his sword, rather self-consciously, and pointing it in that direction, he spurred his mount forward.

As they bore down through rolling country to what was obviously a wide stretch of marshland through which they could see a stream of sorts winding in loops, the knowledgeable Duncan declared that this must be the Peffer, the alternative vale to that of Tyne. And if so, here somewhere must be where their great King Kenneth mac Alpin had helped to win the famous Battle of Athelstaneford, where St Andrew had come to the aid of the Scots and Albannach against the attacking Saxons, and had thereafter been adopted as the two realms' patron saint, these two in time being united by the said Kenneth, and Scotland born. So this was precious, almost holy ground. Cormac hoped that St Andrew was still concerned with their welfare, and would aid and guide them hereafter.

Nearing the first of those smoke columns, they came up with a group of women and children hurrying away, and eyeing the horsemen anxiously. Reining up, Cormac hailed them and asked if they came from the conflagration ahead. He was pantingly told that the Norsemen were savaging their homes at the Druimford there, burning and slaying. Drostan demanded how many of them, the Danes? A couple of score at least, they were told by a younger woman with a babe in her arms. Cormac shouted that they would seek to avenge them, the High King's men, thankfully counting the odds at ten to one in their favour.

Approaching the scene of fire and carnage, he fanned out his following into a crescent-shaped formation. The smoke to some extent obscured their targets, but it would also help to hide their arrival from the enemy, in their preoccupation with swords, axes and torches.

In fact, what followed was no sort of battle at all, however small-scale. The horsemen pounded into a little group of cothouses, barns and sheds, most of them alight, where men on foot, in leather-padded and metal-studded armour, and steel-helmeted, were running wild in shouting fury. Bodies were lying about, men and women, some dogs were barking, and chaos reigned, the smoke clouds billowing, the burning thatch crackling. There was nothing that Cormac could do save spur his horse at the nearest Dane, sword slashing. No born killer, he nevertheless knew a perhaps shameful satisfaction as his blade drove down on the shoulder of a man dragging a young girl by her long hair, and saw him stagger and topple over her – Cormac's first blood-letting. Without pause, he rode on to another, who saw him coming and threw a blazing torch at him. This alarmed his mount, which reared and all but threw him. Plunging aside, his beast was brushed and nearly knocked over by another horse, ridden by Duncan who, axe smashing down, felled the torch-thrower with a single blow, and carried on.

Recovering his wits and seat in the saddle, Cormac wheeled round to seek other victims. But he found none still on their feet. His men were everywhere, getting in each other's way, mounts colliding. In that limited, smoke-shrouded space it was still chaos, only now of another sort. None could honestly claim it as anything to be proud of. But at least no Norsemen had survived their attack; and the Thane of Glamis had led the way and slain his first foe.

What to do now? Cormac's first impulse was to congratulate his people and then to seek out any of the injured inhabitants whom they could help, also possibly finish off any wounded enemies. But Pate the Mill was pointing northwards where, not far away over that ford of the Peffer, a farm was alight, figures just discernible moving around it. The chances were that these, or some of them, could have seen the arrival of the many horsemen across the river, and have given warning. So, attack there before these other killers could organise themselves to resist.

Cormac saw the point, and waving and shouting to his

men to follow, headed for the ford, this marked by the usual posts.

This new assault was very different, even though the smoke and yelling were similar. The Danes here were indeed warned, and had gathered together to face the coming attack. But it being only a single farmery, not any hamlet, there were fewer of them. And, although no doubt fierce enough fighters, they would quickly perceive that they were hopelessly outnumbered and, unmounted, at the mercy of charging horsemen. At any rate, recognising realities, they broke up their formation, no more than a score of them, and ran, this not in any mass but individually, as would undoubtedly be instinctive for self-preservation.

Instinctive or otherwise, however, fleeing men afoot were hopelessly disadvantaged by horsemen in many times their number, however they might run and dodge and turn at bay. In only a few minutes they all were ridden down and slain, and this without a single casualty amongst the Scots. Shouting their triumph, the victors gathered together again, some with collected battle-axes, short Norse swords and even helmets as trophies.

There would have been much celebration, but the prudent and level-headed miller Pate was pointing again. For there was the third smoke column, and a big one, perhaps half a mile away, behind a belt of trees. Whether the attackers there could have gained any indication of danger they could not know, but it was possible. Surely these raiders would take some precautions, sentinels posted and the like? Or were they so assured of their own ferocious dominance and the helplessness of the settled people they assailed that they saw no need for caution?

So it was onward towards this next challenge, over cattle-dotted meadow land.

And, once through those trees, more of a challenge it proved to be indeed. For there, they saw, was a larger establishment, something of a hallhouse with its associated outbuildings, farmery and barns. It was some of the last which were burning, not the main house; probably the invaders were reserving this for their own use. But undoubtedly there were more of them to be seen about the place, despite the smoke, than had been at the other burnings, how many was uncertain. However, nothing like their own numbers, thankfully. The problem here would be that large house, Cormac recognised. But he did not delay, surprise essential.

In fan-shaped formation again, they all spurred forward.

The beat of all those hooves, of course, was to be heard, the ground all but shaking with it, and the busy sackers and burners turned to face the danger. Or some of them. Those around the burning outbuildings, pillaging and driving off cattle, ran together to face the onslaught. But those outside the large house reacted less automatically, standing to stare.

Obviously hopelessly outnumbered, the former group very quickly thought better of making a united stand, and scattered, but by no means fled the scene. Waving his left flank horsemen to deal with them, Cormac led the rest on towards the hallhouse.

The Danes there saw that they would be ridden down also, and did not wait. Turning, perhaps thirty of them, they ran into the house.

Reining up outside the door, Cormac and his people were faced with the problem he had visualised. No riding down was now possible. But to dismount and go in after the enemy through that narrow door would be folly; they would be slaughtered one by one. Yet they could not just leave the Danes inside unmolested.

Pate the Mill knew the answer. "Fire it!" he cried. "Burn them!" Others shouted agreement.

Cormac bit his lip. To burn men alive, in a building! That surely was not the way? He was shaking his head when Duncan reined close and tapped his arm, pointing. There, nearby, against the walling of the next outbuilding, was a pile of heads, bloody human heads, hacked off. Most were on the ground, but three were hanging up by the hair from hooks in the planking, two women's and one bearded man's, a most horrible sight. Some of those Danes who had run inside had evidently been hanging their grim trophies when they perceived their danger.

Those heads banished Cormac's doubts and scruples. Men who could do that . . . ! He nodded, and waved towards the burning barns.

There was no lack of eagerness, nor of fire and fuel, reed-thatch and boarding, such as was not already burning. Dismounting, his men ran to gather it, to bring to heap against the walls of the hallhouse. Torches were readily formed out of twists of reed, dry and brittle, and applied thereto. Quickly the flames shot up. The building was of timber, clay-covered, whitewashed and painted; but the clay, enough to deter fire-arrows, was not sufficiently thick to protect the wood from a full-scale blaze. Soon, as more and more fuel was brought and piled up and lit, that house became a roaring inferno. Yells and screams from within penetrated the crackling chaos.

Some of the enemy chose to die fighting, and ran out or jumped from windows, and were promptly cut down by the waiting Scots with swords and axes, however scorched were the wielders by the heat of the flames.

It did not take very long for the blazing roof to fall in, and to end the howling and shrieking from within.

Cormac, all but sickened in reaction, went over to the pile of bloody heads, steeling himself to unhook those hanging against the walling. What to do with them? Looking around, he saw a small duck-pond nearby. The ground there would be soft. He ordered his men to gather up the heads, and any decapitated bodies of the murdered inhabitants, and dig a grave of sorts with their axes and swords to bury them, but to leave the dead Danes where they lay in their own and others' blood as a warning to their kind. Thereafter, he was eager to get away from that dire vicinity as soon as possible, and the horror of it.

As, presently, they rode on coastwards, he could not

bring himself to congratulate themselves. They had utterly demolished three groups of the invaders, without a single casualty of their own. But . . . !

On a slight eminence at the edge of the Vale of Peffer, they saw the slope of Golyn Hill on the left, and a single rocky mound on their right, with glimpses of salt water beyond, and further east a couple of miles, the cone of North Berwick Law. This, then, ahead of them, by his instructions, must be Dirlington, their goal.

Onwards, seeing the remains of Pictish fortification on that rocky knoll, they came to a sizeable village round a green, or what had been a village, now only the burned-out empty shells of cottages and sheds. More heads were hanging on walling here, but these had been there for some time obviously, and they did not think to start burying them. It was the shoreline, now, for them.

Half a mile or so further, and they saw a belt of low sand-dunes, dotted with buckthorn bushes. Clearly the coast had been reached. What would they find here? If indeed the Danes had based their longships somewhere hereabouts they presumably would not have left them unguarded. So more fighting was likely to be necessary. He reined up his people, and sent a couple of men ahead, on foot, to spy out what lay beyond those dunes.

While they sat their mounts, waiting, they could see smoke rising eastwards in the North Berwick area. How was Connacher faring there? they wondered.

Their scouts came back to report that there was indeed an array of vessels drawn up on the shore beyond, but, so far as they could see, no men. There was a large building, however, on an outcrop of higher ground to the west, quarter of a mile off perhaps. It might well be occupied by guards.

Turning half-left, then, they moved on cautiously behind the cover of the dunes. Through a gap in these, views opened before them. There was a wide sandy beach on the right, changing to rocks and reefs in front and to the left. Beyond, islands rose out of the Scotwater, one directly ahead only half a mile from shore, of a strange formation, almost in two parts and with what looked like a tunnel penetrating it, seemingly stone buildings thereon. A smaller, low islet lay to the west, and further off two larger ones to the east, with the mighty Craig of Bass towering out of the waves a couple of miles away, a dramatic coastline indeed. And along these sands eastwards were drawn up eight or nine Viking longships, single-masted with their upthrusting prows and sterns. In the other direction, westwards, they could see some sort of large house.

Clearly that must be their target now. They swung off to ride towards it behind the shelter of the dunes.

As near as they dared to go, thus, they halted; and Cormac himself, with Duncan and Pate and Dunninald, dismounted and moved up amongst the prickly buckthorn bushes, to peer onwards. The building was quite clear before them, although the light was now failing. It was unusual in shape and style, of the local reddish stone, with high arched windows which gave it a monastic look. The yellow gleam of lamps shone from the said windows, and faint smoke rose from the single chimney.

What, then? It was probably a religious establishment – but who occupied it now? Danes? Or its lawful occupants? Those longships, so nearby, and no men to be seen about them, and with no other houses in sight. It seemed almost certain that the invaders would have taken this over. If so, how many of them? Attack, then? But this was no timber building which would burn. If Danes, could they be coaxed out? If they saw that they were well outnumbered, they would not be apt to emerge. So many questions . . .

Duncan it was who volunteered. He would creep forward, alone, hiding, and try to discover some of the answers. He would go carefully, never fear.

The others wished him well, and waited there.

The tranter was back sooner than expected, and looking grim. Danes most certainly, he assured. He had found the bodies of two women lying near the building, half naked and savaged – but the torn clothing was that of nuns.

And men's loud voices had sounded from the house. It had been some sort of nunnery, evidently.

That was enough for Cormac. But how to assail them, within the stone walls?

The ever resourceful Pate pointed. Those large arched windows. There was the answer. The walls would not burn – but smoke could make the interior impossible to remain in. These buckthorns would burn, and smokily, being sap-filled. Gather much buckthorn. Creep close, and pile it up under all the windows. Light it. Smash the glass of the windows. Keep the fires burning. The Norsemen would have to come out, or be choked to death by the smoke.

All acclaimed that as possible. They went back down to the others and the horses.

The men were set to the unpleasant task of pulling and collecting buckthorn, amidst much cursing, for tougher and more jagged bushes would be hard to find. But that was all that grew on these sand-dunes, apart from marram grass. Dirks had to be used to hack off branches and sprays. But however difficult a crop to gather and awkward to carry, four hundred men were not long in amassing a sufficiency of their fuel.

They left the horses there, watched over by a score of their company, the rest moving on afoot carrying their thorn boughs and twigs, and cursing thereat. Cormac shouldered his share, and was worried that the gruntings and swearings at the prickles might carry on the evening air to warn the foe.

However, approaching cautiously, they reached the nunnery on its eminence without any Danes emerging. A lot of noise emanated from within, drunken-sounding. The door was shut; after all, it was a November night. Cormac posted men at it, just in case. Duncan went off round the building to see if there was another door. There was, so guards were sent to watch it also. Then, working as silently as was possible, the task of piling the buckthorn against the walls, especially under the windows, was commenced. It was as well that the Vikings did not go in for dogs, or all would have been aroused before this.

Cormac's next worry was the actual setting alight of the bushy material. All his men carried tinder, flint and steel for campfire-making and domestic use; but would this be sufficient to torch green thorn, however inflammable when lit? If there had been anything that they could use to help it catch fire, straw or dried reeds or even dead leaves, but there was only the thorn and the marram grass in the dune country. They would just have to be prepared to use up all their tinder and anything else burnable, even on their persons.

The signal was whispered round to start striking steel on flint for the sparks to fly into the tinder, and be blown into flame.

Waiting, waiting, it seemed to Cormac an interminable time before any little gleam and flicker of light developed into anything which could be called a blaze, and only a few of these, at first. But at length smoke did begin to billow up here and there.

Now the next problem was the smashing of those windows. They were all of fixed glass above, which did not open and wooden shutters below which did. These could all be smashed in with axes and sword hilts; but there were the burning bushes below. If they had brought spears or lances, such as had these, it might have been easier, but such had been left at the horses. They could not have done the smashing before the fires were lit, for that would have alarmed the revellers within. Nothing for it, then, but somehow to do the smashing with swords held high, risking being burned themselves in the process. Stones to throw might have served, but there were no stones in these sandhills.

Cormac sought to act the good leader by demonstration. Ensuring that his men stood below all the windows, he took his sword by the blade, drew a deep breath, and plunged forward into the blazing thorns, hilt raised high, and battered at the wooden shutters. Three blows were as much as he could stand, in the heat and flame, and he staggered back. All around the building men sought to do the same.

Some were undoubtedly more successful than others, some even reaching up as far as the glass. But undoubtedly gaps were formed for the smoke to pour inside, fanned by the wind.

Reaction from within was prompt now, the noise changing to yells and bellows of alarm and rage. The Scots at the two doors stood ready, weapons raised, to deal with the enemy who would come rushing out.

And out they did come, or attempted to. But the doorways were narrow, and only one or sometimes two could get through at a time, and however able fighters they might be, sober or otherwise, in that restricted space they were cut down at once, relays of the Scots waiting to take over the slaying. And quickly both doorways were clogged up with bodies piled over each other, denying any further egress. More and more buckthorn piled on increased the choking clouds of thick smoke and would make the confined space within impossible for men to breathe in. It was bad enough outside, with the fire-raisers coughing and choking. Hell must be something like this, Cormac decided.

How long it took for all sounds to die away from within that nunnery none could calculate; but at length they reckoned that they could let the fires die down. None of the Scots was eager to venture inside, over the dead bodies, to see the results of their labours. Assuring themselves that there was no movement within, they all turned and went back to the horses.

But they were not finished yet for that night. The longships. Cormac was determined that these should be destroyed, if at all possible, and promptly, in case Danes from elsewhere came. So down to the sandy shore they rode, in darkness now.

They had no difficulty in finding the vessels; the question, how to wreck them? They had battle-axes, of course, but these were strongly built craft, sea-going, of heavy timbering. Burning would be of no use – they had used up all their tinder. The masts could be hacked down, the rolled-up sails slashed and the oars chopped up. But seeking to smash the thick boarding of the hulls was less than effective. Eventually it was concluded that the best that they could do was to use the vessels' cordage to make tow-ropes, and have the horses drag the hulks out as far into the water as they could go, and hope that the tides would carry them away. This, quite a lengthy and difficult procedure in the dark, they did.

Cormac, like the others, decided that it was enough for one day. They went back to the ravaged and deserted village of Dirlington, tired and hungry, but in the main well pleased with their efforts, and sought to contrive such shelter as the place could offer. All the men carried little bags of oatmeal at their saddle-bows, and these, mixed with cold water from the village well, had to serve for provender. Setting relays of sentries to keep watch, the horses tethered, the company settled itself to sleep in the burned-out cottages. At least it was not raining.

Cormac mac Farquhar's first day as a leader in warfare ended. How had he performed? The thought of all the blood and horror and screams delayed his slumber.

In the morning Cormac wondered what should be his course now. He had been given the task of dealing with this Dirlington area, and that had been done fairly effectively. Should they now go seeking further conquests, or return to Constantine's main host at Inveresk for further instructions? Or should they head on eastwards to see if they could be of any aid to Connacher's people to cope with the North Berwick vicinity?

These questions were answered for him when, a little way inland, they saw a large mounted force proceeding westwards. Since the Danes did not use horses, these could only be the mormaor's own men, tasks presumably accomplished.

They rode to join them.

Connacher himself was no more communicative than usual, nor congratulatory. But others with him were more so, and well pleased with themselves, even if not particularly interested in the Thane of Glamis's exploits. It seemed that their efforts had been on the whole successful and similar. Constantine's strategy of dealing with the invaders piecemeal had proved highly effective. Connacher had had one engagement which could almost be called a battle, when quite a force of the invaders had retreated before them up on the steep sides of North Berwick Law, and there, where horses were disadvantaged, making a stand. The Scots had suffered some casualties, but numbers had told in the end, and the marauders were wiped out. Otherwise it had been small groups attacked at their burnings and slaughters, as had been the case with the Glamis force, and with approximately the same results. They also had destroyed longships in the North Berwick haven, just how was not made clear. But it was asserted that there were no Danes left in that entire area.

So it was on towards Inveresk for them all, going by the coast now, with no hiding.

Rounding the shoulder of Golyn Hill they saw before them, at the head of Aberlady Bay, a large concentration of men. This would be the Mormaor of Strathearn's people, who had been allotted this district to clear. But they saw something else: six longships were sailing eastwards, seawards towards the mouth of the Scotwater, out beyond the bar of the bay. So it looked as though some at least of the enemy had escaped. It was to be hoped that they were now on their way back to Norway or Denmark, and to inform King Olaf thereof that Scotland was not a viable country to take over and settle in.

Strathearn's people were as content with their efforts as were the Angus and Mearns array. They had been unable to prevent that group of longships making off to sea from the western horn of the bay, which the locals called Kilpensandus, but otherwise it was all success.

It was much the same story at Cokainie, the next area, where a group of small communities of fishers stretched westwards along the coast, with sandy beaches and rocky shores all the way to Inveresk. And here they found Constantine himself, who had led the newly arrived Caithness contingent to help comb the extensive inland and fertile country hereabouts, purely farming and cattle-raising territory which the Vikings had easily overrun. Many longships had been destroyed all along this shoreline, a success story such as was becoming almost monotonous.

Constantine commended all his leaders on their efforts and the outcome. He announced that he was going to leave the latecomers, Malduin of Caithness and Sutherland and his force, here in eastern Lothian for a short period to give what aid they could to the surviving local folk in rebuilding their lives and properties. Otherwise the rest of the Scots army would be on its way northwards next day, task accomplished.

There was celebration and feasting that night at Inveresk, the vanquished Danes having left behind much provision and liquor, stolen as it had been.

6

Back home at Glamis, Cormac had to resume his very different duties as thane and laird of his tenantry and people. He found this more to his taste than leading men in warfare, however successful might have been his first experience of the latter. It was, indeed, quite strange for him to see his recent warriors returned to their homes and with their families, farmers, ploughmen, herders, wrights, millers, carpenters, workers of every kind, and to speak with their wives and children. In the process he gathered that accounts of their menfolk's recent experiences had lost nothing in the telling, by no means undervalued or minimised; he had scarcely realised what a band of heroes he had been privileged to lead.

His own mother and sister perhaps had gained something of the same impression? But neither these nor the other womenfolk showed any great concern over the grim fate of the slaughtered, burned and suffocated Danes.

They had not exactly news for him but local gossip as to affairs in the north while the Ard Righ's army had been elsewhere. There were rumours that the Moray and Atholl mormaors, and their allies the MacDuffs, who had not joined the southern campaign, were plotting some form of insurrection. Why they were thus disloyal to Constantine was uncertain. However, the success of the offensive against the invading Vikings possibly might tell in his favour, especially if he proved to be a good monarch otherwise.

Cormac asked whether there was any news from the Red Castle of Lunan, and was questioned as to why there should be? The Lord Aidan and his household were scarcely news-makers. He wondered, not aloud, whether he could contrive some excuse to visit there again. They were not any part of his thanedom, and he had not any valid reason to go. But Drostan of Dunninald *had* attached his group to the Glamis contingent, so perhaps some call there might not be thought strange. After Yuletide, then?

Meantime it was December and the run-up to Christmas. Cormac's father and mother had always made a great celebration of Yule for their people, more of it traditional, indeed pagan festivities than the Christian ones perhaps, for they were not particularly religiously inclined; and the new thane was expected to continue with this. Preparations at Glamis Castle had to be considerable. There was the Mistletoe Bough revelry to start off with, apt to degenerate into more of a saturnalia than any mere ritual. Then there was the Animal Carnival, where men and women dressed up as birds and beasts and went round the houses singing choruses, guising as it was called. There followed, on Christmas Eve itself, the Yule Log bringing, a ceremonial apt to clash with the Church's Holy Night. Christmas Day itself was usually mainly a day of rest after all this, but the activities went on until Twelfth Night in the former pagan usage. All this took a deal of organising and providing for, Cormac discovered; he had taken it all for granted hitherto.

However, his preparations were interrupted, and by no less than the High King himself – or at least his messenger. This courier brought a royal command for the Thane of Glamis to go north to the Mearns on the Ard Righ's behalf, this to visit and assess suitable claimants for the vacant thanedom thereof, and advise. If this seemed a strange task for a young and very new holder of the thanal office, it was apparently part of his duties. Thanes, unlike mormaors, chieftains and lords, were the direct representatives of the monarch himself, hereditary usually yes, but dismissible if so the High King judged. They were not lieutenants of their mormaors, however much they were apt to co-operate with those lesser kings inevitably. They had their especial responsibilities, for instance the collection of royal levies and taxes and Church teinds; the fining of defaulters; the organising and calling up of armed men from their thanedoms to form the royal guard, as distinct from the mormaors' armies; justiciary duties over certain offences, representing the monarch; and the superintendence of royal estates in their areas. The fact that Constantine was giving this present assignment to Cormac was presumably a sign that he approved of what he had seen and heard of him in the Lothian campaign, for he could have chosen another thane for the task, such as Cowie, Garvoch, Stormont or even Buchan. Something of a compliment, therefore.

The need for a new Thane of the Mearns was evident, the evil Fenella's husband dead and her son executed for treason. If there were kin of the family available, it was not to be wondered at that they were not considered. The courier brought three possibles in the Mearns whom Cormac was to interview. One, the Lord of Arbuthnott, he already knew, for he had led a small company in Connacher's army, a young man not much older than Cormac himself, and amiable enough. The other two were the lords of Conveth and Inverbervie. He did not think that either of them had been with Connacher's force.

It was not the ideal time of the year to set off on such an errand, but at least there was no snow as yet. And Cormac's mother and sister could finish the Yuletide preparations. He took Duncan with him, his usual companion, however unsuitable some might think their friendship.

He decided to visit the two whom he did not know first. Conveth, some forty miles away north-eastwards, lay in mid-Mearns, near to the renowned monastery of St Laurence, none so far from Fettercairn and Kincardine Castle. So they went by Tannadice and Brechin, down Strathmore. The Mearns countryside was notably different from that of Angus, strangely, considering that they were so comparatively close to each other, much barer on the whole, with less woodland and much marshy ground, the mountains to the west much more in evidence.

Conveth's hallhouse, set as so often on the site of a Pictish fort, was a fine place overlooking the St Laurence monastery, where, it seemed, the Lord Ewan's brother was conveniently abbot. Ewan was a man of middle age, solid, greying, all but stolid, with a family of daughters. The visitor was greeted well enough, with the usual comment from his host that he had known Cormac's father, always a little off-putting in that it somehow seemed to be implied that the son scarcely measured up to his sire's stature. Perhaps that was so, or seemed so, especially as the guest was somewhat embarrassed in having to explain the object of his coming, even though he did not put it that he was there to sum up the suitability of three candidates for thanedom. However, very quickly this Ewan perceived the object of the exercise, and made his position quite clear, there and then. He had no desire to be Thane of the Mearns, or to be anything other than what he was. He had a sufficiency of responsibilities here at Conveth, with wide lands to see to, the monastery to support, and all his daughters to marry off. The High King must look elsewhere.

Cormac was quite relieved, and was able to pass a pleasant evening in the mainly female company, although hoping that the Lord Ewan did not look upon himself as a possible son-in-law; for although the girls were friendly and attentive, none of them attracted him, or in any way compared with Fenella nic Aidan of Lunan.

He retired fairly early, wondering how Duncan was faring down in the servitors' quarters.

In the morning Ewan took them to see the monastery, one of the most renowned in these parts, Duncan interested to accompany them, admitting quite frankly that he was the bastard of an abbot of another establishment. This fane was dedicated to the Spanish saint who had been martyred by roasting on a grid-iron by the Romans in the third century. But there was a local tradition that it had originally been a refuge for sufferers from the dread disease of leprosy, and called after St Lazarus of biblical fame who was allegedly a leper. And, there being no letter Z pronounced in the ancient Scots tongue, it had become corrupted to Laurence.

From Conveth it was only some eight rough miles over the Hill of Garvoch and by Benholm to the coast, where the Bervie Water entered the Norse Sea at Inverbervie. Here Cormac was able to make his decision in almost moments, for the lord thereof was an elderly man and frail, and although he had a son, apparently they were not on good terms, and he was an absentee. So this one would make no effective thane.

They did not delay at Inverbervie long, then, pleasant place as it was below its striking headland of Bervie Brow and cave-riven cliffs, but turned to follow the Bervie Water up westwards. Arbuthnott lay only some four miles up this river, in its fairly deep and steep valley amongst low hills. Its castle stood between two tributaries of the river where they met to form a strong ravine-flanked little peninsula. Here they learned that Donald of Arbuthnott was out, at what was possibly the last deer-drive of the season, in the Tulloch Hills, to lay in a stock of venison for the ice-house. Although Cormac remembered him well enough from the campaign, and would have no doubts about recommending him to Constantine as the new thane, he felt that he had to ascertain that the man wanted the position and its duties and obligations, unlike Conveth. So they waited at the castle, being well entertained by the lady of the house and her young children, a cheerful family.

It was the darkening before Arbuthnott returned, his men leading a string of garrons laden with the carcases of over a dozen stags, after a good day's sport, a useful meat supply for the remainder of the winter to add to the beef and fowl and fish already in store.

The Lord Donald greeted his visitors agreeably, and when he heard of the reason for it, showed no hesitation in allowing his name to be put forward for the honour of being Thane of the Mearns, even though his wife was somewhat doubtful, wondering how much the functions and affairs would take him away from her and the young people. Cormac sought to reassure her in that *he* did not find his tasks and burdens too onerous, at Glamis; although actually the Mearns was the larger thanedom even if less populous.

At that hour, of course, they had to stay the night at the castle, which they did, Cormac pleased that here Duncan was treated as a guest, his behaviour entirely acceptable.

Before sleeping that night Cormac, recognising that this mission had taken less time than anticipated, and that, near the coast here, they were considerably closer to Lunan Bay than to Glamis, came to the conclusion that it would be reasonable, if not advisable, to return south by that route. As excuse, he could always say that he had felt it his duty to apprise the Lord Aidan of Lunan of the opportunity to have his name put forward as possible Thane of the Mearns, as a mormaor's son and brother, although the likelihood of his accepting nomination was highly improbable. But it would be a gesture, and with its pleasing alternative aspects.

So in the morning it was back down Bervie to the sea, and then southwards around all the bays and cliffs and headlands of that scenic and often dramatic coastline, by Gourdon and Lathallan and the Kaim of Mathers to the sands of St Cyrus and the long Links of Montrose and that place's curious and huge inland tidal loch, all but unique on the east coast of Scotland, save perhaps that of Findhorn in Moray; and on by Ulysses-haven to Boddin Point, the northern horn of Lunan Bay, a score of miles, which they covered in just over three hours. There was a chill easterly wind off the sea, but otherwise the weather was kind.

Gazing ahead, they could see Red Castle, tall on its mound. Cormac was a little concerned that they were reaching it rather sooner than he would have wished, for, of course, he wished to stay the night there if possible, and in fact, at barely noon, they could get back to Glamis by nightfall. He did not detail his priorities to Duncan, although that man probably was not wholly unaware of them.

When they reached the Lunan Water and climbed to the castle, it was to be kindly greeted by the Lady Alena, if more vaguely by her husband, but to learn that their daughter was absent for the time being, at which Cormac's spirits drooped considerably, especially when her mother said that she could not prophesy just when she would be back, that depending on the sport she was having, When the disappointed visitor repeated the word sport, he was led to a window overlooking the sea, and there had pointed out to him a small boat in mid-bay. That was Fenella apparently, at her fishing. She was, it seemed, a keen fisherwoman, her favourite sport, even on a blowy winter's day such as this, which could worry her parents on occasion. She had two men with her for the rowing, fisherfolk themselves, who would be apt to ensure her safety.

When Cormac had explained the ostensible object of his visit and had received the expected declaration of lack of any desire to be a thane from Lord Aidan, who had eyed him askance at the very suggestion, he had to think quickly. He had no valid reason for waiting to see Fenella, and so for staying the night. But if he professed an interest in fishing, seafishing? He could see other small boats drawn up on the sandy shore nearby. Go out in one of those to her?

He did not require to assume an aspect of interest, at least. "I have never tried fishing at sea," he declared. "And always wished to do so. This day I could learn how. Could I take a boat, with Duncan, and row out to her? Lady Fenella might be so kind as to instruct me. Here is an opportunity. And . . . I am not in any haste to win back to Glamis."

"To be sure," he was told. "It is flounders, flatfish, that Fenella will be catching out there. She will show you, I am sure. Those boats all are belonging to our people. Take any one, Lord Cormac."

Well pleased, he led Duncan down to the beach, where they selected one of the boats, oars inboard, and pushed it down to the water, to clamber in, getting wet feet in the process. Neither of them were expert oarsmen, but reckoned that they were quite capable of pulling their way out into the bay, having fished in boats for trout on Forfar and Rescobie Lochs. It was cold out on the slate grey water, and although the sea was not really rough, the waves had their small craft dipping and rolling.

Their progress somewhat zigzag, and preoccupied with coping with the waves – and, of course, with their backs turned to their objective – presently they were alerted by a hail, and a female hail at that, to prove that they were none so far from their destination. Turning on his seat, Cormac saw the girl waving to them, only two hundred yards or so off, obviously having recognised them; to be sure, he was not clad like any fisherman. He waved back, and a roller almost wrenched his oar from his single-handed grasp. Fool! he told himself. They could not afford to lose an oar. He concentrated on rowing until they were all but alongside the other boat.

"Lord Cormac!" Fenella called. "What brings you here?"

He could scarcely answer that *she* did. Panting a little from his unaccustomed exertions, he said, "I had to see your father. Saw you fishing. Always wanted to fish at sea. Never done so. Came out . . ."

Their boat was beginning to drift away from hers, and they were not very clever at manoeuvring it back.

"See you, pull close, and we will tie you to us," she told them. "A rope – we will throw you a rope." She was wrapped in plaiding against the cold but her hair was blowing free, her cheeks flushed pink, those eyes vividly alive.

They endeavoured to pull round closer, and one of the fishermen in the other boat shouted something, and threw a small anchor on a rope, which clattered inboard at the bows, hooked itself against the upper planking, and they were hauled in alongside.

"Fenella!" Cormac got out. "It is good to see you. Good!"

"And you, Cormac. And your Duncan, too. A welcome surprise. So, you would fish for flounders?"

"If you would show me how. I have fished for trouts. But this is different, I judge."

"Yes, indeed. But it is not difficult. You will have no lines nor bait? Then, see you, come into this boat. Both of you. There will be sufficient space." She stood, balancing gracefully, to hold out one hand, a fishing-line over the fingers of the other, to aid him climb over from one heaving craft to the other, quite a tricky transference for those not used to the like. Clutching her, he clambered over safely, and promptly sat down, while the young woman helped Duncan over.

That made five of them in the small boat not really made for so many, which had the advantage of requiring Fenella to seat herself very close to Cormac on her narrow stern thwart, Duncan on the floorboards amongst the slippery catch of flounders, some of them still flapping.

The young woman said that Cormac must be very keen suddenly to learn about sea-fishing, to have come rowing out here this day, to which only a nod had to serve as answer. But she declared that it was not very difficult a sport to learn. She produced from a basket a couple of spindles wrapped round with line, which she pointed out was made from the hair of horses' tails, with, at the loose end of each, a rod of wire some eighteen inches in length and a lead weight attached. From this were hung three short lines of some eight inches, with hooks at the end. She gave one line to Cormac and one to Duncan, and reached for a pail containing wriggling, fat lug-worms dug from the sands. She picked up one of these slimy creatures without any sign of distaste, nipped it in halves, and threaded the still curling sections on the hooks, in the process yellow-brown ooze spilling from them staining her fingers. She took a second worm, broke it, and gave half to Cormac to afix to his line, making sure that it was securely pierced on the hook, for the fish could suck them off otherwise without swallowing the hook.

Cormac thought that it was a rather extraordinary activity for a gently born young woman. She did not seem to worry about her stained fingers.

The three hooks baited, and Duncan heedfully copying her, she explained that the line and attachment were to be dropped overboard and unwound until the fisher felt the lead weight bump on the sandy bottom. Then to be raised the eight inches, so that the baited hooks were just tipping the sand down there, not lying on it. The line was held thus, over one finger. When a fish nibbled the bait it could be felt by the finger, whatever the depth, and a slight upraised jerk was called for to fix the hook in the creature's mouth, otherwise it would probably get away with sucking off the lug-worm. The catcher would soon know if he had got a fish hooked, for the line would jerk and twitch as the flounder twisted and sought to free itself. So haul it up quickly lest the catch won loose.

Even as she explained this, one of the fishermen drew up a flatfish, flapping wildly, detached it from the hook, tossed it down to join the others on the floorboards, and rebaited.

Cormac was going to lower his weighted line over the opposite side of the boat, asking whether ever more than one fish got caught at the same time, for there were the three hooks, and was informed that very occasionally it happened; and was also told not to sink his line on that side but to keep to the same as her own and the other men's, since, with the drift of the tide, it was quite possible for two of the lines to get entangled under the boat, and winning them free again there could be difficult.

So, leaning across Fenella's knees in a pleasingly intimate situation, he let down his line, ensuring that it was fully three feet away from hers, lest even here it might get entangled. Duncan did likewise.

Cormac duly felt the little bump as the lead weight struck sand after perhaps thirty feet of line was unrolled, and raised it for what he hoped was the required height of eight inches. And almost immediately he felt a tug-tug over that extended forefinger. Exclaiming, he jerked, perhaps over-strongly. The twitching sensation continued, and he hurriedly pulled up the wet line, not a little excited, Fenella urging care.

It seemed a lot of line to hoist, splashing water over them both, and then out came the wire with a flailing flatfish on it, twisting this way and that, brown on top and white below, to be hoisted inboard, to the girl's congratulations, she declaring that she had never known quite such instant success before.

He made something of a botch of unhooking that slippery, joggling creature; indeed Fenella had to give her line to him to hold while she did it for him, physical contact very much involved.

While they were at this, both Duncan and one of the fishermen registered catches, so they obviously must be over a very fruitful patch of sand. Sadly Duncan somehow lost his flounder on the way up, although the other man held on to his.

The messy business of halving lug-worms and rebaiting the hooks followed, and the fishing resumed.

Fenella won another flounder, but that was all. Whether the boats had drifted away from the productive spot, or there were just no more fish to catch there, they did not know. The oarsmen tried pulling back to where they could only judge that they had been so fortunate, but without results. However, the young woman declared that it had been a good day's sport, on the whole – her companions counting twenty-two flounders altogether – and enough was a sufficiency. They would return to shore.

Cormac was reluctantly preparing to clamber over to their own boat alongside when Fenella said that there was no need for this, that they could tow the other craft behind them easily enough, her rowers making no objection. So they went back as passengers.

At the beach, they divided up the catch, and Fenella asserted that they would have flounders for supper, which did indicate that she expected the visitors to stay the night.

Well pleased with developments, Cormac and Duncan carried a dozen flatfish up to the castle.

Lady Alena clearly took no exception to the guests remaining; anyway, Cormac was getting the impression that her daughter was probably the one who made the decisions in that household. He decided that there was much to be said in favour of sea-fishing.

Baked flounder, coated in oatmeal, in due course made an excellent repast.

When, after an enjoyable evening by the withdrawing-room fire, Duncan carefully leaving the others early for his downstairs room, Fenella escorted Cormac up to the same attic chamber he had occupied previously, and ensured that all was in order for him there, he wondered how bold he might dare to be. It was evident that the young woman quite liked him, but that did not necessarily mean that she would be open to any sort of intimacy. Yet they had been intimate enough, after a fashion, in that boat, persons close, with himself leant over her knees, hands touching. He certainly did not want to offend, but . . .

So when, after wishing him a good night and she was heading for the door, he took her arm and squeezed it.

"Thank you, kind Fenella, for this day," he said. "It has been a joy. The fishing and, and your good company. I shall not forget it."

"Forget?" she asked. "Why should you – or you are no flounder-fisher! And if you do, you can always come back for other lessons!" And lightly touching his cheek with those formerly brown-stained fingers, she slipped out and closed the door behind her.

After washing in the warm water, he lay in his bed and stared up at the canopy, going over the events of the day – and just occasionally reaching up to stroke the cheek where Fenella had touched it. Was he becoming over-fond of that young woman? Becoming? *Had* become! Was he making more of their association than he ought to be doing, or was wise? Even if she behaved kindly towards him. He would be foolish to build up hopes. After all, she was a mormaor's granddaughter and niece of another. Connacher had no offspring surviving, and if he died thus, so far as Cormac knew, he had no other heir than his brother Aidan. So, however disinclined that man might be, Fenella's father could be the next Mormaor of Angus, one of the lesser kings in Scotland; and the daughters of mormaors could well be far above such as even the Thane of Glamis. Let him remember that.

Next morning it was back to Glamis, after a friendly send-off down at the horses, Cormac reminding himself of the night's cautions, the girl assuring him that there were flounders a-many for him to catch in Lunan Bay when he felt so inclined.

7

Cormac reckoned that the appointment of a new Thane of the Mearns was not so urgent a priority that he must go before Yuletide, now almost upon them, to give his report to King Constantine. Besides, he had been fairly swift in his carrying out of the royal command, so his journey westwards could wait, he judged, until after Twelfth Night.

His mother and sister had been making preparations in his absence, well used to this task, his Glamis people all co-operating. Great stocks of food and drink had to be gathered in for the feasting, the most considerable and all but continuous of the year. It was almost all derived from the pre-Christian ages of sun worship and druidism, to be sure, this mid-winter festivity, preparing to welcome the passing of the shortest day, and leading into the commencement of the new period of the sun's ascendancy, with the growing fertility of the land and the start of the breeding season of the animal creation, the leafing of the trees and the flowering of plants, to mankind's benefit and satisfaction. The fact that Christ's birth was also celebrated at this time was, of course, complementary, coincidental but apt to be rather swamped by the former pagan rites, however much the abbots and monks sought to emphasise the differences.

So the ice-houses had to be filled with beef and mutton, venison, fowl, salmon and the like. The mills were busy grinding grain, the brewers making ale, the baxters baking oatcakes and bannocks.

The first of the twelve nights' activities was that of the Mistletoe Bough, on the twenty-third day of December, when the sun set two minutes later than it had been doing, signifying renewal. Mistletoe was the only plant which flowered at this time of the year in northern lands, parasite as it was, with its yellow petals and white berries, and like holly and ivy was esteemed as conveying promise of fertility and abundance to come. So its praise and augury was always honoured and exalted at this time, as the sun's forerunner and herald, its whereabouts always noted and cherished. And since it required a host tree to flourish, the branch round which it coiled itself had to be honoured also, hence the bough involved.

So that evening, with lanterns lit, Cormac led a party of the villagers and tenants into nearby woodland to a known and guarded hawthorn tree which acted host to a mistletoe plant. All men, they made a double circle round that bent and aged tree and, hands linked, danced around it, chanting. Then Cormac stepped forward, with Duncan, the latter carrying a saw. In the flickering light of their lanterns, it could be seen that the mistletoe had wrapped itself round two fairly slender branches, not apt for their purpose. So the long tendril, some four feet of it, had to be heedfully unwound and detached, care taken to ensure no breakage and none of the yellow petals and white berries amongst the leathery, oval leaves were lost; then this wrapped round a more suitable, thicker branch, with equal regard, the company watching interestedly. Satisfied, at length, Cormac cut with his dirk the stem of the plant about one foot from its base, for enough must be left to ensure that it continued to grow hereafter, and Duncan scrupulously chose where best to saw off the bough with its precious appendage, and went to work. The fact that hawthorns were prickly trees did not lessen the need for care.

When branch and mistletoe were safely detached, Cormac holding it high, all cheered, and recommenced the circling, lanterns swinging eerily. Then return to the crowded castle courtyard was made, in procession, where acclaim greeted their arrival. Fortunately it was a dry night, however chilly, for their ceremony, or what followed would have been a deal less effective and enjoyable.

The mistletoe bough was carried over by Cormac to a specially erected archway of saplings, over which the bough was ceremoniously placed. Then music struck up and singing commenced, and, with the required flourish, the Thane of Glamis placed himself under the archway and bough, and held out his arms invitingly.

There followed a positive rush of women, jostling each other to be the first to enter those extended arms and be kissed beneath the mistletoe, young, of middle years and elderly, competition vigorous. Much of the kissing was equally vigorous, much open-lipped, with hugging and squeezing to match. This was not the first time, of course, that Cormac had gone through this experience, but never before as thane and prime recipient of the salutations, if such they could be called. He did not pretend that it was any sort of ordeal, and enjoyed, at the beginning at least, the female lips and tongues seeking his own, amidst gurgles and murmurs and deep breathings, the feel of rounded persons pressing against him, the clutchings and strokings – and all this by women who at other times were apt to bow respectfully to their lord and behave in modest seemly fashion. The Mistletoe Bough was especial, elemental, basic, as between men and women, just as its flowers were male and female, the enduring symbol and promise of fertility, the need for the one and the other for the continuance of the race – and the need and underlying joy of it.

It was accepted that every woman present should have the right to kiss and be kissed by the thane, and Cormac was pretty sure that some of them came round for a second turn. But presently, all but dizzy with it, he wagged his head and moved away, the competition being promptly changed to taking his place under the archway, and not only by men, indeed scuffles taking place in the process. Not that there need to be, for this could and would go on all night, and would become the more vehement and uninhibited as time went on and liquor flowed.

Then the feasting started, and the castle's busy cooks displayed their worth, while relays of musicians and singers maintained their accompaniment, Cormac acting the host, assisted by his mother and sister. Thereafter it was the dancing, although the eating and drinking, and the kissing, continued throughout.

Thus began the Saturnalia, so named after Saturn the Roman god of sowing the seed – although the druids had called him Mithra, god of light, son of the invincible sun itself. This prolonged festivity signified the start of the seven days of freedom from normal labour and travail and duties of daily life, when in the past even slaves and serfs were temporarily freed and allowed to speak their minds. Now there were no serfs, on the Church's orders; but the freedom was there, and moral bounds relaxed.

That relaxation was in evidence as the night progressed; women's clothing began to become disarranged, and even partly dispensed with, despite the cold, shrieks and yells punctuated the music, some couples disappeared out of the courtyard although not all were so modest about it. Cormac found himself besieged by eager women, for he was quite a good-looking young man, and he was not beyond enjoying much of it, although he kept wishing that it was Fenella nic Aidan who was in his arms rather than these. Indeed he wondered whether some similar activities were going on at the Red Castle of Lunan – and rather hoped not. He was no prude, but . . .

At length, his mother having already retired, Cormac felt that he might decently leave the increasingly noisy ongoings, his sister Bridget apparently quite happy to remain a while yet. There would be much merry-making for hours. He hoped that his sleep would not be too disturbed, for tomorrow was the Animal Carnival, and that was a daytime festivity, although it usually carried on well into the evening also, and he had his leading part to play in it.

* * *

It was in fact noontide before that next development got under way, for much preparation was necessary for this one, and not only by the thane's household. The carnival had everyone dressing up as animals or birds, and parading around the district, making no small demands on the participants, especially after the excesses of the night before, for quite a mileage was to be covered, to villages, hamlets and farming communities, with some sort of reception at each.

Lady Ada excused herself from this, save for the seeing-off of the castle group, for this was mainly a diversion for the younger folk; besides, there was more feasting to provide for the evening. But sister Bridget was all for it, spry, and eager to display the fine costume she had made, representing a swan, with wings attached to the sleeves of her white linen gown, red stockings round her ankles, the head and coiling neck made from the shaven skin of a sheep with feathers carefully threaded in, and a beak formed out of the black tip of a ram's horn, this worn above her tucked-in hair.

Cormac chose to act the stag, a simpler role to devise, with the antlers of a fine twelve-pointer affixed to one of his father's helmets, and deerskins hanging from his shoulders and wrapped round his legs. With all the walking and dancing to be done, these costumes had to be securely attached, and to form no serious impediment to movement.

The castle party, concerned to give a good lead to others, appeared in a notable selection of guises, as tusked boars, horses, wolves, hounds, herons, Duncan suitable as a hawk, his hook-beaked head a work of art. With drummers beating the rhythm, and all chanting, they set off for the village. There was the faintest smirr of rain in the air, but insufficient so far to damp the enthusiasm.

The Glamis community was awaiting them, with a bonfire already lit, and provender and ale laid out even thus early, many young people, variously disguised and garbed, ready to join the walkers, woolly sheepskins, cowhides, horns and feathers being much in evidence. Dancing round the bonfire followed, and then the marchers moved off again, leaving the older villagers to their own celebratory devices.

The thanedom of Glamis covered quite a large area of central Strathmore, and this perambulation could by no means reach most of it. So the custom was for folk, again mainly the younger ones, to come in from the more outlying areas and farmeries, especially from the hillfoots, to certain of the more accessible communities such as Nether Arniefoul, Thornietoun, Cossans, Kinalty and the Mill of Eassie, there to await the ever-growing procession and to greet it with cheer. Each grouping vied with others in their efforts at entertainment and the amounts of refreshment, especially liquid, which they could offer, and at every one the ongoing parade grew larger and more varied, so that presently it stretched, in capering, dancing, singing carousal, for a quarter of a mile at times, although some of the participants did fall out occasionally or not get beyond the next village or two, walking abilities, and also costumes, being unequal. But for Cormac and Bridget and the castle party in general, the full circuit meant a long day's walking, to say nothing of the antics, all of eleven miles indeed, before winning back to Glamis; hence Cormac's concern, the night before, over due rest and sleep after the Mistletoe Bough saturnalia. And completing the extended and so active circuit was not the end of it, for the evening fell to be rounded off with more feasting, bonfires and dancing, even though the revelry was apt to be less boisterous than that of the night before.

Cormac, fond of his bed, was thankful when he could use Bridget's unusual physical weariness as excuse to escort her back to the castle.

There was a day's relief thereafter, thanks to the churchmen. The next day, 25th December, was in fact Log Even; but the abbots and bishops, not only of the Scottish

Columban Church, concerned about the effects of all this licence on the people, had chosen to make a pause in the revelry by naming this day to celebrate Christ's birth, Log Even put off until the morrow; and to celebrate in a very different fashion the Redeemer's coming to mankind. Even the least religiously minded were apt to be glad enough of this opportunity to, as it were, draw breath and relax their persons instead of their moral persuasions. So Christmas Day intervened, and quiet family worship took the place of riot, indulgence and animalism, the Virgin Mary and Babe temporarily superseding Saturn, Mithra and the sun. Cormac, for one, rather pitied the Norsemen, Saxons and other pagans, who did not have this blessed interval, which he could have wished to last longer.

But no, next day was Log Even, and with its own requirements, activities and leadership again demanded of such as thanes. As the name implied, this was mainly a night-time ritual; nevertheless part of it had to be performed by day, although fortunately it required no very early start, the scene, having been selected beforehand.

Once again it was only men who had to be led out, in the afternoon, to bring in the Yule Log. Here, at Glamis, that task entailed quite a lengthy march, for the necessary timber had to be very inflammable, no ordinary green wood being so without much fostering and fanning. Only the resinous fir and pine would burn, newly felled, and even that would have to be anointed with melted beeswax to aid combustion. But the native Scots fir, or Caledonian pine as the Romans had called it, a slow-growing and notably tough tree, was particularly inflammable, excellent for making torches and the like. These did grow in Strathmore, but apt to be away amongst the foothills. So Cormac had to conduct his team some three miles south-eastwards to the slopes of Kincaldrum Hill for the required scattering of Scots firs, there to select a suitable tree, fell it – no easy task with axes – trim its trunk, or a large part of it, and then drag it back to Glamis, and by man-power, not horse- nor oxen-power. This had to be man's labour and tribute, heavy labour over rough terrain. And on the way they had to find both holly and ivy, none so difficult this, to adorn the log in due course, these like the mistletoe being able to conquer the winter's chill.

In the evening, then, the Yule Log, set on a trestle now, had to be treated with the melted wax, the holly and ivy draped on it, and all set alight from torches and heaps of its own shavings. Everyone watched, almost breathlessly, for if it failed to burn, or caught alight only very slowly and feebly, this would predict an unprofitable season's growth, poor harvest and consequent hardship. Happily, on this occasion, the log was quickly ablaze, to cheering. That tough but resinous wood would burn practically all night, and the longer the more auspicious. From its glowing ash and embers subsidiary fires were lit to roast the feast, whole oxen now, part of the thanksgiving. The holly and ivy were offered up in token of gratitude for their providing the fairy people of the forests with shelter from the winter storms.

In the small hours of the morning, Cormac was able to retire, duty done. there were still all those days until Twelfth Night, to be sure, with much revelry to attend, but his major and most demanding responsibilities were over, and he need only take such part as suited him hereafter. His mother assured him that he had acquitted himself adequately.

8

The festive season over, Cormac duly set off on his thirty-five-mile journey to report to King Constantine, with Duncan as usual, going up Strathmore, by Coupar Angus, Glen Carse and Kinfauns to Perth, then over Tay and up Strathearn into Fortrenn to Forteviot. The Ard Righ proved to be at one of his lesser castles, at Rossie, near to Dunning, seven more miles to the south-west. It being still daylight, they rode on thither.

Constantine made no complaints about delay in the carrying out of his mission, no doubt himself having been sufficiently preoccupied with the Yuletide activities; anyway, he was not a difficult man to deal with. Son of King Cuilean, the murdered Kenneth's predecessor, he was the eighth generation in descent from Kenneth Mac Alpin who had united Picts and Scots.

He proved to be quite satisfied with Cormac's advice that Donald of Arbuthnott would make the most suitable new Thane of the Mearns, and said that he would summon him down in due course to instal him as such and inform him of his duties and responsibilities.

This however turned out to be a comparatively minor matter for the High King at this juncture. It seemed that he had much more serious concerns on his mind, which he divulged to his visitor. There was word of renewed Viking raiding in Lothian, despite the crushing defeat and expulsion inflicted on them so recently, and this unusual season for their "hosting", when winter storms at sea would be apt to deter them. As yet these were not on any large scale apparently; but the king feared that they might be only the forerunners of renewed and greater invasion. According to the information sent to him, these were Jutes, that is Danes from the southern province of Jutland, whereas those they had defeated earlier were from Norway, they had discovered. So Constantine thought that there might well be some sort of Viking rivalry in this. He had decided that it might be wise to lead some small expedition down into Lothian in a month or so, when the worst of the snows were over on the hills but before the normal Norse hosting season started, to destroy any such invading parties and discourage further assaults; not with any great army, as before, but with a small fast-moving force, which ought to be sufficient. He might well call upon Thane Cormac for this, possibly with this new Mearns thane. So to be ready.

The other royal worry was even more grievous. He was reliably informed that there was some sort of plot brewing to oust him from the throne, this on the part of those two mormaors who had voted against his appointment after Kenneth's slaying, those of Atholl and Moray. If this was true, he wanted to be kept well informed of any developments. He thought that Glamis, situated where he was, in Angus bordering on Atholl and none so far from Moray, could possibly find out, in a good position to learn of any treasonable moves, and a man that he could trust. Would he make discreet enquiries?

Cormac, of course, was shocked to hear of this, and said so, promising to find out what he could. Perhaps it was all talk, however, idle chatter, stemming from soured men?

The High King thought that it was more than that. The word had come to him from Mar, where the young mormaor had family links with Moray. The talk was of possible armed revolt.

A fellow guest at Rossie Castle that night was the Abbot of Dunning, an ancient foundation. An elderly man, he was much concerned over some of the pagan customs still being enacted over Yuletide, as were all clerics; but his especial distress was over one which was prevalent in part of the area over which he had spiritual responsibility, in Fortrenn, the district of Keillour to the north, in especial that near to Dupplin Loch. This was the heresy of ritual displays against alleged monsters, unchancy creatures of legend and ancient annals, notably those declared to inhabit lochs, with women spurring on young men to do battle with these, with promises of sexual favours if they were bold enough to challenge the creatures in their chosen haunts. This folly was, of course, especially dangerous in winter conditions. They all knew that there were said to be monsters in certain lochs, this Dupplin amongst them, although personally the abbot had never known anyone who had seen one. But this last Yule one young fool had drowned in the loch, allegedly others previously. And the icy water, at this season, must endanger health. And not only the men endangered, for sometimes, it seemed, the women, to encourage them to this sinful folly, would undress themselves at the lochside and reveal their naked bodies in promise. It seemed that the alleged reason for this foolhardy usage was that these monsters were the emissaries of the gods of darkness and blight, and the slaying of them was smiled on by the sun. But if any man died in the struggle, his soul, created by the sun, would go on to a higher destiny and be offered endless delights. This was all anathema to the Church, and to be condemned. The abbot believed that if the Ard Righ was to make it unlawful, lives, and possibly souls, would be saved.

Cormac had heard of monsters in lochs, but had not been told of any supposed to be in the Strathmore waters, nor of this practice being engaged in thereabouts.

Constantine said that he would consider the matter; but Yuletide activities were, by their very nature, outwith the normal laws of the land, and it might be difficult to prohibit any one of them lest others seemed to be threatened. The abbot was disappointed. He reminded that the High King's predecessor and great-grandsire, Constantine the Second had, exactly ninety years before, vowed that he and his successors should protect all rights of Christ's Church; and surely it was an elementary right that heathenish customs which endangered the lives of the king's subjects should be forbidden?

Cormac perceived some of the problems of being High King of Scots.

In the morning, it was back to Glamis, with assurances that Cormac would seek to learn if there was any truth in the rumours of intended rebellion by the dissident mormaors, and to send word to the Ard Righ.

To try to gain the information wanted, Cormac decided that his best opportunity was probably through the new Thane of the Mearns, whose wife, he had discovered, was a daughter of the Lord of Cromdale, in Moray. Through her they ought to be able to discover what was going on in that mormaordom without arousing suspicions. It would also be opportunity for Donald of Arbuthnott to prove himself worthy of Constantine's approval.

So it was north again to Glen Bervie and Arbuthnott Castle, where the new thane-to-be was glad to hear that he had been accepted. He was quite prepared to go on northwards with his wife to Moray to visit her people, and to seek to discover what he could as to any possible rumblings of revolt, taking care to be discreet about it and not to give any impression that he was there to gain information. His wife's sister had recently had a baby, and this would give them suitable excuse for their visit.

Well satisfied, Cormac wondered what excuse *he* could concoct to go home by Lunan Bay, and so soon? He did not expect that any word of possible northern rebellion was likely to have reached the Red Castle family, isolated in more ways than one as they were; but perhaps he could pretend that they might have heard something through their Ethiehaven fisherfolk, who might well be in touch quite frequently with other fishers from northern havens in Mar, Buchan and even Moray. Would that serve? Duncan, with him as usual, declared that the deep-sea fishermen did share common fishing-grounds and were noted for their exchange of news and gossip.

Lunan Bay, then, and in brief snow showers.

If the Red Castle household was surprised to see them back again thus early, they did not show it. Greetings were warm. Cormac was almost too hasty in announcing the ostensible reason for this visit; and his hosts may have drawn their own conclusions, but if so did not voice them. That they had heard nothing of any seditious talk from the north was no surprise, but the enquiry did not sound too unreasonable to make. And if any such word did reach them, Fenella promised to send to Glamis with it. Greatly daring, Cormac suggested that she might even care to bring it herself. Why should he always be the recipient of the hospitality? That was received without evident displeasure but also without comment.

Needless to say, the visitors had arranged their arrival sufficiently late in the day to ensure that they would have to stay the night, this being taken for granted apparently, indeed Fenella wondering whether a second attempt at flounder-fishing might be welcome on the morrow, her guest far from averse. But was mid-January weather suitable? He was told that in fact snow showers usually indicated comparatively calm conditions on the water. They would go well wrapped up in plaiding.

That evening by the fire they talked of Yuletide happenings, Cormac doing most of the recounting, for at Red Castle they engaged in very little of such ongoings, with no community nearer than Ethiehaven, and the fisherfolk apparently being less concerned with the like, their celebrations involved with the sea, pagan also but relating to the sea god Manannan, and this in the spring, not mid-winter. So Aidan's family had, much more appropriately, kept the feast of Christmas, with little of the sun-worship additions, less exciting as this might be, to be sure. Cormac did learn, however, something of the seafarers' spring observances, of sacrifices of lambs and calves to Manannan, these tied marooned on rocks and skerries to drown at high water, this to try to ensure good catches of fish; of torchlight sailings as a sort of prayer against storms; and of the blessing of nets, this last in the name of the fishers of Galilee, more properly.

Cormac asked, eyebrows raised, whether there were any available gestures that they ought to make to ensure good fishing on the morrow, and was told that Fenella did not think that Manannan was interested in shallow-water flatfish.

Taken to his room that night, he risked a kiss on the girl's hand as she said goodnight, this on the palm not the back, and then closing her fingers over it as though in token of some sort of compact; at which she eyed him levelly before leaning forward and kissing his cheek calmly, then departing.

Might he have safely ventured further? he wondered.

The same two fishermen were waiting for them down at the sands of the bay next morning, but with a slightly larger boat, and provided with lines and bait, themselves laden with plaids and a basket of bannocks, hard-boiled eggs and honey wine.

It was proposed that this time they should try another fishing area where there were reports of good catches of flatfish, this just off Red Head, which was the southern horn of Lunan Bay as Boddin Point was the northern, four miles apart. To reach this meant a two-mile row, but the fishermen made light of this, and Cormac and Duncan offered to take an oar each to help, glad enough of the exercise to warm them on a cold morning, even though the other two looked somewhat sceptical as to the worth of their assistance.

Actually, although there were occasional slight snow showers again, mere drifts of frozen rain on the northerly airstream, it seemed less chilly than on the previous occasion, and the water was calmer. They passed Ethiehaven half a mile offshore, and promptly thereafter the ruddy cliffs began to soar impressively. Soon the mighty foreland of Red Head reared before them, Fenella pointing out where, near that fearsome crest, ruins could be seen, once the chapel or *diseart* of the Columban St Murdoch, where he was wont to go for pauses in his missionarising to commune with his Maker, there amongst the winds and spray and wheeling seabirds.

They found two other small boats lying some way out from the headland, and presumed that this was where the recommended fishing-ground was situated, so went to take up a position nearby, after hailed greetings. Fenella reminded her pupils of previous instructions as they commenced the messy business of halving lug-worms and threading the parts on the hooks. Cormac asked about these worms, where they came from and how they were collected. He learned that the innumerable little casts which littered any tidal sandy beach represented their whereabouts, and these could be dug up readily enough with no lack of them. What they found to live on in the sand was not clear, but that was the brown slime with which they were presently staining their fingers.

Once again Cormac seated himself beside the young woman, and proceeded to enjoy the closeness. At first their efforts were less than rewarding, with the twitches of a nibble or two, but no hookings. However, they could see the other fishers drawing up fish quite frequently none so far off, so they got the oars out again and rowed somewhat closer. Presumably the flounders were apt to gather together in groups, like other living creatures, mankind included.

The move proved worth while, for quickly all now began to get bites, and their jerkings on the lines produced results. Fenella herself brought in the first flapping catch, quickly followed by Duncan and one of their fishermen, although Cormac was less prompt in gaining satisfaction, indeed pulling up his line twice to find the worms sucked off. However, since his real objective was not the collection of flounders but the pleasure of near association with Fenella, he did not complain. But clearly fish were there in fair numbers, and in due course he too was rewarded, and began to add to the catch.

They had perhaps three hours, chilly hours, of this, and

an excellent haul of flatfish, when a shower of hailstones, not just thin snow, rattled down on them, and had the fishermen looking northwards, and pointing. The sky was getting notably darker in that direction, whence the clouds were coming, and it was evident that the weather was deteriorating. If the wind rose, as looked likely, rowing back those two miles northwards could be less than enjoyable. It was agreed that it would be wise to call it a day. One of the other boats had already started to head back for Ethiehaven. So the return was made, and this at little more than an hour past noon.

Back at the castle, Cormac recognised that he had no valid excuse for remaining there longer, and certainly did not want to outstay his welcome. So declaring his gratitude for favours received, he said that if they left now they could make it to Glamis by darkening.

With a sack of flounders, they said their farewells, this in a rising wind and hailstorm, so Fenella was dissuaded from accompanying them down to the horses. But she did raise her face towards Cormac's for a parting kiss, there at the castle gateway, and when the man's lips moved from her cheek to her mouth, and lingered there momentarily, she did not draw back nor shake him off.

Duncan's smile as they rode away, to backward waving, was understanding, even congratulatory.

9

Back at Glamis, they had to wait for fully ten days before Donald of Arbuthnott arrived to inform Cormac of what he had discovered on his visit to Moray. There was undoubtedly restiveness in the air up there, folk sensing trouble to come. As yet there was no word of actual armed uprising, but then this was hardly the season for that amongst people from mountainous country amidst winter snows. But there had been much alleged coming and going of lords and chiefs to the Mormaor Finlay's castle at Inverness since Yuletide, and there were rumours that Kenneth mac Duff, son of the former High King Dubh, had been there with his nephew Malcolm, staying for some time; he was the nominee whom the dissident mormaors had put up for Ard Righ against Constantine, which could be ominous. Admittedly all this was only hearsay, less than specific and explicit. But it did support the rumours that the High King's opponents were not quietly accepting his occupancy of the throne.

Cormac wondered whether this was worth retailing to Constantine. After all, it was not much more than he already had heard. Something more definite was called for, if possible; that is, if there was indeed flame behind the smoke. What should he do? Was there any point in sending Duncan, or another, down to Fortrenn with this vaguely supportive information? He doubted it.

But there was the other mormaordom, Atholl, much nearer at hand. He knew various chiefly folk there, indeed was kin to some. It might be sensible to go over to Atholl himself, to, as it were, test the water there. His mother had come from Atholl, a daughter of a former Thane of

Logierait. Suppose he was to take his young and lively sister Bridget there to see their cousins. That would not seem suspicious, and he might learn whether these Moray and Ross rumours were also circulating thereabouts. He asked Lady Ada, who agreed that it might be useful, and could do no harm so long as they were both circumspect. She wanted no trouble with her kinsfolk. Bridget herself was delighted at the notion, even the travel over the mountains in these conditions not deterring her.

To reach the Logierait district of Atholl, a dozen miles south of the mormaor's seat of Blair as eagles flew but three times that for earthbound travellers, it was necessary to cover some sixty miles. Here also, had they been able to go in any sort of straight line, they could have done it in less than half that; but that would have entailed crossing high mountains and ridges, snow-covered. As it was, they would have to thread lofty enough passes on their round-about route; but Bridget was a good horsewoman and expressed no doubts. They took Pate the Mill with them, as well as Duncan, this being a slack season for milling.

They rode north, then, to Kirriemuir at the foot of the high hills, then turned westwards along their flanks, by Alyth, where King Arthur's Guinevere had been abducted and held captive by Mordred, and on to Blairgowrie. Thereafter it was into the high ground and snow, which on the mountainsides was deep but only patchy in the valleys they followed. These led them by a series of lochs, Drumellie and Clunie and Butterstane and Craiglush, a lengthy, winding and challenging progress, reaching high at Butterglen, but in woodland thereafter, where the snow was less of a trial for their horses. By the time they reached thus far it was dusk; but Cormac was determined to win to Dunkeld for the night, where there was a monkish hospice known to all travellers, Bridget making no complaints.

Quite steeply, after the last two lochs, they descended into the wooded valley of the Tay at Birnam and Dunkeld. This was, of course, a famous area, for here, at the dun or place of the Keledei, the Friends of God, a notable denomination of the Columban Church, the great Kenneth mac Alpin, Constantine's ancestor, had established an abbey and monastery to house and care for the sacred objects from Iona, which island had been suffering grievous ravaging by the Norsemen. Here he brought St Columba's relics and later the coronation Stone of Destiny, esteeming this to be the very centre of the united kingdom he had formed out of the realms of Alba and Dalriada, this a century and a half before.

Here, then, at the hospice by the abbey, the monks welcomed them kindly, travellers being comparatively few at this season. They had a women's refuge at the hospice, but Bridget did not want to go there, empty as it was, and the brothers bowed to her will and allowed her to spend the night in a small room near Cormac's. They were in Atholl here, but the visitors forbore to question the monks about matters controversial. Cormac did learn, however, that there had been a meeting of great ones recently at Blair, this mentioned because another thane, of Amulree, had passed nights here, going and coming. This might or might not be significant.

In the morning they rode on up Tay, on its east side, high above the river on a sort of terrace of the hillside of Rotmell and on by Dowally and Guay to the junction of the River Tummel with Tay south of Ballinluig. Here there was an underwater causeway made to form a ford across the larger river, and immediately over it rose a steep isolated hillock, on the summit of which was the castle of Logierait, in a strong position thus guarded by water on two sides. It had replaced a Pictish fort.

The approach of the four riders up the zigzag track had not gone unobserved, and they were met by guards, to be escorted onwards.

Their visit, although a surprise, produced far from any impression of being unwelcome. Neil of Logierait was a man some five years older than Cormac, but little more experienced as a thane, his father having died only some eighteen months before. He was a cheerful character,

heavy-built but active. His wife, Morag, was very much
the proud mother, carrying her baby around with her
even breast-feeding him whenever he stirred, a plump
and good-natured creature. They made an uncomplicated
friendly couple. Bridget found them much to her taste.

Cormac was, in fact, spared any need deviously to
introduce his real objective in their coming, for within
hours of their arrival, after the evening meal when the
womenfolk were with much solicitude settling the infant
for the night, Neil himself more or less raised the matter
on his own.

"This of being a thane, Cousin?" he asked. "How do
you find it? Your duties and dues? Not so much to your
people, your tenants and folk – that is none so difficult.
But this of allegiance and fealty? We have especial duties
to the Ard Righ by our positions. We hold directly of the
crown. We have to collect the royal levies and teinds, to
fine those who default, act the justiciar on occasion. So
we owe homage to the High King. But also we are under
the sway of our own mormaors, and them closer to us.
And if these services clash, what then? How do we act?
Which support?"

"I swore allegiance to King Constantine at Scone at his
coronation. Did not you? Not to any mormaor."

"I was not there. I was abed. Thrown from my horse,
ribs broke. But, yes, I would have done so had I been
present."

"So our duty is plain, no? To the Ard Righ. Not to the
mormoars."

"And – if the Ard Righ was wrongly appointed? Another
more worthy?"

"He that is crowned is the High King, whoever other
may claim. And Constantine is that. Do you hold otherwise,
Cousin?"

"No-o-o. *I* do not. But Kenneth of Atholl does. He
and the others say that Malcolm mac Duff should be
Ard Righ."

"He and Finlay of Moray and Ross were outvoted by

he five others. So there is no question, I say. Constantine s rightful monarch and commands our allegiance. And I ind him worthy. I fought in his train in Lothian. You lid not, I think?"

"No. Kenneth did not answer his call. Nor any from is mormaordom. That is why I ask of this."

"Aye. It is difficult for you, I can see," Cormac said.

"It could be more difficult. For there is a move to unseat Constantine and put Malcolm on his throne. Just how, I now not. But moves are to be made."

"Moves? You mean armed uprising?"

"That, if it is necessary, they say. If they cannot gain Constantine's abdication otherwise. The word is that they, Kenneth and Finlay, will call a great meeting of all the mormaors and lofty ones, thanes also no doubt, and seek greement on change. Only if that fails, then to arms."

"A meeting? And why should the other *ri* desert Constantine, whom they appointed?"

"It is claimed that he does not consult them sufficiently. That he never comes north of Fortrenn. That he sees his main support in the south, in Strathearn and Menteith and Lennox, in Fife. Even over into Lothian. Caring little for Atholl and Mar, for Ross and Moray and Caithness, for he Highland west and the Isles."

"But it is Lothian which has been suffering the Norse invasion since he came to power. And is again loing so."

"There have been raids in the north and west also."

"Only of a much lesser sort. This was *invasion*. Not so?"

"Perhaps. But they have other complaints also." Neil hrugged. "I do not know the rights of it. But, as thane, am between the two sides."

"I would say not, Cousin. You are a High King's epresentative, whoever he may be at any time. You hold he position of him. He could dismiss you or myself, even hough we are our fathers' sons and heirs. The mormaors ould not do that." Cormac paused. "This of a meeting? When is it to be?"

"I know not. I have had no sure word. I will be summoned in due course, no doubt. As will you, I judge."

"And to arms only after that, if it fails to reach agreement? So, some revolt could not take place for some time?"

"No. That would seem to be so."

"And if such rising is mounted, how would you, as Thane of Logierait, act?"

"I, I will have to consider it. I am . . ." Almost thankfully, the other turned to see the women return, and this difficult talking could be halted, as unsuitable for the ladies to have to hear.

But Cormac had learned sufficient. He now had something definite to tell Constantine. He need not implicate Neil as to any blame. But now he had what he came for.

They could not, of course, seek to depart so soon, or it would be obvious why they were there. A couple of days, then?

The two days thereafter were well spent, the company good, the hospitality generous. Bridget especially enjoyed the young female association, of which she did not get sufficient at Glamis, baby talk fascinating her. Cormac grew to like his cousin well, and sympathised with his predicament, although they did not discuss the monarchial situation further at any length. Neil was very fond of hawking and Duncan, as expert, was able to give him useful guidance.

So, on the third morning, in hard frost with the edges of the river icing, they took their leave. In the event, Neil said that he would escort them some little way on their road, which had Cormac doubting, for he had his own ideas about that journey. He hoped that the other would not accompany them over-far. However, his cousin went with them only a few miles, as far as Kindallachan, and they parted in mutual esteem.

Now it was the matter of Bridget. Cormac had decided that there was no point in himself going all the way back to Glamis when he was all but halfway to Forteviot here and could go on and inform Constantine of the situation at once. So he would send Bridget home in the care of Pate the Mill, at Dunkeld. But he had reckoned without his spirited sister. She declared that if he was going on to see the Ard Righ, she was going with him. She had never met a High King, and here was the opportunity. Glamis and their mother could wait. Never fear, she would not lower his credit with King Constantine.

Cormac acquiesced without much fuss.

From Dunkeld it was some sixteen miles to Perth, and another eight down Strathearn to the Dupplin ford and over to Forteviot, so not requiring any overnight halt. By the great Birnam Wood they went, and over the higher moorlands of Auchtergaven to the Water of Ordie, thereafter joining Tay again, which river had made an enormous loop, which, this way, they had cut across, saving fifteen miles, Perth only four miles ahead now. Bridget did not hold them up, interested in all that she saw, new territory for her. The hard, frosty ground may have been sore on their horses' hooves, and they had to crack ice at the banks of the Dupplin ford over the Earn; but they reached Forteviot before dusk, well content.

The High King received them cordially, however surprised he might have been to see the young woman with them. He interviewed Cormac alone, presently, and listened heedfully to all that had been learned at Logierait, expressing his gratitude for the information. He said that it confirmed much of what he had gathered elsewhere. This of a possible great meeting of mormaors and others he was doubtful about, however, for such would inevitably be reported to him by those loyal, and could prepare him for troubles ahead. He thought that this might be merely a device to allay fears. His view was that any uprising would come first, with him and his supporters unprepared. Timing, in that case, would be all-important for his cause. He believed however that there would be no moves against him until the later spring, April or May possibly, for his enemies' men were in the north mainly and the mountain-girt country, and the snow melting, with all the many rivers in flood would make assembling any large army difficult. So he almost certainly had time to deal with these Viking troubles in Lothian. Not only did he owe it to his people there, but the fact that he was doing it, protecting the realm, would commend itself to most of the kingdom. Lothian then, and soon. How quickly could the Glamis and Mearns thanedoms assemble their men and be ready to join him for a swift assault on these wretched raiders?

Cormac thought that two weeks would serve, for Glamis at any rate. The Mearns might take a little longer, a more scattered thanedom.

Mid-February, then, Constantine said. He would have his own people and those of Strathearn and Lennox mustered by then, or sufficient of them. It need not be a very large force on this occasion.

Cormac and Bridget dined with the High King that evening, to her satisfaction. There was no queen, Constantine being a widower. In the morning, it was back to Glamis.

10

At that time of the year, with the spring ploughing and the lambing not yet started and the cattle still confined to the infields, Cormac had little difficulty in raising men. One hundred and fifty of them, he assessed, would be sufficient, with Thane Donald bringing possibly over one hundred, for he had gathered that Constantine sought only about one thousand for this expedition.

They had to wait a few days for the Mearns contingent, which amounted to one hundred and twenty; but even so were in good time for the muster at Fortrenn, with some of the Lennoxmen still to come in. With well over his thousand, the Ard Righ was well satisfied. The Mormaor of Strathearn was with his troops, and declared that he had heard nothing of any meeting of great ones being called.

They set off southwards on the Eve of St Finnian, as before going by Auchterarder and the Allan Water, down to Dunblane, and on to the crossing of the causeway over Forth at Stirling, where scouts were sent ahead to prospect, for the word was that these Jutes were assailing the Forth shores further up-estuary than the earlier and greater intrusions, this more raiding than invasion. As before, however, the enemy seemed to be confining their attentions to the southern, Lothian, side of the firth, possibly looking on the Fife shores as less profitable, and more likely to be better defended, being MacDuff territory.

Instead of heading inland, therefore, by the Tor Wood, and so to the Carron and Avon Waters, making for Dunedin, the force followed the shore of the winding Forth itself, by Throsk and Airth and Kinneil to Abercorn, the estuary now widened to over three miles across. Here their scouts brought back news. Jutes were at Dalmeny, five miles ahead; also at Craigalmond, two miles further. Beyond that also, probably; they had not risked going on to see, lest they warned the foe. How many there was no knowing, but they had counted eight longships beached on the sands at Dalmeny.

That was sufficient for Constantine meantime. He had been here, around the Almond mouth, on the last campaign, so he knew the lie of the land. He detached a company of about five score to ride well inland and then to cut back seawards, to seal off any communication by the enemy between Dalmeny and Craigalmond. Then he told Cormac, who had had experience in the damaging of Viking longships, to take his men directly along the shoreline to destroy these vessels. These sea rovers were all but obsessed with their war-craft, the symbols of their power and the means of their hosting, so depriving them of these would be a blow to their morale.

On their way along the coast they came across the burned-out ruins of farms and hamlets, and not a few dead bodies, but no living creatures, human or animal, save for carrion crows. But inland they could see a distant haze of smoke, bluish this, not black, which indicated old fires still smouldering, presumably where the invaders had been fairly recently busy. Dalmeny village itself was devastated and empty, save for the heads nailed to timber walling, men, women and children, mainly hanging by their hair. Sickened, Cormac led his people on, the more determined direly to punish the perpetrators.

Hitherto the shoreline had been stony, with pebbly beaches; but now commenced a long stretch of level sands. And almost two miles along eastwards they could see the dark shapes of a cluster of vessels beached there, the longships almost certainly. There would be men there, left to watch over them. How many?

As they neared the craft they could see a farmery close by which had not been burned. That would be where the guards were. Would they show fight? These were bound to observe the long column of one hundred and fifty horsemen approaching. Unless there were a great many of the Jutes they would be fools to remain. Would they flee on foot? Or could they launch the boats and get away afloat? Cormac spurred on the faster.

Soon they saw men leaving the farm cothouses and sheds, running, a dozen men perhaps. Four ran off towards woodland, but the rest hurried down on to the sands, towards the longships. Could they get these into the water in time, any of them? They were not small rowing-boats, fairly easily moved, but heavy, sixteen-oared craft, the greyhounds of the seas as they were called. Beached, pushing them back afloat would be no light task, even though they were not far from the tide's edge.

It became evident as the Scots cantered over that last half-mile that the Jutes recognised their situation well enough, and all of them were concentrating their efforts on one single vessel, pushing and dragging. It became something of a race for the horsemen, swords drawn now, to get there before the enemy could launch that craft and pile in. They lost in that contest, the Vikings managing to get the vessel afloat and to clamber in, the long sweeps out, just as the mounted men thundered up. Cormac and some others rode their steeds into the water, amidst much shouting, but too late to get within striking distance. The single longship was rowed out into the firth, escaping.

Cormac now had questions to face, decisions to take. They had captured seven longships, yes. But destroying these, as they had discovered before, took time, especially for men not equipped so to do, for they were substantially built craft necessarily. Holes in the floorbards, then, and take them out to sink them – or six of them, for the sinkers would require one to get back in themselves. How long would that take? Would those four running men, escaping inland, bring back more of their kind to attack while the work was going on? Were there many Jute concentrations? Or might the single vessel reach other enemy groups further down Forth, and bring them up to assail them, by sea or land? His best course, then? Getting rid of ships was the priority, what Constantine had sent them to do . . .

But a thought occurred to Cormac in his debate with himself. Need they actually destroy them? Might not these craft be useful to themselves, the Scots, remaining entire? They were not sea fighters admittedly, however able fishermen. But if they could capture Viking longships, these might prove an asset against further raiders. Could they sail these up-firth then, to Abercorn or wherever Constantine was based now, dispose of them that way? This without weakening his own force overmuch. His men might make but clumsy oarsmen, although some few of them would be fishermen. How many would be needed to propel the vessels those few miles, however slowly? Eight to a ship? Would that serve? Fifty men – that would still leave him with one hundred.

Discussing this hurriedly with Dunninald and Duncan and Pate, they decided that this was probably the answer. They would call for volunteers for the rowing, and the others look after their horses, Pate taking charge of this.

So it was done. There proved to be about a score of fishermen, part-timers most of them, in the company, and these were put in charge of the seven ships to guide the other oarsmen. There followed a great pushing of the craft down into the water, and a distinctly bungled boarding and getting the sweeps out and into position, two men to each oar, long and heavy as these were, amidst much cursing. Unfortunately the wind was from the south-west, so no hoisting of the square single sails would be of help going westwards. Then Pate gave the signal, and in less than orderly fashion the odd flotilla put to sea, somewhat zigzag as to progress at first, to turn up-firth, to wavings.

So far there was no sign of enemy making a return to their boats.

Cormac decided to press on eastwards, the riderless horses being led.

They passed more ravaged homesteads and fishers' cottages, but saw no enemy nor indeed local inhabitants.

That is, until a couple of miles on, with the mouth of the River Almond opening before them, and an offshore island nearby, they saw five longships heading out into the firth from the inlet. Whether these included the one which had escaped them at Dalmeny, and had been warned by it, they did not know, but it seemed probable. They were making eastwards, at any rate.

Cormac led his hundred men into the river-mouth village of Craigalmond, with its hallhouse, wooden jetties, shacks and sheds, a fishing community, drying nets still hanging on rails, but the place otherwise empty, showing signs of hasty abandonment, even uneaten food on tables.

What to do now? Constantine had ordered him only to go and destroy those vessels. Should he return to Abercorn? But he was concerned about those longships he had seen leaving this Craigalmond eastwards. They could be going anywhere, even back to their own Jutland. But if there were other groups of Norsemen along the coast, nearer to Leith and Dunedin, these might be warning or joining them, and readying them for fight. It would not be all flight for these tough Vikings. So it would be best to go on further, along the shoreline some way, to prospect. The High King's scouts had not proceeded thus far.

They rode on, then. The coast now was fairly level and plain, sand, pebbles and rocks, with little of any major features for some miles, inland scattered woods. But well ahead, perhaps six miles or so, soared the mighty landmark of Dunedin, the tall isolated hill of King Arthur's Seat. Its harbour of Leith might well be occupied by the Jutes; they might go as far as that, before turning back.

This proved to be a remarkably empty stretch, with no coves nor settlements, much less havens, and they saw nothing which concerned them for fully four miles. Then they noted two men running into the trees a short distance ahead, local folk by the look of them, and Cormac sent a few horsemen after them to fetch them in, to question.

Two frightened cowherds were brought back, father and son probably. Reassured as to their safety, they said that they had a family in the woods, after their farmery had been sacked, and informed that the Norsemen had landed at Grendun not far ahead where there was a haven, this some days before, four of their dreaded ships. They did not know whether they were still there. But there had been great smokes rising from further eastwards, from the Leith and Dunedin areas, although these had died down now.

So it looked as though the Jutes *had* assailed the Lothian capital of Dunedin, two miles inland from Leith. This would demand fairly large numbers surely, word that they must take to Constantine; not for themselves to try to tackle the like. They would go on as far as this Grendun haven, see how many of the enemy might be there, deal with them if possible, and then return to Abercorn with their news. Those escaped longships from Craigalmond might well have gone there.

But when they reached Grendun it was to find the cove and anchorage empty save for sunken fishing-boats, houses and fish-sheds burned and more dead bodies lying around, none of the enemy. Those vessels had not come here.

They were only a couple of miles from Leith now, and Cormac judged that it would be unwise to venture further. It would be dark before they could get back to Abercorn. Turn around, then, and hasten whence they had come. They were only really acting as scouts now. And they had not slain a single Jute.

But at Craigalmond they discovered that they need not go further. Constantine had moved his main array there, and was going to make this his base meantime. Pate the Mill and his captive longships were in the river mouth there also, having gone on to Abercorn, learned of the move, and rowed back. The Ard Righ was well pleased with the Glamis party's efforts and information, especially this of capturing the longships instead of destroying them. He would have them sent west to the Stirling area, Airth haven probably, for future use. The Dunedin situation was not news to him, however, others having told him of it. That was why he had moved here to Craigalmond, to deal with that himself.

But he had another task for Cormac. On the morrow he was to take his company and ride on eastwards again, but much further than Grendun or Leith. Constantine wanted to be assured that there had been no other landings, nearer to the firth mouth. The word was that these Jutes had been confining their attentions to territories not already devastated by the earlier Norse invasion, namely this area. But that might not be so; or there might even be new attackers descended upon the east of Lothian. So, while he, the king, was assailing the foe at Dunedin and Leith, Thane Cormac was to go on along the coastline, right to the mouth of the firth, to ensure that there was no enemy presence thereabouts, and if there was, to seek to prevent any flank attack on his force from that direction. He was not to hold to the coast only, but to probe inland to the vales where the main communities of eastern Lothian were settled, wisely hidden from sea rovers. Do that, and then return, it was to be hoped, to see these Jutes finally vanquished and driven off. Constantine added that he would not forget Cormac's services.

In the morning, then, the Glamis company attached itself to the Mormaor of Strathearn's contingent to head for Leith, while the High King himself led his main array to Dunedin, or Edinburgh, inland. It was realised, of course, that the invaders now must be well aware of the danger coming to them from the west. What would be their reaction? Would they judge that, facing a horsed army, they would be disadvantaged and probably outnumbered, and take to their ships and flee? Or seek to secure themselves in one or more of the hilltop Pictish forts, possibly the dun of Aiden itself, on its rock, where mounted men would be less than effective, and there make a stand? This Leith force was to try to secure any longships in that great harbour, to prevent flight; thereafter to turn inland and aid Constantine in attack on Dunedin from the north.

But when, presently, they got beyond Grendun without incident, it was to perceive that they were too late for that first part of their task. Quite a fleet of longships was sailing out from Leith, not exactly seawards but towards the island of Inchkeith five miles offshore. What did this mean? Presumably these were not fleeing, only ensuring that they were not captured in harbour by the advancing Scots. If they remained out near that island, then that would imply that they were waiting, probably manned only by skeleton crews, on developments, and available for the main mass of the enemy to use as required, either as a threat of an attack on the Scots rear or to provide escape for their fellows in need.

The contingent rode into a ravaged Leith. The ships remained lying out near Inchkeith: so it was to be a waiting game. The Mormaor Colin decided to leave part of his force here to oppose any landing, and to take the rest up to Dunedin to Constantine's assistance. The High King could have done with a larger army than he had thought necessary, after all.

Cormac and his people, then, pressed on eastwards, as directed, along the coast, heading for Inveresk, which they knew. Indeed, all that shoreline beyond was familiar, for this was where they had operated on the previous campaign. There were many miles of it to the mouth of the firth and the open sea, and they were to search inland as well; so this mission would take some time, even if no fighting was involved.

At the mouth of the Esk, some seven miles on, without sign of the enemy, they made their first turn inland, up-river, going as far as Dalkeith, six miles. No evidence of raiding here, save for unrepaired devastation caused by the earlier invasion. The local people they spoke with were wary indeed, but so far had suffered no hurt.

Back to the coast then and on eastwards for the fishing-haven of Cockainie, another six miles. Here too there had been no recent trouble, although the folk were all too aware of the Viking ships sailing up Forth none so far from their shore.

They rode inland again here, up to the ridge on which

was the community of Travernent, still without incident. Then back to Cockainie for the night, this probing inland taking up much time.

Camping at the haven, Cormac wondered whether this eastwards mission was worth while, since there seemed to have been no raiding in these parts. But he had his orders, and it was always possible that separate Norse incursions could be taking place further on. There were still over a dozen miles, as the wild geese flew, to the Norse Sea, double that by the ins and outs of the shoreline, so their task was going to take them another two days at least.

Beyond Cockainie the coast changed notably to mainly long stretches of sands, to Kilpensandus Point and then the great Aberlady Bay, where the Water of Peffer entered the firth, three miles across, drying out at low water. Here they veered off to follow the Peffer into its wide and marshy vale, scene of Kenneth mac Alpin's battle against the Saxons that century and a half before. Small settlements on the sides of the vale were undisturbed, cattle country this, of the sort which attracted the Norsemen, but here none evident.

They crossed over into the parallel Vale of Tyne, with the Lammermuir Hills looming beyond, to visit Heydon's-toun. This area had suffered grievously before, but now went unscathed. They spent the second night there, wondering how Constantine was faring at Dunedin.

The third day they returned to the coast, wherefrom they could see King Arthur's Seat away to the west, but no indication possible of what went on below its steep slopes, no smoke visible. They proceeded eastwards still, by Golyn and Dirlington to North Berwick beneath its conical law. There they were told that no landings had taken place, although of course the dreaded longships had been seen.

It seemed pointless to proceed further, although they were not quite at the firth mouth. The fisherfolk here would have heard of any trouble beyond. So they spent the night there, task accomplished. Back to Dunedin on the morrow.

It was mid-afternoon before they reached that town, to find all quiet there, no sign of the Scots army. They were told that the Vikings had been there, on the outskirts, but in no great numbers, and that three days ago King Constantine had arrived and driven them off, indeed slaughtered most of them, God be praised. Great was the folk's gratitude. The Ard Righ and his force had remained only the one night at Dunedin, and then returned westwards, it was thought to Craigalmond, presumably Mormaor Colin's company with him.

With something of a sense of anticlimax about it all, their own contribution so unproductive, Cormac set off for Craigalmond, wondering whether the High King and his host, presumably now on their way back to Fortrenn, would be waiting for them there.

They had not reached the Almond when, near the ridge of Clermiston, they came across a group of men, their own folk, in dire distress, some of them wounded, and minus horses. It was disaster, they cried. There had been a battle, a bloody battle. Not with the Jutes, with other Scots. The High King was dead, Constantine slain. At Craigalmond. The Mormaor Kenneth of Atholl had come after them with a large army, attacked them while they were camped at the river mouth, all unprepared. Much slaughter, amidst confusion. It was utter massacre. They had had no chance. And by their own people. The Ard Righ murdered, and many with him. They had been asleep . . .

Appalled, Cormac could scarcely take this in. Constantine dead! Slain by Kenneth of Atholl. And while expelling the Norsemen. It was all but beyond belief. And these men survivors . . .

This, then, was the dissident mormaors' answer to the election of the man they had opposed. The talk of a conference and great meeting to be called had been but a screen to mask this dastardly intention of a swift armed strike, a stab in the back. And to do this while Constantine was fighting for his southern subjects! So Scotland was without a monarch. What would happen now?

Cormac's wondering had to take on a practical aspect. What should he do now? Should they go on to Craigalmond? It seemed that it was two days now since this grievous deed was done. Were Kenneth and his allies still there? Or had they returned back northwards, purpose accomplished? And what would be their attitude towards those who had been aiding Constantine? Would they go on treating them as enemies? After all, they had only been doing their duty in supporting the High King. What about the Mormaor Colin of Strathearn? And the others? Had they all been slain, or at least dispersed? Would it be civil war now?

It was decided to wait where they were at this Clermiston ridge meantime, while scouts were sent forward to spy out the prevailing position at Craigalmond or wherever. Duncan and Pate volunteered to go and discover. It was little more than two miles ahead.

In a state of agitation the pair's return was awaited, Cormac questioning the group of survivors. They were unable to give much more information, the situation when they fled understandably chaotic. But once the Ard Righ had fallen, known to be dead, the fighting, such as it had been there in the darkness, had flagged, flight like their own, or surrender, developing. They did not know what had happened to the Mormaor Colin. These were Lennoxmen.

Within the hour Duncan and Pate were back. Craigalmond was deserted, save for corpses and debris, no sign of armies, locals having fled the scene also. So they had really learned nothing, except that the seven longships were still where Pate had left them, on a strand near the river mouth, these either overlooked or of no interest to the aggressors.

Cormac took counsel with his friends as to what was their wisest course now. Were those who had been part of Constantine's force being looked upon as enemies? If they were, it would be folly to follow after Kenneth's people and possibly catch up with them. Get back to Glamis and Strathmore as swiftly and discreetly as possible then, was the agreed strategy, avoiding the others. How would these have come, and be returning? By the shortest road, almost certainly – that is, inland after Stirling, by the Tor Wood, Ecclesbreak and Linlithgow. So probably back the same way. The longer coastal route for them, then, and seek to cross Forth somehow and somewhere before Stirling.

It was Pate who reminded of those captured longships. They were of value, but could they also be of use in this crisis? They could ferry men across Forth. But horses, one hundred and fifty of them?

They considered it. Duncan thought that, for a very short crossing, they could carry beasts, carefully held secure – if they could get them aboard. Perhaps three to a boat? They could only use perhaps four of the oars thus, but if it was for only a few hundred yards, that might serve. It would demand many crossings, but it should be possible, he thought. It would enable them to avoid that army. They could cross well down from Stirling. For a dozen miles or so downstream it was only a river, before widening to the estuary.

It was agreed to try it, at least. Pate would take his fishermen-oarsmen, with a few extras to help, and row the vessels up the thirty miles to opposite Clackmannan or thereabouts, and the others would ride along the coast, seeking both to keep out of sight of any of the mormaors' force and in view of the longships. It would take a couple of days. So, of course, it was quite possible that Kenneth's army would by then already be past Stirling and beyond Forth, this caution unnecessary. But better to be safe than sorry.

So they proceeded down to Craigalmond, a grim spot now, where they saw Pate and his augmented crewmen into their ships and helped to launch them. Then, although it was already dusk, the horsemen headed on westwards, riding well into the night.

Seeking to remain as inconspicuous as any body of over one hundred horsemen could be, making use of every possible cover of the land, it was mid-forenoon of two days thereafter when they were able to halt at the crossing-place which Pate had selected, where the longships could be hidden in a meander of the river opposite Alloway, this offering a fairly narrow crossing, short ferrying. They had seen no sign of the army.

Here followed the lengthy process of getting alarmed horses into the vessels, using floorboards as plank gangways, three at a time, much patience required. Here Cormac came to a decision, on Duncan's advice. He would remain with the ships, and sail with them up to the Angus coast, lengthy journey as that would be. If the rebel mormaors were of a mind to punish those who had supported Constantine, it would be the leaders whom they would target, not the rank and file. So better that the Thane of Glamis won back to his own territory and Connacher's mormaordom safely, where it was unlikely that he would be assailed. So go by sea, with Dunninald leading the others back by unfrequented routes. Cormac felt a little uncomfortable over this, but recognised that it was probably wise, in his position.

The getting of those horses across Forth, three at a time even in seven ships, took hours, some of the animals being especially awkward. It all must have mystified any locals who could have viewed it. But at last it was done, and without any major mishap. Cormac bade farewell to his mounted contingent and set his mind to the problem of sailing a flotilla of longships on a voyage of possibly eighty miles, much of it on the open sea, with less than expert crews. Fortunately the south-west winds would greatly aid them, allowing them to hoist sails, so much reducing the rowing. If the wind changed, they might find it best to row only four of the craft, with increase of oarsmen, taking the other three in tow?

So, rowing out into mid-river, they raised these large square sails on their single masts, painted with the dreaded black spread-winged ravens as Norse symbols, and headed eastwards. And quickly they perceived that they now did not have to use the long sweeps at all, save for steering, the breeze carrying them along at an excellent pace. These long and slender sea-greyhounds had been built for using the winds of the Norse Sea. Great was the relief. It would probably be even better when they turned northwards at the estuary-mouth, if this breeze maintained.

After all their activities, pressures and anxieties, it was scarcely believable to be able to sit back and idly watch the land slide by. Quickly it became more distant on either hand, and, so much sooner than they had expected, they were passing where they had so recently left, Craigalmond on the one side, Aberdour on the other. How many miles they were covering in each hour they knew not, but they were certainly going faster than their horses would have carried them. For the first time they had something for which to thank the Norsemen.

It was chilly, to be sure, sitting inactive in that February wind, but they had brought their plaids with them, and huddling together, they could put up with that. Cormac calculated that, at this rate, they ought to reach the open sea before darkening. Could they go on sailing northwards throughout the night? There seemed to be no reason why not, provided the wind stayed south-westerly and no storm blew up. If they kept well out from the shoreline there ought to be no risk of striking reefs or rocks in the darkness. Now they could see the Isle of May away ahead of them in the mouth of the Forth. They would have to keep well out from Fife Ness thereafter, the most easterly point of that thanedom; but after that it would be clear going across the entrance to the Tay's firth and on up the Angus coast.

Although some of the less experienced sailors suggested that it would be safest to land on the May island for the night, Pate agreed with Cormac that this was unnecessary, and that the further they could get northwards the better. At a rough calculation they estimated that it might be about forty miles by sea from the May to Red Head and Lunan Bay. If fortune continued to smile on them, they might even be there by dawn.

After they had passed the towering, seabird-haunted cliffs of the Craig of Bass, off North Berwick, they were not long in reaching the May. Already their vessels were heaving much more noticeably than in the estuarine waters, but it was mainly bows-and-stern dipping and rearing rather than sidelong rolling. They did not complain.

After swinging due northwards, they were able to see Fife Ness a couple of miles on their left before darkness descended upon them. How now to maintain their directly northwards course? Cormac, even Pate, was unsure about this, but the fishermen aboard their leading craft did not seem to be concerned. Evidently they had developed some sort of instinct for direction. The others were content to leave it to them to steer.

The wind remained constant in force and course. Most of the passengers slept.

Cormac was eventually wakened to a shaking of his shoulder. One of their fishermen, actually from Ethiehaven, was pointing. There, ahead of them in the half-light of dawn, soared the cliffs of Red Head. They were home, off Angus, glory be!

But now the fisherman had become concerned. The folk of Ethiehaven, when they saw those Viking ships with their raven sails coming in, would be in panic. How to inform them? At that hour, Cormac wondered whether any would be awake, but he was assured that fisherfolk rose early. He suggested that the best course was for six of their craft to lie off the village meantime, well out in the bay, and only one, this one, go in to inform the people that all was well. They knew him there, and his links with Red Castle.

This was agreed, and the other vessels, downing their sails, remained in a cluster, stationary, while the leading boat pulled in to the haven. As they approached, they could see people, mainly women and children, hurrying off southwards along the shore in the direction of Red Head.

The local fisherman stood up in the bows and shouted his name and waved, Pate joining him, and calling out that here was the Thane of Glamis. How effective an encouragement this might be they could not tell.

There was no harbour at Ethiehaven, only the boat-strand below the narrow terrace of houses and sheds under the cliffs. So they had to force their craft as far up on to the shingle as it would go, and then clamber out, still calling their identities. They could see men watching warily from gables and corners.

Their local crewman, Donnie Mar by name, ran forward, was recognised, and explained the situation. So all was well, and the other longships were waved in, the villagers returning, never having seen the like.

Needless to say, Cormac was eager to get over to Red Castle just as quickly as possible to inform and reassure. Their two former flounder-fishing colleagues offered to row him over to save the mile-and-a-half walk.

Excuses to visit Fenella he had manufactured in the past, but such as this had never occurred to him. They would be awake and up at the castle by now, surely. They might well have seen the longships, and feared also . . .

Thanking the fishermen at the boat, Cormac climbed alone up to the gatehouse. But before he reached it, the young woman came running down to meet him, clearly having been on the watch and recognising him.

That was a notable encounter. He held out his arms to her and she did not hesitate to enter them, both exclaiming, panting incoherences, greetings, questions, assertions. And the man did not let Fenella out of his grasp now that he had her, keeping an arm around her shoulders as they turned to walk back up to the castle, jerking out explanations, in no sort of order, squeezing her to emphasise his rambling points, she staring, shaking her red head, gulping. What she made of it all there and then was doubtful, but *he* was a happy man, however sore and shocking were his tidings. He was safely back where he wanted to be. That was sufficient for the moment. The rest could wait . . .

11

When the visitor had settled down to coherent discussion with his hosts at Red Castle, and they could digest the news and its implications which he had brought, they shook heads over the situation. What now? Two High Kings slain within two years!

"This was clearly a long-thought-out plot," Cormac said. "This device of talk of a conference over the succession. Constantine having no son nor brother. And all the time plans being laid to muster an army to strike first, to slay the Ard Righ, a dastardly design! They, these plotters, killers, will have devised further. When Constantine was elected, those dissidents chose for High King Malcolm, son of the late Kenneth, young as he is. Now they will want him to succeed. Will that be accepted? Possible? Will the other mormaors agree? Or choose another?"

"Malcolm was, and is, eligible for the throne," Lord Aidan pointed out. "The son of the murdered Kenneth the Second. Constantine was the son of King Cuilean, predecessor of Kenneth. Both were entitled to be appointed. Kenneth, Mormaor of Atholl, is a younger son of King Duff, uncle of Malcolm on the woman's side. It is complicated, yes, but he also is of the royal succession. But young Malcolm is nearest in line now."

"But after this wicked slaying? Would the mormaors, or the majority of them, vote for him?"

"Who else? Apart from Mormaor Kenneth himself."

"Did King Cuilean not have other sons besides Constantine?"

"No. But Cuilean's younger brother had. One called

Boide of Boyd. More distant. And by a mother not of the royal blood."

"This of succession through the women's line," Cormac said, frowning.

"Matrilineal. Our inheritance from the old Picts. It is strange, uncertain. Other kingdoms go from father to eldest son. Simpler."

"But not necessarily better!" Fenella put in. "Sons are not always suitable successors to their sires! And this gives a choice to lead the realm."

"I am in favour of it," her father agreed.

"So you think, my lord, that the mormaors will choose this Malcolm? Despite, despite . . . ?"

"They have little choice. Save only that Boide. Who is said to be feeble." Cormac rubbed his chin. "And those who supported Constantine?" he asked.

"Such as myself. How will the slayers behave towards them? Towards me? Will they look on us as enemies?"

"Why should they?" the Lady Alena said. "You were only doing your loyal duty. Constantine was High King. As *they* should have done. It is surely every lord's and chief's simple duty to do so. Why see you as an enemy now? And you were not at this battle when they killed Constantine, you say? So I do not think that you need fear. They will not wish to make enemies of all who served the appointed monarch."

"No-o-o. But I judge that I had better remain quiet meantime, probably. Out of their sight and concern. Mormaor Connacher – what will *he* think of this? He was not with us. How behave towards the murderers?"

"I cannot predict what my brother will do," Aidan said flatly. "But he is faced, as are all others, with the succession position. As a mormaor, one of the seven, he must appoint a successor. And the choice is limited indeed."

"Nevertheless, I think that Cormac should indeed lie low meantime," Fenella put in. "Remain inactive in matters of rule, whether Uncle Connacher does or not . . ."

"He cannot remain inactive, lass," her father pointed

out. "Constantine has to be buried. At Iona. All High Kings have to be buried there, however they die. In the mormaors' presence. And thereafter a new Ard Righ elected. All mormaors, thanes and holders of lordships should attend such burial. Cormac must be there – or it would indeed be held against him."

The younger man drew a deep breath. "I, I had not thought of that," he admitted. "I will have to go, yes."

"You will be safe enough, especially if you go in Connacher's train," Lady Alena said.

"When will it be?"

"The body will be embalmed. February is not the best time for sailing to the Hebrides. And the mormaors will be having their discussions first. So it may well be some time before you have to ride."

"Aye, ride. This of riding." Cormac changed the subject. "I have to win back to Glamis. Having come by sea, we have no horses. Can I borrow a couple from you, my lord, to get me home? You will not have many here, I think. Not for all my men who sailed the longships. But if I can get back to Glamis, where the others will arrive in a day or two, then I can return with sufficient beasts to mount these others." He did not add that this would give him an excuse to return speedily.

Horses for himself and Duncan were readily available. Fenella accompanied them back to Ethiehaven, in an exhilarating gallop along the three-mile stretch of firm sands. There she arranged with the fisherfolk to give shelter and provision for the men left behind. Cormac had wondered whether he could just send Duncan to Glamis for the necessary horses, allowing himself to linger meantime at Red Castle, but decided that this was scarcely suitable, with the main body of his contingent, under Dunninald, to be met and dispersed at Glamis.

So he bade farewell to Fenella there, promising to be back in a few days, leaving Pate in charge at Ethiehaven.

* * *

They were back home in Strathmore before dark, to find the mounted company not yet there. Cormac's mother and sister were shocked to hear of the High King's death, needless to say, and much concerned over what would happen in Scotland now. Had only the Mormaor Kenneth of Atholl and his nephew Malcolm been involved in this battle and slaying? they wondered. Or were others of the *ri* involved? Finlay of Moray and Ross? Would there be civil war? Cormac could not inform them. Nor as to what would happen at Iona after the burial. The gravity of the situation was obvious, but the resultant events less so.

Dunninald, with the main force, arrived next day, after their long, round-about road home, quite surprised to find their thane back before them, not having realised what a following wind could do for longships' sails. They had no news as to developments. Cormac allowed them all to disband meantime and go home, but to be ready for a recall if necessary; that is, save for a dozen needed to take the required horses over to Ethiehaven. They would go there direct the next day; but he thought that he himself ought to call in at Forfar Castle on the way to ascertain Mormaor Connacher's reaction to all that had happened.

At Forfar, then, the following forenoon, he saw Connacher. That man, seldom eloquent, condemned the killing of Constantine in no uncertain terms. But he did not seem to see any other candidate for the high kingship than Malcolm mac Kenneth, only twenty years of age as he was, the man Boide being apparently long in failing health. So, presently, he would have to vote for him at Iona. The interment of Constantine was being arranged for one month hence, late March, when it was hoped that the seas would not be too rough for passage. Cormac assured that he would be in his mormaor's train.

Connacher had nothing to say about Cormac's efforts against the Jutes, save for being obviously interested in the capture of those seven longships. He wanted to know about these, judging that they could be useful against Norse raiding along Angus shores.

So it was on to Red Castle for the Thane of Glamis.

Cormac and Duncan, in fact, met the Ethiehaven party, now horsed again, coming up the Lunan Water near Inverkeilor, under Pate. In a way, this scarcely pleased the former, for it might give him no pretext now for calling at the castle. Then he remembered the longships, still at the haven. Arrangements would have to be made regarding these, so there was his justification for a visit again. He rode on. Those vessels were proving an asset.

Whether Cormac's frequent appearances at Red Castle were approved by the Lord Aidan was hard to tell, he, although so very different from his brother, being likewise no conversationalist; but his wife was always welcoming, and Fenella clearly not averse to his company. He explained that he had come to see to the disposal of the longships.

The young woman told him that these were meantime drawn up on the beach alongside the Ethiehaven fishermen's boats. What was he intending to do with them?

Cormac admitted that he was not very sure as to that. Her uncle had been impressed by news of their capture and thought that they could be useful against any Norse raiding, but had not specified just how. On the way here he, Cormac, had been thinking about it and wondering whether they might serve as a sort of offering to commend him to the new Ard Righ to be elected? He supposed that they were *his*, by capture, and therefore, if he could use them in the nation's service somehow, it would be to his credit.

"I too have been thinking about those longships," Fenella told him. "They must not just be left to lie and rot at Ethiehaven, unused. Our fishermen are interested in them, needless to say, they being so very differently built from their cobles and rowing-boats. It occurred to me, Cormac, that we might train our folk to use them! Not for the fishing, but for possible help against attack, raids, if such happened."

"Train them? Lord, that's a notion, lass! Would they do it – the fishermen?"

"Why not? They could soon learn how to handle them,

surely? And there are many fishers along this coast, tenants of my father, not only at Ethiehaven but at Boddin and Dysart and Usan. Enough to man these seven vessels, I think? How many to a ship?"

"I do not know how many of a crew the Norsemen use; that is, apart from the raiders which they carry, fighting men. We managed to bring the craft up here with just over fifty men for the seven. But that was much less, I judge, than the Norsemen use. We had the wind behind us coming north, so the sails were all that was needed, or almost. But in other conditions those long oars, sweeps, take a deal of handling. We had two men to each, but I think that the Jutes use three."

"How many, then, to man all seven properly?"

"Eight oars to a ship, with a steersman. So twenty-five men to each craft. That makes a lot of fishermen to man the seven ships. One hundred and seventy-five altogether!"

"M'mm. A lot, as you say. But perhaps they need not all be fishermen? After all, your men were not, bringing them here. We could train some of the inland folk to help – farmers, herdsmen. Manning the boats *under* the fishers. Let me think, now. How many might we raise from Red Castle lands – fishermen, I mean? The younger men, although some of the old ones are still very active. A score. More, perhaps. From Ethiehaven itself. Boddin not quite so many. Dysart about the same. But Usan, now that is larger. We could win over thirty there, I am sure. And there are other groups, small groups, in coves and inlets along the shore, folk with a few sheep and beasts, and fishing as a lesser occupation. I think that we could find one hundred thus. Then, with the inland folk . . ."

"Here's a notable notion, my clever Fenella!" he exclaimed. They were standing on the wall-walk of the tower-top, gazing out over the wide Lunan Bay. "This could become something quite important, of value to all, to the realm itself. If it led the way. A fleet of longships, available when called for." He paused. "That is – if the men would do it? The fishermen."

"Oh, they would, I think. They are already looking at those longships – the Ethiehaven men. And if they did it, led the way, others would not want to be outdone." She grasped his arm. "See you, let us go down there now. Speak with them. We have time before the evening meal."

Cormac eyed this lively, enterprising and enthusiastic young woman more admiringly than ever, and did not fail to clasp his own hand over hers.

She turned to lead him downstairs.

They rode over those sands again to Ethiehaven, and Cormac saw the longships beached in a neat row alongside the smaller craft, their masts and furled sails towering over the others. Dismounting, Fenella made for a group of men sitting mending nets, a constant task for these folk. They rose at the approach of their lord's daughter.

"Here is the Thane of Glamis again," she announced. "He thanks you for caring for his men. But we have something to put to you, my friends." And she turned to Cormac.

"Yes, I thank you all," he said. "But – this of the longships. The Lady Fenella and I have been thinking about them, a good use for them. They are notable vessels, as you will know, the fastest and most commanding on all the seas. It would be folly to leave them here, or elsewhere, beached and idle. We could *use* them, and to good effect in our nation's cause. We lack anything of the like in Scotland. But they take a deal of handling, as we found out bringing them here after capturing them from the Jutes. With the winds right, under sail, they are indeed greyhounds! And properly rowed, they are swift also, built to be so. If you, and your fellow fishers, learned how to sail and handle them to full effect, they could be of great service. Something new for Scotland. How say you to that?"

"How say you, yes?" Fenella added.

The men gazed at each other wonderingly.

"We did help to beach them, my lord," one of the older men said. "Their oars are very long. Difficult. The sides high . . ."

"Yes. The oars are called sweeps. But three men to

each, pulling together, and they can drive the craft very fast. The Norsemen sing, chant, as they pull, I am told, for the timing. It would mean learning the way of it. And how best to use their great sails. And the steering. But . . ."

"You could master it all quickly enough," Fenella declared. "And be proud to do it. Beat the men of Boddin and Usan at it!" Subtle she was.

They were eyeing each other again. There were nods and grins, no actual opposition evident.

"Consider it," Cormac said.

"Speak with the others here," the young woman went on. "It is over late in the day to try one now. But tomorrow we will come back, and my lord of Glamis will show you how to work these vessels."

"As best I can!" that man added.

Chuckling, the fishermen accepted that, no reluctance voiced nor looked. So it was back to Red Castle, well pleased.

When he heard of their project, the Lord Aidan looked doubtful indeed; but the Lady Alena was very supportive. But she did warn them that Connacher of Angus would seek to take any credit accruing. Obviously she did not love her brother-in-law.

For his part, Cormac was more than delighted, for all this meant that he was going to be in a position to see a great deal of Fenella for quite some time to come, what with the training, and the visiting other havens, and the demonstrating thereafter. He found that he was having to wipe a more or less permanent grin off his face.

That night, when Fenella escorted him up to his room, Cormac sought to ensure that she did not say goodnight just at the door, by asking there whether she considered that an especial one of the Ethiehaven fishermen could be used to act the leader in this of the longships training? He had found one of their flounder-fishing companions a man of some force and character, the one Donnie. Would be serve?

Fenella agreed that Donnie the Crab, as he was known,

was a man of parts. He it was, indeed, who had instructed her in flounder-fishing, as a girl. Yes, he might make some sort of leader.

This questioning had duly brought the young woman into the bedchamber, and to prolong the conversation she was asked why he was called the Crab? Fenella did not know, but said that they would ask him on the morrow.

By this time Cormac had his arm around the other's shoulders and was drawing her into an embrace. She did not exactly free herself deliberately, but moved from him over to the fire to put another piece of wood thereon, and to express the hope that the room was warm enough on a chilly night. He was promptly considering some way of using this hope to say that her own presence was all the warmth that he desired, this without being over-suggestive, when she turned for the door, telling him to sleep well. So he had to hasten to reach her again and renew the embrace before she got out, pressing her close and relishing the rounded feel of her within his arms, managing to plant a kiss on her lips. She freed an arm, and reached up to tweak his ear.

"Ha, my lord Thane!" she got out, as those lips were withdrawn. "It is longship handling which we are to practise, no? Not this of persons and pressings? You are a fisher for more than flounders, I think!" But she let her hand run down his arm as she wished him goodnight, and departed.

He went back to stare into the fire, weighing up progress. He was not really discouraged.

In the morning no constraints were evident. There was little delay, after breakfast, in joining Duncan at the horses and setting off for Ethiehaven.

There they found two of the fishing-boats already off into the bay, but sufficient men still available to make a start on the business of longship handling. Cormac was well aware that he was not really competent as an instructor in this, and that these fishermen knew a deal more about boat operating than did he. But he had picked up something of the necessary usage for these craft on the eighty-mile voyage, as had Duncan: the special demands on the oarsmen over those long sweeps with their different angle of dipping from normal boat oars, and the need for exactly synchronised rowing on both sides of the vessel, not easy for two dozen oarsmen.

So, gathering a group of almost a score of men, young and less so, women and children coming to watch in holiday mood, they went to one of the longships. Before launching it, Cormac gave them what he could in the way of guidance. Then he got six men, including Duncan, to climb into the still-beached craft and to sit next to each other, with necessarily only a small gap in the centre of the bench, to put out a sweep on either side, three men to each, and so to test the feel and weight of them, swinging them in the air in unison, slowly, back and forward, back and forward. Then he had the other men aboard also.

There were insufficient available to make three to each oar of the eight, so some of the boys volunteered to fill the gaps, and nothing would do but that Fenella herself clambered in, hitching up her skirts, the watching women giggling. Cormac repeated his instructions.

At first, thus, there was obvious lack of coherence, of consort, in the pulling, both in the side-by-side sweeps and in the accord with those in front and behind, the men exclaiming at the weight and difficulty of balance as well as unity of rhythm. Whether it would be easier in the water than thus on land remained to be seen.

After a spell of this practice they shipped oars and all climbed out, except Fenella, to push the craft down over the pebbles and sand into the water, most having to wade some distance before the vessel floated, it steeper-sided and less flat-bottomed than were the fishing-boats, none complaining at this. Cormac thought that, at first, it would be best for only the one pair of sweeps to be tried out in the water, to gain the feel of it. So but six men got in, including Duncan and himself, the others waiting and watching, some humorous shouted guidance offered from the beach.

Once again, at first it was less than successful teamwork, the angle of the sweeps and the depth that the blades entered the water being a problem, variance resulting in jostling and confusion on the bench. But in a short while these men, used to single oars, mastered the art of co-operative rowing, and they were able to turn back for the shore.

The three other bench-fillers now piled in, Fenella taking her place, Cormac acting as helmsman at the great rudder, this in itself no easy task in countering the sidelong effects of erratic rowing. Out again they pulled.

This time it was all but chaos, the synchronisation hard to obtain, the four sets of six men seemingly unable to harmonise their pulling and depths and angles. They kept on trying, but always there was one or other of the sweeps at odds with the rest, sometimes more than that, amidst curses and accusations from panting oarsmen.

At length Cormac thought of the chanting. He shouted that this might help. He had a reasonably strong and tuneful voice, and raised it now to render an old ballad chorus of his childhood, working it into a rhythmic ebb and flow in time with the desired beat and swing of the oars. Gradually the chant was taken up by the rowers, Fenella's higher note very evident, a panting, gulping, grunting rendering as it was, and Cormac wishing that he had some sort of drum to tap and regulate it.

Gradually this was effective, as the tempo steadied and the sweep movement with it. Presently, long as it had taken, they were coasting along at a fair pace, and Cormac could devote his attentions to better steering, using the tidal drift. Out into mid-bay they surged, leaving a bubbling, white wake behind them.

What wind there was this day was again from the south-west, which meant that it was mainly abeam on their outward progress. They could have used the sail to help, but Cormac decided that this first day they should keep to oar-work to get the men accustomed to the regular swing of it. Sailing could wait. Ordering a pause, he called the man Donnie the Crab aft to take his place at the helm, he who was probably to be the master and steersman of this craft, while he himself took his turn at the sweep.

Resuming rowing, now near the open sea, they passed the two fishing-boats, whose occupants stared and waved, probably more astonished at what they heard than what they saw, that chanting making an impact.

Cormac wanted the stronger winds and waves of the open water to test his crew further, as indeed presently it did, the sway and tilting of the long, slender vessel in the swells of the Norse Sea making the rhythmic rowing of eight sweeps still more difficult, the steering also. Deciding that he was a better helmsman than oarsman, he was not long in changing places again with Donnie the Crab, to Fenella's amused comment.

At length, reckoning that enough was enough for their first day, he ordered a return to the bay and the haven. Whether out of thankfulness or otherwise, the singing distinctly improved on their reverse journey, even though they were now rowing into the wind.

Back at Ethiehaven, Cormac and Fenella congratulated all concerned over their efforts. They said that the next testing would have to be with the sail up, which ought not to be anything like so trying, an hour or two at it probably sufficient. They recognised that these fishermen had their livings to earn, and so probably would spare them further for a few days, this while similar instruction was offered to their neighbours at Dysart and Boddin. Well satisfied with their day, it was back with them to Red Castle.

They had much to recount to Lady Alena, Fenella admitting that her arm ached.

When it was bedtime that night, the young woman went with her guest only as far as the second-floor landing, where was her own room. There she paused, opening the door.

"Perhaps safest to say our goodnights here, my ship-master friend," she said lightly. "Lest I find your parting attentions more masterful than ever! No?"

He wagged his head. "I . . . I am sorry if I offended," he declared. "My intention was . . . otherwise! Only to show my, my esteem, my caring, my gratitude, lass. For I think more highly of you than, than . . ." He left the rest unsaid.

"Ah, was that it! I fear that I am not worthy of all that admiration. I am a very simple and unremarkable young female, I judge. And frail! But – my own woman! Not that I am therefore . . . uncaring. And I find you good company. And none so ill to work with." She smiled, there in the lamplight. "As well, perhaps, since we seem to be much together these days!"

He eyed her a little uncertainly. "*I* joy in that," he said. "But . . . you?"

"Say that I do not find it a trial!" Suddenly, she reached up to kiss him, and on the lips. "Goodnight, friend!" she said, and entered her chamber, closing the door behind her with something almost of a slam.

Cormac climbed slowly to his own room, emotions roused and varied.

With Duncan, they went the following day to the Seatown of Dysart on its own little bay beside a great rock known as Black Jack. But there they saw five of the seven fishing-boats already out off Boddin Point, so had to content themselves with spending a short time with some net-menders and bait-diggers, telling them of the longships project and saying that they would come back hereafter to explain it all fully, and arrange for one of the vessels to be brought up from Ethiehaven for their possible use, again playing on the friendly rivalry between the villages.

Then on to Boddin, just behind its headland. The haven here was in a neuk tucked in under soft red sandstone cliffs, with small caves in which were stored nets and lobster-creels. At this larger community they found sufficient of the fishermen ashore to hold a satisfactory meeting and discussion, and to stir up quite a considerable interest, even something of enthusiasm. One of their boats, fishing the day before, had actually seen the single longship at some distance at sea, its occupants wondering.

Usan was over a mile further north along a cliff-girt shore, and here was the largest township of that coastal area, and the end of the Lord Aidan's land, with its own little church nearby. With the next day Sunday, Fenella thought it wise to visit the priest there first, and seek to win his approval of their endeavours, which could be of help. Father Ferchar proved to be a vehement young man, another obvious admirer of Fenella, and like her red-headed, his rufus mop unruly about his Columban Church frontal tonsure. He greeted the longship venture with all but fervour; the Church looked on the pagan Norse raiders as the emissaries of Satan, who had so grievously ravaged Iona and many another Christian sanctuary. Anything that he could do against them, he would. Fenella took the opportunity to ask if he would sanction some of his fishermen coming to Ethiehaven on the morrow, holy day as it was, to help bring a longship up to Usan for their use? This was granted at once, with the declaration that it was all part of the Lord's work, and after morning prayer he himself would row south with a party to encourage all.

His visitors, also encouraged thus, went on to speak with the villagers, the priest accompanying them. They found no difficulty in gaining full co-operation at Usan, Father Ferchar's emphatic support ensuring it, if that was necessary. There was no lack of volunteers for the morrow's venture.

Thereafter Fenella took Cormac down to see the remarkable feature for which Usan was famous, Ulysses's haven itself, a lengthy rock-bound corridor, all but a canal through stone, and a sheltered one, probing straight inland from the open water for hundreds of yards, wide enough for two boats to pass each other but narrow enough to offer security from storms. Whoever Ulysses was, he had been a judge of harbours. Cormac thought that he could see where that rock aisle had been improved somewhat by human artifice.

It was back southwards, then. But they were not finished

yet. They were to go on past Red Castle to Ethiehaven again to inform the folk there of the invasion next day from Usan, with its priestly benediction, and to ensure that longships were ready to sail north, one for these callers and one for Boddin.

That duly arranged, the three of them could judge another day well spent.

At this night's bed-going, Fenella did accompany Cormac up to his room, and without comment, in theory at least to see that the maidservant had left all in order for the guest, fire, warming-pan, hot water and honey wine. Satisfied as to this, she turned to the watching man.

"Cormac," she said, almost hesitantly for her, "it concerns me that, in all this of the longships, you may think me something unwomanly, over-eager in this matter. It is man's work, this of ships and crewing and fighting. Making ready for war. I would not have you to see me as, as some female dragon! But I feel that this is all something very important. Important for us all, women as well as men. Something that ought to be done. Especially those who have the lead in the land. My father, son of a mormaor, is . . . less than forward in such matters, a man of thought not of action. So I . . ." She shook her red head.

He went to her. "Save us, lass – here is a nonsense! None could deem you anything but the most womanly of women! Myself in especial! As kindly, gracious, gentle as you are fair. You can be strong and spirited, of mettle, yes – but that adds to your excellence. And coming of a long line of leaders, you are to be looked to for such." He reached out to hold her shoulders, not in any embrace this time but a reassuring grasp, almost to shake them. "Fenella nic Aidan mac Colin mac Duncan mac Kenneth, you are a woman in a thousand! But all woman. All!"

She came into those arms then, close, head on his shoulder. So they stood for moments, his lips on her hair, the scent of it not failing to rouse him. But within him he knew that this was not the time for arousal, but for quiet support. The stirring of her against him did not make his forbearance the easier, but he withstood.

Presently she pushed herself away from him. "I, I am not strong this night!" she got out. "Weak! Feeble! I go, lest, lest . . ." She turned, and ran for the door. There she called back, "I thank you, Cormac. Thank you!" and left him.

The man gazed at that shut door for long, set-faced. But it was not with any grim expression. In truth he was telling himself that he was blessed indeed, that he had advanced his cause in those last moments more, much more, than had he succumbed to the strong urges within him. Good, he told himself, good!

Morning prayer must have been early, or brief, next morning at Usan, for they saw no fewer than eight fishing-boats being rowed south towards Ethiehaven as they were going down for the horses, and these full of men. The good father was nowise failing them.

Reaching the village, they found all in a stir, three longships already being pushed down to the water, Donnie the Crab very much in command, ably seconded by the priest, the Ethie men clearly eager to display their knowledge and expertise to these others. Donnie explained that he was proposing to put eight of their trained men into each of the two craft for Boddin and Usan to guide the novices, and another ten would endeavour to row the third vessel up with them to bring the Ethie men back. It might well be a slow and difficult passage, but they ought to manage it. He was wondering, since they would be going northwards, whether the sails hoisted might be of help?

Cormac agreed that they almost certainly would, once they adjusted to them, the wind being in the prevailing airt. It was four miles across Lunan Bay to Boddin and another two to Usan, no lengthy voyage. He suggested not using the sails straight away. Let the new oarsmen win some experience of handling those long three-man sweeps, lest they thought it all easy, with the canvas doing most of the work. That was accepted. Fenella said that she would go with Father Ferchar in the Usan craft, while Cormac accompanied the Boddin group, Donnie and Duncan in the local vessel.

So, to much good-humoured raillery and shouting, the three longships were floated, Cormac gallantly picking up and carrying the young woman out to her craft to save wetting her skirts in the shallows, and hoisting her over the side, the remaining villagers, oldsters, women and children, offering advice and scurrilous comment, dogs barking. Ethiehaven had never seen the like.

It took quite a while to get started, those sweeps inevitably the trouble, the local men scornful now over the visitors' lack of mastery. And this continued when they eventually got moving, in a very wayward and zigzag fashion, in fact the three craft in danger of collision or oar-clash, Donnie yelling to all to pull well apart, this however no simpler than straightforward steering. But, save for the priest and the three from Red Castle, all there were fishermen and used to boat-handling, if not of this kind, so some sort of forward progress developed, with presently sufficient rhythm for Cormac to start the chanting. This undoubtedly helped, and if they scarcely surged on their way, Ethiehaven did begin to recede behind them.

With quite a breeze at their sterns, Cormac concluded that probably enough rowing had been demonstrated to inform the new men that much training and practice hereafter was required, and led the way in hoisting sail on the Boddin ship. This at first added to the confusion, for the booms swung awkwardly and the craft heeled and lurched, upsetting the sweeps' angles into the waves and causing mishaps on the benches. But once the wind on those raven-painted sails was steadying the thrust, the oarsmen fairly quickly adjusted, and indeed heaved sighs of relief instead of breathless chanting.

Cormac doused sail off Boddin Point as his craft turned westwards for the harbour tucked under the cave-pitted cliffs, and the sweeps had to take over again, the other two ships proceeding on northwards. In sight from this village almost since the vessels had left Ethiehaven, quite a crowd had come down to welcome the first dreaded longship to enter their anchorage. Its mixed crew was concerned to appear competent, and a reasonably effective arrival was staged, although the beaching on the pebble shore did produce some disarray with those sweeps.

Thereafter, while he waited to be picked up again by the returning ship, Cormac gave a sort of lecture to the fishermen here who so far had not tried their hands at this task; he was becoming used to such instructing now. He added some indication as to the usefulness of a fleet of these vessels, expertly manned, not only for the safety of the Angus coastal areas but for all Scotland, with his hopes that such would bring them not only security but possible prosperity and favour, mentioning that the Viking menace did appear to be on the increase again these days. He ended by hinting at the competition from neighbouring communities. It was all fairly well received; after all, these folk were not used to having a thane coming to seek their co-operation.

He did not have long to wait before Fenella, Duncan and Donnie the Crab arrived to pick him up. All had apparently gone well at Usan. So it was for home, the day's tasks accomplished.

In fact, of course, sad as he was to have to acknowledge it, the wider task which had enabled Cormac to remain at Red Castle was also now accomplished, as far as was possible meantime. There was little more that could be done on their project until the various crews had trained themselves expert in handling the longships. He could not decently seek to remain a guest there any longer. Moreover, he was very much aware that he had been neglecting his duties at Glamis, even though what he had been attempting could be claimed to be in the thanedom's, the mormaordom's and the nation's cause. As thane, he had domestic responsibilities towards his own folk in

Strathmore. He had to say as much, that evening, to his hosts.

Understanding of the position was expressed, Fenella declaring that she and Donnie would endeavour to see that progress continued with the crews, and that the Dysart fishers were brought into the enterprise.

When it was time for retiring, the young woman made no bones about going upstairs with the guest, this for the last night meantime, Cormac not failing to emphasise the fact. She said that their association had been as pleasant as, she hoped, it had been fruitful.

All having been inspected as to the bedroom's comfort, when the warming-pan's effect on his bedding was being tested the man elected to sit, and drew her down beside him, she not protesting.

"Fenella, lass, I am going to miss these nights," he told her. "Miss much, but these bed-goings in especial."

"You will couch down on your own bed the more restfully, probably," she said, lightly. And added, tentatively, "And possibly in obliging company, my lord Thane!"

"Company? Not so. I sleep alone at Glamis. Did you think otherwise?"

"A noble lord is apt to have his . . . little advantages! Especially one who appears to appreciate the female person so much as you do, no?"

"It is *you* I appreciate, woman! You altogether. Yourself. Your goodness, excellence, everything about you. And, oh yes, that includes your fair person!" And his arm encircled her.

"Am I so different from other women?"

"You are, you are! For me, you are." His other arm came round her front this time, a hand to cup a firm and shapely breast.

"I think that you are perhaps prejudiced, carried away by, by . . . !" She got no further with that, her lips closed by his. She did not struggle to free them, nor her heaving bosom.

For a little, that is. But presently, as his hands grew the busier, she gently edged herself apart.

"This is . . . agreeable, Cormac," she was able to say. "Pleasing. I, I am woman enough to enjoy it. And your regard, esteem, favour. But I must limit you, I fear. That is also . . . the woman's part! When necessary. Enough, Cormac. Lest we go . . . over-far."

"Could we?"

"Oh, yes. I think so. And I must play the mistress. Of myself, not of you!" Twisting from his grasp, she rose. "I have heard you to say, more than once, sufficient for the day! We must say it again, this night. I leave you to your dreams, Cormac. May they be kindly ones."

Sighing, he stood and escorted her to the door, silent. There she turned, to stroke his cheek quickly before fleeing, and calling back a goodnight.

Long he debated with himself before he managed to sleep. He was learning about women. But . . . this woman? It seemed that he had much to learn yet. How, where, would he learn it? For he would be off in the morning . . .

12

Back at Glamis, amongst the matters awaiting his attention, Cormac found a summons from Mormaor Connacher to attend him at Forfar, no reasons given. Never happy about that man's peremptory attitudes, since the call had come two days previously it could now wait another two while he attended to more local affairs. Lady Ada agreed that he must not let Connacher overbear him. His father had never allowed that. Thanes had a degree of independence, being directly appointed by the High King.

So he coped with a case of rape committed by one of his tenants against the daughter of another, ordering imprisonment for one month in the castle cellars and compensation to be paid to the victim, with further reparations if she became pregnant as a result; a complaint by a miller that one of the farmers within his milling area, a recognised custom, was sending his grain to be ground by another mill outwith it; and a case of theft of liquor from the storeroom of the inn at Glamis, with a certain known miscreant suspected, but no proof as yet forthcoming. These dealt with to the best of his ability, Cormac rode for Forfar Castle.

He found Connacher in doubtful mood, unusual for that man. The news from Blair-in-Atholl was unlooked for, disturbing. It seemed that Mormaor Kenneth thereof was behaving questionably indeed. He had led an army to Lothian to slay Constantine, ostensibly to replace him on the high throne by his nephew Malcolm. But now he was claiming that Malcolm was too young and inexperienced to be Ard Righ, as yet at least, and that he himself should be appointed a High King until his nephew matured sufficiently. He was soliciting the other mormaors so to decide. Meantime the interment of the embalmed corpse of Constantine was to be delayed for two more weeks, to enable the *ri* to consult and come to conclusions.

Cormac knew little or nothing about the young Malcolm, but he did not like what he knew of his uncle. Possibly this had been the real reason behind the murder of King Constantine all along – a bid for personal power. Surely Kenneth would not make a worthy monarch?

Connacher was uncertain, it seemed. Scotland needed a strong Ard Righ, and Kenneth would be that, whatever else. Whereas Malcolm was an unknown quantity, whatever his right to the throne. With Boide not to be considered, the choice was limited indeed.

Cormac asked whether there was not some other possible candidate, of one of the further-out matriarchal lines, who could be advanced as alternative? But the mormaor declared that such would only lead to war and division in the kingdom. If Kenneth could rise to slay one High King, and then put down his own nephew, what would he do about a complete newcomer on the scene?

It appeared to the younger man that his mormaor was preparing himself to vote for Kenneth of Atholl.

However, it seemed that it was not really this that Connacher had summoned the Thane of Glamis to discuss, but the matter of the longships. What had come of that proposition? Was it proving to be a practical project?

Cormac was wary, remembering the Lady Alena's warning that if it all was a success, Connacher might well seek to take the credit; although in just what way it would especially advantage him, as distinct from the generality of the nation, was unclear. He contented himself with saying that the fishermen of the coastal villages had shown an interest, but that the effectual handling of those vessels was very difficult to learn. He did not mention Fenella's involvement in it all; and when Connacher asked what his brother Aidan's attitude was, he merely said that he was not greatly interested.

The mormaor looked somewhat disappointed.

Cormac left, with instructions to be ready to join the Angus party for Iona in probably three weeks' time. He would be notified. Meantime, any advancement of the longships project would be welcomed.

Wondering whether word of this interest in their endeavour was sufficient pretext to make a return to Red Castle thus early, and judging that it was not really to be considered, he returned to his duties at Glamis to await the call to make the required journey to Iona.

Oddly enough, and gallingly, two messages arrived for Cormac in the one day, one from Connacher for him to be at Forfar the day after the morrow, at first light, to make for the far Hebrides; the other from Fenella, brought by none other than Donnie the Crab, to inform that the Usan boat-builder, Ian the Wright, was eager to construct a longship, or to try to, following exactly the Norse design; this a notable proposal which could lead to great things, she thought. The wright required longer, better timbering than was available in the coastal regions, where woodlands were less frequent and trees less well grown than in the inland and more sheltered areas. Could the Thane Cormac help?

This last, of course, set that man astir. Here was the opportunity to visit Lunan, and over a most excellent development. That it should happen just when he was due to set off for Iona was maddening. But he could not delay in this last, not only in that it would arouse Connacher's wrath but because of the ferrying arrangements necessary to reach those western isles. But he was not going to miss this chance to see Fenella, and to encourage the boat-builder. He would go and come back on the same day, the morrow, much riding. He would not be able to stay the night at Red Castle; but at least he would see his beloved. That, and forward their enterprise.

With an early start next morning, he and Duncan were off for the Lunan water, riding hard, sufficiently hard to reach Red Castle before noon, leaving Pate the Mill to assemble the small group of men he required to take with him to Iona.

Welcome by Fenella was nowise disappointing, although she was disappointed to learn that he had to be back at Glamis that same night. Would he be able to see this Ian the Wright at Usan, then? Learn his intentions and needs? It was only five miles from Red Castle to Usan. They could be there in an hour, spend a couple of hours with this man, then back here for a brief stop and some food, and make the return to Glamis by darkening. He might leave Duncan at Red Castle to co-operate with the shipwright and to ensure that his needs as to timbering were met from Strathmore, this while Cormac himself was away in the Hebrides. There was a sufficiency of tall, fine trees on the Glamis lands. The wood could be dragged to the coast by horse-slyps, or sleds.

Fenella rode with them to Usan, despite thin rain.

The man Ian, a brawny character, who acted as blacksmith for the community also, and was a part-time fisherman, proved to be one of the rowers who had been at Ethiehaven. He had a little yard and forge down near the head of that special corridor of a haven, scarcely large enough, Cormac feared, to build a longship in. But the other said that he could enlarge it well enough. He had become fascinated by the construction of their longship, its lines and shaping, heavy keel, its overlapping planking, or strakes, the lower eight strakes lashed to the ribs, not bolted as those above, these of resinous pine, which was presumably the wood which grew in Jutland, their own good Scots pine perfectly suitable. He would probably require different wood for the long sweeps and mast, oak or beech, sufficiently straight lengths required. If such was not available, pine might serve – but the Jute ones were of oak. He could come over to Strathmore to help select the wood, if the lord Thane would permit it?

Cormac assured him of the fullest collaboration. Duncan the Tranter would work with him and see to his requirements. He did not know for just how long he would be away at Iona; the situation might well be complicated and delays involved. But he would get back just as soon as possible, and take a personal interest in the building enterprise.

They left Duncan with the wright and rode back to Red Castle. The rain had ceased.

There, at a meal, Cormac mentioned Mormaor Connacher's noteworthy interest in the longship project, to Lady Alena's head-shakings. He also reported on the Mormaor Kenneth's desire to gain the high kingship in place of his nephew, and this was received with still greater disapproval, especially the seeming likelihood that Connacher would vote for it. Aidan observed that he was thankful to have distanced himself from all such affairs.

Sadly, Cormac could not linger, with his early start from Glamis in the morning. But at least Fenella announced that she would accompany him a little way on the road westwards, since he had not Duncan as companion. He pointed out that *she* would have to ride back alone, but she assured that this did not worry her; none would harm the Lord Aidan's daughter hereabouts.

So they set off, the man much heartened by the fact that this young woman was prepared so to do. Their association was becoming ever closer, that could not be denied, however much it was related to longships. How close might it become? What was possible? That she had a fondness for him she made evident. But could that fondness lead to greater bliss?

After all, she was not only the grandchild of one of the *ri*, and niece of another, but Connacher had no offspring and his brother Aidan was his heir, however reluctant, and Fenella *his* only child. So that made her all but a princess, and in a matrilineal polity. He himself was a thane, admittedly, even if his thanedom a comparatively modest one; but that was a much inferior status to hers. There could be a much more lofty future for Fenella nic Aidan, these affections scarcely relevant.

He could hardly voice such thoughts, as they rode up

the Lunan Water, and they chatted mainly about the longships venture. If indeed this Ian the Wright could construct effective replicas of the Viking vessels, what might not this lead to? Scotland was weak indeed in fighting craft, and this had cost her dear. Some Highlands and Islands chiefs in the west had birlinns, galleys of a sort, but these were not to be compared with longships in speed, manoeuvrability and aggressive qualities, as the Vikings had proved, for their raids on the west coasts were legion and notorious. There were other boat-builders along this Angus coastline, at Auchmithie and Aberbrothack to the south, and Montrose to the north. Usan could lead the way, and . . .

Although Cormac was in no hurry to part with his companion, he was concerned about her having to ride back far, and alone, with dusk approaching. At Balmullie Mill, he drew rein.

"Enough, my fair Fenella," he announced. "This appears to be a saying of mine these days, but it is time that you turned back. Sad as I will be to lose you. In especial as I will not be seeing you again for long, or what will seem to be long. How long I cannot say, but this of Iona, and what will happen there, may take time."

"I know it. That is why I have come thus with you. I will miss you."

"You will, lass?"

"Yes. You are good company." She gave a little laugh. "For a young woman who has only a mother and father to consort with! And fishermen! And flounders! I love Red Castle. But it is . . . isolated."

Cormac did not know whether to be pleased with this information and confession, or otherwise. Was it just young company that she craved and that he was providing? He had hoped that it was rather more . . .

"It is my good fortune that I can help to fill the gap, in some small way," he said, a little laboriously. "For myself, it is more than just the company that I cherish."

"Poor Cormac! You are very patient with me. But, yes,

I will miss your company. Yourself also. In more than this of longships and flounders!"

He reined his horse closer to hers, so that their knees touched, and leaned over to reach out and clasp her, not exactly to him but as nearly so as he could manage.

"Have a care, or you will fall off! Or I shall!" she exclaimed. "Here is no, no convenient way to say goodbye."

"No? Then will this serve?" And, every muscle tensed, he rose on his saddle, reached further over still, gripped her round the middle, somehow keeping his balance, and with a mighty effort heaved her bodily over to him, and deposited her in front of him on his saddle-bow.

"Sakes, what is this?" she gasped. "Am I being . . . abducted? After all?"

"Would that you were! But, better than breaking our backs!"

"You are strong, it seems. And again see me as weak?"

"I see you as lovely, desirable, adorable! Never weak. I had to hold you, for the last time. It may be for weeks . . ."

"Hold me, indeed – or I shall fall! Perhaps . . . I would be safer on the ground?"

"No. Thus, thus I will think of you. In my arms. Held close, secure. At least in, in person."

"Ever one for persons is Cormac mac Farquhar!"

"*This* person." He kissed her hair, and the back of one ear, which was within his reach, of his lips, at least.

She did turn her head then, and her soft cheek and one corner of her mouth became accessible. "Here . . . is something new!" she got out. "Do not break your neck!"

"Then turn your face further, woman!"

She obliged, and their lips met fully, hers open a little now.

So they sat, however uncomfortably, his arms enfolding her, pleasingly rounded even within her riding gear.

But not for long. Presumably she was less preoccupied than was he in the situation, for suddenly she pulled her head back.

"My mare!" she exclaimed. "She is off, straying. See you, we must get her."

Sighing, Cormac yielded, and kicked his mount after the other horse which had moved a little way off. Reaching it, Fenella proved her agility by turning and slipping down to the ground with a modicum of fuss, to go and grasp her mare's trailing reins, mounting thereafter with equal alacrity.

So that was their parting, he bowing from the saddle, she waving as she trotted off, the man watching until she was out of sight behind trees.

13

Cormac was thankful that the new Thane Donald of the Mearns was there for company on the long journey to the Western Sea, for he had no desire to ride beside Connacher. They went, as before, by Blairgowrie and into the hills, over to Dunkeld, Strath Braan and Loch Tay to Crianlarich and up to Tyndrum, and so to Loch Awe and salt water at Loch Etive, three night stops on the way. Then, at the Oban, the problem of leaving all their horses and finding a sufficiency of boats to take them, and all the others travelling to Iona, the fifty-mile voyage. This time it was Strathearn men they had to share passage with, the mormaors going in their own superior craft. Cormac could have done with one of his longships rather than the clumsy scow they had to use. The weather was overcast but calm, fortunately. The talk, needless to say, was all about Kenneth of Atholl's bid to be High King.

At Iona, lovely even in grey weather, with its white cockleshell sands, the colourful seaweeds and green marble rock, they found the island teeming, with its folk no doubt bewailing the necessity for another invasion so soon after the last, whatever they felt about the slaying of Constantine and the ambition of his slayer. But they had other concerns also, which may have been somewhat eased by this arrival of all these great ones and their trains; for the word was of renewed Norse raiding on quite a major scale on the coasts and isles further north, indeed the Mormaors of Moray with Ross, and Sutherland, announcing attacks on their seaboards, this with much anger. Those on the Moray coast were Danes apparently, while the attackers further north in Sutherland were from Orkney and Shetland.

At the distinctly hasty interment of Constantine's remains, nothing being said by the Abbot Maelbrigt as to how the victim had died, Cormac found himself standing between two young men of approximately his own age, one Dungal MacDuff, Thane of Fife, son of Kenneth of Atholl, and the other the oddly named MacBeth, which meant son of life, whose father was the Mormaor Finlay of Moray. The former was clearly wary, if not nervous, no doubt anxious about the general reaction to his father's actions and ambitions, and giving the impression of being no very strong character himself; the other good-looking and friendly, interested in what went on there, and the decisions to be taken. He did not, however, indicate how he thought his father would vote. As they waited, he and Cormac discussed, as a safe subject, the efficacy of the embalming of corpses, since it was now over two months since Constantine's death. This MacBeth said that he understood that the body was steeped in nitre, then smeared with pine resin and wrapped in flaxen cloth, this after the entrails had been extracted, interesting but in the circumstances somewhat gruesome.

Cormac was still a little concerned that those who had loyally supported Constantine, including himself and Donald of the Mearns, might be looked upon as enemies by Mormaor Kenneth – not that his son, this Dungal MacDuff, gave any such impression. His hope was that, if it was so, his longships project might tell in his favour; that is, unless Connacher took all the credit.

He asked MacBeth whether Malcolm, the nephew, was present, never having set eyes on that young man, and had him pointed out to him, standing alone and looking tight-lipped and uneasy, a dark-avised and lean-featured individual, very different from his cousin MacDuff. There were many tensions, obviously, about this Iona burial formality.

The ceremony at the Reelig Oran over, the seven mormaors retired for their crucial meeting, all of them present on this occasion. How long would it take? Would young Malcolm be summoned before them? Or were decisions already made, more or less, beforehand, as had been Connacher's, Cormac suspected? It was not something which he felt that he could ask either MacBeth mac Finlay, nor Dungal MacDuff. He and Thane Donald went for a walk.

When they got back, they found that it was all over, Kenneth elected as Kenneth the Third, Ard Righ, presumably unanimously, possibly the facts of the situation more or less ensuring this, and few of the hearers surprised. Almost certainly Malcolm had not been either. Anyway, he had gone, shaken the dust of Iona off his feet with extraordinary promptitude, which might well indicate that he had foreseen the result and made his arrangements accordingly. MacBeth mac Finlay said that he had seen him hurrying down alone to the haven, boarding a boat there, and being sailed over to the nearby Ross of Mull.

Now what? Would Cormac soon know whether the new High King bore any animosity towards such as himself? Or would that only become apparent in time? After all, there would be more urgent and important matters on Kenneth's mind, many of them, not least possibly his nephew's behaviour and what it might imply. And there were the coronation arrangements to be made. And steps to be taken against the renewed Norse raiding. Not the time, probably, to engage in unnecessary punitive measures.

As they were filing into the abbot's refectory for the traditional banquet, MacBeth brought his father over to see Cormac. The Mormaor Finlay was a stooping hawk of a man, of later middle years, direct of gaze.

"My son tells me, Thane Cormac, that you are much concerned with Connacher of Angus's new purpose of using captured Danish longships to combat the devil-damned raiders of our shores. How far are you advanced in this? Is it a practical endeavour, or some mere wishful notion? Not that Connacher would be one to engage in such, I judge."

Cormac cleared his throat. "It is scarcely Mormaor Connacher's notion, my lord," he said. "I think that you may have taken him up wrongly in this. He has not so much as seen a longship. I captured these in Lothian, and sailed seven of them up to Lunan, on the Angus coast. There we are training the fishermen to work them, difficult as this is. And a boat-builder at Usan is seeking to construct one. And if he succeeds, more. I am finding him the timber, and urging him on."

"So you claim the credit, heh?"

"It is not a matter of claiming, my lord Mormaor. We, my men and myself, have done it all. I think that Mormaor Connacher may have confused you by naming his brother's daughter, the Lady Fenella nic Aidan, in the matter. She is working with me, in this, a notable lady."

"Fenella? The only Fenella I have known was she who slew King Kenneth!"

"A cousin of this one. But different indeed!"

"So! These longships – you see them as being useful against the Norsemen? Or Connacher does!"

"That is the aim of it, yes. They are fast and strong. The greyhounds of the seas – and the killers! We believe that they could be used against the raiders, with good effect."

"Would you bring them up to my Moray coasts, then? Had it not been for this of the burial and a new Ard Righ, I would have been there now, combating the Danes. They are troubling us again."

"I, I do not know that our men will be sufficiently trained, my lord, to face the invaders yet. They take a deal of handling, these vessels. Very different from their own fishing-craft. Eight sweeps, or oars. Three men to each sweep, these long and difficult to use. The beat of twenty-four rowers . . ."

"Come you, and try them, man," Finlay said. "We would show our gratitude. These devils have to be taught a lesson! Come and aid in this. Your men will learn the faster, with the need. Even if only to offer a seeming threat."

Cormac hesitated.

The son, MacBeth, spoke. "I would wish to come to see your ships, Thane Cormac. To take a part. Guide you as to the Moray coasts. I could be of help, perhaps?"

"Yes, do that," his father said, and left them, to head for the mormaors' high table beside the new Ard Righ.

Cormac found himself thus more or less saddled with this unlooked-for and premature venture. What would his fishermen have to say to this? And Fenella?

MacBeth sat beside him at table, demanding details as to the longships, how they were constructed, how they compared with the west coast birlinns, how many men they could carry besides the crew, and so on, he clearly something of an enthusiast. Cormac did like him, but was doubtful about this Moray involvement at this stage.

However, he had something else to think about presently, for the new High King stood to announce that it had been decided to hold his coronation forthwith. The mormaors of the north were anxious to get back to their own lands because of this new Danish raiding, so delay was undesirable. They would all go straight from this Iona to Scone, on the Tay, there to hold the investiture, dispensing with the soil-bringing and treading meantime, the realm's need paramount.

Cormac wondered whether this was indeed the real reason for the hasty crowning, and might it not have something to do with fears of the ousted nephew Malcolm's possible efforts to have his uncle's appointment set aside before it could be confirmed by actual coronation – that hasty departure of Malcolm being perhaps significant?

The Abbot Maelbrigt then declared to all that, boats being a problem for the transporting of all this assembly from the island to the mainland, it would have to be done by stages. Not all would be able to go by sea to the Oban and elsewhere at the same time. So horses would be found for many, over at Fionnphort on the Ross of Mull, a mile away, and they would ride north up the great isle to Craignure, where there were many boats, and they would be carried over to the Oban from there, some ten miles. It was recommended that the younger men present do this, leaving the mormaors and their trains and the older men to sail direct, since it was a thirty-five-mile ride up to Craignure. The evening was barely upon them, so it would be best for the horsed men to get over to Fionnphort forthwith, and they could be on their way north once their mounts had been provided – these used by the monks to transport pilgrims to St Columba's shrine – and win so far as the hospice at Lochbuie, at the head of Loch Scridain, for the night. That ought to have them in the Oban soon after noon the next day, which would not be so long after the seaborne party reached there.

This haste made it evident that Kenneth the Third was going to be an urgent monarch, whatever else.

Soon, then, Cormac, with MacBeth and Donald, were on their way down to the haven, Dungal MacDuff remaining with his father. They did not object to this riding plan, seeing the need for it; they would probably quite enjoy their journey up through this, the largest island of the Inner Hebrides next to Skye.

Over the narrow Sound of Iona they found the efficient monks had a selection of garrons ready at Fionnphort, and set off on these up the extraordinary and lengthy peninsula of the Ross of Mull, a score of miles of it, by innumerable little bays and inlets between the Firth of Lorne and the major sea loch of Scridain, quite lofty inland. At the head of that loch, at Lochbuie, they found a monkish hospice for travellers, and they reached this by dusk, in the company of another dozen riders.

That evening, Cormac learned more about MacBeth mac Finlay, discovering that he was in fact younger than he looked, only eighteen years, but of a strong and lively character and with a sense of humour. Working with him would not be unpleasant, at least.

After the banquet at Iona, they had no complaints over the somewhat plain meals provided by these monks; and in the morning headed on north-eastwards through high mountains now for Loch Spelve, the mighty cone of Ben More dominating all on their left. It made for rough riding, crossing innumerable rivers and rushing burns, but well before noon they had covered the fifteen more miles to the large bay of Craigmure on the wide Sound of Mull opposite Morvern, where they found no lack of craft to carry them over to the Oban. Leaving the borrowed horses, they embarked, and were part-rowed, part-sailed the ten miles, passing the cliff-top hold of Duart, seat of the Maclean chiefs, and the tip of the holy isle of Lismore, the Great Garden, where Columba's colleague and all-but rival, St Moluag, had set up his mission-station those three centuries earlier.

At the Oban, collecting their own better horses again, they found that the High King's and mormaors' party had left there only an hour or so earlier on the long ride eastwards for Scone, some hundred and twenty miles across Breadalbane, the breadth of Alba, from salt water to salt water. There was no urgent need to catch up with the lofty ones ahead, indeed they were better pleased to continue on their own.

The riders got to know each other very well on their three-day journey, and Cormac recognised that he had found a friend in this Son of Life, however odd his name and however doubtful the possibility of the projected expedition of longships to Moray.

At Scone, on the fourth day, an abbreviated coronation ceremony was enacted for Kenneth, the Abbot Cathail officiating, the Ard Righ seated on the Stone of Destiny, and the allegiance-swearing following, this inevitably without the usual handfuls of soil brought from far and near for the High King's foot to rest on. Cormac, for one, had some qualms over kneeling and taking Kenneth's hand within his own and vowing to be a loyal supporter, as he had had to do for Constantine; but as Thane of Glamis he had no option. At least the new monarch gave no sign of hostility towards him when his name was called by the High Sennachie.

As soon thereafter as he decently could he made his escape from Scone Abbey, both MacBeth and Donald of the Mearns electing to come away with him. They ought to be able to reach Glamis before nightfall.

14

Despite all their long riding, they did not remain long at Glamis to rest, to Bridget's disappointment, she finding MaçBeth to her taste. But Cormac was eager to hear Fenella's reaction to this proposed Moray venture. They were off to Lunan Bay without delay, then, dropping Thane Donald on his road to Green Castle on the way. He promised to co-operate with them in any way that he could on this of the longships.

MacBeth was much impressed with the sight and situation of Red Castle on its steep mound above the Lunan's estuary and the vast sandy bay, declaring that it was not unlike Findhorn Bay in his own Moray, but he had never seen such an uninterrupted stretch of fine sands. He was clearly still more impressed with Fenella when she greeted them at the castle gatehouse, she, as usual, having seen them coming from quite far off. Her reception of Cormac was warm if less demonstrative in the circumstances than he would have liked; and she eyed his companion with interest, as he did her.

"Here is MacBeth mac Finlay of Moray and Ross," he introduced. "He and his father are much interested in our longships enterprise. As is Donald of the Mearns."

"Then he is welcome. I have heard of Gillacomgain of Moray, but not . . . Mac Beatha, was it?"

"Gillacomgain is my cousin, lady. I salute you, with much acclaim and respect. Thane Cormac has spoken much of you and your endeavours. Unusual, if I may say it, for a woman!"

"Ah, yes, I fear that it is a most unwomanly concern.

But it is important, and something that I can do. Come you in . . ."

"Have matters progressed, these two weeks when I have been away?" Cormac asked. "I heard, at Glamis, that Duncan the Tranter and Ian the Wright had been there, seeking out and felling timber."

"Yes. They are well pleased with what they got. Ian has laid the keel already. The crews are doing well, or most of them. Dysart is not so keen as the rest – we may have to withdraw their craft from them. But otherwise, they progress at the training."

Later, when the visitor was shown the room he was to share with Cormac, and they were looking out over the bay to Ethiehaven, where four longships could be distinguished amongst the beached fishing-boats, Fenella explained that the other three were at Dysart, Boddin and Usan, for practice. Now Cormac revealed the Moray request, and the urgings of the Mormaor Finlay and his son.

"They would have us take the longships up to the Moray coast. And now, without delay," he said. "They are suffering much from the Danes. They believe that we could greatly help against the raiders. I fear that our men are not yet sufficiently trained, have not fully mastered the handling of these difficult vessels, to do that, to risk using them to fight. Later – that is what we aim for. But so soon?"

"The raiding is costing our people dear, every day," MacBeth pointed out. "That is why we seek help forthwith. Even an appearance up there would be of value. We would be . . . grateful."

The young woman looked from one to the other. "Go north? How soon?"

"So soon as may be. Men, women, children are dying, homes burning, land laid waste."

She nodded. "Perhaps – perhaps it would be none so ill for our men? To challenge them, make them the more eager to prove themselves."

Cormac rubbed his chin. "And if they are not yet fully

able to handle the vessels against these skilled Norsemen? They could suffer . . ."

"They would not engage in a sea battle, no. Not yet. But they could attack men ashore. Even one or two enemy craft at sea. Give aid and hope to the Moray folk."

"Perhaps . . ."

"That would be of great help," MacBeth asserted. "Encourage them to fight back. Not just to flee inland."

"A training attempt, at first. To test them. It could be what they most need." Fenella was clearly in favour of the plan.

"You think that the fishermen would agree?"

"We could go put it to them. At Ethiehaven. See how they thought of it."

"Yes. Then let us do that. See Donnie the Crab. If he and the others are not out fishing . . ."

"They will be back. They go out early in the morning." She pointed. "There are two boats returning now."

So it was back down to the horses, Cormac as ever wondering at the girl's spirit, but not wholly convinced that all this was wise. MacBeth was the more admiring.

At Ethiehaven they found the last two boats coming in from the day's work, and Donnie the Crab unloading fish for the women to gut. Cormac left it to the young woman to put the matter to him.

He listened to her, nodding once or twice, certainly showing no marked opposition. When she had finished, he shrugged.

"We could try it, Lady Fenella," he said. "It would show the men that all this is not for nothing, all the training and the labour. Aye, we could put it to them."

"Do that," Cormac urged. "See how they take it. They may not like it."

Some of the fishermen had already come to greet their lord's daughter, and others were collected. Again Cormac left it to Fenella, deeming that best, after introducing MacBeth of Moray. He watched all those faces keenly as she announced the proposal.

He found it hard to gauge reactions as they listened. These were tough sea fishermen, not the sort to display their feelings and emotions very openly. He saw no actual frownings nor head-shakings, but a few raised eyebrows.

When the girl had finished, he spoke up. "This is no sort of order nor command," he pointed out. "It is for yourselves to decide. Clearly there could be danger in this, much danger. And much toil. But it could be a notable venture. What we all have aimed for, all along. Only perhaps . . . over-soon? Before you are fully trained for it."

"You would win some more training on the way up to Moray!" Fenella added, smiling. "It will be well over the hundred miles."

"Wi' the wind behind us, belike. For the sails!" someone put in.

That simple interjection was significant. There were nods.

Donnie saw it that way. "I say that we should do it," he declared. "Here is what it is all for. A trial, just."

There were more nods.

"If the Boddin and Usan men agree?" Fenella put in.

That raised snorts and sniffs, as it was meant to do.

Cormac, convinced now that the attempt could and should be made, took the lead. "Six longships, then. The Lady Fenella thinks that the Dysart folk are probably not up to it yet. We could take their craft and leave it with the Usan wright for him to build his new vessel from. If the Usan and Boddin men agree, with your own, that is three. Can Ethiehaven provide a second crew? Usan is a bigger place and could crew two, I think. From the three havens, and perhaps with two or three men from Dysart, could we man the six ships?"

There were cries of assurance, with some gibes as to Dysart.

"Perhaps if we had only two men to some of the sweeps it would not greatly hamper us," Cormac went on. "Especially on the way up, if the south-west wind maintains, as it usually does. How soon could you be ready?"

There was some muttering and questioning then, which Fenella interrupted by saying that the next day the other havens would have to be visited and informed, and given time also. They might take longer to persuade? Again her play on the rivalry of the communities.

Donnie said four days, then, sail in four days' time. None contested that, whatever their womenfolk might say.

Thus it was decided. Much heartened by it all, the trio rode back to Red Castle, MacBeth loud in his praise of the people here.

That night, at bedtime, with two of them to be escorted upstairs, Cormac had to be content with only a fairly formal goodnight, although he did get a little squeeze of the arm.

MacBeth thereafter went on at some length as to the virtues, abilities, attractiveness and other attributes of that quite remarkable young woman, with such enthusiasm as to have Cormac hoping that he was not becoming over-interested. He could do without competition from a mormaor's son for a mormaor's granddaughter.

In the morning it was up to Boddin and Usan. They found no difficulty in persuading the crews in both to join in the Moray adventure, using the Ethiehaven agreement as spur. At Usan they could muster two crews, they said, so long as it was not for any lengthy period, this of course applying to the other fishermen elsewhere. It was good for Cormac to see his friend Duncan again, that man electing to help crew a longship rather than remain assisting Ian the Wright. Boddin thought that they could raise a few extra oarsmen as well as their regular crew.

Back to Dysart, then, where they gained a few more volunteers, which more or less ensured that the sixth vessel could be manned. They arranged with these, and some others, to row their longship up to Usan, and returned to Lunan satisfied.

The next day was Sunday, and the Red Castle party

went to worship at the monastery at Inverkeillor, inland. It was on the way back that Fenella asked whether she ought to go north in the second Ethiehaven vessel, leaving Cormac and MacBeth to lead the way in the first, MacBeth of course acting as guide?

Astonished, Cormac stared at her. It had never occurred to him that she would think of accompanying the flotilla on such a foray, highly unsuitable for any woman. He said so, scarcely believing that she spoke in earnest.

But she did, asking whether he thought that, after persuading all these others to go, she could stay behind? They were her folk, and without her urging many might not be sailing. The least that she could do was to accompany them. Women might not have the muscular strength of men, and the ability to pull sweeps and fight, but they need not all be stay-at-homes and lookers-on. It was her project as much as his, Cormac's, was it not?

That man wagged his head. Should he have envisaged this? He could not stop her. Presumably her father and mother could not either, if they had been consulted and knew of her intention. MacBeth actually smote his saddle-bow in approval.

At least Cormac could make one condition. If he was leader of the expedition, he could insist that the young woman sailed in his vessel, so that he could in some measure look after her.

The following day Cormac had to do much riding, for he had to go back to Glamis to inform them there that he would be gone for some indefinite interval, not over-long. Duncan accompanied him. They would be back the same night, ready for the sailing on the morrow. He was a little concerned at leaving MacBeth at Red Castle, with his undisguised admiration for Fenella, but when that young man did not offer to accompany him all the way to Strathmore and back, there was nothing that he could well do about it.

The Lady Ada and Bridget were supportive over the Moray undertaking, the latter asking whether she also could go, as companion for Fenella, another woman being seemly, surely? But her brother was able to draw the line at this, at least.

Pate the Mill also was disappointed that he could not take part, but he had his duties at the castle as Lady Ada's henchman, especially when the thane was absent.

On the ride back to Lunan, they got distinctly wet. They hoped that the weather was not breaking. But at least the wind remained from the south-west.

Fenella told Cormac, when he got back, that she and MacBeth had gone over to Ethiehaven again, and with a practice for the morrow developing, he had tried his hand at the sweeps, or rather his arm muscles. He would take his turn at it hereafter, a fine young man. Not too fine, her hearer hoped . . .

It was prompt bed-going that night, with an early start in the morning – and prayers for better weather.

15

When they arrived, in gusty wind, at Ethiehaven next day they found all awaiting them, fisherfolk being early risers. Cormac, MacBeth and Fenella boarded the first longship, Duncan the second with Donnie the Crab, the two crews now armed with a variety of weapons, axes, dirks, fish-gutting knives, boat-hooks, even mallets – this reminding Cormac that he, and MacBeth for that matter, were not so provided, this aspect of their enterprise overlooked in all the organising arrangements. If they were going to war, weapons surely ought to have been a priority! Swords and the like, of course, had not been any notable feature at Red Castle.

Amid farewells and much advice-giving from oldsters, women and children, they pushed off into choppy waters, these not helping the sweep-pulling. But it was quickly evident that the oarsmen were much more adept at their task than when Cormac had previously sailed with them, nevertheless. There were a few slips and hitches because of the lurchings of the vessels, but no major troubles; and once they were out in mid-bay and the sails could be hoisted, progress improved, and the chanting could be discontinued.

They were soon at Boddin and, spotted from a distance, they were joined by two craft from there, one rather less efficiently rowed than the other. But once these had their sails up, they did not lag far behind.

At Usan they were surprised and pleased to see none other than Father Ferchar in the leading ship, the Church militant it seemed. So, amidst much waving, the six longships sailed in convoy due north, rolling steadily in slantwise seas but demanding little oarwork.

Presently they were passing the entrance to the great tidal basin of Montrose. It was hard to gauge how fast they were moving, but certainly infinitely faster than any fishing-boat could sail. When they saw the mouth of the Bervie Water, easily recognisable with its Bervie Brow cliffs nearby, they reckoned that this being some dozen miles north of Montrose, they must have taken no more than an hour to cover it, less possibly, and this in turbulent seas. That made excellent going. One of the Boddin boats was trailing behind somewhat, but not grievously.

Soon they were level with the cliff-top fort of Dunnottar guarding the bay of Stonehaven. What the folk ashore thought of seeing a group of six longships sailing past was not to be known, probably thanking God that they *were* sailing on.

At this rate they ought to be off the mouths of Dee and Don, at Aberdeen, before noon. They could see why these craft were called greyhounds.

Cormac enquired of MacBeth how far it was north of Aberdeen to the Moray coast, and was told about fifty miles to the great headland of Kinnaird, between Inverallochy and Rosehearty. That was where Moray really began. But it was not there that the raiding had been taking place but much further on, in the Spey Bay area. But, who knew? The Danes might have moved nearer. Spey Bay was another forty miles west of Kinnaird Head. And there were still another nearly fifty miles to the mouth of the Moray Firth. His father's mormaordom was large.

Fenella asked what their tactics were to be once they reached the raided areas? That would not be until the morrow, she presumed. How were they best to use these longships and their men?

Cormac had indeed thought long on this. A battle at sea, with any number of the Danish ships, was not to be considered, if possible, for the raiders would be much more proficient in handling their craft, as well as more seasoned fighters. Two or three longships they might tackle, but not more. He felt that the best policy would be to seek to destroy the enemy vessels while they were beached, and their crews off raiding inland. After all, their own captured craft, with their raven-painted sails, would merely seem like fellow Vikings to the Danes ashore and arouse no alarm. So this should give them a real advantage, surprise. If the Norsemen were not actually beside their ships, but raiding inland, then the destruction might well be easy; and when the enemy returned, they would be much disheartened to have lost their precious vessels. Their tactics, then, he thought, should be to try to avoid outright battle and use surprise and subterfuge as much as possible, especially under-armed as they were.

Fenella cheerfully suggested that they might well capture a sufficiency of Viking weapons in their efforts.

MacBeth asked whether they should attempt to attack at night. Discover where raiders were based, sail past, and then return under cover of darkness. These Danes were reputed to be great drinkers, and many would be apt to be drunken of a night.

Cormac doubted whether this would be wise. His experience of the Norsemen, in Lothian, had been that they seldom ventured very far inland for their pillaging, and returned to their ships at the coast of a night usually. So then they would be in greater numbers, and even if drunken would be tough fighters. That might serve on occasion; but in the main, best to move in during the day, when there would be apt to be only a few guards at their ships. He pointed out, too, that the Vikings were great burners as well as killers and ravagers, and usually their presence in any area could be indicated by columns of smoke in the air. This could help.

It was decided, then, that they should halt for the night somewhere around Kinnaird Head to rest their crews, and in the morning sail openly on towards Spey Bay, on the lookout for the enemy. Now that they were nearing offensive action, Cormac had become increasingly concerned over Fenella's presence with them, danger to her in any fighting. She would have to remain, hidden, in this longship, under its dowsed sail perhaps. He did not enlarge upon this meantime.

Past Aberdeen and on up its long coastline they sailed that afternoon, this part of the Mar mormaordom, new territory for Cormac and Fenella, indeed for almost all their men probably, although MacBeth knew it and pointed out landmarks such as the Ythan estuary, the bay of Cruden and the headlands of St Peter and St Columba. By evening they saw looming up the great cape of Kinnaird, and this could mark their journey's end meantime, a notable journey such as none there had ever experienced, well over one hundred sea miles in the day. Rest was welcome, especially as they rounded the point and promptly recognised that hereafter they would be going west, not north, and with the prevailing south-west wind much more rowing rather than sailing would be called for.

MacBeth was now on, or close to, fairly familiar territory, and urged that they pulled on for another five miles or so to the cove and haven of Pennan, where they could gain shelter and provision for the night.

Actually, this comfort was not achieved without considerable upset and delay, for the sight of six longships probing into their bay produced panic amongst the Pennan inhabitants, and hasty flight of all the population up the steep slopes, all but cliffs, behind, in great confusion, no amount of shouting on the part of the visitors availing in lessening the alarm. They realised that this was going to be a recurrent reaction and problem for them hereafter, and would somehow have to be coped with. Fenella did her best by standing up in the bows of their vessel and waving her arms and calling, obviously a woman, hoping that this might reassure. Father Ferchar called that he was a priest of Christ's Church.

Whether as a result or not, a crowd mainly of men did halt up on the cliff-top, to gaze back down as the longships beached and the crews landed. MacBeth went to stand in a gap in the row of cottages, Cormac, Ferchar and Fenella behind him, to shout at his loudest that he was MacBeth mac Finlay, son of their mormaor, come with captured longships to aid them against the Danes, Cormac adding that he was the Thane of Glamis and Fenella niece of the Mormaor of Angus, their men fellow fisherfolk. This did eventually soothe the villagers' fears, and a deputation of the men came back down to ascertain that all was indeed well. Comforted by what they learned, these waved back to their fellows above, and thereafter the population, men, women, children, even some goats and dogs, returned down that steep slope to greet their mormaor's son, in relief.

They did inform that they were greatly worried about the Danes' incursions, and with reason, for these were taking place none so far off, some having been reported at Portsoy, barely a score of miles away.

In their thankfulness over the newcomers' identity, these were welcomed more warmly than any such invasion might have been, and the crews spent a good night, well fed, Fenella being found a bed in one of the cottages. MacBeth and Cormac chose to sleep in their plaids in the boat, like the others.

In the morning they were off westwards, having to tack now, mainly oar-work but seeking to have the sails made use of in the sideways wind, a zigzag course, chanting once more a help.

They had not gone ten miles when they began to see telltale smoke clouds rising ahead. That would be near the mouth of the Deveron, MacBeth assessed, or inland therefrom, near the small town of Banff. It looked as though their first operation was imminent. All were on the alert.

Presently they rounded a small point, after passing the great Troup Head, and there before them opened a quite wide V-shaped bay, the mouth of the River Deveron. The nearest smoke columns were none so far inland from this. They could see no sign of enemy vessels however.

They rowed on across the bay, peering. They were more than half over before they spotted them, three longships drawn up within the very in-going of the river mouth where, in a sheltered cove, was a cluster of cottages. Standing up, and waving and pointing towards the other vessels, Cormac indicated action.

In file the six craft headed in, the leaders seeking sight of movement, people near those beached ships. It was not long before they saw men emerging from one of the cottages to stare seawards, almost certainly Danes. They could see that some of the houses were roofless now, burned.

As they drew closer, they counted only six men, these displaying no concern. Why should they, with a group of their own Viking vessels approaching? Cormac urged Fenella to lie low; a woman's presence could arouse wonder, if not doubts. The longer that they could remain unsuspected the better.

They were perhaps two hundred yards offshore before signs of unease were evident amongst those watchers. No doubt it was the appearance of the new arrivals' garb which struck them as strange. The six could be seen to draw together. There were shouts therefrom, and two more men emerged from the cottages and came hurrying down.

Cormac, standing in the bows, called and waved. He knew no Danish but hoped that he sounded reassuring. The eight men waited, fairly clearly at something of a loss. Behind them, two naked women ran out of the cottage the others had come from, to hurry off up the slope behind.

Cormac now had his oarsmen row as hard as they could on the sweeps, to run their craft as far up the shingly beach as possible beside the three craft already there, ordering the sail down, the others following his lead. As they grounded, open-handed he leaped down on to dryish land, closely followed by MacBeth, both obviously weaponless. Unfortunately, perhaps, some of the oarsmen behind, drawing in their sweeps, reached for axes and boat-hooks instead, and it was no doubt this which changed the Vikings' wariness into alarm. They all turned and ran back towards the houses, no doubt to collect their swords and battle-axes.

At the sight, the Scots poured ashore, many jumping

into the water, assorted weaponry at the ready. Cormac waved them on, and led the way up towards the houses, very well aware now that he had nothing with which to defend himself. The Danes had disappeared indoors and now two reappeared, spears in hand and one wearing a winged helmet. But they halted there in the doorway. They could see how utterly they were outnumbered; after all, the six longships carried about one hundred and fifty men altogether. No wonder that they, and those behind them, stayed in some sort of cover. But, being seasoned warriors, they would also see that the newcomers were very inadequately armed compared with themselves. They waited where they were, spears forward.

It was now Cormac's turn to hesitate. Blocking the doorway, what could he and his folk do against the Vikings. Those long spears . . .!

MacBeth, beside him, jerked the answer. "Fire!" he said. "The thatch. Fire the thatch. Burn them out!"

That was it – fire! All men carried flint and steel, if not tinder. But that dry reed-thatch with which these cothouses were roofed would demand no tinder. He and MacBeth shouted their orders.

"Fire! Fire the thatch!" And pointed to round the back of the house. So, while the mass of the Scots faced those spearmen in the doorway, standing well back, a dozen or so of the others ran round to the rear. These cottages boasted no back doors. Soon smoke began to arise, to the sound of crackling. The Danes were getting a taste of their own medicine.

The thatch caught alight quickly, and it did not take long for the inmates of the house to recognise that they would either choke in the smoke, be burned to death as the blazing roofing fell in, or die fighting if they ventured out. That these chose the last was only to be expected; but of course they had to burst out all but singly from the narrow doorway and so were not well placed to sell their lives dearly against so many assailants.

Each was met with a hail of missiles as they emerged,

stones picked up from the beach, poles, knives and even axes thrown. All went down, one at a time, without ever being able to strike back, although one did throw a spear, which struck a Scot on the leg, to his hurt. Eight men fell, and were promptly battered to death by axe-blows, in a bloody fury. Cormac for one was all but sickened at the sight.

It was an easy victory for their first action; indeed the greatest risk taken was for those dashing into the burning cottage to retrieve any arms left within.

Cormac sought to collect his thoughts and act the leader. They must not be caught unawares by any returning raiders. So he ordered guards out on the watch. He went back to their vessels to tell Fenella that all was well, only one man wounded; but urged that she did not come and see the battered corpses. Some of their men were already considering how best to destroy the three beached longships.

The thought occurred to him that it would, in fact, be folly to do this, when Ian the Wright was so busy seeking to construct the like. Could they not take these as trophies, captures, also? But – to man them? To do so, however sparsely, would gravely weaken their other crews, handicap their future activities. Take them so far, then, and hide them somewhere? That would be best. Return for them later.

Then another notion struck him. When the main party of these Danes returned here and found no longships, what would they do? Finding dead men only? They would go seeking their vessels. Think that local men had somehow ralied to attack, and stolen the ships? Presumably, then, they might go searching for them, and then try to rejoin other raiding parties elsewhere, possibly using captured fishing-boats?

In a quandary, he consulted Fenella, and they agreed that it might be best to remove those dead bodies, take them out to sea and sink them. Then take the three captured craft back to Pennan and leave them there, to resume their expedition and collect them later. The returning raiders would be at a loss when they found their colleagues and ships gone, possibly taking them off on some exploit of their own?

The priest Ferchar, who had taken no part in the actual slaughter, now demonstrated his Christian charity by saying a brief prayer over the bodies, although they were of pagans, and hoping that the loving Creator might have mercy on their souls hereafter. Then they were carried aboard one of their own vessels, and a scratch crew made up to sail it back down to Pennan, while the other two vessels were towed behind Cormac's and Donnie's craft; fortunately they would have the wind approximately behind them for this short voyage, a blessing, since the rest would be somewhat undermanned. It was to be hoped that no other enemy ships put in an appearance at this stage of events.

All re-embarking, they rowed out from the river mouth and turned eastwards again, duly putting the corpses into the sea, glad to be quit of them.

MacBeth said that he had been thinking of the future. He judged that the Moray men ought to follow the Angus example and learn to fight the Danes with their own weapons. So, while leaving these three vessels at Pennan meantime, why not leave their own wounded man with them to teach the Pennan fishers the rudiments of handling longships, with a view to taking over one of the craft for themselves to use against the raiders? This was accepted as an excellent proposal and to be supported.

Aided by the wind, they made their distinctly erratic way back to Pennan, where once again there was some alarm at the reappearance of longships, this more speedily calmed, and MacBeth telling the folk that they could, and should, give a lead to other Moray people in trying to turn the tables on the invaders. This was somewhat doubtfully received, but no refusals voiced. Leaving the injured Ethiehaven man with them, and asking for a volunteer to take his place on the sweeps, they did get two young men to join them.

The night was spent at the village.

In the morning, it was westwards again. The wind had dropped somewhat, but it was still westerly, so it was mainly sweep-work, the two new volunteers being initiated into their tasks.

Presently they were passing the Deveron mouth once more, and there, a mile or so offshore now, they could see many men at the ravaged hamlet. They wondered what they would make of the six longships sailing past, probably assuming that the three of their own craft were amongst them, and fulminating against their missing colleagues. They left them to it.

It was not long before they saw more smoke rising ahead of them. MacBeth said this would be in the Spey Bay area, a large but shallow indentation of that coast, fully a dozen miles wide, with a fertile hinterland where the River Spey meandered seawards, by Fochabers to Garmouth. That last would be a likely place to look for raiders.

But before they reached Garmouth, approximately in mid-bay, they were passing a little hook-shaped, lowish headland when, just behind this, by a short stretch of sand, were cottages and two beached longships. MacBeth did not know the name of this place. They could see no signs of life thereabouts, although smoke did rise inland some distance.

They held a hasty consultation. Were the Danes still sleeping it off in those houses? None appeared to be burned. Should they seek to repeat the previous day's activity? They could hardly just sail on, leaving these behind them. But their crews might be not far away, out of sight somewhere.

It was decided to sail in, ready for action. Just the two vessels there . . . Cautiously they approached. Still no signs of life. It was mid-forenoon, and surely all the raiders were not still asleep?

Very unsure of themselves, they nosed their ships up on

to the beach beside those others. Quickly all disembarked, armed and ready. Signing silently to the men to line up in a crescent formation, Cormac led the way towards the cottages.

No challenge met them. Fenella was sternly told to wait behind.

On a shed which they reached first, beside drying nets, eight heads were hanging, washed clean of blood, the women's and children's hanging by the hair, the men's nailed through the mouths. That set the newcomers scowling.

A few yards from the first cottage they halted, and Cormac and MacBeth went forward to the open doorway. No sounds met them other than the seabirds' cries. Cautiously they peered within.

One headless body of a woman, naked, lay amongst the bloody shambles of simple furnishings. That was all.

Backing out, they moved to the next house. Three bodies lay therein, none with the heads still attached.

It was the same elsewhere. No one was alive in the hamlet; and no Vikings.

These killers, then, had left no guards for their ships, presumably esteeming them safe enough. So what now? They might not be far away. Taking over these two ships was easy enough. But they had come not just to capture vessels but to assail the invaders. Just to sail away again with their trophies did not seem adequate. And there were presumably only the two crews of Danes hereabouts. Consulting Father Ferchar and Duncan the Tranter, they decided that they must attempt better than that.

They left Fenella and about a dozen of their number, older men, to look after the ships, pushing these a little way into the water again so that, at need, they could be got further out beyond reach of any returning Norsemen. Then, in fairly tight formation, they set off up the side of a small burn, inland.

They had not gone far when a dog barked at them from a clump of whins, gorse bushes. Duncan went to investigate, and there found two scantily clad women hiding. He brought them back, terrified, weeping, the reassurances scarcely of great comfort to them. Gaspingly they told that they had been raped, but managed to flee. One had seen her husband cut down, the other her child thrown from one Dane to another, this same morning. The last feared for *her* husband, now. He and two others had gone upstream earlier to the larger village of Gamrie, a mile or so away, where there was a smoke-house, to cure their fish. It would be there that these sons of Satan were now, wreaking their further havoc . . .

MacBeth told the women to go back to their houses, where Fenella would look after them meantime.

Then onwards. At least they had now some idea as to where the raiders were to be looked for.

Up the little valley they presently came to a levelling and open woodland, in which a few cattle grazed. Through the trees they pressed. Donnie it was who was first to hear it, screams ahead. Warned, they went cautiously, hidden thus far by leafage and bushes. Where their cover ended, they halted. Before them, some two hundred yards off, was the village of Gamrie, quite large, whence came the yells and shrieks, some roofs already afire. They could see men running, waving weapons, chasing. The screaming was continuous.

"Our chance!" Cormac jerked to MacBeth. "They are occupied with their killing. Scattered. Two crews only. Fewer men than we have. Not looking for any attack. You – you take half. That way. I go this side."

There was no need for any discussion, all obvious, task and opportunity. Their company divided roughly into halves. Both groups surged forward, left and right, silent but grim. At least they had now some captured battle-axes, maces, swords added to their miscellaneous weaponry.

Their descent upon the raiders was a total surprise, the Danes intent on their dire work, in twos and threes, none looking behind them. The attackers had to leap over sundry bodies, none of them Danish. But they would alter that.

They did. Smiting, thrusting, stabbing, the Scots fell

upon the killers and ravishers, into and amongst the groups of houses. Amidst all the noise of shrieks and yells and howling and wailing, smashings and the crackling of burning thatch, not to mention the confusion caused by the now billowing smoke, the dreaded Vikings were picked off one by one, without any attempt to come together to form any sort of front, or even little groups backing each other. And all the time the attackers were winning weapons dropped by their victims.

As they worked their way through that village, Cormac noticed folk streaming away from it, but none of them Danes so far as he could see.

Presently he came face to face with MacBeth and his party, their circuiting complete, their endeavours similar, triumph on every face. It was victory. Only the seeking out of any enemy inside houses, or hiding. That was soon seen to.

When they could congratulate themselves that all was over, they counted the dead; there were, significantly, no wounded Danes. Sixty-seven they added up to, an impressive total, however off-put was Cormac, and possibly others, at the sight of the piles of bodies.

They could not just leave the corpses thus; and they must try to help the village's survivors in some measure, victories bringing responsibilities as well as triumph. It was decided that their best course was probably to pile all the dead Danes into a large shed or barn which had escaped burning, then set its thatch alight to more or less cremate the victims. Father Ferchar said his prayer over them. Some injured locals were discovered and given such aid as was possible. A woman, raped and distraught but otherwise uninjured, was found, and persuaded to go off inland after her fled fellow villagers to tell them of the situation and that they could return in safety to put as much to rights at Gamrie as was in their power.

This seen to, however inadequate they felt their efforts to be, the victors returned to the coast.

Fenella was much relieved and heartened to hear of

their success, waiting idly at the ships in anxiety having evidently been an ordeal.

What now? It was only just past midday. They might achieve more yet before returning to Pennan with their new captures. MacBeth thought that Garmouth, where the great River Spey reached the sea, was the sort of place the invaders would be apt to make for, with much populous and fertile country behind it. This was not so many miles ahead. Let them go that far.

They concluded that the two extra longships would be more of a liability than a help at this stage, with the manning problem. They would leave them here meantime and collect them later.

So it was on westwards, their crews all but exultant, so far as fishermen allowed themselves to be. Cormac was less so. They had been fortunate so far, their tasks less taxing than he had anticipated. But they could scarcely expect this to continue. And from MacBeth's description, this Spey area might well have attracted larger numbers of the Danes than the comparatively small groups they had encountered thus far. In which case, they could be faced with greater challenges.

They were, in fact, confronted with testing sooner than expected, and of a different sort. Rounding one of that coast's innumerable headlands, a mere four miles or so on, there coming towards them were three longships, under sail, not making for the land but heading eastwards. Here was a dilemma. Seeing six of their own kind approaching, these were unlikely to sail past without some sort of greeting, exchange or questioning. And when they were close enough to realise that these were not fellow Norsemen, what then? There could scarcely fail to be a clash. And almost the last thing that Cormac desired was a battle at sea with expertly manned Viking craft. But what could they do? They could not turn tail and flee, six before three. They could swing a little more inland, in the hope that these others would pass them by at some distance, but . . .

This they tried, Cormac's craft leading. But less than a mile off a rocky shore, they could not proceed far in that direction. And fairly promptly they saw the enemy vessels turning in towards them.

So there appeared to be no option other than a conflict. Cormac shouted to his other ships to close in. He had never been in a real battle, even on land, but had heard his father say that, in a horsed fight against superior numbers, the strategy was to form a wedge, an arrowhead formation, and seek to drive this through the enemy's line, thus breaking it up, and then to turn and drive back upon the rear in the resultant disarray. Could such tactic be carried out with ships?

For lack of any better notion, he and MacBeth called and waved and pointed to the others, hoping that they perceived something of what was intended.

The enemy vessels, with the wind behind them, came on swiftly. How soon would they recognise that they were not facing fellow Danes? Surely it would not be long. They would be mystified, admittedly, seeing six raven-sailed longships, and not in Viking hands. Any possible confusion must be exploited.

They made a very irregular arrowhead as they rowed on – for they had the wind in their faces – and not nearly so close together as Cormac would have wished, those long sweeps the trouble, and in danger of clashing together. Cormac soon could see the helmeted Vikings staring – and themselves with not a helmet amongst them, it never having occurred to them to wear captured ones. It would be only moments now before the enemy would perceive that there was trouble ahead.

Sure enough, quite suddenly there was urgent activity on those other ships, sweeps pushed out to aid them manoeuvre better, and then swing round. And swinging, they drew away.

It did not take long for Cormac and MacBeth to realise the extraordinary situation: it was the Danes who were fleeing, not themselves. Outnumbered two to one, taken by surprise, and unaware that the six ships were in the hands of less than masterly handlers and fighters such as themselves, they were acting with unaccustomed prudence.

This had Cormac in one more quandary, to be sure. Should he, too, act prudently, and sail off, thankful to have escaped battle? Was that his duty now? Or was it otherwise? Seeming cowardice? Failing? Here was unexpected opportunity to attempt something positive against the foe. Not to seem to run away, but to engage them?

Drawing a deep breath, he pointed at the three craft with the Viking sword that he had adopted for his own use, in a gesture of attack, shouting aggression, he hoped convincingly.

Whatever his crews thought of it all, they bent to their sweeps, to surge forward, however ragged their formation.

Fenella's cry of acclaim and encouragement behind him was only partially welcome, in that it reminded him that he was running the woman he loved into danger which he could have avoided.

Those Danes, once they saw that they were being pursued, reacted like the warriors they were. Possibly they had had time to consider, and reckoned these Scots feeble folk anyway. At all events, they turned their vessels around, and came to meet their pursuers.

So here was the challenge Cormac had so impulsively undertaken, the unseasoned against the skilful, but six against three. One small advantage they had, that in turning back thus the Danes were in no formation. Also, with the south-westerly breeze, the Scots, going eastwards now, out to sea, had the benefit of it. So Cormac and MacBeth were able to yell for those sweeps to be drawn in, let the sails propel them, for those lengthy oars could be a dire danger in any sea battle, liable to collide with the enemy ships and smash back on their own wielders.

Raising his sword high, Cormac stood in the dragon-head bows of his longship and shouted his men on, although within he was praying, not shouting.

The enemy, requiring their sweeps, were late in drawing them in, so that as Cormac's craft came up with the first of them, although he was not able to drive against their oars as he had hoped, nevertheless the Danes were somewhat hampered by their task of getting the lengths in and stowed. As a result, leaning over, Cormac was able to slash at one of the oarsmen with his sword, the first stroke of the conflict. Behind him, others of his crew were able to do the same with their various weapons, Duncan at the stern steering right against the other vessel's timbering. They ground on, inevitably, and past, but leaving some havoc behind.

The second Danish ship had had time to get its sweeps in, so that the impact was very different. And indeed impact it was for, swinging alongside, the two craft crashed not far from headlong, and the abrupt jerk of it toppled Cormac right off the bow-thwart on which he had been standing, to fall over on to the floorboards planking beside three oarsmen.

Possibly that fall saved his life, for a leading, winged-helmeted Dane leaped from his own craft on to the other, battle-axe swinging, and missed his would-be victim by only moments. Followed by two others, he jumped down almost on top of Cormac, amongst the Scots crew.

In that tossing boat, crowded with men and stacked sweeps, chaos ensued, standing, weapon-wielding men stumbling and falling, getting in each others' way, tripping over thwarts, dodging the swinging sail-boom. Actually the first axe-brandishing Dane himself fell over Cormac, and was promptly clubbed into unconsciousness on top of him. Winded, Cormac sought to rise, but was pushed down again in the blundering disarray. Other Vikings leaped in, adding to the mêlée and utter confusion. And in this crazed process, the vessels drifted apart.

The third Danish ship came near on the other side, but before it could close was attacked by two other Scots craft, one on each side, and the three swung away in shouting affray. Cormac, now on all fours amongst struggling bodies, had never imagined battle like this, complete anarchy, and lack of any evident direction or coherence, much less leadership.

By the time he could get to his feet, bruised and unsteady, he found none of the three Danes who had boarded them still there, upright or otherwise, for they had been pushed over into the sea. Some of the Scots crew were wounded, one either unconscious or dead. Fenella was crouching in the stern, with Duncan holding her. Fighting of a sort was still going on between two of the enemy ships and the remainder of the Scots five, but the third appeared to have been vanquished and lay swaying in the swell, with little sign of life aboard.

Desperately Cormac sought to gather his wits and if not take charge, at least try to act the leader. He found MacBeth injured and dizzy, blood streaming from a cut brow. That sail, still up, was carrying the craft on eastwards. Staggering past crewmen in various states, he reached the single mast and managed to bring down the sail, so that at least they did not drift away from the others. Then he shouted to his men to get the sweeps out, or some of them, to pull round and take some further part in the battle, if such it could be called.

In fact that re-entry to the fray was scarcely required. A struggle was going on in one of the Danish vessels wedged between three of the Scots craft and clearly having the worst of it. The other, even as they approached, evidently decided that the situation was hopeless, and set off eastwards with both sail and sweeps, abandoning the scene. With the third already out of action, and there being no point nor room to join in the assault, Cormac hove to nearby, and went to Fenella and Duncan. The young woman was in something of a state of shock but seeking to control herself, fists clenched. Cormac bent to clasp her, unspeaking. What was there to say?

Although Duncan now steered to the remaining fighting, it was indeed all over now, bodies being pitched over the side, Danish bodies. So it was victory again, of a sort, although somehow it did not feel like it, to Cormac at least. Assuring himself that MacBeth was not seriously injured, despite all the blood, he shouted to the other ships to come together, in order to see as best they could to casualties.

It took some time to create a semblance of order out of that confusion. They had quite a number of wounded, mostly not dangerously it seemed on initial inspection, only the one Scot dead, a Boddin man. There was no compunction as to the Danish dead and injured, who were just put over the side, to Father Ferchar's head-shakings. They had captured, incidentally two more longships, the third enemy vessel now being well distant, and swinging back north-westwards it seemed.

Seeking to arrange all in some state of order, Cormac found Fenella was proving her shock mastered by tending the wounded as well as she could.

Eventually, quite a fleet now, they set off back along that Moray coast, all hoping that no more Danish ships would appear on the scene.

With the following wind they made reasonably good time over the twenty or so miles to Pennan, leaving the two earlier captured vessels still waiting at that intermediate haven near Gamrie to be collected later. Even so it was dark before they saw the few lights of their destination ahead, and they had the task of heading in and beaching their eight craft beside the others, getting the wounded ashore, and reassuring the again alarmed villagers.

Cormac heaved sighs of thankfulness as he escorted Fenella to the cottage which she had lodged in before, and kissed her a fond and admiring goodnight. The local women, roused from their beds, were attentive to the wounded. The dead Boddin man was left, wrapped in a plaid, on his ship, to be taken back to his family for burial. MacBeth, bandaged, assured that apart from a sore head, he was in good enough order.

It was thankful rest and sleep for all.

In the morning, Cormac took two craft, over-manned, to row westwards again to bring back the vessels left at what the Pennan folk declared was the Seatown of Gamrie, hoping that they would not encounter any more of the raiders. They were spared this, and were able to sail quite quickly back, wind behind them.

There was no question in anyone's mind but that it was time to head for home. In retrospect they could feel fairly satisfied with themselves. They had been, on the whole, successful, slain a lot of raiders, taught, they hoped, others a lesson that the Moray and Angus coasts were to be avoided in future, and captured no fewer than eight more longships. Mormaor Finlay, and others presumably, would be grateful. The Pennan folk were probably glad to see them go, however much they had almost certainly lifted threat from their area.

They made an extraordinary voyage home to Angus, extraordinary in more ways than one. They had come north six and were returning fourteen, that in itself quite astonishing. But they had no similar increase in crewmen, indeed numbers reduced, owing to the wounded. There had been about one hundred and fifty of them, and now only some one hundred and thirty were able actively to man the sweeps, and this for fourteen vessels. Even with two men to each sweep instead of three, and six oars in use instead of eight, all the craft could not be rowed. So there was nothing for it but to tow four of them. It was not so bad at first, when they were still going eastwards as far as Kinnaird Head, with the sails doing most of the work; but once they turned southwards round that, with the wind more or less in their faces, it was different, sails of little use. Progress became slow indeed. And they had well over one hundred miles to go, towing greatly slowing them. It was hard to calculate speed, but five miles in an hour might be optimistic. And the oarsmen would weary. They would have to halt for the night somewhere along the Mar coast.

As they went, Cormac learned from MacBeth more of the national situation than he had been aware of previously. It seemed that the new Ard Righ had had more enemies than just his nephew Malcolm, and more who sought the high throne than just the said Malcolm. Gillacomgain, younger son of the murderess Fenella's victim Kenneth the Second, was making threats. He was recently married to the young Princess Gruoch, daughter of the ailing Boide, enhancing his claims, owing to the matrilineal system. And the situation was not improved by the fact that King Kenneth the Third was now seeking to have that system abolished and a normal father-to-son succession established. MacBeth knew that his father, Finlay, was much concerned over possible trouble, other mormaors also.

Were all realms as apt for unrest and violence as was Scotland? Cormac wondered.

Thanks to some dropping of the breeze, they got as far as the mouth of the Ythan, in Mar, that evening, the oarsmen all but exhausted. Cormac was now wondering how they were going to find crews for their captured longships; but Fenella told him not to worry, that there were other fishing-havens down the Angus coast to the south which they had not considered as yet: Cuthile, Auchmithie, Carlinheugh, Aberbrothack, Carnoustie and the like. Her uncle, Connacher, she was sure, would not object to them raising men there, since he would certainly claim some of the credit.

They all slept in the ships that night, since there was no village at this river mouth, wrapped in plaids, Fenella between Cormac and MacBeth. Much as the former liked the latter, he could have done without him in this situation.

The wind had dropped almost altogether by the morning, which was a blessing, although an oily swell still made towing difficult, even with steersmen on each towed craft. But they passed Aberdeen and even Stonehaven before noon, and could see themselves reaching their home bases before nightfall.

What to do with the captured vessels meantime, eight of them? At this rate, Ian the Wright could give up constructing longship copies! It was decided to leave two each at Usan and Boddin, and take the other four on to Ethiehaven for possible use of new crews, this last village accepted as base for the entire project.

With much mutual friendly esteem now, as well as banter, to be sure, in due course farewells were said at Usan and Boddin, at the last sadly having to announce the only death of the expedition, although they were hardly able to stress that this represented an extraordinarily modest loss for such an endeavour. Then on to Lunan Bay.

Leaving ten longships beached at Ethiehaven, where they were received as returning paladins, Fenella, Cormac, MacBeth and Duncan returned to Red Castle, tired but fairly well satisfied. Lady Alena greeted them thankfully, and even her husband showed some real interest in their accounts of it all. Cormac asserted that they had a most heroic daughter.

When Fenella accompanied the two men up to their chamber that night, she did enter with them, in order to bathe and dress the gash on MacBeth's brow carefully and caringly, to that casualty's evident satisfaction, so that Cormac was almost wishing that he had also qualified for such treatment. But at least he was able to escort the benefactress downstairs thereafter to her own room, and treat himself to the best and most comprehensive hug he had achieved in six days and nights, despite all the close proximity they had shared. He was not repulsed with more than semi-amused head-shakings.

In the morning, of course, it had to be back to Glamis, with declarations that it would not be long before at least one of them would be back, MacBeth asserting in somewhat laboured fashion that he too would most assuredly be involved further in all this useful activity, and therefore have occasion to renew their association. This was by no means discouragingly received. They rode off.

16

Cormac had seen MacBeth on his way back to Inverness a couple of days later, when, on visiting Forfar to inform Connacher of the longship saga, he heard news which might well trouble his friend, indeed almost all of Scotland as well, as Connacher made clear. Gillacomgain, son of Kenneth the Second, had slain Dungal MacDuff, son of Kenneth the Third – and the assassin was MacBeth's cousin. It had to be assumed that this was a move to forward the ambitious Gillacomgain's bid for the high throne, which he was known to covet. He was, of course, sufficiently high-born, a son of one Ard Righ, his mother a daughter of a Mormaor of Moray, and his new wife daughter of Boide, son of another High King. There was no doubting the eligibility of the man therefore – but must Scotland's Ard Righ always be a murderer? It made a grim thought. How would *this* King Kenneth react?

Connacher feared civil war. A lot would depend on Mormaor Finlay. If he supported his nephew in this, then war would be all but inevitable, and the seven mormaors divided in their allegiance. Kenneth was not popular, and his own murder of Constantine not forgotten. Connacher himself was obviously in doubts as to whom he should support, a worried man.

All this had the effect of rather overshadowing the successful longships venture. But at least Connacher had no objection to Cormac seeking new crews in any of his Angus havens. So the anti-Viking project could further advance.

Not that Cormac could hurry ahead with this, as he would have liked. He was, after all, Thane of Glamis, with quite major responsibilities and duties to perform in his own territories, as his mother was not slow in reminding him. The Glamis folk were in need of a firm hand to keep them in order, or some of them, she declared.

So Cormac had a busy two weeks dealing with a great variety of issues and problems, complaints and grievances, petitions and law-breakings, inspections and adjustments, not all on the negative side admittedly, with some worthwhile developments and improvements. Pate the Mill and Duncan were ever at his side. But his thoughts throughout tended to be elsewhere.

It was now late May, and one of the thoughts which did come to him was that this was the start of the Viking hosting season. Those Danes, of course, had been at it already for weeks. But May to September, while their crops were growing and before harvesting started, was the favoured period for these inveterate raiders, Norsemen, Swedes, Danes, Jutes, Wends and Goths. So the services of their longship flotilla, fleet indeed now, might well be called for, not only in Moray but around other coastal areas. It was time for readiness therefore, and increasing and training new crews.

Leaving Duncan with Pate to assist in the sheep-shearing but to come on in a day or two, on the last day of May Cormac set off again for Red Castle, his now favourite journey. There the Lady Alena informed him that Fenella had been sailing as far south as Aberbrothack, with Donnie the Crab and others, telling the fishermen in the intervening havens about the longships, and seeking their co-operation. But this forenoon she had said that she was off flounder-fishing, and that also she might have a swim in the sea, the weather being so fine and warm. She was fond of swimming apparently. Which she would be at first her mother did not know. There were two boats out in the bay, they could see, but too far off to tell whether she was in one of them. Did Thane Cormac wish to wait, or to go seeking her?

That man was in no doubt as to that. But how to find

her? From the castle's windows he could see no signs of any bather; but if she was in the water, and any distance off, she would be unlikely to be visible. There were miles of sands. Best, then, to ride to Ethiehaven and enquire there whether she was out in a boat, in which case he could seek another to join her; and if she was for swimming first, he might spot her on the way.

He was, in fact, not far along the beach when, passing a little hollow in the flanking range of sand-dunes, he perceived a horse tethered therein. That could be hers; unlikely indeed to be anyone else's. Going to investigate, he found a bundle of clothing nearby, women's gear. She was in the water, then.

He went to peer seawards, but could see nothing more than some rafts of eider ducks floating out there. In those wavelets, a swimmer some way out would not be visible, probably, unless actually splashing about, only head above the surface. Well, he could wait. He seated himself on the warm sand beside the two horses.

It was the scuttering away of a group of those eiders which presently caught his eye. Then he saw a rhythmic slight splashing. That would be the swimmer, alarming the ducks. He rose, to gaze.

Soon it was clear, a dark head and the occasional flash of a white arm. He went down to the tide's edge, to wave.

He got a wave back. He, of course, would be much more visible than she was. He called out greetings and his pleasure.

Fenella came swimming in, using a steady over-arm stroke. Soon she was in the shallows, quite near. She lay therein, her white body very clear, and highly eye-catching for any man.

"I did not know that you were a swimmer," he called. "And you have been far out."

"I swim a lot," she panted. "Do you? Can you swim, Cormac?" She lay still there, on her stomach, hands winnowing the water, her breasts by no means hidden.

"I can swim, yes. I do little of it, I fear. Rivers scarcely inviting . . ."

"Well, here is your chance! The sea is not cold. Or not very! Join me."

He drew a deep breath. He had never bathed with a woman. And to be invited thus to do so! Here was something new indeed. He was not going to refuse, that was a surety.

Even as he was savouring the prospect he was beginning to slip off his clothing, kicking off the riding-boots.

She veered round and swam a little way out again, to deeper water, to await him.

Naked, he left his garb in an untidy heap, unlike hers, and ran down to the water's edge, she turning to wave him on.

He caught his breath again as he strode in. Not cold, did she say? As well, perhaps, in a regard for modesty and manhood. Cold as it was, he quickly plunged headlong, splashing mightily. She waited for him, up to her shoulders in water, her wet hair vividly red thereon.

When he came beating his way up to her, a less practised and effective swimmer that she was, he found his feet on the sand, and stood. Taller than she was, the water came only halfway up his chest, she slightly more fully covered. Nevertheless the water was sufficiently clear to reveal most of what was below, even through the glitter and shimmer.

Cormac took her in his arms, without a word. And despite the water she felt warm, a firmly rounded armful, eminently claspable.

She gave him a salty kiss, before backing away. "How far can you swim?" she wondered. "River paddler!"

He grimaced. "None so far, no. Besides, you have already swum a good distance, I saw."

"I was not finished when you appeared. Come you, then." And she plunged round, and away, her hair streaming behind her.

Less than eagerly he swam after her in very different style, making much splatter.

Soon she turned over on to her back, to be able to watch him, hands behind her head to raise it, feet doing the work now.

"You are labouring, Cormac," she called. "I am unkind. Back to the beach with us."

He did not contradict her, even though his physical labouring was not what was on his mind just then.

She changed direction shorewards. "Perhaps women are better formed for swimming," she suggested as she passed him. "More bulgings and plumpness for floating?"

He swallowed, partly salt water, and followed her round.

Back in the shallows, Fenella lay on her stomach again. "Here is a question," she announced. "I dry myself by running, always. You also will, no doubt. But I fear that it is scarcely decent to be running together, thus! How say you?"

"I, I know not," he got out. "This is . . . new to me, see you!"

"Poor Cormac! Do I embarrass? But if I run one way, and you the other? Will that serve?"

"There is none to see us . . ."

"No. But I would not wish to . . . incommode you! See, I will go off first. This way, we shall dry quickly, in the sun."

She rose in the water, shook herself, flicked a wave at him, and ran out on to the dry sand. He did not pretend not to gaze.

Her loveliness was such as to make him hold his breath, however panting he had been. From long slender neck down to long legs, by those shapely shoulders and prominent thrusting and pointed breasts, to rounded belly and dark triangle thereunder, she was all delectable femininity, beauty personified, all but emphatic. And when she set off running, bosom flouncing, she made a sight to keep him watching, there in the water, until she was only a white gleam against the golden sands and the blue sea, before he too rose to run.

It is to be feared that Cormac did not run very far, whether dry or not, his concern now to repair to his heap of clothing when Fenella returned to hers. In this he was successful, so that when she got back, person heaving engagingly, it was to point at him and to declare that he was not much more of a runner than he was a swimmer, this as she went off into the dune-hollow to dress.

At least he refrained from watching her as she donned her clothes. He was not really dry, especially at his hairy chest and lower, but that did not worry him. In fact, nothing worried him now. He had tasted of bliss, however unworthily.

When the young woman came to him, spreading her still damp locks over shoulders the better to dry them, she gave no impression of being in any way uncomfortable over their encounter, declaring that she doubted whether he was properly dry. Also that once they were riding, her hair would become less of a damp tangle. She had been going to find someone to take her fishing for flounders; but since he had appeared on the scene, and it was not much past midday, perhaps they should find a boat to take them down the coast to the first of the fishing-havens to the south, the first sizeable one, Auchmithie?

Cormac would have enjoyed the fishing and the proximity involved; but since she had suggested this other, he agreed that it was best. So they mounted and set off long the sands for Ethiehaven.

There the sight of the ten longships beached helped to relegate the thoughts of enticing womanhood towards the back of his mind meantime. Would it be possible, he wondered, to raise a scratch crew now, at short notice, and to sail south in one of the craft, so much more effective than going in a fishing-boat? Fenella said that this had been in her own mind, and thought it practical. Inshore fishermen were apt to set out on their day's work early in the morning, and often be back by noon, to dig bait, repair nets and lines, and help their womenfolk with cleaning, preparing and smoking the catch. So there might well be a sufficiency of men available.

This proved to be so, even though Donnie the Crab was not there to act the skipper. And there was no reluctance to take part and to go and show those dullards at Auchmithie what was what.

So one of the vessels was launched, and Cormac at the helm and Fenella in the bows, fully manned with twenty-four crew, the sweeps were pushed out. There was little wind, but what there was came from the south, so it would be oar-work going and sail coming back.

Auchmithie was fully five miles away, and though there were two lesser havens on the way, Cuthile and Rumness, these were too small to provide full crews for longships, so it was agreed that Auchmithie should be approached first, and the men there left to enroll volunteers from these others; that is, if they were prepared so to commit themselves. Fenella had already spoken to them, to be sure, and met with no pronounced opposition.

The Angus coast was a harsh and rocky one, save for the splendid sandy Lunan Bay, and after Red Head it was all cliffs and bluffs, reefs and skerries, mile upon mile, the two small havens Fenella had mentioned mere sheltered indentations in the crags. And Auchmithie itself, when they got there, was no better as a harbour, with a notably steep and narrow pebble beach, so narrow that there was no room for the village itself, the houses having to be set up on the cliff-top one hundred and fifty feet above the shore, with a steep track up and down, no easy access. Yet it was as large a community as Usan, which said something for the hardihood and determination of its fishermen.

Some of these were at their nets when the longship drew in, and greeted the visitors well enough, especially once the Thane of Glamis was identified. Informed that their Mormaor Connacher was interested in this anti-Viking initiative and urging his people to support it, these declared themselves prepared to co-operate. One of their number went off up the cliff track to bring down others of his fellows from the village above, while the remainder listened to Cormac and Fenella explaining something of the project and the problems of handling these longships, but their excellences once the difficulties were mastered.

In due course quite a bevy of men descended the track to them, some women with them to see what went on. Altogether they made a sufficiency to form all but a full crew. So they were divided into two groups, one lot on board the longship with half of the Ethiehaven men for a demonstration exercise at the sweeps, while the remainder of the two parties watched from the shore, saw the mishaps, and were given verbal instructions. Then the second grouping took over the ship.

All this took time, and the Ethiehaven people had to return northwards. It was agreed that another longship for the new crew should be brought down in a day or two. Also that the Auchmithie men should go up to Rumness and Cuthile to try to raise volunteers there likewise. Satisfied, the move was made up-coast, the breeze behind them now, and sail hoisted.

That evening at bedtime, when Fenella checked that all was in order in Cormac's room, no fire needed now, nor warming-pan, but hot water steaming in a tub and honey wine and oatcakes by the bed, the man took her arm to detain her.

"This has been an especial day," he declared. "One that I shall always remember."

"Yes. The Auchmithie men were helpful," she agreed. "We shall have to try Aberbrothack and Callinheugh next."

"That was not what I meant," he said. "It was . . . you! Seeing you, as, as you are! You, not just your clothing! It was . . . beyond all. A, a wonder."

"Was I so wonderful, Cormac? So different from other women you have seen? We females are much alike!"

"You were, you *are*, beyond all in beauty! A dream

of loveliness. Not, not that I have seen many women unclothed. But . . ."

"Ah, perhaps I was immodest? Shameless?"

"You were divine!" he said simply.

"That might not be how my father would put it!"

"Your father, yes." He was silenced.

"My mother might well be less . . . critical."

"She, your lady mother, sees me more kindly?"

"Oh, she likes you well, Cormac. You must have seen that? It was not *you* I was meaning, as to my father. But myself."

"M'mm. And does that concern you?"

"No-o-o. So long as you do not deem me improper? Brazen?"

"I deem you utterly desirable, Fenella nic Aidan."

"Ha – desirable! There is the trouble, no? Desire! Have I done that? Aroused desire in a man? Unworthily. That would be shameful indeed. To provoke, when, when . . ."

"Woman, you have aroused desire in me from the first day I saw you! Think you that I am some cold-blooded fish! One of your flounders! I tell you, you are the most desirable of women, clad or unclad!" He pulled her to sit down on the bed. "Have I not made that clear to you, ere this?" And he put his arms around her, to cup her breasts.

"Desirable, Cormac? Is that . . . all?"

"All? *You* are all! All in all to me. Have you not known it? For long, now. All. I want you, need you, ache for you! I have loved you with all my heart. Loved you!"

"Love! Oh, Cormac, love! You have said it. Said that word. Never before . . ."

"I, I . . . my dear! Was it not evident? That I loved you? You must have known it, felt it? All we have done together . . ."

"I knew, yes, that you liked me well enough. But, but love is different." She turned her face up, to kiss and be kissed.

They clung to each other, there, wordless for long moments, emotions too great for speech, she seemingly as moved as he was.

It was the man who found the need for words first. "My dear, my heart, here is joy, joy! But what is to become of us? You and myself?"

"Become of us? What mean you, Cormac?"

"I mean, our lives. I would have it, our *life*! But that may not be, I fear?"

"Our life? You are saying . . .?"

"That I would wed you, my beloved – *wed*! Make you mine, for ay! But . . ."

"You are asking me to marry you? Yes?"

"Scarce that. Since I fear that it is not to be. But, dear God, would it were! Would it were possible."

"And you deem that it is not?"

"Think you that your father would allow it, girl?"

"He does not mislike you, Cormac. Even though he is not a man for our ventures and the fighting. Even, perhaps, your swimming in my company!"

"It is not that. It is your place, your position in this realm. You cannot but see it? He is a mormaor's son, brother of Connacher. And Connacher has no child. If Connacher died, then the Lord Aidan is his heir. And *he* has only you as heir. There is none other near kin, none that could inherit the mormaordom of Angus. If you wed, and have a son, that child would be the mormaor, one of the seven lesser kings of Scotland. I am not of that degree, that ranking."

"You are Thane of Glamis."

"That is different. The High King could remove me from that. It is a royal appointment, hereditary only so long as the Ard Righ approves. Mormaors are otherwise. Much more lofty. Electors of the High King. They cannot be displaced. Slain, perhaps, but not replaced by other than a son or daughter's son. So . . ."

"You think, then, that I must marry higher? Some mormaor's son?"

"I fear that your father will so see it."

"Yet my cousin Fenella's husband was the Thane of the Mearns. And she was Connacher's daughter and Father's niece."

"Aye, but she had two brothers to succeed to the mormaordom. You have not. If you have a son, one day he will be Mormaor of Angus. Unless Connacher produces a son in his old age. So, I fear, I greatly fear . . ."

"And have *I* naught to say about it? I am my own woman – thus far!"

"Your father spoke much with MacBeth, I saw. Now he *is* a mormaor's son. And he was taken with you, that I could see."

"MacBeth? I liked him also, yes. But not as I like you, *love* you, Cormac!"

"You would? Would indeed wed me, then, lass? If it was possible? Permitted? You would?"

"Think you that I would be sitting here, in your room, on your bed, you fondling my breasts, if I would not, Thane of Glamis?"

He held her the closer. "My dear, my dear! But you are not your father! And young women, although they may know their own minds, as do you, can be overruled by their sires. Especially high-born ones. This of MacBeth does worry me."

"But not *me*. I would refuse to wed MacBeth. I will speak with my mother." She rose. "My love, I think that we have talked sufficiently for this night! My parents' room is next my own. They will know that I am still . . . otherwhere! And also, perhaps wise to go? Lest we . . . misbehave! Enough misbehaviour for one day! No?"

He did not protest, for once, even by inference. What he had learned and gained this night was sufficient for any man. He would go over and over it all in his mind before he slept – and try not to let the Lord Aidan's reaction spoil it all for this night, at least.

They hugged and kissed nevertheless a little more, before Fenella was escorted to his door.

* * *

In the morning they were preparing to go back to Ethiehaven to arrange a visit down to Aberbrothick and Carlinheugh, Fenella presumably not having yet had opportunity for any discussion with her mother, when Pate the Mill arrived at Red Castle, having ridden since dawn. The Lady Ada had sent him with dire news. Gillacomgain, Mormaor Finlay's nephew, had slain his own uncle, burning him to death in his own hall at Inverness, and proclaimed himself Mormaor of Moray, one step nearer the high kingship. MacBeth had not been present or he presumably would have died also. He had been up in Easter Ross, seeking to limit the Danish invasion there. So there would be more trouble in the realm, grim trouble. Cormac should return home at once. Connacher might well call on him to muster and lead troops.

Appalled, they considered these tidings. First Dungal the Ard Righ's son. Now Finlay, the most powerful of the mormaors. Who next, on Gillacomgain's way to the throne? Scotland, poor Scotland, when murder seemed to be how its governance was decided!

Cormac had no option but to say farewell to his beloved and her parents, and head off up the Lunan Water for Strathmore, leaving so much in doubt behind him.

17

Cormac called in at Forfar Castle on his way home, and found that Connacher had indeed sent to Glamis for him to appear, along with his other chieftains and lordlings. The mormaor was much perturbed, needless to say. King Kenneth, it was reported, was in a state of mixed fury and alarm. He called a meeting of mormaors at Forteviot, in four days time. Meanwhile there had been developments, good and less good. MacBeth mac Finlay had declared himself rightful Mormaor of Moray, despite Gillacomgain's assumption of that title, but also Mormaor of Ross. This was just possible, for Moray and Ross was the only dual mormaordom of the kingdom, making it the largest, Ross being even bigger than Moray, with its great West Highland areas, although less populous. So now MacBeth could fill a role as a mormaor despite Gillacomgain. Connacher expected him to be at Forteviot, if he could reach there in time. Gillacomgain was not likely to present himself, in the circumstances. How the meeting would deal with the situation remained to be seen; for the other word was that King Kenneth's nephew Malcolm was supporting Gillacomgain, strange as this might appear.

Bemused and alarmed by this tangle of ambitions and relationships, Cormac headed for Glamis.

His mother, foreseeing the need, had commanded the assembling of the thanedom's manpower, or some of it. Connacher had wanted quite a major turn out of his strength in case of conflict developing at Forteviot. Pate and Duncan saw to the completion of the muster.

A couple of days later, then, it was south-west for Fortrenn, the royal terrain, with a force of eight hundred men, one hundred of them from Glamis, Donald of the Mearns and Dunninald contributing their quotas. Connacher was as uncommunicative as usual, but he did tell them that he assessed Malcolm to be backing Gillacomgain meantime merely as an aid in bringing down his uncle, the High King, whereafter he would use all the powers of the realm to deal with this up-jumped rival. This meeting of mormaors was going to be a difficult and significant one, with Kenneth unpopular and the future uncertain indeed, loyalties tested.

At Forteviot a great host was already gathered, Connacher not being the only one who had judged a show of strength advisable. All the mormaors save Sutherland, the furthest distant, were already present, although MacBeth had not appeared – nor, to be sure, Gillacomgain himself. A tense atmosphere prevailed, King Kenneth clearly an anxious man. Malcolm, his nephew, was not a mormaor, and not expected to put in an appearance.

Next day MacBeth did arrive, together with the Sutherland mormaor, but not with any large train. So the assembly was complete, if MacBeth was accepted as representing Moray as well as Ross.

That young man was well greeted by the other mormaors, sympathies clearly in his favour. Cormac sought him out so soon as he might, amongst all those lofty ones, to express his sorrow over Finlay's terrible death, and to hope that the assassin Gillacomgain would be put down, and MacBeth's succession to Moray as well as Ross would be quickly established.

"My cousin is a very determined man," the other declared. "And if he has the backing of Malcolm mac Kenneth meantime, he will not be easy to unseat, I fear."

"All here will support *you*, I think."

"Perhaps. But how fully? The Ard Righ Kenneth is not well thought of. His nephew Malcolm is more so. And a deal younger. The mormaors may well look to the future. If Malcolm is to become High King they will not wish to side against him now. And he is supporting Gillacomgain. Later, who knows, since these two both desire the throne?"

"It is difficult, yes. But I judge that at present you will be favoured . . ."

This proved to be the correct estimate. The conference of mormaors decided unanimously to support MacBeth and condemn Gillacomgain, denying him any claim to Moray. Malcolm's position was left in abeyance. This was satisfactory, so far as it went.

One decision taken was important for Cormac. His longship initiative had been praised by all, and it was argued that he should muster his fullest strength in the craft and take them up to the Moray Firth, there not so much to deal with further Danish raiding but to help MacBeth unseat Gillacomgain at Inverness, a very different mission, and one over which Cormac was doubtful. Assailing Vikings was one matter, but attacking his fellow Scots was another, however misguided. But he could not refuse a directive, backed by the High King; and besides, he would wish to aid his friend.

It seemed that no other provision had been made to assist MacBeth, presumably for fear of provoking Malcolm. It was to be left to himself and the Thane of Glamis, with possibly some help from Sutherland. Connacher was seemingly not contributing any men to the enterprise, presumably well enough content to claim merit for the initiative of one of his people without himself risking the offence of Malcolm. That perhaps typified the state of the kingdom in general.

Cormac and MacBeth held their own conference later. The latter pointed out that Inverness was a strong citadel on the very neck of land where the Moray Firth joined the Beauly Firth and the River Ness entered salt water. It would be possible to get the longship fleet right to the outskirts of the township; so a conjoined attack by land and sea was to be considered. He would bring down a force from Ross, possibly with Sutherland's aid, to assail the citadel from the north, or rather from the west, for the inner Beauly Firth had to be got round, a dozen miles of it. His own present base was at Munlochy, five miles north into Ross at the head of the long Munlochy Bay, all but a little firth of its own. If Cormac was to sail his longships up there and meet him for a decision as to tactics and timing, that would be best. Say in two weeks' time? He would require to get his own forces assembled, and hopefully Cathail of Sutherland's, or some of them. Would that give Cormac time to assemble his ships and further train his new crews?

Cormac judged that it probably would. The sailing up, all of the over two hundred miles of it, would not take so very long, if this south-west breeze maintained. That ought to give them time to make the force as effective as possible. He ought to have about fifteen longships, some more expertly manned than others. As to total troops, he could not be sure. He had one hundred with him here. He was uncertain just how many each ship could carry of extra men to the crew; that would have to be tested.

Munlochy, then, in two weeks' time; and might fortune smile on them.

Back at Glamis, Cormac left Pate to see to the arranging of the manpower of the thanedom and the bringing of them on to Lunan Bay in a week's time. He judged that almost one hundred would be as many as the longships could take. Then it was off for Red Castle.

Fenella, spotting him and Duncan afar off, came running down to meet them, and as soon as Cormac was off his horse, threw her arms around him.

"My dear, my dear!" she cried. "All is well, very well! We can wed! My father agrees. We can wed, Cormac – wed!"

He all but choked in his joyous surprise. Wagging his head he clutched her, wordless, Duncan looking on and grinning as he led the horses up to the gatehouse.

In all the excitement, Cormac omitted to tell the young woman of what was planned regarding Moray. The Lady Alena greeted him warmly and said that she was happy that soon she was going to be able to call him son. She actually kissed him. Quite overwhelmed, he was led through to the Lord Aidan's retreat, formally to ask permission to marry his daughter.

Seeking to gather his scattered wits, he went in, alone.

The older man was at his table, quill in hand. He looked up but did not rise.

"Ah, Thane Cormac," he said. "I am told that you have expressed the desire to wed my daughter. Is that correct? Not before time, if so I may say, considering how much you have been seeing of her these months!"

That had the younger man blinking. "My lord . . . I, I was afraid! To ask. Afraid that *she* would not wish it. Then that you would not permit it. I wished it, yes, desired it with all my heart. But, but could not see myself as worthy."

"Worthy? She appears to think you so. But, what sort of husband will you make for my daughter?"

"A loving one, sir. Admiring. Adoring, indeed! She is the finest woman that I have ever known."

"She is spirited, yes. Over much so, at times, I fear. And able. Headstrong, perhaps, but sound at heart. I am concerned that she has a good husband. Worthy, yes. And kind. But strong, also. She requires a strong man, see you."

"Strong? As to that, my lord, I do not know. I am . . . what I am. I have my weaknesses and failings. Like others. But I do seek to conquer them."

"She says that you are a leader of men."

"I have men to lead, yes. And to seek to lead them, in this of our longships. But that does not make me a leader."

"You sound unsure of yourself, Cormac mac Farquhar!"

"Unsure of myself as worthy to seek to wed your daughter, my lord. But not of my desire, my need, to do so."

Aidan toyed with his pen. "I have only this one child," he said. "So . . ."

"I understand, yes."

"It is to be considered. Any child of my daughter's will be destined for high places."

"I know it, yes, my lord."

"Then see you that it is not forgotten in the rearing. So be it." And he waved that quill again.

Cormac recognised that the interview was at an end. And, with a surge within him, that his trial, if that was the word for it, was also over. He could wed Fenella. Glory be – she was his!

He went in search of her.

He did not have far to go. She was in the hall, awaiting him. His face told her all, and she was in his arms.

In the circumstances, it was some time before Cormac got round to telling her of the ordered Moray expedition. This had her searching his features.

"Warfare, again! And so soon? Must we? Oh, Cormac, must we? When, when we are . . ."

"I fear so, my love. The Ard Righ and the mormaors order it. And MacBeth needs it. But it need not be for very long, see you. In two weeks to be there. If we are going to oust Gillacomgain we shall do it in a few days, I think – or not at all. So, a month, perhaps? And then . . ."

"Then, if you are still safe, well, not wounded, even slain! But that must not be, *will* not be! For I will see to it to be sure!"

"Never fear, I will take good care of myself. I have now so much to lose, my wife-to-be."

"So you say! But I will see that you do. I will have no victim for a husband! I will keep watch on you, Cormac mac Farquhar."

"You will have to be content with my word, lass; for you are not coming with me this time."

"Who says so?"

"I do. This is war. Not just dealing with raiders."

"I go. You are not my husband yet, to order what I shall do and may not do!"

"But, girl, it is no task for women, any women."

"It is a task for *me*. I helped make this fleet, did I not? The crews are mine, or my father's not yours. You cannot stop me going with them."

He shook his head over her. "What am I for marrying? A female dragon!"

"I told you that I was my own woman! I will be yours also, in due course. But in this I am resolved. If you take the longships to Moray, I go also."

"This, this is not how I thought that we would be celebrating our betrothal!"

"No? Poor Cormac! But I will make up for it! Presently. You will not regret your choice of wife! So now what?"

He all but shook her by her shapely shoulders. "Would that we should go swimming! But I judge that we require to go to Ethiehaven, to warn them there. And to see to the further training. Also, to be sure, the other havens."

"Yes. But the sea will wait for us! Who knows, we may find opportunity . . ."

That they did then, riding with Duncan along to the village, Cormac proud to see the prospect of the nine longships beached there beside the fishing-craft. It being afternoon, most of the crewmen were back from their fishing, and on being told of the forthcoming sally northwards again, none showed any disinclination. One of the ships, they learned, had been taken down to Auchmithie for their use and practice there. Fully crewing nine longships from Ethiehaven was not possible, so another vessel should be allotted to Auchmithie, and one more to each of Boddin and Usan. For this venture it might be possible to make use of some of the extra men being carried north as fighters, for although not fishers they at least had arms and muscles, and if one was placed on each sweep between two trained oarsmen, they could aid in the rowing. Moreover, this project was not intended to assail Vikings but to act as besiegers of Inverness's citadel; so less masterly handling of the vessels might be called for. Admittedly they might come across some raiders, but such would be unlikely to attack a fleet of not far off a score of ships.

All this arranged for, the trio turned back to ride north again for Dysart, Boddin and Usan, on similar errand. The Dysart folk informed that they were contributing half a crew to the Boddin ships, welcome news. At Usan they found something like enthusiasm, Father Ferchar a source of encouragement and Ian the Wright nearing completion of his longship. All was duly organised there, and Duncan was left to assist in the readying process.

It was on the way back, in the warm June early evening, that Fenella pointed to a little sandy cove below cliffs perhaps a mile east of Dunninald, between Boddin Point and a projection which she called Black Jack.

"A swim down there would freshen us after all our riding in this heat, no?" she suggested. "No folk are apt to be about here at this hour."

Cormac was not backwards in agreeing.

Tethering their mounts to a stunted hawthorn, they picked their way down the steep bank to the inlet. No dunes here, only a stretch of some thirty yards of sand hemmed in by rocks.

"No hiding-place," the young woman remarked, but nowise distressfully. "We will just have to look each the other way."

"Why?" he asked, boldly.

"Why, indeed? Before long, we shall be used to a sight of each other unclad, no doubt." She smiled, and began to kick off her riding-boots.

He did not place himself over far away from her, and set about his own disrobing. This was something new for him, actually undressing beside a woman.

She was more lightly clad than he was, and soon, blissfully naked, ran past him down to the water.

"It is warm!" she cried. "Come on, come on!" She splashed in.

He stood watching her white person as she swam out, telling himself that he was the most fortunate man in the land. What had he done to deserve this fair and spirited creature? He did not know – but he was not going to let it worry him. He plunged in and went rather more laboriously after her.

She was on her back, waiting for him, winnowing hands and paddling feet, and nothing would do but that he must go and clasp her, arms around her eminently claspable form. But this was not the gently shelving sands of Lunan Bay but a rock-bound creek, the water deepening quickly. Not realising that they were out of their depth, and with his arms otherwise occupied, down he sank, taking Fenella with him, under water.

Hastily loosing hold of her, beating hands urgently and kicking out, he propelled himself to the surface, gasping, and spewing out salt water.

When he had more or less recovered himself and was able to keep afloat, however pantingly, he found his companion nearby, laughing at him.

"I will have to teach my life's partner how to swim better than this. Amongst other things!" she said. "You do not know how to use your feet, whatever you tend to do with your arms!"

"Your . . . fault! Enticing me!" he got out. "You are . . . too beautiful! You lose a man's wits."

"Am I fated to be tied to a witless creature, then? As well to learn, in time!"

He turned, to splash back to the shore, while she swam in the other direction, seawards.

He was waiting for her, standing at the tide's edge, when she returned. "Now we shall see who requires to be taught a lesson!" he exclaimed, and stooped to pick her up bodily in his arms and carry her kicking over to her clothing. He did not put her down immediately either, but started to kiss salty flesh wherever his lips could reach, she not struggling over-hard.

"I am learning fast . . . what to expect . . . when I am unclothed!" she got out. "I will have to seek to . . . avoid such state. In future."

"Your own fault," he asserted. "Made the way you are."

"I am as God made me. With a little help from my mother and father! You cannot blame *me*."

As he put her down he was very much aware that his manhood was becoming evident in more than mere muscular strength. She did not stare, but nor did she turn away.

"I think that it is time that we donned our clothing," she observed. "The trouble is, we are not dry. And there is no place here to run."

"I will dry you with my shirt," he declared. "That will serve. I have not long wet hair to trouble me."

"It matters not. I will become dry . . ."

But he was not to be discouraged in his gallantry, and set about a very comprehensive patting, rubbing and drying process, which had her protesting here and there, but not sufficiently to halt him.

When she had enough, and broke free, Fenella did not offer to do the same for him, probably wisely. She observed that his shirt was now wet anyway, so little point in drying himself. Wringing out her long, soaking wet tresses, she began to clothe herself.

"No secrets, I fear, for *our* wedding-night!" she mentioned.

"No? I think that there might be, even so!" He did turn away in some degree to pull on his breeches, with due care.

When they were fully clad, they turned to eye each other, and laughter bubbled up in both of them. Hand in hand they turned to face the climb up to their horses.

Back at the castle that night, when it was bedtime, Fenella paused at Cormac's door when he would have led her within.

"Dare I risk entering here this night?" she asked. "Probably unwise, my so eager swain! We have had sufficient clingings and clutchings for one day, no?"

"No," he said. "Never sufficient of *you*. For me. I promise not, not to . . ." He left the rest unsaid.

"A doubtful assurance, it sounds!" But she did enter with him.

"You do not . . . mislike my attentions?"

"Mislike? No. No, I but concern myself that we may go too far! Too soon."

He did not fail to note that she had said we, not you, and was the more heartened. "How far is too far?" he wondered.

"On that beach we went . . . far enough, I would say. And your bedroom is more tempting than any open beach."

He nodded. They were at the bedside now, and she sat down without any pressure from him. "Never fear, lass," he assured. "You have my word. But you must help me!"

"I will try to," she said, as she came into his arms.

For a while the kissing and hugging sufficed, but presently his urgent hands began to stray and press and probe. She stroked his cheek, silent.

"This is where I need the help," he told her.

"I would have thought that . . . you knew your way by now!" And she loosened her bodice so that his hand could slip inside to fondle and caress.

"That is not what I meant," he declared, with something like a groan.

"No? Ah, I see. I am sorry. Shall I . . . ?" And she made to draw in the gap in her gown again.

"No. Oh, no – let it be, my heart. I will hold myself. As well as you!"

"Dear Cormac! Are all men and women, when in love, like this?"

"Some, I reckon, will . . . be more so!"

"Perhaps . . ."

"But all women are not so winsome as you are."

But when his hand, from stroking the firming tip of her breast, slipped down over the warm, smooth skin to her navel, she did offer her help, the sort of help he required if scarcely desired. She reached for that hand, and raised it higher again.

"I think . . . safer above than below," she said. "Indeed, safer still if *I* was below, in my own room, having come this far. One last kiss, my heart, and then . . ." Patting his cheek, she added, "You will thank me, one day."

"No doubt." That was scarcely hearty agreement.

So there was the end of a notable day. Was it always like this, Cormac himself wondered, as she had done, hungry for love, for more, unappeased? For the sake of what? The priests' precepts? Was that sufficient decree? Fenella appeared to deem it so. Then, so be it. Until, until . . .!

18

It was on the fifth day of July, the Eve of St Palladius, that the fleet set out, fifteen longships leaving Ethiehaven, a notable sight, with five more to be picked up at Boddin and Usan, Fenella in the leading craft. Father Ferchar did not accompany them on this occasion, apparently drawing the line at being involved in warfare against fellow Christians, pagan Danes and killers being a different matter. The vessels were all now crowded, of course, with the extra fighting men from Strathmore, these not necessarily popular with the rowers.

Unfortunately such wind as there was came now from the east, so that it was mainly sweep-work, the sails only being of use for occasional tacking. But all were in good heart, the crews vying with each other in handling their vessels, scorn being expressed for the less experienced by the more so.

Cormac knew a very real pride in leading this impressive array of ships, the fruition of a mere notion he and Fenella had had all those months ago. Admittedly he had never thought of them being used other than against the Norse raiders; but their presence on this occasion might assist in bringing peace, and an end to terror and violence in the north, as well as helping his friend MacBeth. He had now no reason to feel apprehensive about MacBeth's association, the saints be praised!

Lacking the following wind, they did not make such good time of it as formerly, and with some of the crews less than expert and tending to fall behind, which occasioned some difficulty for Cormac in keeping his flotilla together. Eventually he appointed Donnie the Crab as a sort of whipper-in, stationing his craft at the rear to round up stragglers.

So that day they did not get so far as hoped for, these long sweeps being very tiring on the arms, and the oarsmen wearying. By the time that they reached the Ythan mouth, Cormac decided that it was enough; the last thing that he wanted was to sicken the new crews. But they did go on a little further, for he was well aware that the sight of a fleet of Viking ships coming in to land would terrify the local population. So they rowed for another mile or two along the Balgownie shore to where the Black Dog Burn entered the sea, and there beached their vessels for the night, with fresh water, wood for fires, and no houses in sight. Fed after a fashion, and wrapped in plaids, they settled for the night, Cormac lying close to Fenella, and able at least to hold her hand until they slept.

It took them until early afternoon next day to cover the forty miles further north to pass Buchan Ness, the most easterly point of all Scotland, and on, to turn westwards round the mighty Kinnaird Head. And now they had the wind behind them, at last, and could draw in the sweeps and leave the sails to carry them on, and at better speed. They had still some eighty miles to go into the Moray Firth, but Cormac reckoned that they ought to be able to reach familiar territory at Garmouth on Spey Bay by nightfall. So the next day should see them at Munlochy, near the mouth of the Beauly Firth, soon after noon. After that, it was up to MacBeth.

Apart from frequently passing fishing-boats, no other sea-going craft were seen on that voyage, no rival longships.

The Moray Firth, wide indeed at its mouth, narrowed in notably to a mere three miles where the great peninsula known as Eilean Dubh, or the Black Isle, projected; and here, at the sudden narrowing, the River Ness entered on the south side, the capital of Moray situated there under its citadel. And a mere four miles to the north opened Munlochy Bay. Their fleet was bound to be seen at Inverness as they crossed. Would Gillacomgain, who almost certainly would have heard of the Thane of Glamis's initiative, guess that this was aid coming to MacBeth? Or would he assume that it was more Viking invaders?

Munlochy Bay proved to be misnamed, not really a bay at all but a sea loch, all but a little firth of its own, less than half a mile wide at its mouth but probing almost three miles inland. Into this the vessels sailed, new territory for them all.

They had no difficulty in finding MacBeth's base, for a little way inland near the head of the loch, a rath or defensive hallhouse within a palisade crowned the tip of a grassy ridge, very prominent. And further identifying it was the large encampment spread over the slopes below, men, many men, gathered there, smoke from cooking-fires rising into the air. Presumably these were not alarmed at the sight of a Viking fleet heading in for them, for MacBeth would surely have told all that the Thane of Glamis was expected.

As they drew close to the shore they saw a group of horsemen riding down towards them, followed by a straggling crowd of men on foot, MacBeth come to welcome his friends.

There was much acclaim and hailing as the ships' prows were driven up on the weed-hung, pebbly beach, and the new mormaor rode his mount right into the shallows, to reach over and down from the saddle to pick up Fenella bodily and carry her ashore in his arms, to save her wetting her feet and skirts, amidst squeals of laughter. Cormac smiled too, reminding himself that he must promptly tell MacBeth that they were now betrothed.

There were warm greetings, and congratulations on the size of the longship fleet, larger than anticipated. This was excellent. They would teach Gillacomgain a lesson! But there was astonishment at the young woman coming with them.

Cormac and Fenella were led up to the rath of

Dunmunlochy, and arrangements made for the provision of the Angus men, much beef, oatmeal and whisky available.

When MacBeth heard of the intended marriage of his two guests, he was nowise grudging in his felicitations, declaring that he had wondered when this would come to pass, but adding that Cormac was a fortunate man indeed, and, with lifted eyebrows, that if his thaneship should happen to fall out with the bride-to-be, or even fall in battle, then her ladyship need not look far for an alternative husband!

They were introduced to Neil Nathrach, a half-brother of the new mormaor, illegitimate but obviously close, whose house this Dunmunlochy seemingly was, a dark-avised slender man, much less tall than his fair-haired brother.

That evening they discussed strategy. Gillacomgain knew, of course, that his cousin had gathered a host here to challenge him, and had summoned a still larger force to Inverness to meet the threat. But MacBeth believed that all these might well not serve him loyally. Finlay, his father, had been well liked, and his murderer would be less than assured of faithful service, calling himself Mormaor of Moray or not. The castle of Inverness was strong admittedly, but the people of its township were known not to favour their new lord. So the scales might be none so unevenly balanced.

MacBeth said that the best tactics might be thus. If the citadel was besieged and all supplies cut off, it could not hold out for very long. It crowned a steep bluff, yes; but the townsfolk could prevent food and drink from reaching it at most points. The river was the problem. It was wide there at its mouth, flowing out of Loch Ness, and it curved in close below the castle at two points. Boats, therefore, could come down from the loch, by night, with supplies, and the local folk not be able to intercept them. That is where the longships would be invaluable. They could form a chain and bar any access.

But before that, to be sure, they would have to deal with Gillacomgain's mustered host. How best to attempt this? The force was much too large to occupy the castle. So it was based around, much of it in the township itself. To stage an assault on the community would entail much hurt to the people there, loss, damage, bloodshed. And no certainty of winning the day, with attack from the castle above a menace. Best if they could coax the enemy out, to battle, this if possible on the open, level ground on the south side of the river mouth. Here again the ships would be of great value to ferry all the men over. The strategy would be to deceive, to be seen to have only a small portion of their host over, most still to come. So in darkness, ferry a large part of the host over, the previous night, these to hide in the scattered woodland there. Then, openly, to bring the rest across, in the hope that this would provoke an attack in force by Gillacomgain, with the hidden troops coming out to assail his rear, in surprise. Did that seem wise, effective?

Cormac agreed that it sounded so. But what if the enemy force did not move out to them? Remained in the town?

Then they would just have to wait, MacBeth said, the longships blockading the citadel from the river. In time Gillacomgain would have to come and fight. But, being the man he was, and with a large force, he almost certainly would not delay in meeting the challenge.

When, then? When to start this offensive?

Right away, they were told. That very night, if possible. These July nights were short, only six or seven hours of darkness. So the ferrying would have to be speedy. They would go down this afternoon to inspect the position. It would not matter if they were observed from the citadel; they would seem to be prospecting the site for the next day – whereas it was for that night.

So presently MacBeth, Cormac, Duncan and Donnie the Crab, with Neil Nathrach, rode southwards the four miles to North Kessock, where they looked across the narrows between the firths to Inverness, only half a mile off, it seeming strange to be able to approach so close without danger. Gazing over, they could see quite an area of level ground, cattle-dotted, clearly the town's common grazing, with trees and bushes, possibly a square mile of it. Cormac wondered that the enemy were not using it for the encampment of their own troops; but MacBeth said that ground at the other side of the town was being used for this, that being the way any attack would be expected to come from the north, having to work round the head of the Beauly Firth, as would be necessary without ferrying.

Cormac surveyed the shoreline here to see where his ships could best operate, and perceived no difficulties. They calculated that for the short half-mile row, each longship could carry across some thirty men at a time. Their score of craft then could take, say, six hundred. So taking their own Strathmore men first, they could ferry MacBeth's first thousand or so quite quickly, leaving a mere four hundred to be moved over openly next day, this smaller number hopefully tempting Gillacomgain to attack.

They returned to Dunmunlochy.

Waiting until darkness, the larger section of MacBeth's force set off to march for the river mouth. The Angus contingent reboarded their ships and rowed down the loch again to the Moray Firth, and so southwards, a longer journey, double the distance. There was no real problem in finding their way, despite the gloom, for once out of Munlochy Bay they had only to skirt the shoreline south by west till the obvious narrowing of the firth, and there found the host of Ross men awaiting them, MacBeth and his half-brother included.

The loading-in process commenced at once, MacBeth and Neil going over with the first groups, to inspect the terrain beyond and ensure that hiding-places were adequate, possibly the most difficult part of the night's work. Fortunately they found an area at the southern side of the Kessock projection – it was scarcely a peninsula – where there were sand-dunes formed by the winds off the sea, and these would give ample cover for any number of men.

Leaving Neil Nathrach in charge of the hiding hundreds, they returned, to find the ferrying over; and it was back to Munlochy for a brief sleep.

In the morning, it was a repetition of the night-time procedure, the march down of the remaining men, around four hundred, and the rowing of the longships, this all now openly, and inevitably obvious to all at the citadel of Inverness. The business of ferrying the men over the narrows was carried out with much to-do deliberately, to make it very clear to watchers as to numbers involved. And when all were over to the Kessock shore, the ships drew off again seawards, to disappear from view round a small headland on the north shore, called Craigton apparently, where, out of sight of Inverness, they lay to meantime, the intention being that they would be thought to be going back to Munlochy for further troops, this to encourage Gillacomgain to attack swiftly before any reinforcements arrived. The crews' contribution would come presently, it was hoped, Duncan and Donnie left in command.

Cormac stayed with MacBeth and the four hundred.

They marched on southwards, in no particular formation, to a point some six hundred yards from the bluff-top citadel, and there went through the motions of preparing for battle, forming groups, cutting down bushes and tree branches to form barricades of a sort, all with much shouting, and all the time their leaders watching for reaction from the enemy.

They did not have long to wait. From the castle's gatehouse issued a group of horsed men, a quite small company. These did not move far down, but halted, delaying. But only for a few minutes. Then round both sides of the citadel men came afoot, large numbers of men now, group after group. The mounted party came down to join them.

Now it was time for MacBeth's tactical moves. As though

alarmed at the size of the approaching host, he ordered his four hundred to edge back, and keep on edging back, deserting their barricades. This brought on the enemy the faster, as its two great sections joined, and being led by the horsemen.

Timing now was highly important, vital, for the Munlochy men. Precipitate flight in the face of vastly greater numbers would not do, or it would all become a mere chase and rabble. The foe must be coaxed onward sufficiently far, without suspecting any trap. Back towards the sand-dune area they withdrew, the enemy getting close indeed, and shouting slogans and war cries now. It was to be hoped that Neil Nathrach was fully alert and ready to play his part; also Duncan and Donnie and the ships.

There was a sort of wide indentation in the sand-hill line, and in towards this MacBeth and Cormac backed their retreating folk, thus far without a blow having been struck, their foes now jeering and mocking as they came on; for of course the retreat could not go on much longer, with salt water just beyond those dunes. Cormac, for one, was in a state of anxiety. Mere minutes could dictate the difference between success and disaster.

It was the longships which signalled a change in the situation. The score of them emerged from behind Craigton Point, and, with only half a mile of water to cross, the yells of their crews drew the required enemy attention to this very obvious threat on their left flank. Gillacomgain may have assumed, to be sure, that these were merely coming to try to uplift the retiring Rossmen, to escape. There was no slow-down of the advance.

Then, from the other side, the east, came the major impact. Out from the cover of the dunes surged Neil's thousand men, brandishing swords, axes and spears.

So, suddenly, all was changed. The enemy force might not be outnumbered, but it was outflanked, unexpectedly threatened on three sides, front, east and west. Consternation and uncertainty was very evident. MacBeth, waving his sword high, changed retreat into advance with ringing cries.

Gillacomgain could have perhaps saved the day had he been prepared for a defensive rather than an attacking role. His people, formed into a great square, or groups of squares, with spears projecting before them like giant hedgehogs, could have faced and possibly held an assault, and made the attackers pay a heavy price for any victory. But that did not develop. Not a few of his men were probably less than eager to give their lives for the man who had murdered their Mormaor Finlay, and it may have been such who initiated a move back. With the crews now landing from the ships and beginning to advance also, at the run, this enemy retiral quickly became not exactly a rout but a very pronounced retreat, the leadership ignored, and this before any real battle was joined. Some clash did take place, but it was on a relatively minor scale considering the numbers involved. The fact was, of course, that almost all those involved were fellow countrymen with no hatred of each other, the entire conflict lacking the necessary spur for determined fighting.

After some futile shoutings and wavings, Gillacomgain and his leaders saw that recovery was impossible. They turned and spurred back to the bluff and on up to the citadel.

Seldom could there have been a battle with so few casualties. The crews from the longships had not even become engaged.

MacBeth did not order his people to pursue the men fleeing back to the township; no point in that. Gillacomgain was the enemy, not these. He was going to hold the citadel, apparently, so that must be their objective now. Siege. This had been foreseen should the initial battle be successful. Now to operate their plans.

The Munlochy force was divided up, most to surround the castle hill, some to base themselves in the town itself, and the longships to form their chain in the River Ness to prevent supplies reaching the besieged, especially by night.

So all this was set in order. Full crews were not required on the ships, and the Angus men would take their turns at manning the vessels, the rest joining MacBeth's people in their various duties. That man, with Cormac, and some others, went to occupy a house in the town which his mother had used when she tired of the restrictions of citadel living.

In comfort, then, and not a little pleased with themselves, they all settled down to wait.

They had five easy, idle days and nights there at Inverness, with no incidents to cause concern or indeed activity other than the necessary collection of food for all their men, and checking that all was well with the ring of besiegers; also having scouts and guards placed at various far-out points to ensure that no help for Gillacomgain came upon them unawares.

After two days, with no developments, it was thought safe for Fenella to be fetched down from Dunmunlochy to join them in the townhouse, she having been kept informed as to the positions meantime, and sending demands to be allowed to do so. Her escorted arrival added to the satisfaction and indeed the sense almost of unreality of the situation, so utterly lacking in any warlike atmosphere, more of holiday than military endeavour. Cormac rejoiced in her company as, clearly, did MacBeth.

It was on the sixth day that a man was brought to the mormaor, one whom he knew, the head cook from the citadel. He came with news. Gillacomgain had slipped away the previous night, dressed in servant's clothing, and so clad had managed to pass through the besiegers' lines without arrest. Where he was going was not known, but clearly he had accepted that he could not withstand further siege.

They considered, then. Gillacomgain might be going to try to raise another force to try to retake Inverness.

But after the débâcle here, he would find that difficult. If his host had failed him, all but deserted him, was another likely to rise for him? What would he be apt to do, then? Probably disappear into the far western Highlands to, as it were, lick his wounds meantime. That one would not give up readily, but he might need some time to recover and regain his strength and initiative. Meanwhile there might well be peace in Moray and Ross. It was to be hoped so, at any rate; and MacBeth could increase and solidify his hold on the two mormaordoms.

The Angus contingent, then, could return southwards. Loud and long were the thanks and praise accorded them, although Cormac declared that they had done really very little, however much of a show their longships had made. They would be back if required.

Homewards then, friendship demonstrated and duty done.

19

Cormac now had his own priorities, other than demonstrating the worth of longships and that fisherfolk could be fighters. Marriage was the goal, and just so soon as was possible, Fenella nothing loth. But the union of such as thanes and the heiresses of mormaors, it seemed, was not to be effected in any hurried, simple or hole-in-corner fashion. There seemed to be an endless succession of details to be settled first – succession indeed being a significant word in the matter. Apparently such heiresses could not be wed without certain conditions fulfilled. First of all, they had to have the permission and agreement of the reigning mormaor. Then the order of succession had to be decided on for offspring, male or female. A worthy and sufficient dowery property had to be provided for the bride by the groom, and duly inspected. In the event of the woman dying without offspring, her husband had to agree to sign away all interests and rights in the mortuath to the next legitimate heir, and to retire therefrom. And if the man was subject to the mormaor of another mortuath, he had to renounce all allegiance to that *ri* and commit himself entirely to his wife's sub-kingdom, this fortunately not applying to Cormac, already an Angus laird.

So much had to be settled and argued over before the wedding itself could be organised, not to mention personal concerns of the pair, much to Cormac's frustration. Connacher at least did not make any objections to the match, he having assumed for long that this would happen, and anyway tending to bask in the fame and celebrity of the longships saga initiated by one of his thanes. And it was not as though he had had any other nominee lined up for his niece.

The finding of a dowery house and land gave the couple opportunity to go touring round the Glamis properties, even though sister Bridget volunteered to accompany them on occasion to help in the choice. They settled eventually on the rath and farmery of Kinnordy, north of Kirriemuir, that remote and hilly area, beside its loch, much pleasing the bride-to-be.

The Lady Ada was much taken with her son's choice of daughter-in-law, presenting her with some of her own jewellery, but not failing to point out that if they produced two or more sons, while the first would one day become Mormaor of Angus, the second would succeed his father as Thane of Glamis. Fenella was duly impressed.

All the necessary conditions coped with at last, the marriage arrangements could finally be fixed. Although Connacher would have had his niece and heiress wed in the large monastery of Aberbrothack, the greatest church in Angus, the abbot of which was the custodian of the famous Brecbennach, or emblem, of St Columba, nothing would do for Fenella but that Father Ferchar should marry them in his little chapel near Usan, there being no religious establishment near Red Castle. This would be a strange place for a wedding such as this, but it was the bride's choice and meant something to her, more than any abbot's seat. The Lord Aidan and his wife had no complaints to make. And all the crews of their longships were to be invited to be present.

They were now into the second half of August, and it was decided that the ceremony should be held on the last day of the month, which was the Feast of St Aidan, Celtic Church Bishop of Lindisfarne, who had died three centuries earlier, this being also the Lord Aidan's birthday.

There had to be much organisation for the great day also, if all the fisherfolk were to be got up to Usan from the various havens. It was agreed that it was only suitable that the longships should be used to transport them all;

and to save Fenella's mother and father riding there, they agreed to be carried up in the vessels also, weather permitting. Since Connacher was honouring the occasion with his presence, he was invited to join them at Red Castle and also sail up, since he took an interest in the longship venture. Here was his opportunity to sample one.

The great day dawned at last, fortunately fair and warm. It being a tradition that bride and groom did not associate on the wedding day before the nuptials, Cormac spent the night in Donnie the Crab's house at Ethiehaven, Duncan and Pate the Mill being put up nearby. They would sail in different vessels from the bridal party.

Joined by the craft from Rumness and Auchmithie, amidst much excitement the Ethiehaven ships pushed off, all men dressed in their best, however humble such might be. At Red Castle, Cormac's ship stood well off, so as not to be too close to the bride's vessel; but he did see the group boarding, and managed to forbear to wave. A dozen craft, they rowed on, and, with the wind back in the south-west, were able to hoist sails to aid them, Cormac wondering how Mormaor Connacher felt sailing under the dreaded raven-painted canvas.

At Boddin they could have been joined by three more longships, one from Dysart, with Dunninald; but as Ferchar's chapel actually lay on the clifftop between Boddin and Usan, it was thought best that Cormac's craft should beach there, and with its crew and these others proceed on foot the barely a mile to the church, leaving the main fleet to go on to Usan and then approach from the north.

Great surprise awaited them at the chapel, for who should be present, with the distinctly nervous Ferchar, but MacBeth mac Finlay himself. He had been informed of the wedding date, yes, but not with any expectation that he should attend. And not only MacBeth but Donald, Thane of the Mearns. This was going to be a notable occasion, and for a small cliff-top church, remote and undistinguished.

Small wonder that Ferchar was in some agitation, with two mormaors and two thanes present.

All that company, of course, could not get into that little chapel, no larger than a cattle-shed and entirely plain, with only two wall cavities at the east end for keeping the bread and wine and the holy oil. So the ceremony would be held outside in God's open air, and only the final blessing to take place before the altar within. The Celtic Church had always been very open-air-conscious anyway, with Columba, its founder in Scotland, having deliberately adopted some of the druidical practices in his campaign to convert the sun-worshippers, even using their stone circles to contain his chapels and cells.

So Cormac waited there in the sunshine, with MacBeth, Donald and the others, a man not exactly nervous, like the priest, but tense with anticipation, the moment approaching for which he had waited for what seemed like years – or the first of the moments. There would be others.

Fenella did not exercise the bride's privilege of being late. Soon they saw the large company coming along the cliff-top track, well over one hundred strong, not only saw but heard, for they were led in triumph by two pipers and a drummer, these competing with the screaming seafowl disturbed from their ledges on the cliffs.

As they came up, Connacher and his brother not walking together, Cormac had to avoid contact with the young woman, although they did exchange glances.

Ferchar now took rather hesitant charge, somewhat in awe of at least some of the company. He kept the two groups slightly apart. Then calling for a drum-beat for due attention, mounted a louping-on stone outside his chapel, a set of steps to assist female worshippers into the saddles of their horses; and from there treated all to a short homily on the sanctity of marriage which, he declared, was symbolic of Christ's marriage with His Church. Let no man nor woman, high-born or low, forget its import and purpose.

He then called forward Cormac mac Farquhar, Thane of Glamis, with his supporters.

This Cormac was prepared for, but only just. For, not anticipating that MacBeth would be there, he had decided that Duncan the Tranter, his constant companion and friend, should be at his side, despite his humble rank; but the appearance of the Mormaor of Moray and Ross in his company, lofty associate of both groom and bride, rather complicated the issue, after he had come over one hundred miles to be present. So he had them both to support him. One on either side, they moved to the louping-on stone.

There, with all the company, great and less so, in a great semicircle watching, the priest addressed Cormac as to his responsibility before God in entering the holy estate of matrimony, briefly but tellingly.

Then he beckoned forward the bride and her father, Fenella clad simply but most attractively all in white, to symbolise virginity, and looking radiant. Still a little way apart from the men, Ferchar gave similar guidance to the bride, reminding her that she represented their Creator's primeval concern for the continuing survival of mankind, made in His own image.

The couple were then waved together, to stand side by side, and there told to take each other by the hands, this to Cormac's joy – that hand-in-marriage. He would not let go of that hand now for all the rest of his days.

That was, in fact, the theme, concept and essence of the brief ceremony which followed, hand in hand. So they were to remain, to love and cherish each other, for this life and into the next, man and woman made one by their Father in heaven. Eternal love and eternal life were God's greatest gifts to mankind. Here both were shown forth, in a new oneness made and displayed before all these witnesses. This day God created something which had not been before – let all perceive it.

So now these two were to be made one, hand holding hand. And they had been given tongues as well as hands. Use them both now, and worship, praise and promise. Both to swear their marriage vows here before all.

Cormac all but shouted his, Fenella less loud but no less gladly. They raised their still-clasped hands high, and so held them for moments.

"I now lay another hand on these two," Ferchar said, and raised his own to grip them there. "In the name of God the Father, God the Son and God the Holy Spirit, with the laying-on of hands, I, Ferchar, God's humblest servant, name you one, man and wife. Take each the other."

Most willingly they came now into each other's arms, while all the company shouted acclaim. On and on went the praise, the drum-beat joining it.

When the acclamation died away, Ferchar led bride and groom, with their supporters and intimates, into the chapel, where they knelt before the altar to receive the oil of gladness, in the form of the Cross, on their brows. The benediction followed, and then it was outside again to receive the further benediction of all in congratulations, good wishes and felicitations.

There followed a surprise. Aidan, or more properly his wife, had arranged for a dinner for the happy couple and a few others, little as Red Castle was used to providing festive meals. But now it transpired that Ferchar, Ian the Wright and others of the Usan community had organised a wedding feast on their own, a great spread of beef and mutton and roe-venison, of fish and lobsters, of porridge and cream, of soups, mushrooms, of ale and whisky, plenteous enough for all and to spare, a major effort. This was to be partaken of before the cottages of the Seatown, with the women and children all taking part. So northwards along the cliff-tops all now paraded behind the pipers and drum, a lengthy procession, for the track was narrow and winding. Surely never had that rugged seaboard witnessed the like.

Settled between the village and the drying nets, no speeches were made at that feasting, for which Cormac at least was thankful, since he would have had to answer anything such; anyway, so great was the noise and general jollity that little would have been heard. Connacher, and indeed his brother, not used to the like, sat throughout in some unease, but all there clearly enjoyed the occasion, doing full justice to the provision.

When those with the more moderate appetities had had a sufficiency, it was Fenella who rose from her bench and went over to call on the pipers and drummer and ask them to strike up their music for dancing, there on the cropped, shell-scattered turf. Nothing loth, the instrumentalists obliged. When the skirling strains of a reel resounded, and Cormac jumped up to partner his wife, Fenella waved him away imperiously, and went to dip a slight curtsey before MacBeth instead, and offered him her arm. Laughing, he rose, waved over to his friend, and the pair led the dance, to the delighted cheers of the company. Cormac, pulling a face, went to his new mother-in-law and escorted her out in more sedate fashion, she murmuring that he would have a task in proving himself the master of her wayward daughter, now made one as they might be.

With the reel ended and another dance commencing, Cormac now sought out his recent hostess, Donnie the Crab's wife, to wait on; so it was Fenella's turn to toss her red head and go seek the still-dining Donald of the Mearns and lead him out. It proved to be a vigorous romp, and Donnie's plump spouse was soon breathless; and so at the necessary pause, sought relief and a seat. Thane Donald, seeing the bridegroom left on his own, smilingly led Fenella over to him, and bowing, handed her to her husband for the remainder of this cantrip.

"So, there is no escape for me!" she sighed. "I am now to be tied to Cormac mac Farquhar foot as well as hand!"

"Did you not vow it, woman! For all your days, here and hereafter. Too late to repine now." Arm encircling her, he stepped out. She did not hold back now, indeed she squeezed his arm lovingly.

Presently it was time to depart, and all the Usan visitors trooped down to the longships amidst much ado, and still to musical accompaniment. Farewells and cheers resounded as they put to sea.

Back at Red Castle, further feasting was scarcely desirable. Moreover it was now late in the evening, and Cormac for one had other preoccupations, and was not slow in communicating them to his wife. She tapped him on the arm, and observed that they must not fail in courtesy and hospitality towards guests; to which he answered that the guests here were her mother's and father's, not theirs. However, MacBeth soon announced that he claimed the privilege of conducting the newly-weds to the bridal chamber, whichever that might be – and no one contested that. So it was goodnights fairly promptly, the Lady Alena giving her daughter an especial embrace and caring murmurs before the three younger ones went off to mount the stairs.

Fenella paused at her own room door, and innocently asked whether Cormac would prefer to share the upper chamber that night with his friend who had travelled so far to be with him? Or was that extending the courtesies too far? To which her husband replied by pushing MacBeth towards the further stairs in no uncertain fashion – no way to treat a mormaor.

Alone together at last, and the door shut behind them, Cormac took his bride in his arms and all but shook her.

"My dear, my dear!" he exclaimed. "So long to wait! Long. Endless! And now, now . . . !"

"Aye – now?" she echoed. "Now I am at your mercy, no? Delivered up. Will you *be* . . . merciful? Or, or . . . ?"

"What mean you by merciful?"

"Just that this, now, is new to me. All new. In your hands, as well as your arms. All . . . unversed as I am. A woman lacking in experience. No longer my own mistress. So, at your mercy, indeed!"

"What mercy do you seek of me, girl?"

She gave a little laugh. "That is the trouble. I do not know! Just your loving care. As you teach me . . ."

"Teach? Think you that I have had other wedding nights?"

"No-o-o. But do not tell me that you have not bedded with other women – you, the Thane of Glamis!"

"Not so. Bedded, no. I have had, had exchanges, with the farm and village girls. In the hay. Or behind some bush. But that is . . . different. This is all as new to me as it is to you, lass."

"I doubt that. Not your word, but the lack of . . . knowledge."

They were over at her bed now, and sat. Despite her pleas, Fenella's arms were round him, and they changed from debating to kissing. But soon male hands were busy, and Cormac freed his lips for long enough to declare that he demanded the right to undress her.

"But you have seen me naked," she protested.

"That is different. I want to unclothe you myself!"

"Then have a care for my wedding gown!"

"You will not be requiring *that* again."

Nevertheless, she helped him somewhat with the disrobing process; but again protested when, with all her sheer loveliness so close and within his grasp, he began to push her flat on the bed.

"Have *I* no rights and privileges?" she asked. And sitting up again, she commenced to undo his doublet and tug at his shirt.

That, of course, presented problems, especially when it came to his breeches, and some guidance was called for, he having to get to his feet. And while so, she rose also, and declared that it would be a pity not to use the tub of steaming water which the maid had provided for their ablutions. It had been a long and busy day, and some freshening would not go amiss, surely?

He was less eager than was she for delaying tactics, however good for them, but he went across with her to the water, a little embarrassed by his so evident physical arousal. At the tub, after he helped her to step into it, he insisted on climbing in after her. They had to stand, to be sure, for there was no room for two to sit. It was even over-close for effective washing, but Cormac was not to be denied the opportunity to attempt it, at least, his companion's person, not his own, however awkwardly, especially as he was fairly selective in the doing of it.

Fenella submitted, but when she had had enough of that she had the sense to step out of their tub before she acted the dutiful wife by washing her spouse rather more thoroughly, even though she too was heedful as to territory, if more tactfully.

The drying process was only superficial, and quickly deeming it sufficient, Cormac picked the still-damp girl up in his arms and carried her back to the bed, she a little tense now.

Cormac, urgent as he was, told himself to be gentle, caring, unhurried. And however much of an effort this was for him at first, presently he found himself to be not merely restraining himself but actually able to enjoy the delaying process, in the touching, stroking, fondling, feeling and kissing, as well as the sensual body contact itself – and best of all, in a little while the sense of response on Fenella's part, the awareness that she was reacting to his caresses.

This last, of course, had its counter-effects in that it made the man's own self-control the more difficult, and it was not long before, on top of her now, panting his need, he sought ultimate possession. Gaspingly she admitted him, and their one-ness now was completed, she committed physically at last as well as in spirit and in feelings.

The summit of fulfilment, to be sure, came to Cormac first, and with a cry he had to let nature take its course, a man spent, for the moment at least.

Fenella uttered a cry also, but it was different, questioning, doubting, all but demanding, as he rolled off her and she gripped his arm tightly, turning to gaze at him at her side, both deep-breathing.

Aware of her doubt, her need, her chaos of mind and body, he drove himself to aid her and explain.

"Give me . . . a few minutes. Only a few. I will . . . do better, lass. And it will . . . be well. With you. I promise. *You* to have the mercy now!"

"Is all . . . is all . . . well? I have not failed you?" she wondered.

"Far from it. Wait, you." His hand went down to her, as he leaned over to kiss her breasts, while she gazed up at her bed canopy, biting her lip.

He was as good as his word. In only minutes he was able to replace that hand to good effect. And now, quickly, she had no more doubts. It was not long before she was gasping again, this only to end in a cry of intense ecstasy, acclaim, consummation.

Cormac, this time, was able to prolong his attentions, to her satisfaction and his own. Eventually, after rich reward, sighing, he sank back. She stroked his chest with gentle lingering fingers, whispering endearments.

Presently they slept, bliss attained.

20

Needless to say, the happy couple were eager to be off on their own next day; and after seeing MacBeth off with his two attendants on their long ride north to Inverness, they took leave of Fenella's parents to head for Glamis. Not that they intended to stay there. Cormac had thought long over where he should take his bride after their wedding and, considering her delight in the remote, uplands dowery house of Kinnordy, he had decided that two or three days there and then excursions into the empty mountains behind, his own favourite haunts ever since boyhood, would suit the two of them. This plan very much commended itself to Fenella.

So, after a suitable spell with Lady Ada and Bridget at Glamis, in which he had some discussion with them as to where they should stay and dwell, with the castle having a new mistress, Fenella insisted that they should not leave their long-time home, and that she and Cormac should stay most of the time at Kinnordy; and when he had to be at Glamis for his duties as thane they could lodge in the other and larger dower house, normally reserved for widows and unmarried daughters of the family, nearby very happily, her husband agreeing heartily. This settled, to mutual satisfaction, after two nights the couple departed north-westwards, leaving Duncan with instructions to come in search of them should need arise, particularly if news came of serious Viking attacks demanding the attentions of the longship fleet. They would leave word at Kinnordy as to where they were to be sought in the Angus glens.

On their own, then, and joyfully so, the pair rode off.

The House of Kinnordy was not large, and was sparsely

furnished as yet, having been empty for long. But it had its small farmery close by, which could supply them with food and service. Not that the latter was likely to be needed to any degree, for Fenella was as practical as she was spirited, and not only capable but desirous of looking after themselves adequately for their simple needs, neither of them anxious for more than basic living and each other's company.

Settling in, for two days they did little or nothing but laze around in the pine woods, swim in the loch and go fishing for trout. There were roe deer in these woods, and Cormac managed to shoot one with a crossbow, which added juicy venison to their larder.

But on the third day it was the uplands for them, riding sturdy sure-footed garrons from the farm; that is, part way, for they intended to walk afoot also, leaving the horses tethered. Fenella, reared on the coast and an only child of less than active parents, had never had the opportunity to explore and climb the hills inland, and mountains fascinated her, called to her. Now she could indulge her hankering, and Cormac eager to indulge her.

Their first day's expedition was comparatively modest in conception, for they would have to see how the young woman managed on the hill, inexperienced as she was. So they rode through lowish uplands and braes, making for the valley of the Quharity Burn. On the way they halted to try a climb, that of the Weem hill, no major summit but a favourite of Cormac's youth because of the caves in its upper corrie, the name weem being the Gaelic *uaimh* for cave. Tying their mounts loosely to trees at the foot, where the beasts could graze, they commenced the ascent.

Quickly it was evident to Cormac that he need have no fears as to his wife's ability to climb. Sure-footed as she was light, she picked her way up as though born to it, requiring little in the way of guidance or warning, whether on grass or heather, rock or scree, joying in it all and saying so, breathless as she became inevitably, to the agitation of her bosom and her husband's appreciation.

They explored the caves, one deep and with a spring of

welcome cold water at its head, this allegedly the dysart or retiring hermitage of one of the Columban saints of four centuries earlier, they picking out his shelf bed in the rock and his fireplace.

Then on up the now steep ascent to the summit where, breathless or not, Fenella was vehemently voluble in her exclamations of delight at what she saw, views over great distances, southwards over the wide vale of Strathmore, west to the Sidlaws and the Perthshire hills, the east somewhat limited by nearby high ground, but the north tremendous, to the vast and endless mountain masses, serried ranks of soaring peaks and blue ranges to all infinity, the heather now coming into fullest bloom. This last vista all but intoxicated the girl with its scope and challenge, she never having seen the like, beckoning her, she declared, pointing, pointing. Cormac assured that they would probe into those heights and glens and learn their secrets. Now that he knew that she could climb, and so nimbly, he would be able to take her deep therein.

They descended after a spell, almost reluctantly, to the garrons, and on to the Quharity Burn, to follow it westwards to its source high in the Ascreavie Hills. They climbed one of these, but it was less dramatic than the Weem. Fenella would have gone on to scale the much more impressive Crandard ahead, almost a mountain this, but Cormac warned that enough was enough; she might well be stiff next day if she overdid it now, which would not help the day's efforts.

So it was back to Kinnordy, well content.

That night was no disappointment either.

The young woman's eagerness to tackle those distant mountains had Cormac revising his plans and scrapping any further breaking-in projects. They would head up long Glen Clova, which would require a ride of a dozen miles before they could leave the garrons to seek to conquer the mighty peak of Manywee, strangely named but dominant. So they would have to make an early start at it.

Glen Clova was over a score of miles in length, and their

walk would start over halfway up. But they had to ford the River South Esk before that, at the shepherd's house of Gella, near where their chosen route left the main track to branch somewhat eastwards. Cormac said that this could be a dangerous ford in winter, or when the snows were melting from these high tops in late spring, with sudden spates flooding down; but at this time of year it would present no problems.

Beyond Gella, two more miles, they came to another cottage, a cowherd's this, called Glasslet, backed by scattered woodland. Here they turned off. They could use their horses still for the best part of a mile eastwards and upwards, before the climb became too steep and rocky even for garrons.

Once out of the tree area, the vision of Manywee soared before them, a huge mountain massive as it was lofty, rugged with corries and outcrops for the final five hundred feet or so, but with a flat summit, and a long subsidiary escarpment, slightly lower, stretching for well over a mile southwards. They would walk that narrow ridge after their climb, for the views therefrom, on either side, were spectacular.

Leaving their mounts on long tethers, for they would be gone for hours, they started their ascent, Fenella, skirts hitched high and tied, eyeing the challenge of it warily but nowise reluctantly. She would get there.

There was no hurry, Cormac advised. A steady pace, with pauses, that was best.

It was not long, indeed, before they had reason to pause, with Cormac gripping her arm, and pointing. There, above them, on a broad shelf of the hill, a large herd of red deer were grazing, perhaps three hundred yards away, no more. Such breeze as existed was from the east, or they would not have got thus far without the creatures having detected them, and gone, for they relied on their noses rather than their eyes for warning, keen of scent as they were.

Fenella had never seen the red deer of the mountains. The smaller roedeer, yes, denizens of the woodlands and lower slopes, which might even venture on to beaches at times, for she had seen their tracks in the sand although never sighted an animal itself. But these deer of the heights were more than twice the size, and handsome creatures, graceful, long-legged, the males, stags, with their great forked antlers, a proud sight. Crouching down amongst the heather and rocks, Cormac explained to the young woman how difficult it was to approach them. They could smell mankind quarter of a mile off, and depart. So to seek to stalk them it had to be done with the wind from them to you. But the deer had keen eyes too, and any approach, to get close enough to shoot with a crossbow, had to be done on the man's belly, creeping cautiously through long heather, making use of every possible projection or outcrop to hide behind in order to win within range, say fifty, or at the most sixty, yards. Most such stalking efforts ended in failure. But when a kill was attained, great was the feeling of triumph. Most deer killed, of course, were slaughtered otherwise, in deer-drives, when herds were rounded up by many men spread out on foot in great semicircles, causing the animals to flee in desired directions towards gaps in the hills, passes or in artificial ramparts, where the archers could hide and shoot as the creatures streamed through, a deal less challenging sport, even though the targets were running, but much more effective for the filling of larders and ice-houses.

Fenella was not greatly interested in all this but in how the deer managed to live and survive in such high and seemingly barren territory, this often under snow, conditions inhospitable to say the least. That her companion could not answer convincingly; they were as God made them, was the best that he could do. There were woodland stags, of course, which normally avoided the high ground, but these were comparatively rare, in these parts at least. He had heard that there were many in Lowland wildernesses such as the Forest of Ettrick.

But the pair of them were there to climb Manywee, not to observe red deer, and they could not crouch thus in cover for long. They would start climbing again, slowly, using any uneven ground they could find to hide them, in the hope of getting nearer before the herd spotted them.

This they did – but did not get far. Suddenly, up there, the deer were off, speeding away in the opposite direction, but somehow not giving the impression of running, but drifting, more like swift-moving cloud shadow than a group of perhaps fifty animals, the roughness of the terrain seeming not to affect them, all wild grace, Fenella delighted at the sight.

The couple continued with their ascent, inclining now somewhat to the north, to follow roughly the course of a burn which led them upward reasonably conveniently, until it became only a series of small cascades and waterfalls as the ground grew ever more steep. They avoided the corrie or wide hollow wherein it rose, and faced the final few hundred feet, some of this having to be surmounted all but on hands and knees, so beetling it became. But the girl faced it well, dogged now rather than spirited, halting frequently to regain breath, and accepting Cormac's advice not to look back down on some of the almost vertical parts.

And then, suddenly, they were out on to the top, this a little circular plateau of bare rock, gravel and a few lowly creeping plants, vistas abruptly boundless before them in every direction, Fenella gasping at the utter immensity of it all; that is, until her attention was distracted by the sight of the scuttling off of two grey-white, dumpy birds, as large as pigeons, with loud cackling cries, not flying, their legs thick-seeming because covered with feathers right down to their claws. Ptarmigan or snow-grouse, Cormac called them, strange inhabitants of these bare heights. Something else new to her. What did *they* find to live on?

But it was the views which regained her attention, possessed her, a bewildering, all but unbelievable and limitless succession of ranges and ridges, of peaks and pinnacles and heights, wherever she looked, the low ground which must intervene between them all hidden, but indicated by shadows, purple against the unending blue mountains which eventually merged into the azure of the sky. Too overwhelmed to speak, she gazed and gazed, scarcely heeding her companion's pointing out of prominences and identifications, north, east, south and west.

It was not the far-flung prospects however which in time broke in on her absorption, but Cormac's grabbing of her arm and pointing, now upwards. There, high above them, two more birds were spiralling in wide circles, wings apparently unmoving, very different fowl these from the ptarmigan, the height indicating the size of them. Round and round they soared, seemingly in perpetual but tireless motion.

"Eagles!" he cried. "See – eagles! Kings of the air! At their hunting."

"Hunting?" she questioned. "Eagles? Hunting up there? How can that be? What is there to hunt?"

"Their prey. On the ground. Or else nearly so. Their sight is beyond belief. They can see, and that at greater heights still, any creature, any movement on the ground, any low-flying bird, however small. And when they so choose, drop on it like a stone!"

"Sakes! I have heard of eagle-eyed. But never thought . . ."

"They are a wonder, great creatures. They can be three feet tall and more, with broad wings which tilt up at the tips. And fierce beaks and talons. These can pick up a lamb or a deer calf in flight. But stoop on even a mouse or a sparrow from thus on high. Small wonder that they have been used by the ancients as their symbols of power and mark."

Presently the birds appeared to abandon their circling over this area, and slid away eastwards, wings seeming never to move nor flap. Fenella wondered what next she would experience.

They started on something very different, no climb this but a ridge walk. More than a mile south from the summit of Manywee rose a lesser peak which Cormac called Craigthron. But this was connected to the major mountain by a long and narrow spine of rock and grit, with steep, almost sheer drops on either side, these of three or four hundred feet. Although in parts it was sufficiently wide not to cause alarm, however exciting was the sensation of negotiating it, at others the passage was dizzy-making indeed, only a few feet in width and uneven as to surface. Cormac pointed this out before they started along it, in case Fenella felt disinclined to risk it; but she asserted that she had no fear of heights, having been reared in cliff-top surroundings, indeed one of her youthful activities being the collection of seabirds' eggs from nests on ledges of the precipices. Nevertheless their progress along that escarpment, as well as exhilarating, had its moments of tension of a sort, this mainly caused by the effect of sheer drops on *both* sides, which left even the most sure-footed and steady-nerved climber extremely aware of being precarious as to position, movement and balance. The man was heedful for his companion's safety, if such he could call it, and they took no undue risks, even when a buzzard flew out from a cranny just below them, and they peered over to see if it had left a nest, holding hands prudently. They wondered whether it was on one of these cliffs that the eagles they had seen had their eyrie.

Elevated in more senses than one by their experience, they reached Craigthron, itself even steeper-sided than Manywee, and decided to descend from there, down one of its less difficult flanks, and so to slant back north-westwards the two miles to their horses. They saw more deer on their way, a smaller number, so probably not of the same herd.

Delighted with their day, they returned to Kinnordy. Cormac said that there was a still higher mountain called Glamsie, more remotely sited up the Noran after some four miles east of Manywee, but only reachable by a lengthy, round-about ride. Perhaps they could tackle that another day, if Fenella felt like it? But a restful break might be called for meantime?

There were more sorts of allegedly restful breaks than one, for the newly-weds, before their holiday was over and they returned to Glamis.

PART TWO

21

There was no lack of excitement, challenges and problems for Scotland in the run-up, those years up, to the millennium, that is the year 1000 from the birth of Christ Jesus; and a sufficiency for the Thane of Glamis and his wife and folk to do, beyond the normal managing of properties, maintaining the peace and dispensing approximate justice amongst squabblesome tenants and dependants, plus of course home-making at Kinnordy.

The longships were called for fairly promptly for service, not this time to the aid of Moray and Ross but for still further afield. This was on account of two distinct circumstances. First of all, Thorfinn Raven-Feeder, as he was known, MacBeth's half-brother, and son of Sigurd, Earl of Orkney, a Norseman himself but one with a Scots mother, Donada, came to the help of the Moray folk with his own longships, and established a base at Torfness, otherwise called Burghead. This had the desired effect. Viking raiding ceased thereabouts, meantime, and along this eastern side of Scotland.

However, the second circumstance counteracted this relief by transferring the menace to the other side of the realm. It so happened that Malcolm, the High King's disgruntled nephew, had been given the overlordship of the former kingdom of Strathclyde, that is the south-western portion of the land from Argyll down to Cumbria, in order to keep him quiet, as it were. But he was of an assertive nature, and finding that the Cumbrian section of his new domain had yielded to Viking pressure, and was indeed paying substantial tribute to the Norsemen yearly, this he promptly refused to do. This resulted in almost as prompt longship raiding thereabouts from Norse bases in northern Ireland and the Western Isles, with much slaughter and plunder. Great was the outcry. So the appeal came to Connacher and Cormac: come and help us with your fleet against the dastardly Vikings.

Thus the idyllic period of post-wedding bliss came to an end, and it was back to longship-manning.

Having become a wife and consort to a thane by no means altered Fenella's insistence on being involved in their fleet's activities. She would take part in this new venture, whatever other folk thought of the suitability, her husband now knowing better than to attempt any real opposition. And she had never been to the parts of the land concerned, the west coasts of Scotland and Cumbria; now she would see it all.

Towards the end of September, then, the assembled flotilla of about one score of longships set off from the Angus havens, actually on the Eve of St Adamnan, to sail northwards, this time heading far beyond Moray. But, as it transpired, they were not to avoid diversions; for, on the second day out, towards evening, as they passed Burghead in the Moray Firth, between the mouths of the Rivers Spey and Findhorn, out came another fleet of Viking ships, somewhat fewer in number than their own but led by a large and imposing dragon-ship, this flying the flag, the giant raven banner, of Thorfinn Sigurdison, the Raven-Feeder, MacBeth's half-brother, to challenge them, on the assumption that they were Danes, Jutes or Norsemen come hosting from the south.

On the bows platform of the large vessel, twenty-benched and with four men, not three, to each sweep, behind the high-beaked prow in the shape of a snarling dragon, stood a huge man wearing a golden helmet adorned with black raven wings, and clad in a black leather tunic studded with armoured scales, breeches bound with leather straps at the knees, bare arms hung with bracelets of gold and bronze, a polar-bearskin cloak hanging from one shoulder. This extraordinary character held high a sword, and demanded who sailed the Moray coasts without the mormaor's permission – the impression given that *he* was the mormaor.

"I, Cormac, Thane of Glamis, and friend of the Mormaor MacBeth mac Finlay, do," he was answered, in as stout a tone as could be mustered. "But . . . we sail further. To round the north of this land. To reach the western lands beyond. Where Norsemen, such as yourself, are at their raiding. You, I take it, are Thorfinn, brother to MacBeth?"

"I am that, yes; to aid the Son of Life who, poor brother, appears to require it! I have heard of you, Cormac of Glamis. And how you are learning to fight. I could teach you further!"

Was that a threat or an offer? Cormac eyed this giant of a man doubtfully. "On another occasion perhaps, Raven-Feeder," he said carefully. "Now we have other lessons to learn, far from here. Dealing with lesser Vikings."

"Ha, they are but the scrapings of our Norse pot! From Dublin and the like. But they can fight, Angusman! So, heed you at it."

"We can fight also, Orkneyman," Cormac managed to announce. The two vessels were close alongside each other now, their sweeps all but clashing.

"You needs must use women to help you do it?" the other enquired, mockingly, pointing to Fenella, who was standing beside Cormac. "*I* see women as for other purposes!"

"Perhaps, then, *you* have also much to learn, Norseman!" That was the young woman, calling clearly.

A great hoot of laughter came from the big man. "Hear her! The hen-chicken seeks to crow! I have heard that her father crows not, nor even clucks! So she crows for him?"

"You speak of my wife, the Lady Fenella," Cormac said. "I ask that you do not forget it, Raven-Feeder."

"No? I shall not. One day, perhaps, I shall teach *her* some small matters? My brother, I understand, finds her to his taste."

"The teaching, Sir Jarl, might be two-sided!" And Fenella flicked her hand dismissively.

Again the shout of laughter. "So be it! We shall teach each other. But meantime, I will instruct your husband in some little fashion as to fighting longship men. Since he appears to be ignorant of it. See you, Angusman, you should hang shields over the sides, between the sculls, the sweeps, as do I. Even you should know that?" He turned to his crew. "Shields, then, I say shields. For these cockerels!" And stooping, bearskin cloak flung back, the giant snatched one of the round bucklers from the bulwarks of his craft and hurled it over the gap at Cormac, who had to dodge to avoid it, as did Fenella. Made of leather, padded, and bound with iron rings, these were weighty as well as strong, and could knock any man over.

This danger became very evident in the next minute or so as the shower of these shields came spinning over from the dragon-ship, thrown by the crewmen on that side, amidst yells and howls, the Scots having to duck and flatten themselves to evade them as best they might, cursing. So much for instruction in naval warfare.

Cormac signed for his helmsman to veer off, and their other craft were only too ready to do likewise. Thorfinn presumably decided that he had demonstrated superiority sufficiently, and ordered his vessels into a wide turn away.

So the two fleets drew apart, with no love lost, however friendly both might be to MacBeth mac Finlay, the Scots to continue northwards, the Orkneymen to return to their base of Torfness.

Cormac had those shields collected. Little as he had enjoyed that lesson, he perceived that here was something worth the learning in ship-fighting. He would have some sort of shields made, not necessarily like these ones, for protection of craft and crews in sea battle.

They had still almost one hundred miles to sail up the coasts of Easter Ross, Sutherland and Caithness before they could round the north-easterly point of mainland

Scotland and turn westwards towards the Hebrides. With the wind south-westerly, they made good time, and were able to put in at the sheltered large bay of Wick for a night's rest, with only a score more miles to go to the great foreland of Duncansby Head, and their turning.

They were off early in the morning, Cormac heedful over the possibility of more Orkneymen at sea, who might not be so friendly, if that was the word, for this Caithness area, although part of Scotland, had long been dominated from the Northern Isles. However, all they saw were a few fishing-craft, and they were able to turn Duncansby Head, giving it a wide berth, and face the west at last.

Now it was all oar-work, the sails of little or no use. In a few miles they passed the cliffs of Dunnet Head, this the most northerly projection of all Scotland's mainland, the Orkneys starting less than ten miles off, and plainly visible. Cormac eyed that prospect warily, although Fenella said that a fleet of longships of their size would almost certainly be taken to be Thorfinn's, and not challenged.

All that day they rowed due westwards, for this northern brink of the land was another hundred miles long, and with the wind largely in their faces they did not make such good headway as formerly. Indeed they got only as far as an out-jutting, narrow promontory, at which they put in for shelter for another night, and which an alarmed local fisherman told them was called Strathy Head, with still nearly fifty miles to go to Cape Wrath, the mainland's north-westerly tip. Cormac had not realised that such distances were involved.

Food was becoming something of a problem for their many crewmen, the stocks which they had brought beginning to run out, and these northern parts being but sparsely inhabited, with little of cattle or sheep to be seen. Fish they could get, and oatmeal, that was all. No doubt the proximity of those Orkney Isles was responsible for the comparative depopulation.

The next day's sailing became ever more dramatic as to scenery, with great mountains soaring, and three deep sea lochs probing far inland, west Highland landscape now, before, in forty or so miles, they came to the mighty turning point of their journey, Cape Wrath, or Am Parbh, the Turning Point indeed, in the Gaelic, the towering pyramidal headland of lofty beetling cliffs and jumbled rock-stacks, against which the seas broke unceasingly in surging fountains. They swung southwards, now, prudently well offshore to avoid the menace of reefs and skerries, with the Butt of Lewis, northernmost tip of the Outer Isles, just in sight to the west.

They were into the Minch now, the great alleyway between the Highland mainland and the Hebrides, which would lead them southwards for three hundred miles to the Irish Sea through the wildest and most picturesque area of all Scotland, with its myriad of islands and sea lochs, its gleaming white cockleshell sands and colourful seaweeds producing translucent multi-hued waters, its green machairs and seal-haunted rocks, all backed by the endless peaks, ridges, escarpments and shadow-filled corries of the blue mountains. Here was beauty, infinite and vivid, scarcely to be comprehended, enough to impress even the most unheeding viewer. It all had Fenella in rhapsodies.

They got as far as the sea loch of Bervie that evening, oar-work still in the south-westerly breeze, the swell of the tides in this Western Ocean notably greater than in the Norse Sea, the rowers having to adjust to it. Noting a herd of red deer on an island at the mouth of it, they pulled in on the far side of it, and Cormac, Duncan and Donnie the Crab went stalking, with crossbows, and in the dusk, the wind in their favour, managed to shoot a young stag and a hind. They dragged the carcases a little way, but soon decided that there were plenty of men at the ships to come and cut up the beasts and carry the pieces down. They would have red meat to complement their fish and oats that night. Perhaps this seaboard would prove kinder for hungry men than had been the eastern.

They saw their first Viking ships the next day, three of

them heading westwards towards the Outer Isles. These did not change course nor approach them, a fleet of a score being best left uninvestigated, whoever they might be.

It took them five days of rowing to cover the three hundred miles down the isle-strewn coastline, passing Skye, itself over fifty miles long, Rhum, Eigg, Muick, Coll, Tiree, great Mull with Iona at its foot, then Colonsay, Jura of the twin breasts, and Islay, until they reached the lengthy Kintyre peninsula. On their way they saw many longships, but never in any large numbers, and all keeping their distance if not actually seeking to avoid them. Fenella suggested that these possibly thought that they might be Thorfinn Raven-Feeder's fleet from Orkney, and therefore not to be approached. Cormac began to wonder whether, with their own numbers, they might not have to do much fighting in the end, the sight of them all sufficient to warn off the raiders?

Once round the tip of Kintyre they were at the mouth of the Firth of Clyde, and Cormac judged it sensible to turn in thereat to visit Dumbarton, the oddly-placed capital of Strathclyde, sited at the very north end of the one-time kingdom which extended southwards for over another two hundred miles. Malcolm mac Kenneth might well be residing there meantime, and it would be wise to report to him and to learn what was required of them.

So it was northwards now, up Clyde, at least with the wind behind them, passing the mountainous island of Arran, sixty miles to where the firth suddenly narrowed. And there, guarding the jaws of it, rose the conical hill of Dun Briton, corrupted to Dumbarton, crowned by its strong castle, dating back to the famous Arthur's time, when he was High King of the Britons, the fortress indeed formerly known as Castrum Arthuri.

Anchoring off the township, and no doubt causing some alarm amongst the folk, Cormac and Fenella, with only a small escort, landed and approached the citadel hill. They had the usual difficulty and delay in gaining access, castellans ever suspicious of strangers; but when admitted, learned that Prince Malcolm – he was calling himself that here, it seemed – was in residence but off hunting deer on Ben Lomond, to the north, at the moment. Sending word back to the ships, the visitors settled down to wait, feeling strangely cramped, confined, indoors, after two weeks of sailing in open ships.

Eventually Malcolm arrived, to greet the newcomers scarcely warmly, for he was not a warm young man, but well pleased that they had come, saying that he had counted their ships and believed that they would be required.

"The devilish raiders are at it daily," he declared. "They come across from Ireland, slaying and ravaging and burning. I have many men down there to counter them, but with their ships they can draw off and laugh at us. And land somewhere else, to continue their savagery."

"How many ships?" Cormac asked. "How many to each raiding party?"

"They vary. Sometimes only the one. Sometimes three, four."

"But never a fleet?"

"No. They all may come so far as a fleet, or a large group, and then divide up, to raid in smaller companies. Over wide lands. I do not know."

"Yes. That is the same as in the east. Where is this raiding taking place? Not here, in the Clyde?"

"Not here, no. They dare not venture near me here, I think. It is mainly down in Cumbria. That coast. But of late they have been pushing north into Galloway: Whithorn, Luce Bay, into the Solway. They grow the bolder, the barbarians!"

"When they see a fleet of longships come to deal with them, they may think better of it, and depart," Fenella said.

"That is my hope, lady." Malcolm eyed her questioningly. "*You* have come to the fight?"

"Not with my hands, no. But there is more to warfare than swordery, I say. And a woman's wits may sometimes rival a man's!"

"M'mmm."

"My wife has accompanied us when dealing with raiders in our own parts," Cormac added.

The other shrugged. "As you will. But rid me of these Norsemen and I will not forget it, Thane Cormac. My men in the south will be at your command. Any aid that I can give you, I will."

"If you will supply my people with food and drink, Malcolm mac Kenneth, that would be welcome," Cormac said. "We have been two weeks at sea, and supplies for some hundreds of men can run out."

"I shall order it, yes."

They received some refreshment from their host, but there was no suggestion that they should linger, nor spend the night there, although it was late afternoon.

On their way down to their ships, Fenella said, "I think that is a hard man. He sees narrowly, for his own weal. I would not like to be wed to him!"

"Would you like to be wed to any other than your own lawful husband?" she was asked.

"Only at times!" she said, and squeezed his arm.

They lay in their vessels overnight, nowise complaining, for they had grown used to this by now, and preferred the company to that of any stiff host. In the morning, supplies of meats, more fish, meal and ales were delivered, and thereafter they rowed off, with no further contact with Malcolm mac Kenneth. All were grateful to see that the wind had changed into the east, which meant that they could now use the sails to better effect and all but dispense with the sweeps for much of the time, a relief after all the hundreds of miles of rowing.

They made good time down Clyde, therefore, holding fairly close to the Ayrshire coast, and by midday were passing the towering isolated rock stack of Ailsa Craig, so very similar to the Bass Rock at the mouth of the Forth estuary, all white bird-droppings and screaming seafowl. It was drawing towards evening when they saw the smoke rising inland near the mouth of a deep bay or sea loch.

Had it been a single column they would not have drawn in; but there were three clouds some little way apart, and that might well indicate burning thatches, houses, raiding. So they pulled into the loch mouth, and there, on their right, after a mile or so, they saw three longships drawn up on the shingle.

Cormac ordered his vessels to move shorewards in crescent formation.

What followed was almost a repeat of their previous engagements in the east, as was almost inevitable. These Norsemen tended to act in the same way, leaving their ships under only small guard, and raiding inland to where were the larger settlements, farmeries, cattle and sheep, although not usually venturing for any great distances from the shore. The guards here, seeing the fleet clearly drawing in on them, evidently decided on discretion, whoever the newcomers might be, and departed towards the smoke columns. So Cormac and his leading craft had an unopposed approach and landing, beside a group of abandoned fishermen's cottages, with the usual series of heads hanging from drying nets, and decapitated bodies lying around, no living souls to be seen. Sickened, as always, Cormac and Fenella had their men take down those heads, of men, women and children, and gather up the corpses, a distressing task. There were peat-hags nearby, with their heaps of cut fuel, and two of these were used to form makeshift graves, covering the bodies and heads with the brown turfs, and using posts lashed crosswise to erect above them to mark Christian burial.

While this was going on under Fenella's eye-blinking supervision, Cormac decided that they should take two of the enemy longships to add to their own fleet, and burn the other as an example, the while setting watchers to warn of any approach of the raiders.

None appeared, and there arose some question as to procedure now. Three ships might signify well over one hundred men. Although their own numbers would far outmatch these, was actual battle to be sought? Their task ıere was, in the main, to discourage raiding, not necessarily o engage in fighting unless this was called for. Casualties mongst their own men were to be avoided, if possible, specially with captured craft to man. So, go a little way nland, to some higher ground, to see if any force of Vikings vas approaching. If not, sail off on further duties.

Leaving Fenella at the shore, Cormac took perhaps ne-third of their men to mount a small grassy hillock earby. On the way, it was a dog barking at them which drew heir attention to a little group of two terrified women and hree small children hiding amongst whin bushes. These ook a deal of reassuring, despite the newcomers' dress eing so different, that they were not more Norsemen but riends. The gabbled incoherencies about what had befallen hem and their neighbours were all but unintelligible, but hey did reveal that the village inland, a mile or so, now roducing some of the smoke, was Kirkcolm, called after St Columba, who had not come to their aid, and the loch alled Ryan.

There was nothing that could be done for these unfor-unates other than sympathise, and advise that they hid urther away from their burned cottages, for the raiders vould undoubtedly return presently, seeking their ships. On that hill-crest they saw no sign of an enemy presence neantime in the scattered woodland country.

So a return was made to the shore, where their colleagues vere making their own smoke cloud in the burning of one of the longships.

When this token message of threat and warning was atisfactorily completed, it was all aboard again, and off outhwards, volunteers taking over the two extra vessels. Was this going to be the pattern of this campaign? It eemed probable, unless somehow the individual raiding arties managed to arrange to merge together to form joint force to confront them, although that seemed ınlikely in the circumstances. These Norse raiders' ıostings were very much separate ventures, no sort of ınited assaults, a form of individual enterprise from various

bases, grim way of seeking satisfaction and diversion a
it might be.

What would happen to the stranded raiders whose ship
were lost to them, who could tell? They might join u
with others of their kind, similarly deprived, to be sure
but with Malcolm's men on the lookout for them, surel
their objective would be to get home to wherever the
came from, Ireland or Man or the Isles presumably. S
they would probably steal local fishing-boats and seek t
use them to depart, chastened if not wiser, it was to b
hoped.

The hosting season usually ended in the late autumn
So, a month or so, and it ought to be back to Angus fo
themselves.

Their forecast of events proved to be fairly accurate. The
saw no more fires on the Galloway coasts, after passin
the night in a bay near Portpatrick. Then they crossed th
mouth of the Solway Firth to the Cumbrian shores. Ther
the tell-tale smokes began to appear again, not widesprea
but scattered, and with large gaps between.

Their first actual encounter, however, took a differen
form. This coastline was not indented by deep bays an
sea lochs as it was further north, and that second day the
were rounding a small headland to investigate a drift o
blue smoke when there, coming out towards them, wer
four longships, less than half a mile away.

Great was the excitement amongst the Scots as to wha
would happen now. Cormac had devised a strategy to see
to deal with such a situation; but of course it all depende
on the Norsemen's reaction. He ordered his ships int
three divisions, two to seek to outflank the enemy an
the third to come up to where aid might be needed. Thu
they rowed on.

The four Norse vessels had little option as to thei
tactics. They would not know what the large approachin
flotilla might represent, but being longships they migh
possibly be friendly. On the other hand, they woul

lmost certainly be rivals for hosting and gaining booty. o they would be best avoided probably. At any rate, the ttle group evidently so decided, and veered off to the eeward, south-westwards, for the open Irish Sea, and did ot delay.

Cormac wanted no warning of his fleet's approach to be iven to this Cumbrian coastline, so it was intervention, if ossible. It became a race, as he waved on his many ships, word drawn and pointing.

With the wind easterly, sails aided by sweeps, progress as fast – but on both sides. Shouting encouragement to is men, and leading the panting chanting to aid the rowers' hythm, and beating the time on shields and timbers, e leaders urged the utmost efforts; but no doubt the orsemen were doing the same. The gap between did not eem to narrow. And gradually the Scots pursuers became trung out, the less well-manned slipping behind, not all e crews being equally adept. Cormac began to wonder hether this was a worthwhile activity? Indeed, fairly oon he would have called off the chase had it not come him that the further off he could drive these invaders estwards, towards Ireland or Man, the less likely were ey to return and be able to warn others. So the pursuit ontinued.

It was Fenella who first pointed out to him that one f the Norse vessels was itself lagging somewhat behind e others. They could not guess the reason, whether ndermanned or perhaps the men wearied with their land activities, or drunken, who could tell? But one as certainly dropping behind.

Cormac shouted to Donnie the Crab, whose vessel as nearest to his own in the lead, to take four of his raft to deal with the straggler, while he himself led e rest after the other three enemy ships to ensure at they were driven ever further from this Cumbrian oast, since he had little hope of actually bringing them action.

Soon they were passing the one labouring Norseman

at some hundreds of yards' distance, the Scots crews too breathless to shout or jeer.

On and on they went, the gap between not obviously lessening. How far to go? They must be at least five or six miles from the shore now, the Isle of Man none so far to the south-west, the way they were going. Was this sufficient?

Deciding that it was, and those three going to escape anyway, they turned back. It took them a while to reach Donnie's group, for now the wind was in their faces. When they did, it was to find all over, not a raider to be seen, all disposed of and consigned to the waves, with one more captured ship to add to their fleet. Ian the Wright would be able to give up building longships. There were a few Scots casualties, but none seriously wounded, the odds in their favour having been too great.

Reasonably satisfied, Cormac ordered a return landwards, with now three extra vessels to crew. Inevitably the others were becoming undermanned. This problem would have to be dealt with hereafter.

Malcolm mac Kenneth had advised, indeed ordered, that they should make contact with his lieutenants in Cumbria, particularly one Murdoch mac Neil, based at Maryport. Cormac reckoned that this was none so far south of where they had reached now, perhaps a dozen miles. They would head for there for the night.

There were not many harbour communities of any size on this seaboard, with the hills beginning to rise fairly close behind now, some quite lofty; and when, with the light beginning to fail, they saw quite a township ahead of them, they decided that this would serve. There were two jetties here, and while most of his vessels anchored out in the bay, Cormac had his own craft and Donnie's pulled in to one of these, and landed. They learned from some anxious fishermen that this was indeed Maryport, and that the Lord Murdoch and his party occupied a hallhouse some way inland. These locals were told to go and inform the said Murdoch that the Thane of Glamis had arrived with his fleet, sent by the Prince Malcolm, and desired attendance.

They reboarded their ships. They were going to be their own masters here.

It was almost dark when a group of horsemen arrived, and hailed them from the jetty. The man Murdoch mac Neil, a Scot and no Cumbrian, proved to be a burly character with an abrupt manner, but obviously impressed by the size of the visitors' fleet. He declared that he was a cousin of the Thane of Monteith, and was in charge, under Malcolm, of operations here in Cumbria. Cormac, who knew Monteith slightly, suspected that the cousinship was far out or perhaps illegitimate, but did not say so. He did assert that he was not there to take orders from anyone, but that he would be glad of information as to the current situation hereabouts. He mentioned that they had already had two encounters with Vikings, none so far off, and one in Galloway.

Murdoch reported that the worst of the raiding was taking place further south, beyond Workington and Whitehaven, and advised that Thane Cormac based himself at the last named, which was a fair-sized port and could provide his crews with the necessary supplies. He, Murdoch, had groups of men, mainly horsed, all the way down between coast and mountains, right to Millom and Balton, and these would co-operate with the thane. But the difficulty for them was, of course, that the raiders were never very far from their ships, and when attacked could always retire to these and escape to sea, then land somewhere else to resume their pillaging. Hence the need for ships to contest them. Of all of which Cormac was well aware, and said so. This Whitehaven – Murdoch to send orders that they were to be well received and aided from there, with full association. He was concerned, here, to remain in control.

This was accepted. Murdoch, as a seeming afterthought, asked if the thane and his lady wished to come up to his house inland for the night; but this invitation was civilly declined. They would stay with their ships, and leave in the morning.

Fenella agreed with her husband that in this campaign they must make it quite clear that they were self-sufficient, save for supplies, independent, taking orders from none, they the benefactors, Malcolm and his underlings not to act the lords, as it seemed they might be all too apt to do.

They passed one more night aboard.

In the morning they sailed southwards again, along a fairly barren coast, seeing no signs of current raiding, passing one major river mouth, and then a township which would be Workington. In under a score of miles, with a great jutting headland ahead of them, which they had been warned of, St Bees, they came to Whitehaven.

This was the largest community they had seen since leaving Dumbarton, and with a good sheltered anchorage for ships. Not that there were many vessels presently there, save for fishing-boats. There were many houses scattered over quite a wide area behind, before the hills began, with livestock and rig-cultivation, all of which indicated a suitable base for the newcomers. Well content with what they saw, whatever the reaction of the residents, the seafarers moored their ships and prepared to stay.

The name of one, Lakin, the Cumbrian headman of this place, had been given them, and indeed they did not have to go seeking him, for he came down to the harbour to greet them, having been apprised of their coming, a man of middle years and grave manner but not unwelcoming, and respectful, with a son little younger than Cormac of a more lively disposition. Clearly excited by the arrival of this formidable-seeming company, he was voluble. Cormac got the impression that these folk would be more easy to deal with, and probably effective.

Lakin declared that they were all grateful for the Scots coming to aid them against the ravagers – he named them Danes – and hoped that they would be successful in their efforts and at no great cost to themselves. He had been instructed to give them every assistance and hospitality required, and had so informed his people. He was sure that they all would co-operate, everyone being well aware of the benefits their coming could bring. Houses, barns and sheds had been set aside for their use, and there would be a sufficiency of food and drink.

Much appreciative, Cormac asked whether any of the local fishermen, whose nets were much in evidence, might be prepared to join their longships' crews temporarily, they having captured three vessels and requiring additional oarsmen. These craft were difficult to handle, at first, but newcomers, placed between the seasoned crewmen at the sweeps, would soon learn the way of it. He was told that the fishers would be asked to provide volunteers, and his son, named Art, promptly backed that by offering himself as the first trainee.

It seemed that they had found a satisfactory base for their operations.

Fenella accompanied her husband up to the houses – it was more than any village – and they were introduced to Lakin's wife and two daughters, who promised their services in respect of care and hospitality, taking them to a cottage for themselves.

The visitors were beginning to think well of the Cumbrians. Their own somewhat guarded attitudes eased.

So it was down to the business of settling in, their crews appreciative likewise, especially of the female company available, although considerable competition was not long in developing, since there were by no means sufficient hostesses for all of them.

Cormac asked Fenella whether their enterprise might be going to develop into more of holiday than battling?

In the days that followed, lengthening into two weeks, that question recurred more than once. For although the Viking-hunters achieved what they had come to do, and effectively, they seldom missed a night at Whitehaven, and did not fail to make the most of its opportunities. They found the local people grateful for their successes in freeing them from the menace of the raiding, and demonstrating this approval in various ways; so that coming back to base of an evening became something of a priority. The local volunteer crewmen also proved an asset, a sufficiency of them quickly learning to play their parts, usually one man set between two Scots on a sweep.

As to combative action, they totalled six engagements in all, and without any serious losses to themselves, this on account of the Norsemen's own habitual preference for small isolated forays, in which they could be dealt with piecemeal. They captured three more ships, burned four and sank one in the driving off of others, this with little of actual fighting and small hurt to themselves. The predictions of Cormac and Fenella proved accurate. These Vikings were vulnerable to assault from the sea by superior numbers of their own kind of vessels.

When, eventually, three days passed without any sign of raiders, and it was nearing the end of the usual hosting season, it was decided that probably their task could be considered as over, meantime. They would leave three of the captured vessels with these Whitehaven fishers, in the hope that they could use them to good effect for their own defence in the unlikely event of more attacks over the winter, and train others also in the handling, the young man Art to act captain.

So then it was farewell, with suggestions from some that they might be back the following year, if needed; and much appreciation mutually expressed, sometimes almost embarrassingly.

On the way north they called in on Malcolm mac Kenneth at Dumbarton, to report. He would have had them leave some part of their fleet with him over the winter months in case of further Norse attentions; but it was pointed out that their crews were fishermen and with their livings to earn and families to look after, and they had already been away from home for six weeks. The three ships left at Whitehaven might serve as some deterrent. Satisfaction at their efforts was only briefly expressed – but that was Malcolm.

At least he did provide horses for Cormac and Fenella, with Duncan the Tranter, to ride hereafter north-eastwards, while Donnie the Crab led the fleet on the long journey homewards. After all, the Thane of Glamis had his duties to attend to in Angus, much neglected, and it was only some hundred miles overland thereto as against something like six hundred and fifty by sea. Cormac felt rather guilty in leaving his crews thus; but he had the responsibilities of his inherited position, and they weighed on his mind somewhat. Moreover, he was longing to be home alone with Fenella at Kinnordy.

A change then from shipboard to horseback, and November upon them.

22

They returned to an atmosphere of some anticipation and tension in the Scottish realm, not to say excitement. The year 1000 was almost upon them, and many, not only the clergy, were filled with a sense of curiosity, expectancy, over this. None prophesied what would happen at this millennium of their Saviour's birth, but most assumed that it must be marked by some special events, God-given or by man's own devising, or both. Celebrations there must be, of course, but more than that was looked for, not only by the churchmen.

This expectation was paralleled by a sense of foreboding as to national affairs. For King Kenneth was not popular, his reigning erratic and unsure, his favouritism notorious. Not a few of the mormaors were condemning him, including Connacher of Angus, and many of the land's lords and chieftains were saying that they would have been better off with Malcolm his nephew. Also there were rumours that the English king, Ethelred the Second, was casting acquisitive eyes on parts of south Scotland, in especial the Cumbrian part of Strathclyde and the Merse area of the Borderland. Malcolm had not mentioned this to Cormac at Dumbarton, but presumably it had been on his mind.

None of all this greatly affected Cormac and Fenella on their arrival home; but two more personal items did. The first was that the Lord Aidan had fallen ill at Red Castle, and was showing little signs of recovery – so visits had to be made promptly to Lunan Bay. And the second was the announcement made by Fenella, just after they had welcomed their fleet's safe return to the havens in early December, that she was fairly sure that she was pregnant.

This last, of course, was the occasion for great satisfaction and rejoicing on Cormac's part, their own celebration of the millennium. But he also became much concerned over his wife's care and well-being, fearful for any least mishap, strain or weariness, infinitely more so than she was herself, Fenella declaring that she was perfectly fit and able to continue a normal active life for months yet, and intended to do so, refusing to be in any way restricted or confined. As well that it was wintertime and no longship adventures anticipated, or there would have been dire arguments as to her sea-going. And she certainly was not going to be dissuaded from frequently riding to see her sick father.

An aspect of his brother's illness was Connacher's anxiety over the future of his mortuath. Aidan was his heir, however feeble a one; but there was a far-out cousin, the Thane of Doune, who was known to nurse an ambition to be Mormaor of Angus one day, whom Connacher loathed and was determined should by no means succeed him. His reaction to the news that his niece was expecting a child was that pray God it was a boy, which could unstring Doune's bow; the thought of a daughter of Aidan's daughter would be stretching the required succession overfar.

So Yuletide, Christmas and the New Year came amidst festivities, celebrations and revelries, although no earth-shaking signs came from above, and some seers and diviners said that perhaps they had got the date wrong, and that Christ's birthday had been erroneously calculated, and the great occasion yet to come. The Celtic Church bishops and abbots pooh-poohed this, and declared that if the good Lord was not marking this millennium with any especial wonders, it was because of the sinful failings of Christian folk, and repentance and betterment demanded.

At any rate Cormac sought to mark the occasion more or less suitably at Glamis, with religious services, feastings and Yule observances, even though some of the latter were of pagan origin, long preceding the coming of Christianity. He also publicly announced that the Lady Fenella was set to bear him a child in this millennium year, and all prayed that it would be a good augury, both for the thanedom and the mormaordom.

Fenella reckoned that the birth would probably be in July, going by monthly indications; so there was no need to restrict her activities for a long time yet, doubtfully as this assertion was received by the expectant father.

Back at Kinnordy life went happily.

Then in March the Lord Aidan died, being found dead in his bed one morning, his passing as quietly undramatic as had been his life. In the circumstances, prepared for it as they all were, there was little of shock, however much wife and daughter might grieve. Lady Alena took it all with a typical calm acceptance. She declared that she would continue to dwell at Red Castle, it having been her quiet home for so long; but she hoped that Fenella would come and stay with her on occasion.

The interment was a modest and private affair, as Aidan would have wished. There being no graveyard nearby, Father Ferchar was invited down from Usan to consecrate a piece of ground beside the Lunan Water where it entered the bay, just below the castle's mound; and here the funeral rites were conducted briefly but movingly thereafter, with only the widow and daughter, Cormac, the castle servants and a few local people attending, Connacher not putting in an appearance. It was a secluded but attractive spot, amongst a scatter of bushes, and Aidan mac Nechtan's body was to rest, to the gentle sounds of the birds' cries, the rippling flow of the river and the more distant sigh of the waves on the shore – to wherever his reserved spirit had retired.

The Lady Alena, self-sufficient always, was content with her lot.

Whether or not Malcolm Mac Kenneth judged that the Norse raiding of his Cumbrian and Galloway lands would be deterred from resuming that hosting season, about to start, by the Angusmen's longship activities of the autumn, he alarmed the nation in April by making the resounding declaration that the present Ard Righ, his uncle, was unlawfully on the throne and was proving incompetent to reign and rule. Therefore he, Malcolm, son of the previous Ard Righ, challenged him to vacate the high kingship in his favour; or, if he was not prepared to do that, either to meet him in battle, or, better, that innocent blood be not shed, to fight a duel with him to decide the issue. This extraordinary pronouncement was the stranger in view of the talk of Ethelred the Unready's supposed intention of invading Scotland, Malcolm presumably either discounting this or judging that such threat might work to his advantage, in that his uncle would not wish to risk the dangers of civil war at such a time, and the mormaors and lords be disinclined to support him in arms in the circumstances. Whether that was his reasoning, it all made a most notable impact on the nation, the which Cormac by no means escaped. If it came to war, whom was he to support? He had taken the oath of allegiance to the High King at Scone; so in theory he was committed. But on the other hand, Malcolm would probably make a better and more effective monarch, especially if English invasion was in the offing.

Fenella said that he should support neither, whatever her Uncle Connacher's attitude, but stay at home with his pregnant wife.

A period of waiting ensued while the Ard Righ made up his mind; or perhaps he had no decision to make, and merely assessed his nephew as playing insolent games, and could be ignored meantime. At any rate, he did nothing.

Word from MacBeth at Inverness was that desultory raiding having started again on the Moray coasts, his half-brother Thorfinn was coming down again from Orkney and, it was hoped, would put a stop to it. No need for the Angusmen's help, as yet. And there was no call from Cumbria.

The lull continued.

Fenella began to show signs of child-bearing, although she was by no means over-bulky and carried herself well.

She was still not prepared to limit her activities. The couple heedfully rode down to Red Castle frequently, to pass a night or two with Lady Alena. Fenella's condition did not seem to interfere with her fondness for sea-bathing any more than with flounder-fishing.

Connacher's concern for his niece now was all but embarrassing, he who had never taken any real heed of her previously. What would happen if the child was a girl was a matter for conjecture. No doubt the loving parents would be urged to go on procreating until a son was born.

However, in early June, the mormaor sent for Cormac, to inform him that he had consulted a locally renowned spae-wife at Rescobie, none so far off, and she had examined whatever signs and portents she claimed would reveal the future, and assured Connacher that he would shortly be presented with a grand-nephew with red hair. How much reliance could be put on this forecast was not to be known; but the prospective great-uncle was well pleased, and Fenella herself had said for some time that she was fairly sure that she was bearing a son. Indeed she had decided that he ought to be called Nechtan, after her paternal grandfather, the previous mormaor.

Cormac had no complaints to make about that.

At the end of the month the dreaded English invasion took place, in Cumbria, not in the Merse, Ethelred leading it himself. If it had been in the latter, or Lothian, King Kenneth would have been in duty bound to do something about it; but Cumbria was a different matter, purely his misliked nephew's responsibility, not really part of Scotland at all. So he elected to do nothing, however much some of his mormaors urged him on, saying that a success there would only whet Ethelred's appetite for more, and that the Merse could well be the next target. Malcolm did not call for the longship fleet either, presumably assessing its usefulness as only to counter the Vikings, the English assault only by land. For this Cormac was thankful indeed, for the very last thing that he desired was to be away from Fenella's side when her giving birth was expected at any time; in fact he would have refused to go personally, and have sent the ships, or some of them, under the leadership of Donnie the Crab, who had proved to be a worthy lieutenant.

Then, in mid-July, they got heartening news. Malcolm mac Kenneth had defeated the elderly Ethelred in battle, without the help of others, the English monarch presumably living up to his by-name of the Unready or ill-advised. This was, of course, a great triumph for the young would-be High King, and did his cause no harm in Scotland, where he was becoming seen as a worthy successor to Kenneth, and that succession the sooner the better. Perhaps the Norsemen would hear of it and take note, and decide that Strathclyde, like Moray and Ross, was unsuitable territory for their hosting.

On 22nd July Fenella was brought to bed, and after a fairly lengthy labour, hand held for much of the time by her anxious husband, was delivered of a small son, Nechtan mac Cormac.

That night, the bells of churches were rung, not only at Glamis, Kinnordy and Usan but at Aberbrothack Abbey and all over Angus. The spae-wife of Rescobie no doubt received her measure of praise also.

23

Scotland decided, whatever the exact and correct date, that this millennium was a good thing for the realm, however unfortunate for England and other kingdoms. An almost unprecedented spell of peace and comparative harmony prevailed, and men and women could get on with the business of normal living without the everlasting dread of war, and fighting for their rulers, homes and lives, this despite misrule on the part of the Ard Righ and murmurings amongst his mormaors and lords. None judged that this state of affairs would last for very long, especially with Malcolm's ambitions so well known; but praises be for present mercies!

So said the Thane of Glamis. Fenella made a swift and complete recovery, and became as active as before, while being a good mother, even while suckling Nechtan. That infant presented them with few problems, a healthy normal child, with a strong appetite and lungs, and left his parents in no doubts as to his wishes. Cormac said that he took after his mother.

The Lady Alena was greatly taken with her grandson, and requested the more frequent visits, so that Red Castle began to rival Kinnordy and Glamis as a place of residence. One day, of course, it would be Fenella's property, and then Nechtan's. That young scrap of humanity indeed seemed destined to become lord of vast lands.

The winter came, still without any serious troubles, and whether the millennium date had been a year out or not, there were still no miraculous happenings that Yuletide either, folk however content with peace.

During all this time Connacher's attitude was strange.

Until the child had been born he was all care and anxiety. But now that the hoped-for heir to the mormaordom was safely delivered, he appeared to lose interest. Any hint of the child's ailing would presumably have greatly worried him; but so long as Nechtan was fit and thriving he did not concern himself with him. Cormac wondered whether perhaps this had something to do with *himself*? As the father of the eventual Mormaor of Angus, did Connacher fear that he might interest himself and perhaps interfere in the mortuath's affairs? It was a possibility, with that strange man.

Their blessed period of peace was not paralleled elsewhere, however, and the troubles of others, even of their enemies, could possibly affect them in Scotland sooner or later. Of particular relevance that spring and summer was the rivalry between King Olaf of Norway and King Sven of Denmark, related as they were, the sudden death of the Emperor Otto creating a power vacuum and leaving these two to fulfil their contrary ambitions. Sven instituted a series of major attacks on the east and south of England, no mere raiding this but full-scale invasion led by himself, to take advantage of Ethelred's incompetence. The object seemed to be not actual occupation of the land but the stripping of its wealth and possessions for export to Denmark, Kent in especial suffering, but also right round the Channel areas to South Wales. To compete with this, Olaf of Norway assailed the Northern Isles, especially Orkney and the lands dominated therefrom in northern Scotland, Caithness and Sutherland. This had the effect of causing Thorfinn Raven-Feeder to withdraw from aiding MacBeth in Moray and Ross to return to assist his father, the Earl Sigurd, in countering Olaf's attacks. Noting it, Cormac feared that it might not be long until more, as it were unofficial, raiding started again on his friend's domains, and the longships' presence be required once more. What was it about these Scandinavians that they were so set on plundering other folk who had done them no hurt?

Nechtan's first birthday was celebrated with great acclaim. They introduced him to salt water at Lunan Bay, to his splashing and chuckling collapse, taking to it like any duck.

That autumn the first signs of an end to the unaccustomed and blessed tranquillity began to appear. And they emanated from Strathclyde again. Malcolm mac Kenneth, after his victory over Ethelred, perceiving that there were unlikely to be any further English attacks in the near future, and with the Norsemen occupied otherwise, felt strong enough to repeat his challenge to the High King, and this time to put a time limit upon his demands. The Ard Righ was to abdicate in his, Malcolm's, favour, or fight, and this within the year, or it would be outright war.

This renewed and ominous threat, clearly no idle one, had Kenneth much perturbed, sufficiently so to call a meeting of his mormaors, this for the beginning of November at his seat of Forteviot. Would they all attend, dissatisfied with the monarch as most of them were?

MacBeth mac Finlay at least did. He arrived at Glamis two days before the conference was due to start, the first Cormac and Fenella had seen of him for many months. Proudly they introduced their small son to him, in a pleasing reunion.

MacBeth was much concerned over the monarchial situation. He believed that if it came to war the majority of his fellow mormaors would not rally to the support of Kenneth, and some might actively aid Malcolm. The present Ard Righ's behaviour was alienating them all, not least his declared intention of abolishing the ages-old and all but unique system of appointing the High Kings by election, by the mormaors, of the most suitable and worthy candidate from the separate branches of the ruling line; and substituting the principle of eldest son succeeding father on the throne, such as was usual elsewhere than in Scotland. Apart from this being contrary to cherished tradition, it was in present circumstances the more objectionable in that Kenneth's surviving son, Giric, brother of the late

Dungald, was a young man of no effective character, a nonentity, whose nominal rule of his father's Athol mortuath was feeble in the extreme. For him to be the next High King was not to be considered. So this meeting of mormaors was likely to be a stormy one.

MacBeth himself was in a difficult position in all this. For although he would favour Malcolm as the best choice of Ard Righ for Scotland, that man was said to support Gillacomgain in his ambitions, he who had murdered Finlay, MacBeth's father. So if he did ascend the throne, he might well appoint that unworthy cousin to be Mormaor of Moray and Ross, displacing himself, MacBeth, a grievous thought.

At this suggestion, Fenella it was who pointed out that Malcolm owed Cormac and herself some gratitude for the longships' aid in ridding his Cumbria of the Viking threats. Could they not approach him, send him a message perhaps, urging that he repaid his debt to them by renouncing his support of the murderous Gillacomgain and favour the excellent MacBeth, the rightful mormaor? Cormac agreed that this might well be done. Malcolm, himself not a mormaor, would be unlikely to appear at the Forteviot meeting; but they could visit him at Dumbarton and press MacBeth's case.

Grateful, their friend informed them of the present situation regarding Gillacomgain. He had not sought to retake Inverness or other of the Moray and Ross strongholds, but remained hidden away in the Highland fastnesses of Strathconon and Glen Orrin, his family lands. But that he had not given up his hopes of taking over the mormaorship, and possibly of rising even further, seemed evident by the fact that he had recently contrived his marriage with the Lady Gruoch, little more than a child, daughter of the ineffectual and ailing Boide, head of the alternative branch of the royal line. This was ominous, to say the least; the match could be for no other purpose than to further Gillacomgain's ambitions. The girl was an only child, and in their matrilineal system could place him in a position of influence.

It occurred to Cormac that this marriage could hardly commend itself to Malcolm of Strathclyde, who undoubtedly would want no possible challenges for the throne from the alternative line. So, a point to be made in MacBeth's favour?

They saw their friend off to the mormaors' meeting encouraged.

MacBeth returned three days later, sooner than expected, and had to travel down to Red Castle to see them, on one of their visits to the Lady Alena. He told them that the conference, if such it could be called, had been anything but a success, at least as far as King Kenneth was concerned, criticism of his regime predominating and little in the way of support against Malcolm voiced. All these sub-kings in theory were bound to use their strengths in the cause of the reigning monarch whom they had elected, and could not threaten him overtly; but they could indicate fault-finding and disapproval, and this they had done, Kenneth's demands that they all rally their fullest forces in his cause, in the event of his nephew's threatened uprising, being greeted with very evident reserve. The son, Giric's, strident dictates, as acting Mormaor of Athol, that they put down his wretched cousin Malcolm without waiting for further threats, by no means helping his father. MacBeth feared that civil war was inevitable, and before very long, with consequent dire bloodshed. He almost wished that enemy raiding might start again – but not on Moray and Ross – in order that Malcolm might be restrained, and time given for some sort of compromise to be reached. Not that any likely compromise on either side was to be envisaged meantime.

MacBeth went off back to Inverness, a worthy man with much on his mind, the couple promising to pay their suggested visit to Dumbarton before the worst of the winter weather set in.

* * *

Judging that Nechtan was old enough now to be left in the care of his maternal grandmother at Red Castle, she doting on him, the pair, with Duncan as usual, set out on the long ride south-westwards in windy and overcast but passable conditions, Fenella's first major expedition since giving birth. They halted overnight at Auchterarder in Strathearn, passing near to Kenneth's Forteviot but not venturing into the royal presence. By late afternoon of the second day they reached the Clyde, by way of the Doune of Menteith, Drymen and Strathleven, having made good time.

Malcolm received them questioningly, far from effusive; but they had not expected any warm welcome from that man. When he realised that they were not on their way anywhere else and had not called in merely to spend the night, he was typically direct.

"What brings you to my door, then, all the way from Angus?" he asked. "In especial yourself, lady?"

"I support my husband in most matters, Prince Malcolm," she answered easily. "Not only in the uses of longships. And this seemed an issue of some importance. For the realm."

"Indeed? And the Thane of Glamis esteems his presence here sufficiently important to ride over one hundred miles?"

"We do," Cormac said, a little stiffly. He could not like this individual, however highly he might assess his qualities of drive and leadership. "Since we have been given information by MacBeth, Mormaor of Moray, which we feel concerns yourself and the nation both."

"MacBeth sent you to me? For his own purposes?"

"No. It was our own decision to come here. For we understand that you favour Gillacomgain, who slew MacBeth's father, Finlay."

"What if I do? Finlay was no great loss."

"Gillacomgain seeks to take the mormaorship from MacBeth. And he is ambitious! Would you wish him to become Mormaor of Moray and Ross? If he got rid of

MacBeth, slew him also, like his father, it would mean war with the Orkneymen. Thorfinn Raven-Feeder, MacBeth's half-brother, would see to that! Would you wish it, with the other Vikings, the Kings of Denmark and Norway, already assailing England?"

Malcolm pursed his lips. "I have no reason to believe that Gillacomgain would slay MacBeth. He may seek to *succeed* him, his cousin. As might be his right."

"MacBeth is a younger man than he is. Not likely to require a successor – unless he died an untimely death!"

"This is all mere supposition, Thane Cormac. Fears, with little to support them."

"He has already attempted to grasp Moray. Took Inverness. Until he was driven out by MacBeth."

"With your aid, I understand?"

"Yes. We used our longships to help MacBeth. As we did to help *you*!"

"Yes. But that was different. Norse invaders of our nation. Not a family contest. The realm's concern."

"And are Gillacomgain's designs not the realm's concern also?" Fenella asked. "He is, we say, ambitious, for more than Moray and Ross, we deem."

"What mean you?"

"Why has he wed the Lady Gruoch nic Boide? Not just to gain Moray, in which this child-bride has no interest."

"Wed! Gruoch . . . ? Gillacomgain!"

"Yes. Had you not heard? It is recently."

"Why would he do that?" Cormac demanded. "Other than to produce a child who would be in line for the throne?"

Malcolm stared, eyes narrowed. Clearly he was much concerned – and Malcolm mac Kenneth concerned was a notable sight. He turned and strode away from them across his hall, and back again.

"This is truth? Assured? No mere hearsay?" he charged them.

"MacBeth himself told us. And he knows the truth. No secrets from him in Moray!"

The other let out a long breath. "Then I have a second cause for thanks to you," he said. "I shall not forget either. I would have heard of this in due course, to be sure. But the sooner that I knew the better!" He waved a hand, changing his tone. "You have come a long way to tell me this. You will bide the night here? Before you return?"

This was hospitality indeed for Malcolm mac Kenneth. They did not see much of him however that night, for all his gratitude, well provided for as they were. He saw them on their way home next morning, in thin rain, without further evidence of thanks. But they judged their objective achieved. What would be the results of their mission?

It was, in fact, next spring before they gained an answer to that. Young Gruoch was a widow. Gillacomgain had been attacked in a house in the Highlands, the building set afire, and he and fifty of his men burned to death. Malcolm had not been wholly successful in his designs however, for MacBeth reported that Gruoch, despite her youth and short period of marriage, was pregnant.

24

A more happy marriage than Gruoch's was celebrated that spring, at Glamis, with Bridget nic Farquhar wedding Drostan of Dunninald. That young man, a firm supporter of Cormac's, had been a frequent visitor, his property only a score of miles away. Sometimes the latter had wondered a little at Drostan's needs to consult him, over and above his help with the longships, now he knew. Bridget was joyful, and Ada glad that her daughter was going to be living so comparatively nearby.

Such pleasant family affairs however were soon superseded by the developments so long feared by many in Scotland. Having so swiftly disposed of any threats to his designs by Gillacomgain of Conon, Malcolm mac Kenneth did not delay in seeking to do likewise towards his twice-threatened uncle, King Kenneth himself, and marched north in force. He had raised men from all over Strathclyde and Cumbria, won others from the Argyll Highlands north of Dumbarton, and now called on all men, great and small, who cared for the weal of the realm to join him. When he heard of it the Ard Righ did the same, asserting that his traitorous nephew must be taught once and for all who ruled the land, and the penalties for treason. All mormaors, thanes, lords and chieftains to rally to the royal-boar-on-silver banner.

So, like all the others, Cormac was faced with the dire decision: whom to support? Like most, he believed that Malcolm would make a better monarch, and as son of the murdered Kenneth the Second had an undoubted claim to the throne. But he had taken his oath of allegiance to Kenneth the Third, and held such oath as no mere gesture, but binding. He had a notion that Connacher, and probably most other mormaors, would be equally unhappy, and he doubted whether many would throw their full, or indeed any, weight behind the High King. But that did not solve his own problem, salve his conscience. What to do?

Fenella, practical as always, asked exactly what he had sworn to do at that oath-taking. He said that it had been to honour the Ard Righ, to sustain him in the realm's cause, and to heed his call at all times.

"The realm's cause? And heed? You can heed, my dear. But that need not mean swift action! And the *realm's* cause? If your heeding makes you doubt whether the action is to the realm's good, need you so act?"

"That, I think, is but hair-splitting, lass. No honest plea."

"A man is permitted, indeed expected, to use his wits, his judgment, in all matters, no? You can surely judge rightly only when you know all the facts. So, no need to rush into action, I say. Heed, yes. But take your time. And see matters so."

"I fear that you are but playing with words in this, my hitherto so-assured wife!"

"Not so. I but see it as the correct use and understanding of words. The words of your oath to Kenneth. That you may not hazard yourself and those you lead in a cause in which you do not believe."

"What do you say that I *do*, then?"

"Call your people, yes. But in no great haste. Ride for Forteviot. Discover Kenneth's intentions. What forces he has. How the mormaors are supporting him. Urge a meeting with Malcolm. Discussion, not bloodshed. Come to terms, in some sort. For the realm's weal. Others will say the same, I swear! And if Kenneth refuses, then you make your decision, conscience clear."

He stared at her. "I know not whether it is an angel or a devil that is advising me!" he declared.

"It is neither, Cormac my heart. It is your wife, part of your own self. We were made one in marriage, were we not? Here is how *one* part of you sees this matter, so important. For you, for us both, and for others. Heed, yes – heed *me*! I have thought long on this . . ."

Cormac doubtfully heeded. His decision admittedly could affect the lives of others, of many. Had he the right, because of the tugging of his conscience, and that possibly mistaken, to hazard his life and those of his people? But anyone, any commander of men, could so debate. And no great issues ever be decided.

He called for a rally of his thanedom's men for two days hence.

He learned that Connacher was allegedly doing nothing – which was of no help to him.

Another day, and he bade farewell to Fenella. At least, with Nechtan to cherish, she could not propose to accompany them on this possibly fateful mission. She did not further press her advice on him – not in words, at any rate; but her looks were eloquent. They embraced, and then she turned away almost abruptly.

At Forteviot in Strathearn they learned that King Kenneth and his son Giric, with no very large host, had already departed westwards, apparently only one mormaor, young Mar, in support, leaving instructions for others answering his call to come on after him, with all haste. It seemed that he was heading up the River Earn towards the skirts of the Highlands at Loch Earn itself, there to seek to prevent the Argyll forces whom Malcolm was known to have summoned from joining up with him. If he could defeat these first, it would be a notable advantage. Since the Argyllmen were coming from the Inveraray and Oban and Tyndrum areas, the presumption was that they would have to thread the passes of Glens Ogle or Lednock to reach Malcolm's army, which was reported to be coming north by Glasgow and Stirling and Menteith. These narrow Highland passes were ideal for surprise ambushing, the unsuspecting enemy inevitably strung out and vulnerable, leadership detached from most of the led.

Cormac wondered who was thus advising Kenneth as to strategy?

He and his pressed on, with only a modest party of the Thane of Gowrie's people as company.

Strathearn was a long and wide vale, reaching westwards from Perth for fully thirty-five miles, by Madderty and Crieff to the narrows of St Fillans between Comrie and Loch Earn itself, where the river rose. Having already come all the way from Angus and Gowrie, they camped for the night at Gask, where they learned that the King's army had passed the previous noontide.

In the morning they continued to ride westwards. Cormac knew this country, for they had traversed it coming back from Iona burials to Scone for coronations. How far ahead was Kenneth? And how far south was Malcolm?

It was just after midday that they learned the answers to that. They were nearing Innerpeffray, still on the Earn, when they were surprised to see a hard-riding company of perhaps two score coming towards them from the west. As these came up, Cormac recognised their leader, Colin, Thane of Struan; and he had a bloody shirt bandaging one bare shoulder. Others of the party looked the worse for wear also.

Drawing up but not dismounting, this Colin shouted his tidings. "All lost!" he cried. "All over! Too late. A massacre! Kenneth dead. His son with him. We had no chance . . ."

Cormac and the others stared.

"Malcolm came up behind us. Come further than we thought. The Argyll force already through the passes before us. We were held, back and front. Kenneth sought only to flee. Malcolm trapped him, sought him out, slew him with his own hand. Back there, at Monzievaird near to Crieff. It was a massacre!"

Scarcely able to take it all in, the hearers gasped out exclamations, questions, demands.

These were not answered, for over the slight ridge ahead

came another band of horsemen, in equally determined flight, more so indeed, for these did not draw up beside the first but pounded on eastwards, past them, without pause.

Their urgency transmitted itself to Struan and his men, who promptly spurred on after them. And not only Struan, for Gowrie, cursing, waved his people round, to ride off also whence they had just come.

Cormac and his men were left there, most of the latter clearly preparing to do likewise. But summoning his wits desperately, Cormac tried to consider aright. What was it to be, now? Was this flight the answer? Kenneth dead, Malcolm would certainly become the High King. Flight from him not the answer, surely? They had not taken part in the fighting. And Malcolm owed him something. Flight would seem as though *against* the winner. Better to go on, then, meet him, hail him, the victor?

Pondering, undecided in this sudden exigency, the sight of Fenella's face rose before his inward eye. What would she say to this, his other half? He had little doubt, really. She would be for going on, congratulating Malcolm on his victory. Not saying that he had been on his way to join Kenneth, however doubtfully. Supporting *him*, Malcolm, now. For the good of the realm. All debating now pointless.

That was it, then. He told Duncan and Pate of his decision, and they accepted it without question. What his rank and file thought, he did not ask himself.

So they rode on westwards, distinctly off-putting as it was to pass other fleeing groups from the battle going in the other direction. Cormac was not sure just where this Monzievaird was. Struan had said near to Crieff. He knew Crieff, at least, another five miles perhaps.

Approaching that quite large community set in the Highland foothills, they found it in a state of high excitement, word of the battle on all lips, some fugitives already amongst them, fears expressed as to what this

Prince Malcolm would do now. So far no victorious troops had entered the township, but . . .

Monzievaird, it seemed, was a hilly area to the north-west, barely three miles away. They rode on.

From a ridge, presently, they saw the smoke of campfires rising ahead. But also they saw a group of horsemen coming towards them along the slight height, no hurrying refugees these but obviously a sentinel party. Cormac turned his one hundred and fifty towards these.

"Who comes?" was shouted at them by a sword-pointing leader. "Who comes, thus late in the day!"

"The Thane of Glamis, to speak with the Prince Malcolm mac Kenneth. Of possible aid to him," was the careful answer.

"The Prince of Strathclyde needs no aid from such as you!" was jerked back at him.

"He did once! None so long ago. In Cumbria."

The shouter shrugged, and leaving his party under another, said that he would conduct the thane to Prince Malcolm, whatever his reception might be.

They rode down amongst the grassy braes and hillocks to a quite wide valley in which the waters of a loch glittered. The area was clearly full of men and horses, those campfires amongst them.

Approaching, it was very evident that this had been the scene of the battle, bodies of men and horses littering the ground, bloody gear and weapons everywhere. They were led towards the lochside where, dismounting, Cormac was escorted alone forward to one of the fires where Malcolm mac Kenneth sat with some of his chieftains, including kilted Highlandmen, eating and drinking.

Recognising him at once, Malcolm pointed authoritatively. "Ha, Cormac mac Farquhar! Come late in the day! And to whose side?"

Cormac had had time to consider well his reply to whatever reception he was accorded. And he desired to sound honest.

"I come in some doubts, my lord Malcolm," he answered.

"The Ard Righ summoned us all to his aid. Some held back, did not move. I chose to come on, delaying yes, with this small company. To discover the rights of it. Not to fight, if that was possible. To seek mediation. What was best for the realm."

"Ah, a careful man, the Thane of Glamis! Heedful for his own welfare, as well as that of the realm!"

"Was I so heedful of myself and mine in your Cumbria? I had sworn allegiance to the High King at Scone. But judged that *you* would serve the realm better. So I came thus."

"To see which side would gain the mastery? And to join that!"

"To seek mediation, discussion, a settlement, rather than bloodshed. Are we not all fellow Scots, our duty not to slay each other, but to choose the best for all, for the kingdom?"

Malcolm eyed him keenly, assessingly. "And if you had come earlier? While still we battled, my uncle and myself? Whom would you have supported?"

"Once battle was joined, I would have preferred yourself, Prince. But I still would have sought mediation." That was the best that he could do.

"A careful man, as I said, Cormac of Glamis!"

"Is care not called for, in those who lead? As we both showed in the matter of Gillacomgain!"

The other stroked his chin, glancing over at his interested companions. Then he reached over and drew a rib of roasted mutton from beside the smouldering fire, and held this out to Cormac.

Swallowing his relief, he accepted that offering, and what it seemed to represent, and raised the meat to his lips.

Malcolm patted the plaid on which he was sitting. "Come, and tell me more of your caring for the realm's good," he said, not without a trace of mockery. "Who knows, I may need it? Now that I am to become Ard Righ."

That simple statement, so almost casually rendered,

made entirely clear that Scotland was now going to have a monarch whose rule would be as unassailable as it was firm and assured. Cormac sat, however warily, and chewed at that rib, tough as it was.

"Connacher, your mormaor?" he was asked. "Where is he? Where stands he?"

"He is still at Forfar, I would think. He was never strong for King Kenneth."

"He had better be strong for me, then! Tell him so. Or your small son may become Mormaor of Angus sooner than you might expect! And then *you* having to make the right decisions for him!" Malcolm was well informed, clearly. There was a hint of menace behind that.

Chewing, Cormac was spared having to answer.

"Your friend, MacBeth of Moray? How sees he the nation's cause? Is he grateful to me over Gillacomgain?"

"I judge that he will be, yes."

"Tell him that he ought to be. In your caring for the peace and well-being of the realm."

This appeared to be developing into a session of threats and warnings. More tearing off of undercooked meat was indicated.

"Have you paid your respects to the remains of him to whom you swore fealty?" he was asked. "His corpse lies yonder." And Malcolm pointed across the encampment. "Iona for him, although he did not deserve it!"

Taking this to be a form of dismissal, and also a reminder of dutiful attendance at the formal interment, and thereafter the so-assured coronation, Cormac thankfully rose, and made his way over to the spot indicated, beside tethered horses, where, on a sort of platform contrived out of spears and lances and shields, plaiding covered the shape of a man. Biting his lip, he went to raise the corner of the cloth – and winced at the sight of the diagonally slashed face, all dried blood, one eye gone, the other staring blindly. Cormac looked no further. This was the third High King's body he had seen in those so few years. Clearly it was a hazardous position to hold. He wondered how long the next incumbent would manage to retain it. Somehow, he judged that this tenure would be a considerably longer one.

There was nothing to detain him there now, he reckoned. It was only mid-afternoon, and if they set off for home now, they could be back in Strathmore by the next evening. He, like others, would have to attend the Iona burial, which would not be long delayed. But at least he ought to have a couple of days with Fenella and Nechtan before he must leave for that, and the coronation presumably to follow.

He would have much to tell his wife. And to commend her judgment.

25

There was no question in any of the mormaors' minds, after the interment of Kenneth, as to whom to elect as Ard Righ. It was taken for granted by them, and by all, that Malcolm the Second was High King of Scots, and the return to Scone merely made to confirm the fact formally. That man was now being given a new by-name, Malcolm Foiranach, the Destroyer. He had earned it.

So Cormac had to swear allegiance once more. MacBeth also.

Malcolm Foiranach did not delay in using his new power. He informed all mormaors that their allegiance was no mere gesture but a firm commitment to support him with all their strengths in all matters to do with the nation, or be ousted from their mortuaths. Whether he had indeed the right to threaten this was very doubtful; but he emphasised his declaration by promptly marrying his daughter, Bethoc, to the hereditary Primate of the Celtic Church, Crinan the Thane, lay Abbot of Dunkeld, and thereafter creating him Mormaor of Atholl in place of the late Giric mac Kenneth; thus ensuring that he had the important influence of the churchmen behind him, with their ability to refuse the Christian rites of baptism, marriage and burial to transgressors. Malcolm had no son, only two young daughters; but in their matrilineal system, daughters were the more important where the royal prerogative was concerned, although they could not ascend the throne. The late Kenneth had wished to change this rule to the usual father-and-son succession, but not Malcolm, thereby further strengthening his position with the Church.

Other moves he made to limit the powers of the mormaors and enhance his own, and with the reputation he had earned for himself, got away with it.

Little of all this affected Cormac at this stage, however much it did Connacher and his like, and he and Fenella enjoyed a period of peace to get on with their own lives, for which they were grateful. Nechtan continued to be a great joy to them both, developing fast. At two years he was a bundle of activity, never still while he was awake, but a happy child however demanding.

The nation's demands, for such as his father, were likewise not to be ignored, if less rewarding. The first trouble of the new regime came from the north. King Olaf of Norway's rivalry with his Danish counterpart took a new turn. He, until fairly recently a pagan like most Scandinavians, had succumbed to Christian teaching and been baptised. In his new-found faith and enthusiasm, and possibly in the hope that this Christ-God would prove effective in forwarding his competition with Sven of Denmark, he insisted that the Earl Sigurd of Orkney and Shetland, his vassal, should also turn Christian. Sigurd refused, and Olaf changed his concern with Orkney into downright occupation, Sigurd and his son Thorfinn becoming prisoners in their own isles, paying a high price for their adherence to the old religion of Thor and Odin. As a result of this, the Raven-Feeder was unable to come to MacBeth's aid; and noting it, the Norse raiding recommenced on the Moray and Ross coasts. So Cormac and his longships were called upon once more, after a lengthy spell of inaction.

Fenella made her first complaint about Nechtan, in that he was still too young to be left with either of his grandmothers, to allow her to accompany the fleet.

The fishermen of the havens were by no means reluctant to resume their anti-Viking activities, with the booty they were apt to gain thereby, as well as the sense of achievement; and Cormac and Donnie the Crab took a flotilla of fourteen ships northwards, seen off at Ethiehaven by a frustrated Fenella and a shouting Nechtan.

They had their accustomed long sail up the coastline to the Moray Firth, and it was at Garmouth in Spey Bay before they saw the usual signs of raiding, smoke rising inland from various points. Four Norse ships lay beached at this Garmouth, and the Scots had little difficulty in taking over three of these, although the Vikings left to guard them chose to make their escape in the fourth one rather than to flee afoot westwards to warn their fellow raiders on land.

Cormac decided to continue with his previous policy of not actually engaging in fighting with the stranded enemy inland, where possible, but to leave them ship-less for MacBeth's armed Moray forces to deal with, his fishermen crews more useful as sailors than as soldiers. So seventeen vessels continued on northwards.

They saw only one other sign of raiding, this at Findhorn before the firth began to narrow in towards Inverness, and here they arrived too late, for the Norsemen had evidently finished their hosting, and seeing the fleet approaching, took to their five craft and headed seawards to make their escape. Under-crewed again, with their captured ships, the Scots recognised that they had little hope of catching up with these and doing battle. They followed them north-eastwards for an hour or so to ensure, if possible, that they did not return for further ravaging, before at length turning westwards for Inverness.

Landing there, they discovered that MacBeth himself was away with a force seeking to deal with raiders further north, in Ross. So they set sail again, and went as far as Nigg, at the mouth of the Cromarty Firth, before they saw more telltale smokes from burning thatches, and drawing in, were able to capture three more longships, their guards putting up a fight on this occasion, however hopelessly outnumbered. Two or three survivors escaping inland, Cormac and his men followed them some way, and presently were confronted with the Norse compatriots retiring towards their ships in the face of horsed attackers, a running battle. Caught between two opposing forces, the Norsemen were trapped, some fleeing individually but most dying fighting, for whatever else they were brave men, however disadvantaged they were against horsemen with lances and spears.

While, thereafter, the two groups of Scots were congratulating themselves on this encounter, who should ride up to them but MacBeth himself, with a third party, come from dealing with another group of invaders further inland. Joyful was the reunion.

In discussion as to further action, MacBeth said that he had heard of no raiding to the north; but on Cormac's suggestion that they might sail on thither for some way, in case there might be, he, MacBeth, said that he would accompany them in the ship, leaving his men to return to Inverness meantime, to rejoin them presently.

This they did, the two friends relishing each other's company. They went as far north as Tarbat Ness, the Ross border with Sutherland, but saw no signs of the enemy, before turning to head back for Inverness.

There the Angus contingent spent a couple of days being entertained and feasted, to their satisfaction, before a return was made southwards, Cormac promising further help should raiding resume. It had been a rewarding mission.

As it transpired, raiding did resume, and on a major scale, consisting of invasion indeed. For it seemed that these Norsemen had come from Orkney and Shetland, and those escapers had appealed to King Olaf, still there, and he decided to teach the Scots a lesson. So, that early autumn, he personally led a descent upon Moray and Ross, spreading devastation.

The first Cormac heard of this was from King Malcolm, not MacBeth. A messenger came to Glamis from the Ard Righ, declaring that this incursion by the Norwegian monarch on *his* domains was insufferable, and must be dealt with adequately and at once. Cormac was to muster his maximum strength in longships and take them north, while Connacher and the other mormaors were to join him, the High King, with their forces, for all-out war. Olaf would learn why Malcolm was called the Destroyer!

So it was all activity. The Ard Righ would mark his advance northwards by lighting hill-top beacons, which could be seen from the sea, so that the longship fleet would be able to sail more or less parallel with the army, a combined operation.

Fenella was the more frustrated than ever that motherhood prevented her from taking part in this great occasion.

Now with two dozen ships, the Angusmen set sail, a little doubtful as to this beacon-signalling arrangement.

Their doubts grew as they proceeded northwards. They did not know just when Malcolm was starting out, nor where from. Presumably he would march fairly near the coast, not only that he might keep in touch with the ships but because the Norsemen were very much coast-conscious, their vessels all-important to them. Even Olaf would not venture far from the sea, it was reckoned.

Cormac, in consequence, was getting anxious before they saw their first beacon, or what they assumed was one, a single column of smoke, quickly getting dispersed in the breeze, rising from a prominent summit near St Peter's Head in Buchan, well north of Aberdeen. So Malcolm was indeed on his way, and was taking the coastal route. They saw another of these signal-fires some ten miles further, at the headland of Inverallochy.

Soon they would be off Moray. Where would they find King Olaf's invasion? Would it be concentrated in one area, or spread out over a wide front? Cormac had to be concerned about this, for even his enlarged group of ships would be in no position to assail the sort of fleet the Norse monarch was likely to bring on such a major foray, indeed must bring to transport his troops.

The beacons ceased after the headland of Pennan, and the question was whether to continue on, westwards now, or to heave to for a while? They might be getting ahead of the High King's army, and that was not advisable. They drew in to a small bay, to pass a second night. All seemed peaceable here.

In the morning there was still no sign of beacons, nor yet inland fires. No enemy shipping either. At something of a loss, Cormac hesitated to put to sea again. If Malcolm was not yet as far up as this, the last thing wanted was to proceed on into enemy-held waters. Indeed he was in some doubt as to what part the Ard Righ expected him and his to play in this campaign. He was to pose a threat from the sea, presumably, in support of the land army; but so much would depend on the numbers of the enemy force left with their ships, and where these ships were based. It was all very uncertain.

They waited near Pennan for much of that day, with no indications of other than the local folks' activity to guide them. But eventually, feeling that this waiting was of no use to anybody, they moved on.

For about thirty miles they rowed, without being any the wiser as to the situation. Then, at the eastern horn of Spey Bay, they saw smoke ahead, no beacons this but widespread and hazy, giving the impression that it was not new, coming from old fires. Could this be the area of Olaf's landings? Spey mouth and its vicinity was fertile, populous country, the sort of terrain that the Vikings ever sought. Only recently they themselves had had that encounter at Garmouth.

That ravaged community was approximately at the centre of the great bay, the river mouth itself forming a lesser inlet. And as they drew near this, in the fifteen-mile wide stretch, they saw ahead of them a positive forest of timber upthrusting, the masts of longships innumerable. Here, then, was the invaders' base.

What now? They could not even begin to count the numbers of ships berthed and beached there, sufficient to transport an army. No previous experience applied here. Any idea of major assault on these marshalled vessels seemed out of the question. They had come to aid Malcolm, yes – but how to do it? Presumably the main enemy force was not here, but somewhere inland, where all that smoke arose?

If *they* could see all those ships, their guards would be as able to see them. So some decision must be made swiftly. To wait there, offshore, posing some sort of threat: would that help the High King? Very little, Cormac assessed. Surely action of some sort was called for. It occurred to him that all those ships, drawn up in close-ranked lines, hemmed each other in. Most could not move until the formation was somehow broken up and space given to use sweeps, to manoeuvre in some measure. So, in fact, only those at the outer, seaward, edge would be able to put up any sort of fight in the first instance. Therefore, a swift descent upon these, a limited attack, and then withdrawal out into the main bay again? Would that have some useful effect? It was all that he could think of.

There could be no delay in this, if it was to be worth while. Cormac shouted to his nearer craft to spread the word. An assault on the outer row of the enemy ships, then back out here before any large number of the Norsemen could gather thereon to oppose them. Set fire to the ships as far as possible; furled sails would burn. Sweeps could be broken or thrown overboard. Their own strategy heedful not to get in each others' way. Then withdrawal. He would signal when, with his horn.

Cormac's ship led the way in.

As they neared land they could see much activity amongst the enemy vessels, activities of men, not of ships, these more or less wedged in position. How many men had been left at this Garmouth they could not estimate, but, fairly clearly, many. These would not be certain that it was a Scots fleet approaching, longships like their own; but if these Norsemen were from Orkney and Shetland, they would know about the Angusmen's initiative, and would not be unprepared. But they could not know the tactics intended, and might well not all come out to defend the first ranks of their ships. So they, the attackers, might be given time to do considerable damage before they had to retire.

This of using fire was the obvious course, but it might be difficult in the limited time available to get much set alight. His men would all have flint, steel and tinder, for campfires and the like; but apart from sailcloth and possible blanketing and spare clothing left aboard, there might not be much that would burn promptly. Getting rid of the sweeps could be more effective perhaps.

Bearing down on the enemy, Cormac assessed that there were about a score of longships ranked in what constituted the outer tier, five or six times that behind and more beached. So he ordered his vessels into a line-abreast formation, and so drove forward at the foe, who must by now be in no doubts as to the hostility of the newcomers.

Norsemen were leaping out from one vessel to another, swords and axes in hand, but, so far as could be gauged, in insufficient numbers adequately to protect every forward ship, their defence unco-ordinated and haphazard at this stage. Some came jumping over other craft to one ship, some to others, leaving a proportion unguarded. Even so, those reached did not obtain more than perhaps half a dozen each, no effective defence against the fully manned Scots vessels.

The one Cormac's longship bore down on, roughly central in the line, had in fact only four men awaiting them; and as the two vessels collided, Scots sweeps inboard, and fully a score of attackers clambered over the side and upon them, these wisely turned and leaped back whence they had come, on to the boats behind. As far as this craft was concerned, it was a bloodless victory.

Two or three of the Scots had battle-axes now, captured from previous Norse affrays, and these were set to smashing enemy sweeps stacked there. Others sought to set fire to anything which might burn, with less success, although the great raven-painted square sail, in folds at the mast-foot, did catch alight, and its flames burned the ropes and rigging satisfactorily, even though little else was consumed.

Cormac allowed his men to deal with all this, himself urgently watching the overall situation, both to check on how the other crews fared and to look landwards to see what other Norsemen might be coming out from the shore. Some he saw, but insufficient greatly to alter the situation. And so far as he could tell, their own men all seemed to be succeeding in their efforts, the clash of some fighting sounding, as well as oar-smashing, others having no opposition to cope with, smoke now rising from many ships.

He wondered now whether, in the circumstances, to proceed on to the next row of moored vessels; but decided against this. It would give time for more enemy to come out; and his people be delayed in getting back to their own craft.

When he judged that sufficient havoc had been wrought, he blew the horn that he carried for signalling to distant crews, three long blasts, which ought to sound clear above the din, indicating withdrawal. There was fairly prompt obedience, although some inevitable delay in getting into their ships and seated six to a bench and the long sweeps repositioned.

As far as Cormac could see, they pulled off without casualties, leaving satisfactory chaos behind them. Well out from the land, they hove to, to gaze shorewards.

So far as they could see their assault was producing the desired effects. There was confusion and much activity, but no sign of ships putting to sea for combat. That might come, but not yet.

They waited. Cormac did not see what else they could usefully do. Another such attack would be difficult, with the enemy prepared, and those damaged craft to be got over first before others could be reached. Posing a threat out here seemed to be their only practical contribution meantime, however little idling appealed to him. For how long they lay there watching was difficult to calculate before they perceived different movement landwards. And landwards it was, men coming streaming down from the grassy slopes inland, a few at first and then more, a stream erratic as it became unending, with no horses. The watchers gazed, and sought a reason. And the only reason that presented itself was that these were Norsemen hastening back to their ships. And if so, why? It could only represent defeat. They were fleeing from a battle, therefore, and a victory – but not for King Olaf.

Was that wishful thinking? But as hurrying men continued to appear, their thinking seemed to be confirmed. All these coming in haste to the ships could only spell Norse disaster.

Then, to be sure, decision fell to be taken by the watchers, major decision. These fugitives, if such they were, would not be coming merely to sit beside their ships. They would be for off, to sea, escape. A solid mass of them, if pursued, could make a stand, but not this straggling rabble. So vessels would presently be coming out from this Garmouth. But they could not help but see two score of Scots longships waiting there. What would they do?

It took some time for them to gain an answer to that, and all the while new escapers were arriving. Which, of course, meant that the number of ships liable to come out would be the greater. Needless to say, Cormac would have preferred that they sailed out singly or in twos or threes.

The first to emerge did, in fact, meet his requirements, four craft issuing from the great pack of vessels, sails hoisted and sweeps busy. Wisely, from their own point of view, these quickly swung off sharply at an angle, heading towards the northern horn of the great bay.

Promptly the Scots set to cut them off.

It became a race, and the Norsemen, more expert longshipmen, and possibly driven by fear, had the advantage. In consequence they reached that headland first, and disappeared round it.

Cormac perceived that he was being out-manoeuvred, especially when, looking back, he saw that three more vessels had come out, and were heading in the other direction, southwards. No hope of intercepting these. He had miscalculated badly.

What was best, then? Possibly to resume their previous position in midbay and, on seeing escapers emerging on the flanks, send off groups of his ships to try to head them off, the main force remaining central in case of any major break-out.

This strategy worked in some fashion. Another three ships came out presently, and headed northwards, keeping close inshore. Cormac sent Donnie the Crab with six of their craft to try to intercept, and these managed to cut off the would-be escapers, fought with and captured two of them, although the third got away. Some of the Norse crewmen jumped overboard and swam for the shore.

Presumably discouraged by this failure, no further attempts at seaborne flight were made meantime.

Nevertheless, men continued to come hastening back from the up-river area, and in large numbers. Cormac recognised that it was only a question of time before the total of these escapers became sufficient to man at least some major proportion of the ships lying there, and they were able to make a mass exodus; and this his own smaller fleet would by no means be able to tackle, for he did not underestimate the Vikings' fighting abilities, given anything like equal numbers.

In fact they did not have to wait very long for this development. Possibly it was the appearance, on the western skyline, of a group of horsemen, instead of the fleeing stragglers, which expedited the major exodus, these presumably the first of the victorious Malcolm's pursuing forces. At any rate, much commotion amongst the ranks of the longships resulted in no very orderly but large-scale putting to sea of the majority of the vessels, sufficient to leave only a score or so, including those damaged in the first Scots assault.

So Cormac decided that duty was done. His part had been to pose a threat, and to put enemy ships out of action as far as possible, not to slay maximum numbers of Norsemen. The High King did not seem to be requiring further assistance. He gave orders for a judicious retiral.

Seeing that the mass of enemy ships was heading north-eastwards, he withdrew his flotilla in the opposite direction – and no move was made to turn towards them by the others. The two fleets drew ever further apart.

Three more Norse craft came out shortly, after the others. That was all.

The Scots could see more and more horsemen appearing behind the anchorage. Might they themselves risk venturing in to meet and consult with these? They could only be Malcolm's men.

They turned and headed back shorewards.

No hostile moves met them, any Norsemen left behind evidently having preferred to flee by land. But, working their way in past the damaged ships, they had to face threatening gestures from the new arrivals, the horsemen, arriving at the waterside in increasing numbers. These, to be sure, would assume that this fleet of longships coming back was part of Olaf's array returning for some reason. Cormac decided that, in future, he should provide his ships with the saltire blue and white banner of Scotland, to identify them when necessary.

When, sufficiently close for shouting to be heard, he blew on his horn and called out that he was the Thane of Glamis from Strathmore, and men, who had been engaging the Norse ships. What of King Malcolm?

Accepting this, shouts came back that it was victory, Olaf defeated. Other shoutings followed, but these they could not make sense of, and they pulled on in, to learn details.

It seemed, from these Buchan men, none so far from their own territory, that the Scots had met Olaf's army at a place called Mortlach, where the Dullan and Fiddich Waters joined, perhaps a score of miles from here; and Malcolm had managed to entrap the Norsemen between the two rivers. Nevertheless, the battle had not gone well at first for them, until, appealing to St Moluag for divine intervention, apparently the favoured saint of this area, and promising to create a chapel, a church, even a bishopric's see here, dedicated to Moluag if given the victory, reminiscent of the adoption of St Andrew as Scotland's saint at Athelstaneford nearly two centuries earlier, he had in a burst of heroic leadership dashed forward and personally slain one of the Norse leaders, not Olaf unfortunately who was well guarded. This proved to be a turning point in the struggle, and led by their king, the Vikings began to retreat seawards. It became a running battle, and presently a rout, over so many miles. And here they were.

Cormac congratulated all concerned, including St Moluag.

It had been a long, taxing and uncertain day. However, the invaders had left behind a large haul of stolen beef, mutton and other provisions, and these were done justice to by the victors before they settled down for the night. They all thought that they could safely assume that the Norsemen were unlikely to be returning.

On the morrow it would be back to Angus for the fleet, with a new supply of longships, the largest catch yet, which would make for slow progress. So be it.

26

While the nation resounded with praises for the new monarch's victory and leadership, Cormac mac Farquhar and his wife had a new issue to consider. It had occurred to them ere this, but the accession of this latest levy of longships, the largest ever, made it the more valid. Why, they wondered, should this assault on the Viking menace by sea be confined to the folk of the Angus coast? After all, there were literally thousands of miles of coastline around Scotland, with fisherfolk dwelling at much of it. Others could and should be enrolled and trained for this duty.

The obvious area to start with was Moray and Ross, which had suffered so much, and where MacBeth could surely be relied upon to assist. If he co-operated, other mormaors with coastal lands might be persuaded to do likewise.

So, before winter set in, a preliminary voyage up to Inverness with two or three ships for demonstration purposes; and since this would be no warlike venture, Fenella could bring young Nechtan along, and look on it all as something of a holiday. Let them hope that the weather was kind.

With Duncan and Donnie, and crews from Ethiehaven and Usan, they set off in four longships; they now had over thirty usable craft, and some of these could be sent up to Moray later if volunteer crews were forthcoming. Conditions were grey but reasonably calm. Fenella had had contrived a roofed-in shelter in the bows of Cormac's vessel, scarcely a cabin, where the child could be bestowed on occasion, although that active infant was unlikely to remain therein save when asleep. Surely never had a Norse longship been so equipped.

They reached Inverness on the third day, after calling in at Spey Bay to show Fenella the scene of their last action, and to find that four of the badly damaged ships left behind still were beached there. These could be repaired and used, no doubt. MacBeth greeted them warmly at his principal castle, and expressed fullest sympathy with their objective, admitting that he had thought of something of the sort himself but had never got down to doing anything about it. He suggested Munlochy as a likely and suitable starting point, on its own little firth. It had not been raided, and had a sizeable community of fisherfolk, also smiths and woodworkers who could repair damaged vessels.

He accompanied the four ships up to Munlochy, and there had a successful meeting with the villagers. As their mormaor, MacBeth could have commanded his people to co-operate; but they wanted good teamwork and collaboration, if not enthusiasm, and therefore volunteers. And they won no lack of these, especially when they were told that MacBeth would be going on to Cromarty thereafter on a similar mission, and rivalry came into it.

A couple of days were spent, one of them wet unfortunately, but seas not stormy, showing the new crews how to handle these ships with the long sweeps, and how to use leather and iron shields to protect the oarsmen, hung over the sides. They left one of the longships there, with its Angus crew meantime, to be picked up on the way back, and sailed on with the other three to Cromarty at the mouth of the next firth.

It was a similar story there, no lack of interest and responsiveness. All had heard of the Angusmen's exploits of course, and were not averse to showing that they were no less capable. Another two days of demonstrating.

Cormac was faced with the situation of providing these fishermen with a ship to work on, otherwise they might lose both interest and their newly acquired skills. So only two overcrowded craft went back to Munlochy to pick up the crew of the vessel left there. It was going to be a tight-packed journey back to Lunan Bay. But the Norsemen themselves carried many extra warriors on their longships; they themselves could do the same.

They enjoyed two days of rest and refreshment at Inverness on the way home. MacBeth told them that Malcolm had called a meeting of mormaors at Forteviot in mid-November, for purposes unexplained; and there he would make known Cormac's plan for wider-spread longships use, and his own efforts in that direction, with hoped-for emulation.

All the while young Nechtan had been enjoying himself, causing considerable amusement, indeed hilarity, amongst oarsmen, especially in his efforts to assist them at the sweeps, but on the whole creating little trouble, although not infrequently his parents had to dash over benches and bodies to try to ensure no closer contact with the water; likewise the dangers of the parapet walk of Inverness Castle. Nechtan mac Cormac looked as though he was going to be a bold longshipman one day, whatever else.

MacBeth came back from the mormaors' meeting in late November with the information that King Malcolm was planning further conquests. Much of Lothian was now being raided, not by Norsemen but by Angles from Northumbria, not so much raids these as with intentions of settling. Lothian, especially the eastern portions, was more fertile and worth inhabiting than where these came from, and was easily accessible. So, in early spring, there was to be a major offensive southwards, all forces mobilised. No doubt Cormac's people would be needed, whether by sea or land.

He also said that he had told the other mormaors, and the High King himself, about the expansion of the longships initiative; and the reaction had been favourable, especially from young Mar who, of course, had a vast seaboard, from the Mearns right up to Moray. He would be approaching Cormac for guidance. Malcolm had been interested, but thought that after the crushing defeat of King Olaf the Norsemen would be chary of raiding the Scottish coasts, for some time at least. MacBeth was not so sure, nor was Cormac. After all, most of the raiding was done, as it were, on a personal basis, not on a major armed scale. There was little reason to believe that this would cease. And it could be sufficiently dire for the localities assailed.

Mid-winter was not the time for raiding, nor for counter-measures. So they had an interval of peace at Glamis, Kinnordy and Red Castle, and Cormac could fulfil his somewhat neglected duties as thane. He did have a visit from Ethernan, Mormaor of Mar, however, and was able to advise him, and promise instruction and help for crews in due course.

It was in February that Fenella announced that she believed herself to be pregnant again. Cormac for his part declared that he required another son, to be Thane of Glamis while Nechtan was Mormaor of Angus.

The word duly came from the Ard Righ in March. All forces of the realm to assemble, horsed if possible, at Forteviot in two weeks' time, to ride for Lothian, nothing said about longships.

So the fishermen were largely spared this time, and it was the farm folk, shepherds, woodmen, millers and the like, who were to play their part on the nation's behalf, their numbers limited by the horses which could be raised. With one hundred and fifty or so, the Glamis people joined the Angus contingent at Forfar. Cormac found himself, to his some embarrassment, to be put in command of it all, almost one thousand men, this because Connacher, not in the best of health, decided to absent himself. He was never keen on warlike activities anyway. No question of Fenella coming, this time.

All rode to Forteviot, where they found a large host assembled, the largest Cormac had ever joined, Malcolm the Destroyer's name and reputation ensuring fullest support. The Angles in Lothian were going to receive no minor shock.

The Lothian situation was a strange one, some seeing it as scarcely part of Scotland at all. It had, of course, been a separate kingdom, under King Loth of the Southern Picts, he who had given it its name, and his successors; but the Northumbrian Angles had always cast envious eyes on it, the eastern areas in especial, and had occupied it off and on for centuries, interbreeding with the local inhabitants. They even gave it a different name, part of Bernicia. Kenneth mac Alpin and his successors had pronounced it part of Scotland, and frequently backed their claim by force of arms. But always the Northumbrians came back; after all, the border of Lothian with the Merse, inland, was only some twenty-five miles north of the Tweed's mouth and Northumbria. Malcolm was determined that hereafter there should be no doubts as to who ruled there.

They rode two days later, over fifteen thousand of them, horsed, the foot, to the number of perhaps half that, to come on behind at their own pace, all the mormaors present save Connacher, Cormac finding himself almost accepted as in that position, MacBeth and Ethernan of Mar treating him as an equal. Going by Stirling, to cross Forth, they headed eastwards to the start of the estuary, and followed its southern shoreline to enter Lothian at Inveravon, near to Linlithgow.

Enquiries here revealed that no Northumbrian occupation was being suffered thus far west. Reports gave it as all occurring east of Edinburgh, in the fertile vales of Tyne and Peffer and the Dunbar area, fine land for settlers and easily accessible.

The army pressed on to Edinburgh, under its towering Arthur's Seat. This was all familiar territory to Cormac, of course, from the campaigns of King Constantine. There they were told that the nearest community of Angles, apart from their probing bands, was at Cockenzie or Cockainie still almost a dozen miles off, a fishing-haven with much good land behind. It was onward, then.

Cormac had wondered, as no doubt had others, why Malcolm required so great a host for the elimination of these comparatively small settlements of intruders. Now they learned. After they had dealt with these Angles they would proceed on into Northumbria itself, to teach those folk the lesson that they deserved, and to ensure that they did not trouble Lothian again. Outright war was the objective, no mere clearing of Lothian.

Thereafter followed what amounted to a parade through the territory east of Edinburgh, with nothing remotely resembling a battle, their large array ensuring that the intruding Angles fled before them from villages, new settlements and farmeries, leaving behind somewhat bewildered original inhabitants, some of whom themselves fled also. For these Northumbrians had not been like the Norsemen, there to kill and ravage almost for sport, their objective to instal themselves on the land. On the whole they had not come to blows with the local folk, unless these had taken arms against them; indeed it had largely been a gradual and peaceful penetration. But now Earl Uhtred of Northumbria was laying claim to Lothian, or some of it, as part of his domains.

The approach of so large a force could not be hidden and what happened at Cockenzie was fairly typical of the next few days' proceedings. The local people, many Scots as well as Angles, fled before the army could arrive on the scene. In eastern Lothian the Lammermuir Hills rose only eight to a dozen miles inland from the coastal plain and the fertile vales, and provided ideal and convenient hiding-places for refugees and their cattle and sheep, some two hundred square miles of grassy ridges, hidden valleys and heather moors. So thither the folk largely went, and Malcolm's host found little to assail. They burned a number of hamlets, communities and farm steadings, but this was largely a gesture. There was some riding up into the hill-skirts after fugitives and their flocks, but this again was more warning than serious pursuit.

Malcolm himself seemed nowise concerned over this less than triumphal progress, and the under-employment of his great force. Ever more clearly it became apparent that Northumbria, the land, was the real target, this only a preliminary flourish. They went on by Aberlady Bay, Golyn, Dirlington and North Berwick, inland by Travernent and Haddington and Hamer, eventually to Dunbar. Thereafter, with the hills coming down almost to the shore, the Norse Sea, no longer the Firth of Forth or Scotwater, and where Lothian reached the east coast of the Merse, land worth the settling on was minimal, and there was no further demonstrating called for. The army was directed to ride due southwards now, just inland from the cliff-girt and dramatic shoreline, which reminded Cormac of the Angus and Mearns seaboard with its cliffs and precipices, to make for Berwick-on-Tweed. They had so far seen nothing of the foot contingent coming on behind, Cormac wondering what their role was.

Twenty-five miles on they came to the mouth of the great River Tweed, beyond which lay Northumbria. They camped for a night at the edge of it, and Malcolm held a conference with his leadership.

He outlined his intentions now. Northumbria extended southwards for fully one hundred and twenty miles, to the border of Deira and Durham, it indeed having once been a kingdom of its own. It was, in essence, less than a score of miles wide, however, before the Cheviot Hills were reached, like the Lammermuirs all but empty country. Uhtred of Northumbria had three great strongholds, at Bamburgh, Dunstanburgh and Alnwick, the first two on the coast. Malcolm's plan was to divide his force into three, approximately five thousand in each. Not knowing where Uhtred was based meantime, they would assail or besiege all three castles in the hope of penning him in, so that he could not rally his full strength and lead it against the invaders. Bamburgh was almost certainly the strongest and the nearest, some twenty-five more miles south of Tweed; he would lead that assault himself. Crinan of Atholl would take another five thousand and head inland by Etal and the Till and Wooler, along the Cheviot foothills, for Alnwick. And MacBeth to head for Dunstanburgh with the remainder. All to keep in touch by scouts and couriers. If they could keep Uhtred walled up in one of these fortresses, then the rest of Northumbria, more or less leaderless, would be open to them to pillage and spoil, the required lesson for the Angles. Uhtred might, of course, not be in any of these three strongholds; but if not, he would probably make for one when he heard of the invasion, Bamburgh the likeliest. But all three sections of the army must be prepared to come together again at short notice in case of the earl managing to muster a major strength against any one contingent.

In the morning, then, the force split up into three, crossing Tweed by fords some way inland, the Berwick crossing being highly defensible. Cormac would have elected to go with MacBeth for Dunstanburgh, but being in command of the entire Angus array he found that being retained by Malcolm himself, and was told that since he was expert in boat-handling, and Bamburgh was on the coast, he might be useful in assault by sea. So they crossed the river where the Whiteadder joined it, creating shallows; MacBeth's force proceeded on to near Paxton, and Crinan further still to the Fishwick ford, the vital importance of keeping in touch by frequent messengers emphasised. And no delays with preliminary local engagements; the three fortresses were the prime objectives.

Malcolm's contingent rode southwards along the coast, by the ancient monkish hospice of the Spital, and on by Cheswick and Goswick to the great bay formed by the oddly shaped Holy Island of St Cuthbert. The shore hereabouts was sandy, with ranked dunes, not rocks and cliffs, very different from the seaboard they had left. Cormac did not see it as likely to provide seaborne aid to any assault, even if boats, fishing-craft, could be found to use.

Bamburgh was a surprise however, when they neared it, a mighty fortalice set on the summit of an isolated towering red-stone outcrop of rock, extensive and highly defensive. Even Malcolm was off-put when he saw it, recognising that the only way to take this hilltop hold would be by prolonged siege in order to starve out the occupants, even battering-rams, balistas and stone-hurling catapults, with which they were not equipped, being of little use owing to the steepness of any approach. However, if Uhtred was within, and they surrounded its every access effectively with these thousands, he would nowise win out, their objective partly achieved. Cormac saw no prospects of seaward assault, only long sandy beaches, reminiscent of Lunan Bay.

They settled down to encircle that daunting fortress, camping in tight-packed fashion so that none could pass, day and night guarded. Fortunately there was water available from a stream, and wood for their campfires.

Malcolm was soon fretting for the arrival of the foot section of his army. This was what they were required for, it seemed, to take over the siegery and free the cavalry for further advance. Apparently the Ard Righ was actually aiming to reach Durham. He declared that he was eager to recover the remains and relics of St Cuthbert, a Scot from the Merse, these held by the Angles at Durham, and to convey them to Mortlach where he had won his victory over King Olaf, there to found the bishopric which he had promised. Cormac for one was distinctly surprised by this declared intention, for Malcolm the Destroyer had never struck him as a man of religion.

They had to wait two days there before the foot arrived. Meanwhile they had heard from both MacBeth and Crinan that they had duly besieged the castles of Dunstanburgh and Alnwick, each announcing that, lacking the required equipment for assailing such strengths, they could only seek to starve them into submission. So all three sections of the mounted army were similarly placed. And none could know whether Earl Uhtred was in fact in any of those holds. It was not a satisfactory situation.

But, at least, once the weary footmen arrived, Malcolm could move off, and use his five thousand to harry the land, leaving the foot to immobilise Bamburgh. And this they did, most thoroughly, descending on the communities of

Belford and Doddington, of Wooler and Chattan and Chillingham, the inhabitants, such as escaped the sword, fleeing into the Cheviots. They did not pursue these, but pressed on southwards on a wide front with their destruction.

Cormac did not enjoy this kind of warfare, demolishing peaceful villages and their populations, very different from fighting aggressive Norsemen; but he supposed that it was necessary if the Angles were to be taught that invading Lothian brought down this sort of retribution.

They reached Alnwick in due course, where Crinan of Atholl was confronting another strong castle, the furthest south the Scots had so far penetrated. Malcolm left his son-in-law to it, but took two thousand of his men, assessing that the remaining three thousand should be sufficient to maintain the siege.

Tynemouth was the next major target, although there were a sufficiency of lesser places to assail on the way: Warkworth, Amble, Ashington, Bedlington and Cramlington, to name only a few. Their now seven thousand left a trail of devastation behind.

It was just short of the Tyne that Malcolm made his decision. This Tynemouth was a large town and port, the greatest in Northumbria, from which much of the wool from the Cheviot sheep flocks was shipped. So there would be many vessels there, and some of them could well sail off southwards, not only to escape the Scots but to warn others of the menace, warn Durham in especial. And Durham was the High King's especial objective, to gain those precious relics of St Cuthbert. On to Durham forthwith, then, avoiding Tynemouth; they could deal with that on their return.

So the force made a quite wide detour westwards, reaching the great Roman Wall, and crossing the River Tyne at Pons AElii, now called Monkchester, some ten miles west of the port. They did not assail any villages or hamlets now, anxious not to arouse the country before Durham was reached. It was fast riding for them. They still had twenty-five miles or so to go.

By Usworth and Birtley and the Rivers Team and Wear they drove down on Durham. This had long been a very special place, first in the Celtic polity and then, when the invading Angles and Saxons became Christianised, they took it over and made it their principal religious centre in the north. But being the folk they were, they combined their new-found faith with their urge to possess land and wealth, and turned Durham into a military as well as an ecclesiastical base, setting up a monastery and great church which was as good as a fortress, this on a large mound within a meander of the Wear, where the river all but enclosed the site. They put a bishop in charge, but a warlike one, and this tradition continued, the present incumbent being Bishop Aldhun, who had a few years before brought the bones of St Cuthbert here from Ripon, much further to the south, to join those of the Venerable Bede, fetched from Jarrow. It was this adoption of the relics of the Scots missionary from Melrose in Tweeddale which had apparently so offended Malcolm, and was now to be rectified.

Reaching the Wear, they followed it down until they came in sight of their goal. And there they quickly recognised that this was going to be no easier a conquest than any of those three other fortalices, within its encircling river, the only access thereto being a narrow causeway, with a gap in it spanned by a drawbridge, which, even as they looked, was raised, the approach of their host perceived. That river would be as effective a defence as any cliff-sided rock. Here was another hold to be starved into submission, religious or not.

There was the usual supportive community nearby, and this the Scots took over with little in the way of opposition, the inhabitants fleeing at the sight of the thousands of armed horsemen. At least here the leadership could settle down to wait in comparative comfort; the rank and file could, as ever, fend for themselves.

Malcolm ordered his men to surround the castle-monastery-chapel most securely, and to check that there were no boats available for egress nor ingress. So no food could reach the inmates save by that drawbridge, which could be heedfully guarded day and night. Assuming that the bishop and his people had not been warned of the swift approach of the invaders, they were unlikely to have large stores of provisioning on hand.

So, nothing for it but to wait, with what patience they could muster, as their other three groups were doing further north.

For four days they waited there, idle, with no developments from the besieged fortress. And then the situation changed, and drastically. Their guards posted around came to inform that a large horsed host was approaching from the north.

At first Malcolm assumed that this must be either Crinan or MacBeth, or both, objectives achieved and possibly bringing him the Earl Uhtred as prisoner. But, alas, shortly thereafter, another scout came hurrying to announce that a second large mounted company was bearing down on them from the west. This made that hoped-for explanation unlikely. Could this represent a threat of some sort, a major threat?

The Scots reaction was prompt now. But all their men were spread out in a wide circle, no ideal position to face possible assault. So orders went out to reassemble, to mass in to form a strategic whole, capable of obeying commands to split, divert, outflank and the like. But for those four days the men had been settled, inactive, horses unsaddled and tethered. As a result, many were slow in responding to the command, especially those placed behind the besieged citadel and aware of no cause for alarm. The assembling was delayed, to Malcolm's anger.

And his anger was justified, for before his thousands were marshalled in any sort of order, long lines of horsemen appeared among a rise of ground to the north, and it took only seconds to recognise that these were not their fellow

Scots, banners making that clear. And even as Malcolm urgently shouted orders to seek to cope with the now so evident threat, another array came in sight, only a little further off, to the west.

The High King did his best in this suddenly dire situation, seeking to divide such of his force as was at his command to face these two menacing approaches. Which was the larger was difficult to assess, probably that to the north; but both could have others coming on behind.

Cormac found himself, with Ethernan of Mar, given that western force to face, Malcolm ordering attack, attack, arrowhead formations. More used to sea warfare than cavalry charging, he sought to group his people into some sort of spearhead-shaped parties, and this while already on the move. It was not a very successful development, any more than was the Mar contingent's, but at least they were advancing, not waiting to be attacked – that is, if the newcomers were indeed attacking. Could it be that this double arrival was not in fact hostile? And here *they* were charging at them!

Any such doubts were swiftly dispelled as the oncoming host aligned itself into a roughly crescent-shaped formation and, spears and lances lowered, spurred onwards. It was going to be headlong clash, and Cormac reckoned that the enemy could be at least double their own numbers.

Chaos ensued. Leading one of his arrowheads, close supporters just slightly behind him on either side, sword slashing in figure-of-eight fashion before him, Cormac crashed his horse into the front rank of the oncoming foe, the beast rearing high as it did so and all but unseating its rider. Possibly that rearing saved him, for the spear aimed at him was knocked aside, merely glancing off his saddle. Admittedly his own sword likewise failed to find its target, as the other man plunged on past him.

Then Cormac was into the second rank of the enemy, and he was aware that the supporter on his right was no longer with him. This row of horsemen did not have their lances lowered, since that could have speared those in front. So it was swords, maces and axes raised. But the Scots impact on the first rank, its momentum and collision, could not fail to have its effect on those immediately behind. To avoid crashing into them, they had not exactly to rein in but to swerve and jerk their animals this way and that, which did not aid their weapon-wielding, any more than it did Cormac's own thrusting. As a result, he hurtled on into the mass further behind, which, less than prepared for this so early confrontation, did not effectively bar the Scots charge through them. Nor did he achieve a satisfactory stroke against one of these, although he saw him all but topple from the saddle. Cormac recognised that the enemy's wide crescent formation, however good for an advance against a waiting foe, was not the ideal one to counter arrowhead-shaped charges of a number of smaller groups. Malcolm had known what he was at with that last command.

Unhurt, however breathless and unsure of what next, he found himself right through the foe's ranks and amongst only a few stragglers anxious to avoid him. Gazing back over his shoulder, he saw that his personal following, hardly an arrowhead now, seemed to be fairly intact and compact. Right and left other similar groups were emerging also, their tactics having clearly been reasonably successful. How many casualties they had suffered was not to be known at this stage.

With no sign of Ethernan of Mar, Cormac perceived that his was the responsibility for the further action. Pulling his mount round, he gestured to all who were in a state to pay attention, made the sign of an arrowhead with his upraised arms, then pointed his sword at the enemy rear, which was still plunging on in the same direction. He repeated his signals, and then kicked his horse into motion, hoping that another V would form itself behind him.

It was a strange sensation to be riding into the backs of the onward-charging enemy. None of them appeared to be turning to face any threat at their rear. Warfare was most evidently as much confusion and error as challenge, courage and endeavour. A distant commotion on his right now seemed to represent Mar breaking through there, in whatever force. But no point in holding back now and seeking to operate in common, even if he could have halted and diverted his charging groups. On they pounded into the hindmost ranks of the foe.

The confusion, great enough on the outward charge, was much worse on the return, almost ridiculously so. The Scots found themselves cantering alongside their enemies, although some of these clearly did not realise this, and were astonished when they were assailed. To add to the disarray, not all the Scots force had yet battled its way through their antagonists, and were now coming face to face with their own folk returning, and not always recognising the fact either, in the chaos. So friend could be striking at friend.

There was nothing that Cormac could do now but to press on regardless, with such of his people as were still approximately behind him. Because they were all mainly going in the same direction now, he did not greatly outpace the enemy, so that he and his must have all seemed to be part of the now disorderly host bearing down on the High King's array. What Malcolm must have made of it all was anybody's guess.

But almost certainly that was the least of the Ard Righ's concerns at this stage. For he was in full combat with the other and larger enemy force coming from the north, and inevitably in a defensive role, outnumbered and with not all his besiegers yet rejoining him. The battle was scarcely going well for him.

Nor did the arrival of the curious western horde help, whatever its composition of friend and foe. Certainly its impact was less shattering than had it been a unified and well-commanded whole. But nevertheless the effect of the many hundreds of careering horsemen reaching the flank of the already beleaguered royal force could not be other than detrimental.

Cormac did what he could to lessen the damage, but to

little effect. His men were now much dispersed amongst the enemy, and Mar's, presently coming behind, were out of touch. The struggle became the more desperate.

Malcolm, destroyer as he might be, was also a shrewd tactician. He would not fail to recognise when a military situation was hopeless. Presumably this was his reading of it now, for he evidently gave orders for a withdrawal to as many of his leaders and people as could receive and accept them. And his line of retirement, probably wisely, was westwards, whence the flank attack had so recently come. So, headed by the Scots monarch and his nobility, all who could disengage streamed off through the disorganised mass of friend and foe, smiting all and sundry aside in their determined exodus, although leaving not a few battlers still involved behind them.

Cormac, for his part, waved to his own followers to join in this departure, Mar just arriving in time to turn back, with *his* men, whence they had just come.

The Battle of Durham could be reckoned as being over.

The escapers soon turned northwards, slowing the pace a little to allow others to catch up with them when they assessed that there was no enemy pursuit, as yet. However galling it was for Malcolm to find himself thus in unaccustomed flight, he retained firm command. He declared that it was Earl Uhtred himself who had descended upon them. Presumably he had been at Tynemouth when the Scots army had avoided it, and had hastily gathered a large force to come after them in the two arrays. It had been a sorry episode, and they had sustained a serious blow; but it was not a disaster. They still had their thousands at Alnwick and Dunstanburgh and Bamburgh, however fruitless their siegery. So they would not suffer further defeat if Uhtred came after them. Cormac asked whether it was the High King's intention, once he had gathered his full force again, to turn back and confront the Northumbrian earl. But Malcolm said no. A defeat, even a comparatively minor one, could be dangerous in its effect on any host, men all too apt to fear another, and fight the less confidently. Also, here in his own Northumbria, Uhtred could possibly muster a much greater host, vastly outnumbering themselves. Better to go back to Scotland with most of his army intact, and come to deal with the Angles here another day. At least they would have taught them that Lothian was not for them.

They had picked up Crinan of Atholl and were collecting MacBeth at Dunstanburgh when some belated escapers caught up with them, not to report any immediate pursuit by the Northumbrians but to tell of Uhtred's cutting off of the heads of the Scots slain in the battle, and hanging them from the walls of the fortress-monastery. Presumably he had heard of this barbarous Norse custom, and decided that it was worth emulation.

That sent Malcolm and his people homewards vowing vengeance. One day . . .

27

It was good to be home after an absence of almost six weeks, and to return to the arms of Fenella, who was still showing no signs of her pregnancy although she calculated that the child was due in early September. Nechtan seemed to have grown even during that interval, and demanded much attention from his father. As did the affairs of the thanedom, including the sad duty of informing, sympathising and seeking to compensate in some measure the wives and families of the casualties of warfare, fortunately not many in the Glamis contingent.

An added responsibility returned to was over the continued illness and incapacity of Connacher of Angus. Cormac had suspected that his claimed sickness had been largely accounted for by an unwillingness to embark on Malcolm's military expedition; but apparently it was more than that, for the man was undoubtedly unwell, not bed-ridden but slowed in his speech and unsteady on his feet. This worried the younger man, for although he had no real affection for his mormaor, he realised that with only young Nechtan as his heir, much obligation was going to fall upon himself, Cormac, in the affairs of the mortuath, his acting as its armed forces commander, as recently, only the beginning of it all. He was one who preferred a quiet family life to leadership, rule and the administration of great lands.

At least there were no calls from the High King for military activity for some little time thereafter. Uhtred of Northumbria did not seek to exploit his victory at Durham by any ventures into Lothian or the Merse; indeed he preoccupied himself by marrying the daughter of the Bishop Aldhun thereof, an unexpected development. Moreover, King Olaf had returned to Norway, having at last converted, if that was the word, Earl Sigurd of Orkney to Christianity, but taking his eldest son by his first marriage, Hundi the Whelp, with him as hostage for continued adherence to the true faith; a rather strange form of missionary activity. So now Sigurd and his other sons were again free men and might be expected to demonstrate the fact, and that not only in Orkney and Shetland. Noting it, Malcolm took precautions. Aware that MacBeth and Thorfinn Sigurdson were half-brothers, and knowing that Cormac and the former were close friends, that summer he appointed the pair as his envoys to go to Orkney and offer an alliance with Scotland to Sigurd, to their mutual advantage, and if agreed, to have him created Earl of Caithness and Sutherland also. If this might seem an over-generous offer to the potentate of a comparatively small island nation, it fell to be remembered that Sigurd already dominated Caithness and Sutherland, and also controlled the Outer Hebrides and the Isle of Man, as well as having toe-holds in Northern Ireland, all of which could be useful to a King of Scots.

Cormac was a little concerned that this errand could have him absent when Fenella was brought to bed in September. Somehow that must be avoided. An earlier start, then, than Malcolm suggested? Fenella solved that problem for him as she had done others. Since they must go by ship to the isles, she and Nechtan would accompany him. In summer conditions it ought to be a pleasant voyage. When, highly doubtful, Cormac said what if she was brought into premature labour on board, she answered that there could be worse places than a longship in which to be delivered. And he could prove his husbandly worth by assisting in the process – not that that greatly reassured him.

So when, in due course, they set off from Ethiehaven, it was in family form again. They used the vessel on which Fenella had had her shelter constructed; but Cormac had decided to take another two ships as well, as looking better than the one for an official visit. All aboard viewed it in the nature of a holiday.

When, three days later, they arrived at Inverness, it was to find that MacBeth had had the same notion, and was waiting for them with four of his own small fleet now gathered there. So it was quite a flotilla which went on northwards.

When last Cormac had been off the coast beyond Ross, Sutherland and Caithness it had been to turn into the Pentland Firth on his way to the western seaboard of Scotland, making for Galloway and Cumbria. But now they headed across the mouth of that firth, making for the Orkney Isles, Ronaldsay less than ten miles away and clearly visible. They had been warned to beware of dangerous waters hereabouts, roosts as they were called, whirlpools and turbulences caused by sudden great holes in the seabed, with consequent overfalls and tide races. However, the weather was calm, and although there was a long swell coming sidelong from the Western Sea, they encountered no hazards. Soon they were passing the Burwick tip of Ronaldsay and on into the Sound of Hoy, past Flotta to the major island of Hoy. This proved to be much larger and higher than they had anticipated. They had deemed the Orkneys to be fairly treeless isles, flat, obviously fairly populous but anything but dramatic save in their inhabitants. But this Hoy had not only fearsome cliffs, riven with chasms and caves, and with down-pouring waterfalls, but quite high and dominant hills. They kept well offshore, for it was guarded by reefs and stacks and skerries. It would be a dangerous place to approach in hard weather.

MacBeth had been instructed by his half-brother how, if needed, to reach the Broch of Birsay, the earldom's principal seat on the main island of the group, locally called Hrossay. They were to swing left round the head of Hoy, through the narrows between it and the Stromness, Hrossay's southern tip, these narrows accentuated by a small, elongated islet in the middle named Graemsay, which created channels on either side known as the Sounds of Clestran and Burra. These could be dangerous, and so useful for defensive purposes, for the tides raced through these and with their rocky shallow beds produced much riot of waters, often wild indeed. Here, threading the western one, Burra, they encountered their first roosts, which had their oarsmen in much agitation, their sweeps thrown out of alignment and rhythm, their craft swaying and dipping and rolling alarmingly, some spray coming inboard, to young Nechtan's crowing delight. His elders were glad when they were past Graemsay and out into the open sea, with only the regular swell to deal with.

Up the west coast of Hrossay they sailed, cliff-girt but less daunting, with much grassy and fertile land behind, cattle-dotted, although they could see little of cultivation, these Orkney Norsemen being evidently herdsmen rather than true farmers; that is, when they were not at their preferred hosting and winning other folk's farm products.

They rowed on for some fifteen miles, MacBeth on the lookout for the landmarks Thorfinn had told him of. When they had passed the deep-indented bay of Skaill, the only one of its dimensions, with its prominent ancient Pictish settlement of Skara Brae on the one horn and a towering broch on the other, he knew that they were two-thirds of the way to their destination.

Cormac and Fenella were interested in these brochs, new to them, circular stone fortlets, tall and wide to the air at the top, with a central open space for cattle, and mural chambers in the thickness of the walls for folk to take refuge in from marauders. These were of Pictish origin, rather than Norse, the latter scarcely requiring them.

Another half-dozen miles, further than MacBeth had thought, and they reached a thrusting headland, at the tip of which rose a rocky islet, half a mile wide, roughly circular, with a high flat top, the Broch of Birsay. There was indeed another broch on the summit, but this was surrounded, all but hidden, by a former Pictish settlement which had been turned into something of a palace, of hallhouse, outbuildings, barns and the like, principal base of the earls.

Finding this was one problem solved, reaching up to it quite another. The entire islet seemed to be fenced in with sheer precipices, ringed by savage reefs, these last spouting fountains of water alarmingly. Yet there must be an access somewhere. They had to circle it almost entirely before at the north-west corner they came to a narrow gap in the cliffs, opening into a very cauldron of a basin, denied the sunlight by the steepness of its high walls. And even this could be closed off by a great chain hanging with spikes, presently below the surface of the water but which could be raised by handled winding-gear. Presumably their approach, which would certainly not have gone unobserved, had been considered innocuous, the blue and white saltire banner at Cormac's ships masthead noted, or the chain would have been up.

They rowed in, and there, in something of a corner, were two longships and three or four fishing-boats drawn up on brief shingle. There was not much room for their own seven vessels on that small beach, so they had to moor close alongside, sides touching, and clamber from boat to boat to land, Nechtan leading the way, Cormac urging care on his pregnant wife.

They saw three men coming down the steep track, largely steps cut in the naked rock, one of them most obviously the enormous person of Thorfinn Raven-Feeder.

It seemed strange indeed to be preceded up that difficult ascent to the so warlike citadel by a small boy, who clearly saw it as a personal challenge and was not to be held back.

As clearly not at all impressed by the huge Thorfinn and his companions, Nechtan hurried on past them and up, ignoring calls from his father. The Raven-Feeder gazed after him, and hooted laughter. Then he turned, waved and shouted.

"Ha, Son of Life! And Thane Cormac. And lady. Here is surprise. Led by a warrior of modest size but of iron will! What brings you all this way, to the end of all lands?"

"You do. Or your sire, Thor," MacBeth called back. "Hail to the converted – newly Christian as you may be!" This was not strictly fair, for Thorfinn's mother, Donada, had been a Christian and had taught her son something of her faith, and to respect it. "How is my good mother?"

"Well, well. And asking why you have not come before this?"

The meeting of the brothers was sufficiently hearty, although the big man had his eye on Fenella from the first, and noting her most evident child-bearing.

"Is this a mission of the Earth Mother rather than any Christian pilgrimage?" he asked, and bowed elaborately to the woman.

"Could it not be both?" Fenella demanded. "Womenkind are needed by all faiths, Norseman!"

"Do I not know it, lady! Thane Cormac is to be congratulated."

This exchange was interrupted by high-pitched yells from aloft, where Nechtan had discovered further excitements and was beckoning. So the ascent was commenced, Thorfinn solicitous for Fenella's care, holding her arm and all but hoisting her up those steps, she nowise shaking him off.

At the summit, it was the raven-winged helmets of the guards on duty at the palace gates which had the small boy fascinated, he flapping hands at each side of his own head to indicate wings, and pointing. Cormac grabbed him; and his mother, distinctly breathless, told him to be less bold. This was another's house, not Glamis or Red Castle.

They entered the citadel, and there was a stocky, heavy-built man waiting to receive them, Sigurd Hlodvison. Elderly now, he was strong of feature as of body, not handsome but striking, his yellow hair greying. He eyed them all and said nothing.

"I greet you, Jarl Sigurd!" MacBeth declared, giving him his correct style. "Here is the Thane of Glamis and his Lady Fenella, niece to the Mormaor of Angus. And their son, who will one day be mormaor. We come at the behest of the High King of Scots."

"Which one? There have been not a few of them!" That was gruff, deep-voiced and scarcely welcoming.

"Malcolm mac Kenneth, Jarl. You will not have failed to hear of him!"

"My father grows old. He cannot keep pace with all your kings!" Thorfinn interjected easily. "You change them over-often."

"This one, I think, will last longer!" Cormac put in. "He is made of lasting stuff!"

"The Jarl Uhtred did not esteem him so!" was jerked back at them. Sigurd was evidently better informed than he had sounded at first. "But come you. My wife would see the son that she bore so long ago."

Thus distinctly doubtfully received, they were escorted into the hallhouse.

There they were accorded a very different treatment, the Lady Donada welcoming her elder son with open arms, and offering his companions kind cordiality, picking up the little boy and hugging him. She was considerably younger than her husband and did not look old enough to have been MacBeth's mother, a handsome woman.

Their hostess entertained them well, despite lack of warning of their coming. They began to realise that Sigurd was not quite so inimical as he seemed, his manner merely abrupt, and his tongue sardonic but not actually sour.

Presently the men were left alone to discuss their mission. MacBeth led off.

"King Malcolm sees some understanding with you, Jarl Sigurd, as of advantage to both, an alliance of sorts. He knows that King Olaf can be difficult towards you, has your son Hundi hostage in Norway. Also that the Danes in Ireland are threatening your isles of the Hebrides, or some of them. Also Man. And Brian Boroime, King of Munster is seeking to become High King of all Ireland, and would have the Danes out. He, Malcolm, believes that this would be to Scotland's advantage, as well as your own. He says that both should support King Brian."

"So?"

"A stronger Orkney, Shetland, the Hebrides and Man, in alliance with Scotland would, he holds, keep King Olaf and the Norse in check. Also Uhtred of Northumbria and King Ethelred of England. Do you not agree?"

"It might do, yes – to your king's advantage. What of mine?"

"Olaf came here, did he not? To your hurt. He could come again. But if he knew that *Scotland's* strength was there at your call, he could think twice. The Ulster Danes also."

"I see this as of some worth," Thorfinn put in. "And we have naught to lose."

"But little to gain. And Malcolm Kennethson is a grasper. Is he not so named? The Destroyer!"

"Destroyer of foes, not friends," Cormac said.

"Was that other Kenneth his foe? His own kin and king. Yet he destroyed *him*."

"He deemed him a sorry king for Scotland, Jarl. As did many."

"He is a strong monarch," MacBeth emphasised. "Better as your friend than one possibly to fear. And he offers you token of his friendship. He would make you to be Earl of Caithness and of Sutherland, in the Scottish realm."

Sigurd looked up keenly. "I already hold Caithness and Sutherland," he said.

"With the sword and axe, not as of right. But as an

earl of Scotland, all but a mormaor, you could, if you wished, sit in the council and have some say in the affairs of the land."

"And be a subject of your king?"

"Not so. You would hold the earldom free of tribute."

Sigurd tapped the table-top. Despite his tone, Cormac now judged him sufficiently interested to consider the proposal.

Thorfinn evidently thought the same. "That would have its advantages," he said. "With Ross and Moray in my good brother's hands, we could control all, right down to Buchan and Mar. I say that it is a worthy offer. And if Malcolm fails us, we can call off the alliance."

The jarl eyed him for long moments, and then nodded. "It is enough," he said.

And that appeared to be that. No writings nor sealings, no formal declaration, not even a handshake. Sigurd Hlodvison's nod was apparently sufficient. Their task was accomplished. They could rejoin the ladies, and gladly.

The visitors spent three interesting days being shown round the Orkneys by Thorfinn, sailing as far north as Eday, where one of his other half-brothers, Brusi, acted lord of a group of islands, including Egilsay, Faray, Sanday and Shapinsay, a cheerful man who laughed uproariously at almost all that was said, and carried Nechtan round on his shoulder. Like his father, he chose to dwell not on his main isle but on a little offshoot at the northern tip, the Calf of Eday, as more defensible. The other two brothers, Somerled and Einar Wrymouth, it seemed ruled the Shetlands between them.

Cormac was a little anxious to be off for home, this on account of Fenella's condition, even though she declared herself untroubled. So, although MacBeth would have stayed longer with his mother, he agreed to a departure thereafter, Donada promising to have Thorfinn bring her to see him at Inverness before long; they had been parted over-much. And her husband might well be visiting

Scotland on occasion, as one of its earls, in which she would encourage him, so it should all be better now. She had prayed for this.

It was southwards then for the seven Scots longships.

28

They reached Glamis in ample time; indeed they were able to ride to Kinnordy, Fenella's favourite domicile, before, three weeks later, she presented her husband with a little girl. They named her Marsala, and Nechtan seemed to consider her his own property. The mother promised another son, in due course, but Cormac was making no complaints.

They came back to word of war in Ireland, the northern clans there, usually at each others' throats, uniting for once under Brian Boroime of Munster to assail the Danes who were all but taking over Ulster. Malcolm was sending Ethernan of Mar with a quite large force to aid them. Cormac was thankful that a similar command was not being sent to him for the Angus men. He was tending to wish, now, that Connacher had indeed had a son, and the Thane of Glamis could have led a more retiring existence on the national scene.

However, no serious calls were made on him that autumn, despite King Brian suffering a major reverse against the Danes and Mar returning to Scotland having suffered large casualties. Perhaps fortunately, the ensuing winter was one of the hardest for years, with snow, ice and storms all but prohibiting military activities, so that peace of a sort reigned. Fenella asked why it took such weather to restrain men from fighting and killing each other? Cormac could not answer that.

It was in belated spring before a message came from King Malcolm, and this blessedly no summons to warfare but a very different command. The Thane of Glamis, with the other men of rank, including the mormaors, of Scotland, was to attend the Ard Righ at Mortlach in Moray, where he, Malcolm, had won his great victory over Olaf the Norseman those years before, there to celebrate suitably that event, and on the Feast of St Serf, 20th April.

This was a mission, surely, which ought to make few demands on Cormac, other than a ride of well over one hundred miles. With Duncan the Tranter he set off five days later, another four days before St Serf's, to ensure arrival on time. After all the melting snows, the rivers would be running high, and there would be much flooding, and with over fifty such to cross, many major ones, diversions might have to be frequent and delays inevitable.

They went north by Kirriemuir, passing Kinnordy, and up Glen Isla, the river having inundated much of the haughland; and so they reached Glen Shee after very ploutering riding. As night fell, they got as far as the monkish hospice of the Spittal, where they were able to sympathise with the brothers who had been cut off from their fellow men for months, with few travellers to provide for, food stocks now running low. In the morning, it was on up and over the very high pass of the Cairnwell, one of the loftiest in the land, where the snow still lay thick and their mounts had to pick their way warily indeed, and savage mountains glowered down on them on either side.

Then down by the rushing torrents of Glen Clunie into upper Mar and the Dee valley, this running at right angles, with more flooding. From Braemar and Crathie they went north-eastwards to find a crossing of the River Gairn, this only with great difficulty. Then it was on, under great Morven, to the headwaters of Don, and more hold-ups. But thereafter, up Avon, they did reach Tomintoul, one of the highest-placed communities in all Scotland, where again monks welcomed them to their so useful hospitality, that word deriving in fact from just such religious hostelries and hospitals. They learned that the Mormaor of Mar had passed the previous night there.

On through the Ladder Hills next day, still northwards, lesser mountains these, but their valleys the more waterlogged, to Glen Livet and so down Fiddich to Mortlach, the wettest journey that Cormac had ever undertaken. But they had done it in three days, and felt quite proud of themselves, although in fact it was their garrons which deserved most of the praise; other horses, however much bigger and swifter, could never have managed it.

At Mortlach, close to the site of the battle, they found a large company already assembled, but less large than King Malcolm would have wished, it seemed, the travelling conditions having delayed or defeated not a few. Indeed there were only three mormaors present; MacBeth, who had had the least distance to come, Mar and Crinan of Atholl. But the Ard Righ was not going to postpone his celebration to give time for others to arrive. On St Serf's Day it was to be. For St Serf had been a contemporary of Columba and Moluag, the real begetters of Celtic Christianity in what was to become Scotland, and his feast day was significant in the Columban Church. He it was who had christened St Kentigern, whom he had called Mungo, or mannikin, who had founded Glasgow and the see thereof; and this dedication at Mortlach was aimed at perpetuating that tradition. Normally it was the Primate of Holy Church who established bishoprics, not monarchs, however potent they might be. But Malcolm was determined that this was to be *his* dedication. He claimed that Angus mac Fergus, High King of Alba, who was father-in-law to Kenneth the First, mac Alpin who had united Picts and Scots to make Scotland, had founded the Primate's own see of St Andrews, claiming St Serf's authority so to do, Serf's own diseart being in Fife. So although Bishop Malmore of St Andrews was present, also Crinan of Atholl, hereditary Abbot of Dunkeld, and Murdoch, Abbot of Iona, as it were to homologate the appointment, he it was, the Ard Righ, who was establishing this new bishopric as acknowledgment of divine help in winning the victory over Olaf – and incidentally seeking to establish himself as supreme in Church as well as in the realm.

The lordly ones spent that night in the nearby hallhouse of Balvenie, belonging to a vassal chieftain of MacBeth's, in welcome comfort; and next day, St Serf's itself, the Mormaor of Strathearn and MacDuff, Thane of Fife, arrived just in time to witness the ceremony. The scene of it was the little chapel of St Moluag, he who had allegedly come here all the way from his mission base on the inner Hebridean isle of Lismore, off Mull, to convert the pagan Moravians. The building was very modest, consisting merely of four walls, with an earthen floor below a thatched roof, with one doorway at the west end and a single window behind the altar facing east towards Christ's birthplace. The altar was flanked by an aumbry in the walling to contain the sanctified bread and wine, and opposite it a holy-water stoup for baptisms. It seemed distinctly humble as seat of a bishopric, but Malcolm announced that he would increase its size by three spears' lengths, to indicate the battle, himself pacing out the required dimensions and giving orders for an improved addition to be built, with a stone-slabbed roof and two windows.

This announced, he summoned forward a youngish man named Bain, whom rumour had it was illegitimate kin of his own, and called on the Primate to lay hands on him and consecrate him bishop, not of Moray but of Mortlach itself, even though the diocese he said was to extend from the Spey down to the Dee, this to commemorate the God-given victory.

Somewhat doubtfully, it seemed, and very briefly, Bishop Malmore did this, all kneeling save himself, this outside the chapel which was much too small to contain the company.

Then the new prelate rose and went within, with the Primate and the two abbots, to bless the bread and wine, and to present the holy elements to a select few, all done in simple, brisk, almost businesslike fashion.

That seemed to be the end of the proceedings, Cormac for one deciding that they had all come a long and difficult way for such a limited and odd occasion, however significant Malcolm seemed to deem it.

Thereafter MacBeth conducted all back to Balvenie, where something of a banquet had been prepared for those in charge, and whole oxen roasted outdoors for their escorts and followers, much noisy celebration continuing into the night, not perhaps the usual way of celebrating the foundation of a bishopric.

It was dispersal next day. MacBeth asked Cormac whether he could spare another day or two before returning to Angus. He would be glad of his advice in a matter of some importance which had developed recently, a matter which had its personal concerns. It would mean going up to Rosemarkyn, on Cromarty; but a couple of hours' ride would take them to Garmouth, on Spey Bay, where three of his longships were based, and one of these could take them up to the Black Isle of Cromarty by next midday. Cormac agreed to do this.

When they had taken their leave of the High King and set off northwards, they asked each other why Malcolm the Destroyer should have involved himself in this new bishopric project, he who seemed no man of religion? MacBeth thought that perhaps it was as a means of ensuring that the churchmen could be relied upon to support him in any possible conflict with the mormaors. Cormac considered that it might have something to do with his attack on the Church's famous centre at Durham, and his defeat there, a means of placating the clergy or even higher spiritual powers. It could be both.

MacBeth told him why they were heading for Rosemarkyn in the Black Isle – and this had some concern with Malcolm also. It involved his own cousin Gillacomgain's widow, Gruoch, and her little son Lulach. She was the daughter of Boide mac Kenneth mac Malcolm, and so the boy was in direct line for the throne, why indeed Gillacomgain had married her, as a mere girl. Now Malcolm the Destroyer had his eye on her, whether to marry her himself or to wed her to some nominee, whereby he could control young Lulach, she did not know. But she did not want to be further used as a pawn in power struggles, and she had appealed to Donada and through her to MacBeth for aid. Thorfinn had brought her and the boy from her retreat in Wester Ross to MacBeth's summer residence at Rosemarkyn, where she ought to be safe meantime, guarded by his people.

Concerned over all this, Cormac wondered what advice he would be able to offer in such grievous situation. MacBeth then came out with it. He himself would wish to marry Gruoch; not for any desire for power or the throne, he assured. But she was a fine woman. Fair. Spirited. And kind, despite all that she had suffered.

Cormac tried not to stare. "You would wed!"

"I would. I would."

"And . . . Malcolm?"

"Aye, there is the question! Malcolm the Destroyer. What would he say to that? What would he *do*?'

"You say that he has designs on her, himself?"

"So she believes."

"Then he might be dangerous, that one."

"Yes. But . . . how dangerous? And to whom? I care not for myself. I could face Malcolm mac Kenneth. But Gruoch! And her son. I would not, must not, endanger her, them."

"What could he do to her?"

"Take her. Imprison her. Lock her in some hold. And the boy Lulach. As hostage for her. Make her obedient to his will."

"Would he do that? And make bitter foe of the Mormaor of Moray and Ross? And of Thorfinn, of Sigurd Earl of Orkney, Caithness and Sutherland? Turn all north of Spey to Shetland against him, after going so far in making that alliance? I think not."

"This is the question. Why I wanted your guidance, Cormac my friend. Who knows Malcolm best, think you? To guide me."

"I would say his daughter Bethoc. Your aunt. And her

husband Crinan, whom he has made Mormaor of Atholl. Your own mother?"

"*She* has not seen him for years. Up there in Orkney. And they were never close, I judge, But Bethoc is close. But would she guide *me*? Would she not favour her father in this?"

"She and Crinan have a son, have they not? Duncan is the name? Will Malcolm not see him as his heir rather than this Lulach?"

"Lulach is closer to the royal succession. By a generation, although younger in years. The Council of the *Ri*, the mormaors, might well choose him. They choose, on the death of an Ard Righ."

"Yes. But does this Lady Gruoch desire that? The throne for her son?"

"I think not. I judge that all she seeks is peace and a good life for him."

"Then, if you were to tell Bethoc that. She and Crinan will wish their son Duncan to succeed. So she may aid you . . ."

They left it at that, meantime.

Rosemarkyn, which meant the Chanonry of Ross, once that bishop's seat, was now the summer dwelling of the mormaors, the bishop moved to more central Dingwall. And there, the following evening, Cormac was introduced to Gruoch nic Boide mac Kenneth mac Malcolm. And at his first glance he saw why his friend would wish to wed this woman. She was beautiful, dark of hair and eyes, gracefully carrying herself, proudly but the reverse of pridefully; but it was the sheer warmth of her personality which made the greatest impact. MacBeth had called her kind, and that was what her presence said to Cormac. His friend would choose aright if he wed this one. But, the consequences?

"Lady Gruoch, Princess, I salute you!" he said, bowing. "I have heard much of you. But, but naught to rival what I see and esteem now!"

"Ah, the Thane of Glamis is a man of the courtesies, as well as of the sword and the longships! I have heard much of you also, Lord Cormac," she said. "And of the Lady Fenella. She must be as notable a woman as you are a man!"

"Much more so, I judge! You and she, Princess, would warm to each other."

"I hope that they will have opportunity so to do," MacBeth put in. "And before long. I must take her south to Glamis . . ."

That was interrupted by the arrival, from a room off the hall, of a boy, not so much older than Nechtan but so very different, a diffident, uncertain, great-eyed youngster, who looked at Cormac doubtfully and went to take his mother's hand: Lulach mac Gillacomgain, closest heir to Scotland's throne.

"Lulach, here is a great man, the Thane of Glamis," Gruoch said. "He has captured many of the wicked Norsemen's ships, and used them to drive away the raiders. Is that not splendid?"

The boy made no answer.

"He is shy with strangers."

"I have a son, younger than you are, I think," Cormac said. "He is fond of the sea and the longships. Have you ever been in a longship, Lulach?"

No answer.

"The Lord Thorfinn brought us here in one of his," the mother informed. "That was the first of the sea for this one. It was all very strange for Lulach."

They went out into the orchard, where Cormac tried to involve the apprehensive youngster in a game of pitching little fallen apples at a stake, but with scant success. But the process did win him a pleasing association with the mother. They got on very well together, so well indeed that when MacBeth left them for a space to give his steward some instructions, Cormac was emboldened to say how much he admired the Mormaor MacBeth and how much they had done together.

"I admire him also," Gruoch told him. "He is one of the best of men, and has been very kind to me, to some small risk to himself, I fear. Done much for me and Lulach. I doubt if I can ever repay him."

"I judge that perhaps you might!" he replied carefully. "From what he has . . . hinted."

"Would that I could," she answered simply.

He eyed her directly. "May, may I tell him so?" he wondered. "He is my good friend."

"I do not see why not, Thane Cormac. I would have him mine, also."

That was sufficient for that man. "I think that that knowledge would make him well pleased," he said, and changed the subject.

Later, alone with MacBeth, Cormac told him of this conversation, and found the other heartened indeed. He had never before played matchmaker.

"You encourage me," his friend said. "Encourage me to make my wish, my hopes, known to her. But, aware of the dangers as she is, think you that she will do it? Agree to wed me? Arousing Malcolm's wrath, it may be."

"Since she it was who told you of the situation, I do not think that she would have said what she did to me had she been . . . averse. I say, ask her, my friend."

That night, after the boy was put to bed, Cormac deliberately yawned once or twice, and declared that he was weary and would seek his couch, this in order to leave the pair alone. He did so, and it was considerably later before he heard the door to the next chamber to his own, where young Lulach was bedded, shut quietly. Had his small efforts borne some fruit?

In the morning, at the breakfast table, it seemed that they had, for when Gruoch and the boy arrived presently, she went to kiss MacBeth. And as an afterthought came to salute Cormac also, if not quite similarly. He took this as a hopeful sign, for his friend had not kissed her when they had arrived here from the south, or on other occasions that he had seen.

And in a little while, he noted MacBeth's hand lingering over the woman's shoulder as he went to fetch her more cream for her porridge.

It was when, in mid-forenoon, he was seeking to involve the still hesitant Lulach in the game of apple-pitching that his friend came to him with his announcement.

"You will be eager to get back to Glamis and your wife and son, Cormac," he said. "I think that we should sail all but forthwith. Myself to go on to see my Aunt Bethoc at Blair-in-Atholl. As we spoke of. Learn how she judges that Malcolm will act when, when he knows that Gruoch will marry me!" That last came out abruptly.

"So-o-o! That is the way of it! Success, my good Son of Life! I salute you. Salute you both. Here is satisfaction for you. I had my hopes . . ."

"Yes. She is willing, to my great joy. Last night she accepted me. It was good, so good. The question now is, when? When shall we wed?"

"Would you not say the sooner the better? Present Malcolm with the fact. Not have him seeking to prevent it."

"It might provoke him to anger. Against *her*. To take steps against her, and this boy. That is the fear. I must see Bethoc."

"You are a mormaor. And with powerful friends. He would hesitate, I think."

"I would hope so. But he is the Foiranach, the Destroyer. See you, we will sail south. Take Gruoch and the boy with us. Leave them with you and Fenella at Glamis, while I go over to Atholl to see my aunt. Then . . ."

"Then?"

"Then decide whether to wed at once or to inform Malcolm first. That, I recognise, we ought to do. He is the Ard Righ. And this Lulach is his possible heir, indeed rightful heir. He ought to be informed if the boy's mother weds. Which would be worse, think you? His anger at not being told, asked permission? Or his decision to try to stop it happening?"

"Myself, I would wed first. And face the consequences, if any, later. Rather than risk him seeking to ban it."

"Aye. You may well be right. *She* would have it so. But I have her weal to think of."

"MacBeth, here is a notion! Suppose you got Bishop Bain to marry you? At Mortlach. He whom Malcolm made a prelate. He, Malcolm, could scarcely condemn him for his first important act. Not the Bishop of Ross, at Dingwall but this Bain, who is in fact Bishop of Moray. He would not refuse the Mormaor of Moray, I think. And Malcolm the more tied."

The other slapped his thigh. "Here is a notion, indeed! Bishop Bain. If he would do it . . ."

"Why should he not? He is a long way from Fortrenn and Malcolm. He would not know of any reason to refuse you."

"It is worth the trying . . ."

So it was decided. They would sail down to the Angus coast. MacBeth would leave Gruoch and her son with Cormac and Fenella at Glamis, Red Castle or Kinnordy, wherever she presently was, and borrow horses to ride to Atholl, then come back with his aunt's views and advice. Then, unless it was very much against her guidance, go on up to Mortlach. And go in company. Cormac declared that, if so it was decided, he, and he was fairly sure, Fenella also, would be happy indeed to attend the bridal couple for this so special occasion.

In the event, when MacBeth returned to Red Castle from Atholl one week later, it was to announce that his Aunt Bethoc, and her husband agreeing, advised that he wed, and this as promptly as possible. Much better to present Malcolm with an accomplished fact rather than allow him the opportunity possibly to forbid the marriage, on whatever grounds. They did not think that the Ard Righ could seek to take punitive or other action thereafter, with so much at stake in probable offence to so much of the power in the land, not only Moray, Ross, Sutherland and

Caithness, but other mormaors who would resent the royal interference in the private concern of any of his *ri*. They had not added, apparently, that they would expect MacBeth, at some future date, to support their own son, Duncan, rather than Lulach, as the next High King, but that was more or less implied. All this coincided with Cormac's own view of the situation, Fenella agreeing. The marriage would go ahead, therefore, and without delay; and if Bishop Bain refused to officiate, which seemed improbable, some other priest could be found without much difficulty.

Much relieved and indeed delighted by this decision, preparations were made for an all but immediate journey northwards again, swiftest and surest by the vessel which had brought them down, and with one of Cormac's own craft accompanying them to fetch the Glamis pair home in due course. The children could safely be left with their grandmother, the Lady Alena, for the two or three days.

To sea again, then, Nechtan objecting that he was not being taken with them, when Lulach was.

At Mortlach they found the new bishop busy superintending the building of a suitable house for himself at the same time as extending the church to the dimensions ordered by Malcolm, an active man. Whether he was equally active in his pastoral duties, as yet, was not clear. But at least he showed no reluctance to marry his mormaor and the widow of Gillacomgain, however surprised he might be at their sudden and unannounced arrival.

It was a very brief and simple ceremony, held in so modest a building in process of alteration, but none the less effective for that, with only Cormac and Fenella, Duncan and Donnie the Crab, and two or three of MacBeth's people as witnesses, this nowise upsetting the two principals, who were only too happy to be declared man and wife by whatever means and process. Young Lulach was the only doubtful one present, he, hand held by Fenella, eyeing all uneasily.

The nuptials, such as they were, over, the participants

did not linger there, leaving the prelate to his building activities and setting off on the twenty-mile ride back to Garmouth-on-Spey. There, although MacBeth hospitably invited the Angus party back up to Rosemartyn, Cormac and Fenella, feeling that the newly-weds should be left on their own for a while, elected to return home forthwith, the children left at Red Castle as excuse.

The parting was not without certain anxieties expressed over what Malcolm Foiranach's reactions might be, but no doubt expressed over having taken the right course. If the worst came to the worst, MacBeth could always take Gruoch and her son up to his mother in Orkney, where they would be safe.

The ships sailed off, north and south.

29

No word of the High King taking any action against MacBeth and Gruoch reached Cormac in the weeks, indeed months, which followed. He was, of course, much preoccupied with the position in Cumbria, Man and Ulster, especially the last, where the Danes were in control now of most of the land, with Brian Boroime's Munster holding out against them although itself frequently assailed. Fortunately the alliance with Sigurd of Orkney held, and this prevented the Hebrides being attacked and with them the seaboard of north-western Scotland. But the Isle of Man was being seriously raided and Sigurd was calling on Malcolm to prove that the alliance was not merely one-sided, and to send help to deal with the Manx situation, so far from the Orkneys. Cormac feared that this might well involve a call on him for the use of his longship fleet, since seaborne any aid must be; but no such call arrived, although Malcolm led a force as far as Cumbria, to discourage Danish activities there and to make at least a gesture towards Man.

Peace and normalcy, then, reigned meantime in Angus, save in that Connacher, now almost permanently bed-bound, left all the mortuath's duties and problems to Cormac, so he was a busy man indeed. He took young Nechtan with him on not a few of these visits and missions, both to emphasise his authority and to show all who their next mormaor would be, the boy nothing loth. He also took him to Connacher's bedside on more than one occasion, that both the old man and his successor might establish some sort of rapport. Whether this was successful or not was hard to say.

Little Marsala continued to be a delight to her parents as well as to her brother, and was not long in showing that she had a lot of her mother in her by refusing to allow Nechtan to order her around, as he seemed to think was his right, however fondly. They made a lively pair.

That winter was a lot less severe than the previous two, and travel was less of a hazard in consequence. Cormac and Fenella were delighted, in March, to receive a visit from MacBeth and Gruoch, with Lulach, this by ship, now the accepted means of communication. They learned that Gruoch was in fact pregnant, the cause of much congratulation, with MacBeth eager to have an heir to the mortuath. They learned also of an extraordinary move on the part of the High King, far removed from any obvious action hostile to Gruoch's marriage, and on the face of it strange in view of the situation with regard to Danish aggression. Malcolm had devised a system of written laws for the realm, something hitherto unknown, which he was calling the Leges Malcolmi, these on the face of it just and worthy, although whether they would be accepted by the mormaors, and by future monarchs and generations, remained to be seen. This Ard Righ certainly had the ability to surprise. Not exactly one of these laws, but the preamble thereto, was quite significant, and at first glance strangely liberal, not to say unselfish. He announced that hereafter all the land of Scotland was to be gifted to his vassals and lords, in perpetuity, with the single exception of the Moot Hill of Scone, which alone was to remain the sole property of the monarch, this mound being traditionally composed of soil from all over the kingdom presented to the newly crowned High King at his coronation by the said vassals under their oaths of allegiance. In return, the lords were to grant to the Ard Righ the firm assurance of their feudal services in manpower and support.

When Cormac, who had not heard of this, expressed his wonder at Malcolm's seeming generosity and vision, MacBeth pointed out that he saw it perhaps rather differently. Could it not be a move to limit the powers and privileges of the *ri*? If all the land was to be owned, in theory, by the lords, chiefs and vassals, what of the mormaors? They were traditionally the minor kings of their mortuaths. If now all the land-holders were to own their properties direct of the crown in return for their consistent and certain armed support, what authority remained for the *ri*? The men who elected and appointed the High King? Would they not become mere names, masters of their personal estates, little else, great lords perhaps but no longer kings? They were not so much as mentioned in this preamble to the new Laws of Malcolm. Was the Destroyer to become the destroyer of the mormaors, as well as the kingdom's foes? Was he changing the realm's system of governance, rule and succession from the ages-old patriarchal and matrilineal to the feudal, copying that of so many nations elsewhere in Christendom?

On considering, Cormac saw that this might be the result. Were the mormaors not only going to be reduced in power but all but superseded, become at best something more like earls? And would they tamely let this happen?

MacBeth foresaw a fairly prompt and concerned conference of the *ri* to consider all this, and what it might lead to. If they were united against it, could Malcolm have his way? Perhaps not. Only, the mormaors were not presently at their strongest. Connacher of Angus was useless, Crinan of Atholl was Malcolm's son-in-law and desiring his own son Duncan to be the next High King, so would probably not contest Malcolm's will. Strathearn was aged and feckless. That left, of the seven, only MacBeth himself, Mar, Menteith and Lennox. If only one of these refused to contest the High King's conception, then it probably could not be halted. Almost certainly Malcolm had considered all this before he acted. And he would bring strong pressure to bear.

Cormac saw that, and wondered. Wondered whether there was anything that the *ri* could do about it? His son was not mormaor yet, and *he* had no real authority, only what was delegated by Connacher. So it did not look as though he could help. Wondered also whether Scotland would be greatly disadvantaged by the decline in status and power of its mormaors, ancient as their prerogative was? Other nations did not have the like, and seemed to fare well enough. He promised MacBeth, who seemed to see it all as a dire threat, that he would speak to Connacher; but knowing Fenella's uncle and his present state, he was not hopeful of any positive results.

When he discussed it all, later, with his wife, Fenella said that she did not think that MacBeth would be wise to take any lead in countering Malcolm in this matter. After all, his happiness and good life with Gruoch were what was most important for him, surely, not power as a mormaor? And he had already risked offending the monarch by his marriage. She thought that Cormac should advise his friend to take no direct action, unless his fellow *ri* should show a united front, which seemed improbable. And she was fairly certain that Gruoch would say the same.

MacBeth saw the point in that, and agreed to caution.

As events turned out, Malcolm was not in any position to implement his plans for feudalising his realm for some considerable time to come. This on account of Ethelred of England. Unready as he was styled, he was yet not backwards in seizing opportunities to advance his kingdom's cause. He saw such in these Danish assaults on southern Cumbria and Man, and evidently decided that these could well be added to his own realm, to which they were contiguous; indeed the Isle of Man was a bare thirty miles off his own coast, even though it had been held by the Celtic peoples since the time of the High King Arthur of the Britons, until the Vikings had taken over, and Sigurd of Orkney now held it. Admittedly he would encounter and assail the likewise invading Danes in his efforts, which had its advantages for the Scots, even though they saw the English threat as infinitely more urgent than the Danish. Earl Sigurd demanded

Malcolm's fulfilment of their alliance, in a joint effort to expel both sets of invaders.

In consequence, both Cormac and MacBeth found themselves faced with demands from the High King, and nothing to do with the marriage situation. They were ordered to muster their fullest numbers of longships, not to assist in any assault on the Cumbrian coast or the Isle of Man, but to sail down the eastern seaboard of England, right to the south, to pose a threat thereto, especially into the Thames estuary and to London town, this in order to force Ethelred to recall his own shipping from the Irish Sea to deal with it, the anticipation being that he would be using most of his available vessels there, with few if any left to combat such Scots menace on the eastern side. It might take some time for word to reach Man to this effect, so the fleet was to linger thereabouts, even if necessary sail round into the Straits of Dover, to coax Ethelred back. They were not advised actually to attack any areas, just to show a presence. Outright war with England was not the objective, just the threat by sea, while Malcolm and his land forces made similar gestures to the west, leaving Sigurd to do the real fighting.

So the gathering of a maximum number of longships from Angus, Moray and Ross was put in hand. And some ten days later a great fleet of over thirty vessels, flying the saltire banners of Scotland, set sail southwards from Lunan Bay, waved off by Fenella and Gruoch, who had elected to pass the waiting time at Red Castle, with Nechtan complaining that he was not allowed to accompany his father but left to companion the feeble Lulach.

They sailed in convoy down and past the Tay and Forth and Tweed estuaries, and on past the very different Northumberland seaboard, largely lengthy sandy stretches interspersed by occasional rocky headlands as at Bamburgh and Dunstanburgh, with the Farne Islands to be avoided, their impressive array no doubt arousing dire fears amongst the folk ashore. They did not push on in any haste however, that not being called for, using the sweeps but little and tacking this way and that to make use of their sails in the prevailing south-westerly breeze. So they did not cover more than seventy direct miles each day – and they had five hundred to go before they reached the Thames – putting in at sheltered bays overnight, and appropriating such cattle, sheep and provision as was available for their sustenance, this without actually harrying the local population, however much these would fear it.

Once past the Northumbrian coast to that of Durham and Deira and York, none of the Scots knew the seaboard, save by repute, so it was very much guesswork as to where they were at any specific time. Fortunately the weather remained reasonably fine, indeed they could have done with more wind; and it all made fairly carefree sailing, the crews relaxed, and declaring that this was an excellent form of warfare. They did see other vessels on occasion, mainly fishing-boats but few larger craft, and these all, needless to say, gave the fleet of Viking longships a very wide berth.

MacBeth accompanied Cormac in his leading craft most of the way. They vied with each other in trying to assess, each day and night, approximately where they were on that English coast, this complicated by the amount of tacking which they had to do, confusing their judgment of the distances covered, so that they could not be sure whether they were off the Tees, the Humber – although Flamborough Head did help them, together with in time the wide mouth of the Wash – or thereafter down at the Deben, Stour, Blackwater and Crouch estuaries, none of these so identifiable as their own great Scots firths. Calculating perhaps seventy miles each day, depending on the wind, did not aid them much.

However, when eventually they reached a wider gap, even more so than the Wash, in and out of which many ships came and went, they reckoned that this must be the Thames, leading into the great centre and trading port of London, which the Saxons had made their capital. Into this they turned, sweep-work now.

Cormac strung out his fleet in a mile-long column, making it seem even more impressive and menacing from the shores, to row up the almost seventy more miles to London itself. The local inhabitants' reaction to this lengthy file of the dreaded Viking ships would be to spread alarm almost certainly. The orders were to row slowly, so that such alarm would go ahead of them, that being part of their objective. It might arouse opposition, admittedly, some defensive measures, but in view of their own numbers and aggressive appearance no major assault was anticipated. However, keen watch was kept.

It was obviously notably populous country on both sides of the narrowing estuary, low-lying ground, with many villages and havens of a sort. At length, towards evening, they saw ahead of them, like a high mist, the smoky sky which indicated a large town. They drew in, and lay for the night in their ships near a harbour, which a hailed and apprehensive fisherman drawing in his nets told them was called Purfleet.

On the morrow they made their protracted demonstration towards England's capital, rowing up and down the winding course of the broad river between its now built-up banks, parading their menace without actually landing anywhere. And no ships, large or small, came out to challenge them, although they could see many vessels moored. They could only hope that the message was being received ashore with the required disquiet, and would be somehow transmitted eventually to King Ethelred, presumably by riders to some southern port and by ship westwards thereafter. At any rate, this was what they had been ordered to do, effective or otherwise as it might be.

For two days they continued with this curious procedure without arousing any evident counter-measures, until food and patience ran out. Cormac and MacBeth were in two minds as to whether to risk going ashore for the required provisioning, but decided against it. Once their men were off their ships they would become vulnerable, their numbers, substantial as they were, as nothing compared with the forces which could be brought against them. Better to head off down-river again to some farming area where they could purloin the necessary beef and meal, and thereafter to sea again, duty done, however much of merest display it had been.

This satisfactorily carried out, they rowed back to the river mouth. At least they ought to have the wind largely behind them on the way north, and save them all the tacking process.

Once out of the Thames, wind they did have but also rain, which in their open craft made the journey less than pleasant. But they were on their way home, and clearly taking little more than half the time to go as they had taken to come. Complaints were minimal.

Sails hoisted all the way, the crews largely sheltering under their plaids from the weather, they covered fully one hundred miles each day; and landing for the nights at chosen wooded areas where there was ample fuel available for fires, dried their clothing and roasted their beef and made great quantities of soup with their mutton and meal. In five days they were back off the Angus coast, this with the sun shining again, having been away just over two weeks.

Welcoming them, and hearing her husband's account of it all, Fenella declared that she, and Gruoch also, might as well have accompanied them, on this occasion as on others; she would have been interested to see England.

30

Whether the longships' demonstration had anything to do with it or not, the Cumbria and Man campaign, if so it could be called, proved to be a success, Ethelred retiring and the Danes heading back to Ireland, Sigurd claiming most of the credit, and probably with reason. But Malcolm had played some part, and gained advantage from it, actually out of all proportion to his efforts; for the sub-kingdom of Strathclyde, of which Cumbria was a part, although for long a dependency of the Scottish realm, now came to accept the fact that it was unable to protect itself from such aggression, English or Scandinavian. Its merely nominal monarch, Owen the Bald, an elderly man, conceded that his subsidiary role was now ineffective and untenable, and made formal resignation of his ancient kingdom to the Scottish Ard Righ in perpetuity. Since Strathclyde had always laid claim to all Cumbria, indeed right down to Lancaster, this accession might have more than mere superficial advantage to a monarch of Malcolm's character and ambitions.

At any rate, Malcolm made something of a display and flourish of this incorporation, summoning his mormaors to Dumbarton, Strathclyde's capital on that river's estuary, for a symbolic taking over, in effect reducing the ancient nation to one more mortuath. MacBeth duly attended, and took part. He came back to report to Cormac that there had been no mention made of his marriage to Gruoch; nor had anything been said about the proposed feudalising of the land, and its effect upon the mormaors' position. It looked as though Malcolm Foiranach might have decided to tread more warily in some of his projects, in the circumstances, with sufficient to cope with meantime.

For his part, Cormac was able to tell his friend that Fenella was with child again, and he had hopes of a male heir to the thanedom of Glamis, as distinct from the mormaordom of Angus.

It was only two days after MacBeth had left for Inverness that a messenger arrived hotfoot from Forfar. The Mormaor Connacher had breathed his last, after sorry illness. It was a sad end to an old story.

What of the new one?

Despite having been prepared for this news for long, Cormac found himself in some doubts as to what was to happen now. Did Nechtan, child as he was, perforce become mormaor, even in his sixth year? So far as he knew, there was no other recognised heir. Would some other claimant announce himself? Did some process of appointment have to be instituted? Some proclamation made? Did he, as the boy's father, have to act mormaor meantime, or some sort of council of lords and thanes of the mortuath become involved? Connacher had never given any guidance in the matter, and Cormac had not liked to broach the subject to an ailing man.

At the interment ceremony, although there was a good turnout of notables, Cormac remained little the wiser. The situation had never arisen before in Angus, and none there was any better informed. And for once, Fenella was of little help, she knowing no better than anyone else.

However, at Glamis they did not have long to wait for presumably authoritative information. A courier arrived at Forfar Castle from Forteviot. The High King commanded the appearance of the Thane of Glamis and his son, in Fortrenn, and promptly. Clearly this must be over the mormaorship.

Fenella, pregnant as she was, insisted on accompanying her husband and son, as was of course her right, it being through her that Nechtan could succeed his great-uncle. Leaving Marsala with the Lady Ada, the three of them, with attendants, set off for Strathearn, a ride of over fifty miles. Fortunately Nechtan was good on a horse, having had ample practice. His father and mother sought to explain to him, as they went, something of the significance of the occasion, the eminence of the High King, and the respect due to be paid to him, this from a not always notably respectful youngster, who in fact was much more interested in all that he saw on the way.

At Fortreviot in Fortrenn, they found the Ard Righ absent meantime, over at Dumbarton regularising the Strathclyde situation, but expected to return on the morrow. Cormac and Fenella were quite thankful for the delay, which allowed them to settle themselves in the royal residence reasonably comfortably, and to school their son, hopefully as to behaviour.

Next mid-afternoon Malcolm duly arrived, with Aoidh of Lennox, who was the closest mormaor to Strathclyde, and was taking some responsibility for managing affairs there, Owen the Bald being less than effective.

In due course, the trio from Glamis were ushered into the royal presence, Nechtan being held firmly by the arm by his father. They bowed, at least the boy bobbed a head but stared keenly, assessingly, his first sight of a monarch. Malcolm's gaze was likewise assessing.

"Ha! The Thane of Glamis and the Mormaor of Angus!" he jerked. "Greetings! And to the Lady Fenella." That at least was an encouraging start, in seeming acceptance of Nechtan as mormaor.

Cormac bowed again. "Highness! We come at your royal command. In duty and loyal respect."

"That I require, yes. This time you have had to travel without those ships of yours!"

There was nothing to say to that, by Cormac at least. But the boy thought otherwise. "We rode horses," he said. "A long way. We saw deer on a hill. And men with nets, on a river, catching fish."

"That is scarcely unusual," the Ard Righ said, raising his brows.

"Oh, it is. For the deer were all stags. No hinds amongst them. A hundred. I have never seen that before. Have you?" Cormac's grip on his son's arm tightened, all but shaking him, to little effect. "And the fishermen were getting sort of snakes out of their nets. Amongst the fish. They were, were . . . ?" Nechtan looked up at his father for help.

"They would be eels," Malcolm said. "Which river was that?"

"The one near where my father said that you had sat on a great stone. On a little hill. And men held your hand, many men. Why did they do that?"

"Highness, forgive my son!" Cormac interjected. "He does not mean disrespect. He can talk over-much. I ask your pardon . . ."

"Eels!" Nechtan declared. "I had never seen them before. Can you eat them?"

"Hush, you!" Fenella made her first contribution, less than hopefully.

"I have never done so," the monarch said. "But I know that some do."

"These men were throwing them back into the river. They wriggled and twisted. Like that!" And the boy swung and rotated his free arm dramatically.

"I see that the Mormaor of Angus is like to be a man of some force," the High King observed. "We shall speak more later." And he waved a hand to indicate that this preliminary audience was over.

They bowed themselves out, Nechtan waving when he realised that they were leaving the hall.

Thereafter the boy got something of a lecture on his behaviour in the royal presence, although his previous instructions did not appear to have made much impression.

At the meal which followed, a high-pitched young voice was not infrequently raised, and Cormac wondered whether they should have left him in the care of Duncan; but that would have meant the boy eating in the servants' hall, which Fenella said was unsuitable for a mormaor-in-the-making. More than once they saw the Ard Righ eyeing the youngster from his seat on the dais. Nechtan was making an impression, of whatever sort.

The dining over, eventually, Malcolm indicated that the Angus party were to attend him in a private room off the hall. It was the later evening now, and Nechtan's bedtime, but since it was the boy's position and future which fell to be discussed, it seemed desirable that he should be present. He was taken, with strict warnings as to conduct.

The High King, at a table, was accompanied by the Mormaor Aoidh and a monkish clerk with quill, inkhorn and paper. Malcolm waved the trio into seats across from him. But after sitting for a moment or two, Nechtan preferred to stand. The monarch commented.

"None may sit while the High King stands, young man," he said. "But when *I* sit, you may!"

The lad shook his head, and remained on his feet, leaning over the table. "*You* sat on that stone on the mound, when they all held your hand. Did they have no chair for you there?"

"That was an especial seat, only for the Ard Righ," he was told, in Malcolm's gravelly voice. "The Stone of Destiny, it is called. One day you will no doubt have to kneel there, before it. But, let us hope, that will not be for a long time!"

"Why?"

"Because it is used only at the coronation of a High King. So, if so you do, it will mean that *I* am dead!"

"Dead? And I will have to hold someone else's hand? Why?"

"You will. As Mormaor of Angus. To swear allegiance."

"What is that?" This despite the tugging at his arm.

Malcom was very patient for such a man, but his rasping tones did not show it, nor did the boy find it so. "It is your promise to obey, honour and support the man on the Stone of Destiny all your days, you and all your power. Your father has done this. And so has the Mormaor Aoidh here. To myself."

"I have told him of it, Highness. But a child forgets," Cormac put in.

"I will not forget this time. Not when this was the man who sat on that stone."

"Name him Highness, Nechtan."

"High? Why high? He is not very tall."

"Nechtan!"

"*I* will have him remember this day," Malcolm said. He had neither frowned nor smiled once during all this exchange, but in fact had almost seemed interested in the boy's attitude and questionings. He waved now. "Come, lad."

Nothing loth, Nechtan went round the table to the Ard Righ's side.

"You recognise what it means to be one of the *ri*, a mormaor, do you?"

"Oh, yes. It is to lead. To tell men what to do. Go in the first ship, to kill Norsemen."

"It is more than that, boy. Many lead, but few *rule*. Govern the realm. Mormaors rule, under the High King. And support the High King in his greater ruling over the nation. You will be one of these. Important!" A frown. "You understand?"

"I think so. Like my father."

"More than your father. He is a thane, not a mormaor. A leader, yes, but not a ruler. He will teach you, guide you, until you are old enough to rule, but *he* cannot rule Angus. Even for you. So *I* rule over Angus, as well as over all the realm, until you are of age to rule, yourself." And Malcolm looked over at Cormac as he said that.

"You will come to Glamis? And Red Castle? To rule there?"

"No. I may visit, yes. But you will come to me when I call. As now you have come. And be always my trusted liegeman, my helper. This is for you to remember.

There are seven *ri*, lesser kings. You will be one of them."

"A king can do anything? What he likes to do?"

"Scarcely that. But he is not ruled by anyone else. That means that he must rule *himself* also! So that he rules his people well. Do not forget it. So, this is to help you know it, remember it. Kneel, boy."

Nechtan looked at him doubtfully, and then over at his father, brows puckered.

"Kneel, I say."

"Do so, Nechtan," Cormac told him. "There, beside the High King."

Less than eagerly the youngster got down on his knees.

"Now, here is my hand. Take it in your two. No, not like that. Not clasp it. Hold it, three hands side by side. That is right. Now, say after me. 'I, Nechtan of Angus.' Say it."

"I, Nechtan of, of Angus . . ."

"Swear before God and these witnesses."

"Swear . . . What are witnesses?"

"Others who can vouch, testify, prove that you have done and said this. These other four persons here. Say, 'I, Nechtan, swear before God and these witnesses, that I will uphold your rule at all times.' Say it."

In something of a gabble, he got it out approximately in order.

"And I will give all in my power and of my power, to aid you, even my life."

"My life . . . ?"

"Yes. Your life. I will give *my* life for the realm of Scotland. You will, if need be, give your life also."

Nechtan again looked over at his father and mother, who both nodded.

"Yes."

"Say it. Holding my hand still." After a fashion he said it.

"Good! Then rise, Nechtan, Mormaor of Angus. You

are accepted by me, Malcolm mac Kenneth, Ard Righ, as one of the *ri* of my realm. Be you a true mormaor until your life's end."

Relievedly the boy got up, releasing the man's hand, which was raised to pat his shoulder instead.

"Something to remember," he was told. And somehow the way that was said held not only approval and congratulation but warning also, almost threat – for that man was Malcolm Foiranach. And there was a glance at the boy's father. Cormac was on his feet also, and Fenella after him. It was a moment of strange significance, augury, even portent, silence in that room.

HISTORICAL NOTE

Malcolm the Destroyer reigned for twenty-nine years, the longest of any Scots monarch before or after until that of James the Sixth. But it was no peaceable reign, battles and warfare predominating. He was not present at the great battle of Clontarf, in northern Ireland, in 1014; but he sent a force to it, under the Mormaor of Mar, who fell there, as did so many others including Earl Sigurd of Orkney, and indeed King Brian Boroime himself. But it did help to purge that land of the Danes. At Carham, in 1018, Malcolm redeemed his defeat at Durham, gaining an important victory over Earl Eadulf, brother of the late Uhtred of Northumbria, with all present-day Scotland south of the Forth becoming permanently part of the kingdom. But in 1034 he suffered defeat by Cnut or Canute, King of Denmark and England, at Stirling, and was forced to agree to pay tribute of a sort to the invader. He died shortly afterwards from wounds. His grandson, Duncan, became High King, but his inglorious reign lasted only six years, until MacBeth rose in arms against the misgovernment, and replaced him.

Such a century was that for Scotland, after the first millennium.